STARRING:
Adrian (Blaze) Shaw & Raquel Ash

GUEST APPEARANCE:
Ashton Kent & Jada Scott from
HIS MOUTHPIECE: ASHTON & JADA

Merrick Alexander & Jocelyn Milner from
HIS MOUTHPIECE: MERRICK & JOCELYN

Des and Piper from **THE LOVE IS SERIES**

Copyright © 2024 by Nicki Grace

ISBN: 9798870635682

All rights reserved.
No part of this book may be reproduced in any form or by any electronic or mechanical means, including information storage and retrieval systems, without written permission from the author, except for the use of brief quotations in a book review.

Dedicated to Sie Sie and Quiana. I still can't believe you are gone. My world isn't the same without you and I miss you both so very much.

Prologue
ONE YEAR EARLIER...

My hands trembled, tightly gripping the black folder that contained several copies of my resume, a thick legal pad as a space filler and a much too fancy ink pen. I nervously tapped my foot and kept checking my slightly distorted reflection in the elevator doors, hoping I looked professional enough.

In less than ten minutes I was expected to make a good impression on Monica Respress, the Humans Resource manager at Vex and I felt like I was experiencing every emotion known to man.

Not only was this the first job I had taken in fifteen years that had no relation to my modeling career, it was also the first job I had agreed to since the accident.

The accident.

I squeezed my eyes shut, willing the dreadful anxiety that always followed to cease, and focused on happier things, such as this interview with HR. It was merely a formality.

According to Jocelyn, the owner, Blaze, who was a friend of her fiancé, had already decided that he would give me a chance, so I really should calm down.

I took a deep breath, shoving away the memories that still haunted me. The accident had changed everything - my confidence, my sense of security, my very identity. But here I was, taking a brave step forward into the unknown.

I am resilient, strong, and deserving.

I didn't really believe any of that, but it sounded good and it would make my therapist happy.

The elevator doors slid open, and I stepped inside, immediately pressing the button for the second floor.

Mentally, I rehearsed my answers to potential interview questions. Where did I see myself in five years? Why did I think I was a good fit for this company? How did I respond to challenges?

My phone chimed, breaking into my thoughts. It was likely my friend Jocelyn, sending me yet another message with the wink emoji.

All morning, it had been…

"Good luck with your interview." *Wink*

"You're going to do amazing." *Wink*

"I'll be waiting for your call when you leave." *Wink*

Was my friend having a stroke? What was with all the winks?

Arriving at my desired floor, I exited the elevator, taking a brief moment to glance down into my purse and silence my phone. Formality or not, a phone ringing during an interview was unprofessional.

"Woah," came a deep, commanding, masculine voice. It was accompanied by two strong hands on my shoulders, halting me in place.

Glancing up from my purse, I realized that I'd almost had the misfortune of walking directly into a file cart that was left in the middle of the floor, a few feet from the elevator door.

However, as my eyes lifted even higher, I reconsidered. It wasn't misfortune at all. I was lucky as hell, because I was now being held in the clutches of every woman's fantasy.

He was tall, so tall. Dressed in all black, wearing a bulletproof vest with intense brown eyes, kissable full lips, and a gorgeous face. He sported huge, tattooed arms and his broad chest was begging for me to rest my head on it.

The man was a human action figure, and I had one question. Well, technically three.

Where did they make these? Could I get directions to the factory? Or did I need a special subscription?

He released me and smiled. My knees got so weak I thought they disappeared.

"Hi," I said, sounding like some breathless, ditzy chick. I hated it, but damn, it was hard to act normal. He was a lot to take in. "I'm umm–"

"Raquel Ash," the larger-than-life size action figure said. "It is a pleasure to meet you. I'm Blaze."

No way! This was Blaze?! This would be my new boss?!

Now all of Jocelyn's winks made sense. She had set me up.

I could not work for this man. My entire check would be spent on replacing my underwear!

"382," I said absentmindedly before blinking a few times to clear my head.

Shit! I'd just announced how many days it had been since I last had sex. I was going to kill Jocelyn for this.

Blaze's brows furrowed. "Excuse me?"

I located my most professional smile and to him I said, "It's nice to meet you. Thank you for this opportunity."

And to myself, I thought, *how in the hell was I supposed to survive this?*

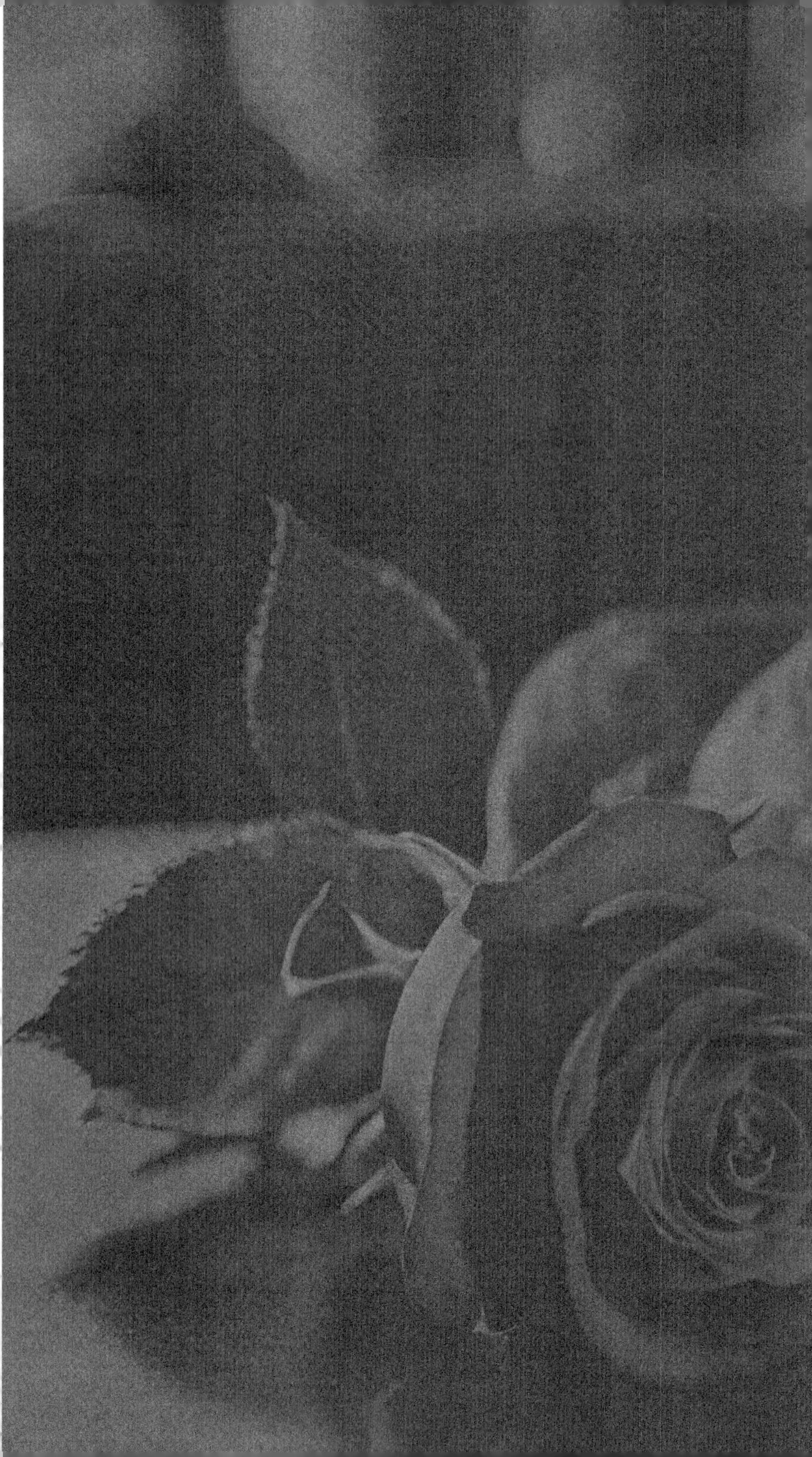

Chapter One

"She was going to cum, and I was cumming with her."

I licked my lips and picked up my vibrator from beside me on the bed. This porn was getting good. The tall, golden brown, muscular fireman looked yummy.

Damn, I love a man in uniform.

He was shirtless, dressed in only his red pants, black straps and helmet.

The woman lying on the bed in front of him was naked and ready for action. I pressed the power button on my pulsating toy and joined her.

"Where's the fire, ma'am?" he said in a deep, yet poorly executed acting voice.

"Right here," the woman replied, sliding her fingers between her legs and spreading her pussy so wide, everyone within a fifty-mile radius could have gotten a good look. "Do you think you can put it out?"

The cheesy exchange almost ruined the moment for me.

However, when the fireman loosened his straps and those pants hit the floor, my attention was drawn to the dick on TV that was pointing directly at me.

It was thick, not as long as I'd hoped, with only a few visible veins leading from base to tip.

Instinctively, my head tilted to the side as if altering the angle would give me a more detailed view. The view remained the same, but I decided I liked what I saw.

Now that is a dick I could suck all day and ride all night.

The thought startled me. I would never in my life say something like that aloud, and my extremely short list of sex partners proved that I also wouldn't do something so adventurous either.

Nonetheless, my shyness about sex didn't stop how wet my pussy was currently getting.

In my mind, I was free to live out my fantasies, and in them, I wished to have a guy like him ruthlessly invading every hole in my body.

Actually, not a guy like him. There was one specific guy that I'd wanted for a while, but he was, and would sadly remain, off limits.

The firefighter crawled up the bed toward the lucky woman and I closed my eyes, blocking her out and envisioning it was me having the time of my life.

My pleasure toy hummed as it repeated the automatic pounding motion in and out of my pussy. It felt so good a squeal escaped my lips, and I quickly steadied it, blindly searching for the speed button to slow it down.

I was never good at allowing myself to relax into pleasure. The more intense and enjoyable it got, the more tense I became.

Hitting the button several times, I found a speed that didn't have my toes gripping the sheets and sunk deeper into the bed.

This is more like it.

Closing my thighs to hold the vibrator in place, I slid my hands over my breasts, and gripped each nipple between my pointer finger and thumb, twisting them hard and feeling a surge of erotic sensation rush down to my center.

I loved how the brief presence of pain increased my sensitivity.

Risking a peek at what the fireman was doing to the woman so that I could pull it into my current fantasy, my mouth fell open when I spotted his face buried deep between her legs, eating her pussy like it was his last meal.

A guy had never done that to me before, and even if they tried, after the embarrassing mishap I had years ago, I was now insecure as hell and would say no.

But this... this was what I wanted.

To let go of all my inhibitions and be free. The woman on the screen certainly was. She was crying out in ecstasy, moving her hips, and so lost in the moment she was pulling me in with her.

I'd always been a good girl, and not in the dirty, sexy way I preferred it, but in the traditional sense.

I followed the rules, built a successful career for myself and stayed away from trouble. Come to think of it, I may have been my parents' most polite and level-headed child.

Nonetheless, I wasn't a pushover by any means.

Standing up for myself was an automatic reaction when someone forced my hand, but unless provoked, I didn't like to ruffle feathers or make others uncomfortable and, overall, that worked for me... in public, anyway.

When it came to private, I was someone different entirely.

The type of sex I craved would make a nun have a heart attack, and because I was reluctant to explore my desires, I'd never experienced fucking the way I wanted it.

Watching the porn play out on the screen, my eyes widened as the fireman's tongue swept hungrily over her pussy, licking at every spot and sucking her clit so hard I noticed it swell from one moment to the next.

Without thinking, I reached down and massaged my own clit to relieve some of the building pressure that the vibrator just wasn't reaching.

She was going to cum, and I was cumming with her... or then again, maybe I wasn't.

My vibrator made a grunting noise and stalled before starting up again, with a weaker thrust and a quieter roar.

"No, no no no no," I said aloud. "Don't give up on me now."

I pushed it in and out, hoping to help it regain some power to finish the job, but it was fading fast and I couldn't stop it.

I glanced back up at the TV in desperation, wanting the couple to wait for me. I wanted to cum too, dammit, but it seemed my vibrator was clocking out for the night.

As soon as it went silent, the woman got loud, screaming from an impressive release that I was jealous not to be part of.

I tried to restart the feeling with my hand, but it wasn't the same. It was too long of an interruption and I'd lost my sweet spot. I would have to start all over.

Sitting up, frustrated, I was suddenly very aware of the puddle beneath me. I was still turned on.

These days nothing got me off like a good porn and a strong vibrator. I had to finish the job.

Besides, there was no reason I shouldn't.

It was a Friday night. I was alone, couldn't sleep, and horny as hell. I hadn't gotten laid in so long and hadn't cum in even longer. I deserved this!

Refusing to let dead batteries stand in my way. I searched my apartment for some replacements and came up empty.

Turns out the vibrator required two double-A batteries, and it was on this night that I discovered that every device I owned used triple-A.

Looks like I was fucked, and not in the good way.

Still naked, I placed a hand on my hip and sighed. Then the thought of how ridiculous I must have looked hit me, and I couldn't help but laugh.

I was a thirty-three-year-old woman, successful, smart and, until a year and a half ago, worked as a professional model.

I had no problems getting sex, let alone a date.

Nevertheless, here I was, standing in my living room, sexually frustrated and rummaging through my house like a madwoman, searching for batteries so I could get off.

"Get it together, Raquel," I said to myself.

Spinning around, the glow of the moon and something else caught my eye out of the window. Moving closer, I peered out of my partially opened blinds down at the store on the corner. Zens was still open.

I guess I am going out.

Hurrying to my closet, I spent five minutes trying to locate an outfit that didn't make me look like I was ready for a photoshoot.

After all these years, I guess old habits were hard to break. I barely had any regular clothes, like sweats or an old ratty pair of jeans.

For as far back as I could remember, everything I wore was about representation and putting my best foot forward.

Not because I was some world-renowned model, because I wasn't, but because it was how my parents raised me; my mother specifically.

Like me, my mom spent many years putting her best foot forward on runways and anywhere else her long legs and striking looks were requested.

The importance of fashion was akin to breathing for her. Which meant if she could see the faded pair of pink sweats and matching hoody I was currently pulling on, she'd nearly suffocate.

And then because she is the sweetest and funniest woman I know. We would laugh and she would pull me in for a hug and say that she still loved me, despite my wardrobe choices.

I caught the elevator, exited the building and was inside the door of Zens in less than five minutes.

"Raquel!" Lenny Zen, the owner, shouted from the front as I entered. "My favorite girl. What brings you in tonight?"

I make a right and then a left, quickly locating the battery section. Thanks to all my late night cravings, I'd been here many times and knew this store like the back of my hand.

"Oh, you know me," I said, pulling a six-pack of double-A batteries from the shelf. "I couldn't sleep, so may as well check on Lenny."

"Well, I'm honored."

Tapping the batteries in my hand, I glance around the store. It would be a shame to not pick up some butter pecan ice cream and a root beer.

Collecting my items, I make my way to the front. Another customer enters, heading towards the back, and Lenny gives him the same warm greeting.

Lenny was a good guy, always smiling, and knew most of his customers by name.

The man could definitely teach major companies a thing or two about customer service.

"How's Maureen and the boys?" I asked, placing my merchandise on the counter.

"The boys are good, but Maureen is still bitter about me forgetting our anniversary last week." Lenny bagged my items. "I must thank you again for getting me that necklace last minute. If you didn't, I think I'd be sleeping outside."

I laughed.

"I'm sure Maureen would never do that. She loves you. How much do I owe you?" I said, after seeing there was no amount displayed on the register.

He waved a dismissive hand and slid the bag toward me. "Maybe, but this is on the house."

"Lenny, your thanks is enough. I don't need any special treatment."

He pushed the bag closer.

"I won't take no for an —"

"Face down, hands behind your head!" shouted someone behind me.

Lenny's hands shot up into the air, and my reaction mirrored Lenny's as absolute terror filled my soul.

I turned, hands in the air, and watched a man dressed in all black wearing a ski mask advance towards us with a gun pointed straight at me.

"I said on the floor, hands behind your head!" The man repeated to me in a menacing tone.

I dropped to the floor and assumed the position. Half because I was obeying orders and half because my knees gave out on me. I couldn't think, breathe, or speak.

"You too, fat ass!" the robber shouted to the customer that had entered the store a few minutes ago. "I see you over there trying to hide behind that rack. Get over here and get down!"

I heard the squeak of the guy's shoes behind me and felt the air shift as he got face down on the floor less than three feet away.

My cheek brushed across the cool, dusty tiled floor as I discreetly turned my head a little toward Lenny. He took a step back and drew the attention of the man with the gun.

"If you try anything, I will blow your fucking head off. Empty the register now."

Lenny's voice was shaky and scared when he said, "Okay, okay."

"Hurry up," the robber yelled, as if a gun in his face wasn't enough incentive for Lenny to move as fast as humanly possible.

Please God... please God... please God.

I didn't know exactly what my request was. I just needed help. If anyone died, I'd have another nightmare to add to my lineup and if I got killed, well.. at least the nightmares would be over.

With my hands pressed firmly behind my head, I could feel tiny strands of hair that had gotten caught in the band of my watch being yanked out when I trembled too hard.

Lenny thrust the money at him, dropping some of it in the process. The guy took the money, shoving it into his pockets.

My face was getting further and further from the ground as I strained to continue watching what was going on.

"That's it?" the robber said in disgust when he was done. "Where's the rest?"

"It's... it's all I got," Lenny said. "Just take it and go. I promise I won't call the cops."

The man stepped closer, touching Lenny's head with the barrel of the gun.

"You won't tell anyone because you will be dead," the man said in a low growl. "Open the safe."

"It's empty. I took the money to the bank earlier. This is all I have, I swear. Don't kill me, please," Lenny pleaded.

The robber cocked his gun. "Wrong answer."

This was it. This was it for Lenny. I was about to watch him die.

"I can get you more money!" I shouted from the floor.

What the fuck? My thudding heart screamed at me. *Don't throw us to the wolves.*

But I had to. I refused to witness Lenny's death. He had an entire family at home. A wife and two small kids that loved him.

I, on the other hand, only had parts of a man at home. Parts that needed batteries, two stupid double-A batteries, in fact, to love me correctly.

I had way less to lose than him.

The scary guy walked over and instructed me and the other hostage to get up on our knees. Now, I was the one staring into the round, dark hole of the gun.

Fear paralyzed my body.

I was going to die and there were so many things I'd miss out on.

Seeing my family again, adding things to my bucket list I knew I'd never truly do, finding a guy that could give me mind-numbing orgasms, getting married...

Oh shit! The wedding.

Jocelyn was going to kill me. I was one of her bridesmaids and if I missed her wedding, she wouldn't care that I died. She would literally dig me up so that she could kill me again.

"Someone wants to be a hero, I see," the guy said.

On the outside, my words came out calmly, but on the inside, I was already in cardiac arrest. "You don't have to hurt anyone, okay? If you want more money, I have my ATM card. I can get you more money."

The man said nothing, and I risked a look up at him. All that was visible were his eyes, and one of them was strange and unlike anything I had ever seen.

The pupil was keyhole-shaped, and the iris was an odd green. Almost faded looking, like the light in his body was being consumed by darkness.

I knew at that very moment he had no soul.

He was going to kill us all. The only delay he was having was deciding just how quick to put me out of my misery.

"A beautiful woman with guts," he finally said. "Maybe I will accept your offer and afterward, you and I can have some fun together. Give me the wallet."

He extended his hand, but unfortunately for me, the hand holding the gun remained aimed at my temple.

I noticed a snake tattoo that wrapped around his pointer finger, continued up the side of his hand and disappeared underneath the sleeve.

It looked so realistic it made my skin crawl.

I swallowed hard and removed one hand from behind my head to reach for my wallet.

Alright, I'm buying time. Maybe we won't die after all.

However, when he tapped the gun against my forehead several times, I almost pissed myself.

"Slowly," he warned. "I wouldn't want to ruin that pretty face."

At a snail's pace, I retrieved my wallet and passed it to him. He opened it, momentarily removing the gun so that he could use both hands to pull out my ID.

Holding it up to the light, he began reading the information aloud.

"Raquel Ash. Dark brown hair, brown eyes and look at that..." he let out a low whistle. "5 feet, 10 inches in height. Now, that's tall."

Robber guy continued reading my ID aloud, making it very clear that he was committing my address to memory.

Well, I'd surpassed cardiac arrest. Now I was flatlining.

That's when I noticed him. Another man, also dressed in all black but not like the man that stood before me. This man was bigger, faster, and undoubtedly better trained.

He was coming up from a rear aisle, crouched low and silently moving towards us, dressed in a dark uniform that I'd grown all too familiar with.

We made eye contact, and I knew everything would be alright.

"It's your lucky day," the robber said, staring down at me. "Get up."

As I stood, my brain scrambled at what to say to keep him facing me. If he turned around, this was going to get real bad, real fast.

"I only came here to get batteries for my vibrator," I blurted.

That threw him off guard. Hell, it threw me off guard, too. I wasn't planning on revealing so much.

For a split second, I could feel everyone's eyes on me in the store. Judging me, perhaps?

But I didn't care, because it worked. The robber shifted back to me, about to say something when everything went to shit.

The other hostage spotted our approaching hero and in a panic yelled, "Please help us! He has a gun."

The robber swiveled so fast he knocked me over.

I screamed, and in the next second, a shot was fired, and the robber fell to the floor. A single bullet hole in the middle of his head.

Everything thereafter happened so fast, and the commotion was overwhelming. Cops were everywhere, reporters were interviewing people and our hero had disappeared into the darkness.

The cameraman turned his bulky black device on me, the bright lights causing me to wince.

Next, the reporter asked a question that I was much too discombobulated to answer before shoving a microphone into my face.

"What?" I said in a deep fog.

"I said can you give us a recount of the story? Were you afraid for your life?"

Afraid was an understatement, but I was too in shock to tell her so.

"So no comment." The reporter asked, pushing for me to say something. "I heard you were a big deal inside. Is that true?"

Suddenly, Lenny was there, throwing his arms around me.

"Yes, it's true. She was amazing! It is because of her I am still alive."

"How so?" The reporter probed, eating the story up.

"She sacrificed herself and distracted the robber to buy the mystery guy enough time to take him down. Raquel is an absolute... what do the kids call it?" he said, snapping his fingers. "Badass," he announced, satisfied with the word. "Raquel is an absolute badass!"

Lenny took over the interview after that, and I sank into the background.

Funny thing, I didn't feel like a badass. I only felt bad. My heart was in my throat. A man had just died, and all I could think about was the guy that had saved our lives.

He was not only a hero, but the dirty star in all of my wildest fantasies and, unluckily for me, my boss.

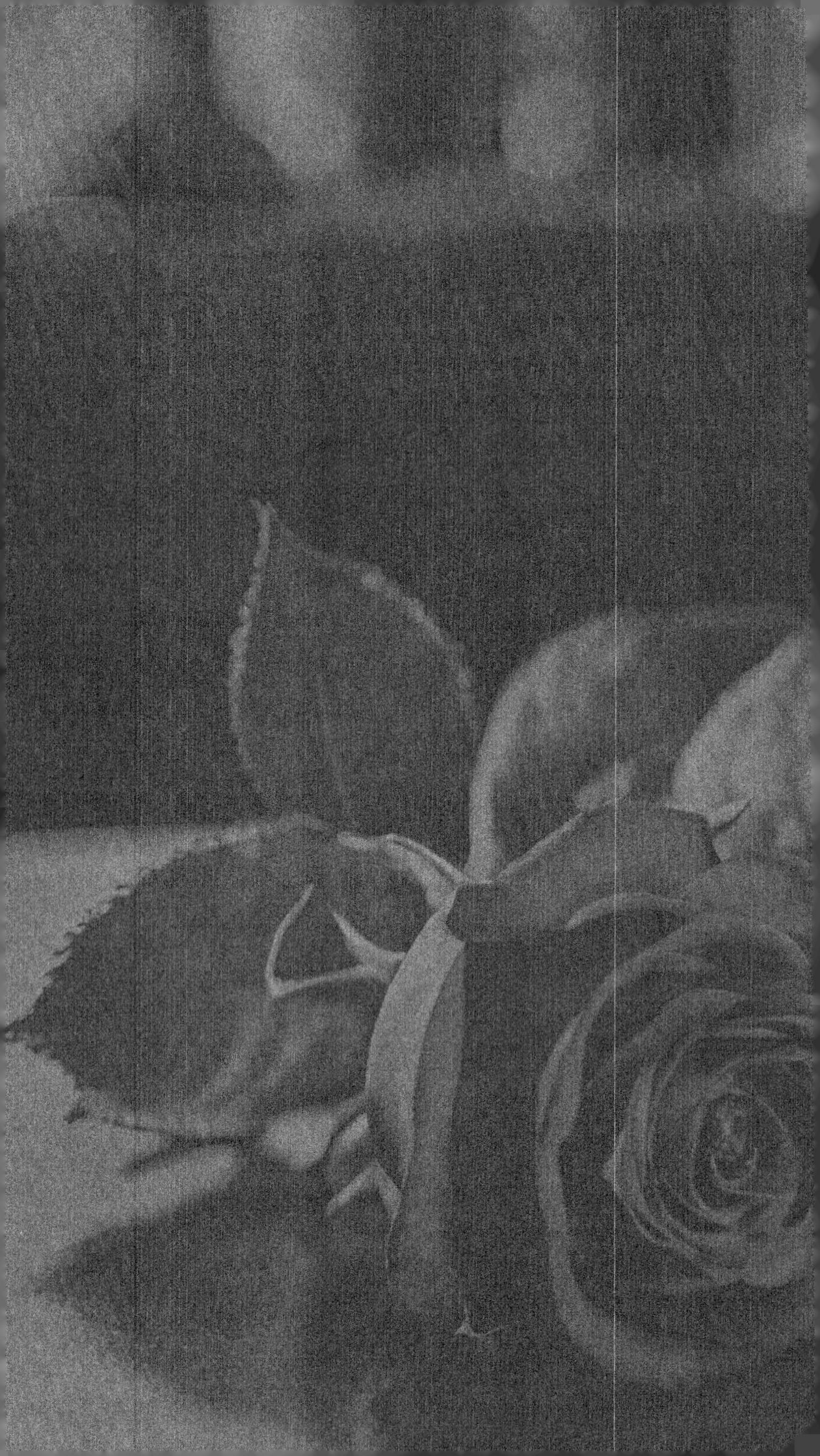

Chapter Two

"I'LL BET HE FUCKS LIKE A MACHINE."

I swiped my employee badge and pulled the door open before stepping into the small, plain lobby.

Two black leather chairs were positioned on either side of the door and less than ten feet ahead was the security desk that I approached with a smile.

"Good morning Miss Ash," the security guard, Trenton, said. "Glad you made it out alive."

Digging deep within, I pulled on my business face.

Based on his statement, I could tell it was going to be a long day.

Which was why I'd taken extra special care this morning in choosing something nice to wear.

When people saw me I wanted them to think put together and serene. Not disheveled and miserable, like the way I felt on the inside.

Therefore, I went with my red skirt suit and silver heels. I even took extra time with my makeup, using a silky, light liquid that gave my honey brown skin a dewy glow.

And what happens?

I'm in the office for less than thirty seconds and all my efforts are wasted.

There was no amount of makeup or stylish suits that would deflect the attention from what happened.

I should have stayed at home. Escaping the questions and comments would be impossible.

The incident had been all over the news and is partially the reason I barely got any sleep this weekend.

Between the calls from my family and friends, reporters wanting a sound bite, and waking repeatedly from the certainty that a gun was still pointed at my head, I was a mess.

Coming into work, a place where varying levels of threats and chaos were part of the day-to-day, I'd thought my personal mishap wouldn't raise a brow and I would finally get a break from it.

Based upon the way Trenton was looking at me, I wouldn't hold my breath.

"Thank you," I replied graciously. "I'm glad I made it out alive as well."

"Did the cops find the person who stepped in to help?"

"Beats me," I answered, moving forward and dropping my purse and phone into a tray to be scanned.

After walking through the metal detector and collecting my things, Trenton motioned for me to move ahead, and I did so with my right hand extended, placing it flat against the digital screen on the wall.

I watched as the green light worked its zippy zappy magic, verifying that I was, in fact, an active employee and allowed access inside the building.

I had been getting my hand scanned every day since I began working here a year ago and I still couldn't believe this was my new life, an assignment processor for Vex—a top-notch security firm.

They provided protection detail for high dollar clients, such as government officials, actors and even aided the FBI with classified missions.

That last one wasn't public knowledge. Very few people that worked inside the building knew about the secret missions Vex was involved in. However, based on the NDA I had to sign, I understood why.

The assignments were perilous and as a processor, even though I was never privy to the full details of any FBI case, I knew the outcomes could, and did, often lead to the threat being eliminated, permanently.

The scanner chimed its approval, and I wished Trenton a good day before stepping into the elevator.

Put on a brave face. Do not break down. Do not cry.

The pep talk I'd been giving myself all morning lasted for two seconds, before I caught myself blinking rapidly to keep the tears at bay.

I couldn't stop seeing flashes of a dead body in my mind. First Loni, now the guy in the store. My mind was becoming a cache of macabre images, and I wasn't a fan.

My therapist would insist that meant it was time to increase my sessions, but I was tired of talking about death and pain.

It was bad enough that thoughts invaded my mind at random times throughout the day. I was no longer interested in also paying her once a week to relive it in vivid detail, no matter how comfy her couch was.

I was going to try it my way for a while, which was nothing special. My only plan was to wing it, shake things up. Maybe join a gym, dye my hair green, or finally attend some of those outings my coworkers invited me to.

Anything but the ordinary.

My phone suddenly vibrated in my purse, and I didn't acknowledge it. I knew it was only my mother calling to make sure once again that I hadn't somehow "expired" on my way to work.

She hated the word, died, so she always used expired, stating that it made the conversation lighter when it sounded like she was only talking about something as simple as a gallon of milk.

Needing a distraction, I pondered what top secret training

they must be doing today in the basement as the elevator rose to my desired floor.

I'd gotten a peek at their training list a few times and they did some pretty extreme stuff. Gun handling, scaling walls, and even crawling across a thin metal wire without falling.

The intensity and focus required were obvious, resulting in the general staff being prohibited from accessing that part of the building.

Once the elevator reached my floor, the doors slid open, and I was immediately aware of two things: how hot it was on this floor and the way several sets of eyes locked on me.

Great.

"I'm glad you're okay," Tammy, from accounting, said, patting my shoulder gently.

"Why is she even here today? I'd never leave the house again." Monica, the HR rep, mumbled to Joe.

And then there was Phillip, from the tactical team who asked, "Do you know who the mystery person was that saved you?"

These were all questions and comments I had endured on the way to my desk while my phone vibrated furiously in my purse. Reminding me that if my vibrator worked as well as my phone, I wouldn't be in this mess.

I didn't want to appear ungrateful to anyone, because I wasn't. It touched me that so many people cared, but I was feeling a little closed in. The constant concern from everyone was a reminder that I almost got my head blown off by Louis Murphy.

Louis Murphy. That was the name of the guy Blaze killed at Zen's. I'd learned it from a news report that I had the guts to watch. However, as soon as the story switched from talking about Murphy to me, I turned it off.

His name never left my mind all weekend.

I kept rolling it around in my head, or saying it, trying to see if it sounded as bitter and cold as the man himself. It didn't, and to my dismay, the haunting memory of the gun he used was equally unforgettable.

The hard steel pressing firmly against my temple, the slight tilt of it when he placed his finger on the trigger, the...

"Earth to Raquel," Melanie said.

I looked up to see the other assignment processor, Melanie, leaning over my cubicle, fanning herself and looking down at me.

That was odd, because I didn't recall sitting down or putting my things away. I really needed to get some sleep.

"Hey, Melanie," I said cheerfully.

She gave me a prolonged stare before speaking, and I inwardly sighed.

I hadn't worked here long, but Melanie and I had become close really fast.

She reminded me of friends I had for years because not only was she kind, honest, and loved a good laugh, but her bullshit radar was top-notch.

"You can drop the act, Raquel. I know you aren't alright. Why didn't you call me back yesterday? I was worried about you."

"I'm sorry, I forgot," I said, giving her my best innocent smile. "I can make it up to you by doing all the ACRs for this week."

I lifted my brows playfully, and Melanie laughed and pointed a finger at me.

"Who do you think you are kidding? I know those are your favorites."

She was right. The Assignment Close-out Reports were like reading miniature drama stories. Any disasters security personnel experienced on a job, no matter how big or small, had to be disclosed in case it was ever necessary from a legal perspective.

Such as the time a celebrity couple got into a fight because the wife was caught banging three men from their waitstaff and the husband, in a fit of rage, stabbed two of them.

Luckily they lived, but that story lasted months in court, and I followed every juicy detail.

Melanie stopped laughing and regarded me soberly.

"You didn't spend all weekend suffering endless panic attacks like I did when I got robbed, did you?"

My expression turned empathetic.

Melanie got mugged at gunpoint three years ago and still avoided going out after dark.

"I wasn't having endless panic attacks," I assured her, pushing the memory of being huddled in the shower and crying my eyes out aside. "I'm digesting it all, but I'm fine. You don't need to worry about me."

Melanie wasn't convinced, but she left that part alone for now and moved on to the infamous question. "Is it true that some unknown person came to the rescue?" she whispered.

"Appears so."

"And you have no idea who they were? Man, woman, the Hulk?"

I shook my head, feeling a twinge of guilt. Melanie had signed the same NDA as me and knew that the work Blaze and his team did for the FBI could be, well, rather messy for lack of a better word, but I still thought it best not to share.

Wasn't the point of the contract to not reveal any details I learned about a case, even if it was with a fellow team member?

Besides, it would only open the door to more questions, and I had zero answers. I didn't even know if that robbery had anything to do with a case Blaze was working on.

Why else would he have been there? The logical part of my brain questioned.

Melanie was staring at me, awaiting some big revelation, but all I gave her was the same statement I'd given the police.

"It all happened so fast, I was unable to get a good look at the person," I stated with a shrug and before she could dig further I asked, "Is someone coming to fix the AC today?"

"HR said it will be up and running by tomorrow," Melanie replied, pulling her hair back into a ponytail. "It's hotter than my weekend with Calvin in here. How come you're still wearing that jacket? Aren't you burning up?"

"No. It's not that bad," I lied, subtly shifting closer to my small desk fan.

This jacket really did need to go, but that wasn't going to happen. Revealing the marks on my upper shoulders and back was unacceptable. I'd rather die of heat stroke first.

"So let's backtrack," I said to Melanie. "You mentioned something about a hot weekend with hubby?"

Melanie's face lit up. "Yes! We left the kids with my mom and I finally got some." Melanie wiggled her brows. "A whole lot of some."

I released a sound of annoyance. "Don't rub it in."

She rolled her eyes. "Raquel please, everyone knows that between your stunning sense of style and that gorgeous face you could have any guy, anytime. It's not our fault that you are so picky."

"I am not."

Melanie leaned further over the edge of the cubicle. At this point, she should have just come over to my desk.

"Oh yeah," she challenged. "What was wrong with Eric?"

I rolled my chair closer before replying, thankful for the excuse to get in better alignment with the fan.

"Eric was... was... not a good fit."

"Yeah right," Melanie muttered. "Those are called excuses. Nothing was wrong with him, and he still wants to date you."

"He does not."

"Well, why is he coming over?"

"Why is he what?!" I said, spinning around in my chair

just in time to see Eric approaching.

"Raquel, I'm so glad you're alright!"

A hug accompanied his words, and I was caught off guard, so my arms just kind of hung there while he squeezed me tight like a grandmother would.

Out of the corner of my eye, I noticed Melanie lowering herself slowly out of view. First her mouth, then her eyes, and eventually her entire head disappeared behind the dividing wall.

Melanie wasn't fooling me. I knew she was listening.

Eric was reasonably attractive, nice, and we had gone out on a few dates since I began working here, but unfortunately for him, he wasn't my type.

As one of Vex's security guards, I think he fascinated me because of my newfound attraction to men in uniform.

However, upon further dating and even a few rounds in the sack, I realized the only thing I loved about Eric *was* his uniform.

Eric was much too clingy. Showing up at my home unannounced repeatedly, belching all the time mid-sentence, and for a guy that worked security for a living, he was rather clumsy.

It was too much.

Maybe, if the sex was amazing, I could have dated him longer, but it was mediocre at best. Which was a major turn off because I am pretty simple to please.

For one, I had only had sex with four men in my entire life, so the bar for what I expect wasn't exceptionally high.

Two. Thanks to an awful experience in my past, I don't require or even allow guys to give me oral even though I do it for them.

And three. I was too nice.

As it pertained to sex, anyway. I was reluctant to reveal my true desires to a man, fearing his judgment or manipulation.

Therefore, I'd fake an orgasm and cheer him on like he's made a touchdown, even if he already screwed up in the preliminaries.

Eric released me, and I clasped my hands together and gave him a pleasant smile.

"Yes. I'm okay," I said.

He took a step back, looking me over again as if my mere physical presence wasn't enough to convince him I was alive.

"Do you need anything? Want to go out to dinner tonight and talk?"

"Umm, that's unnecessary, but I appreciate it, though."

"You sure?" he asked, his hand rubbing over mine. "We can go to that place you like?"

I rolled my chair a few inches back. Hoping to stave off any further touching.

He'd been asking me out on another date for months since I broke it off. I guess he was trying to use this misfortunate incident as an opportunity to restart things.

"Eric, I just want to go home and get some rest."

He looked a little hurt, and that made me feel awful.

"Another time then?" he asked hopefully.

"Let's see how things go," I replied, refusing to commit officially.

Finally, Eric gave me two thumbs up and left.

"He's gone now. You can stand up," I said to Melanie.

Her head popped back into view so fast she bumped into the thin cubicle wall, causing it to shake.

I got up and went around to her side so that we could stop this awkward socializing over the wall. As soon as I set foot in her area, Melanie jumped up and down, excited that Eric asked me out again.

Between Melanie and Eric, I wasn't sure which of the two wanted Eric and me back together more.

"You should—"

"No," I said, cutting her off.

"But Eric is so—"

"No," I reiterated.

"He really likes —"

"Absolutely not!" I said. "Eric has been fired as a potential boyfriend and if we don't get to work, you and I will be fired from our jobs."

Melanie opened her mouth to protest, but quickly shut it when he walked in.

He, being the owner and CEO of Vex, Adrian Shaw, better known as Blaze.

My knees weakened and everything around me moved in slow motion, as I fought not to stare, but I couldn't resist.

Blaze was the most attractive, yet intense man I had ever seen, and being a model for most of my life, I'd seen a lot of men.

Confidence rolled off of him like ocean waves, taunting and teasing me, making me wet and willing to be drowned in his grasp.

No matter if I were seeing him at work, or a casual function between our mutual friends, Merrick and Jocelyn, Blaze had this effect on me.

The man awakened every part of my body, especially the lower half.

I could, and often did, masturbate to the thought of him, confirming that as corny as the thought was, the man was like catnip to my pussy.

Blaze was ten years older than me, placing him in his early forties.

Never had I been so attracted to an older man, but the maturity, experience and no doubt sexual knowledge he possessed were hard to ignore. It laid the groundwork that enticed my mind while his physical attributes called to my body.

The man was six feet six inches tall, with golden brown skin and dark brown eyes so captivating they spoke volumes even when he hadn't said a word.

He'd trained in the military, successfully led a SWAT team for five years, and since opening Vex, Blaze had secured and closed over one hundred confidential cases for the FBI.

The man was a force all his own.

I mentally drooled as I gazed at his tattooed arms that promised his tough and dominating demeanor was not just for show.

My eyes traveled to his shoulders and chest, broad and hard, sporting a black t-shirt covered by a bullet-proof vest that clung to him in ways I wish I could.

Shit, I need to get laid.

Blaze was perfection in the physical form, a trained killer and the type of man I should avoid. He was setting me on fire, and this office was already hot enough, but it was so hard to look away.

Why did I feel so weak around him?

Melanie, humming in a low voice to herself, pulled me from my fantasy and I finally tore my eyes away from Blaze and noticed his four team members following close behind.

They were the only people at Vex with clearance to work on all the covert operations with him and, although Blaze was in a league all his own, his team was also pretty impressive.

They were a diverse, highly respected and equally dangerous combo.

Jolli, the country boy that kept everyone laughing, hence the nickname, was an expert with explosives. Vadim was an intense Russian and the best marksman in the building. Axel was from Jamaica and remarkably skilled with knives, and Hannah, well, Hannah was who I wanted to be when I grew up. A badass Colombian beauty that was fierce in hand-to-hand combat.

ADRIAN SHAW

SKILLS: Psychological Manipulation, Hunting and Tracking, Polyglot, Jiujitsu, Survival Specialist, Boxing

BLAZE

KILLS: 154

HANNAH ESCO

SKILLS: Jiujitsu, Boxing, Hand to Hand combat, Weapons, Psychological Combat

HANNAH

KILLS: 101

AXEL BENNETT

SKILLS: Psychological Combat, Hunting and Tracking, Survival Specialist, Bladesmith

AXEL

KILLS: 93

VADIM DMITRIEV

SKILLS: Psychological Combat, Marksman, Hunting and Tracking, Hand to Hand combat

VADIM

KILLS: 122

SAMUEL VANT

SKILLS: Explosives Expert, Psychological Combat, Hunting and Tracking, Weapons

JOLLI

KILLS: 87

"I'll bet he fucks like a machine," Melanie said, fanning herself. "If I wasn't married...the things I would do to that man."

There was no question regarding who Melanie was referring to. Jolli, Vadim and Axel were handsome, but Blaze was the prize. Every woman in this office noticed him.

I swallowed hard, pretending, like I too, wasn't having a naughty daydream.

"Put it back in your pants, Melanie."

"What? I'm just admiring the view. The very tall, hot, mouthwatering view." Melanie said. "You know what? Forget about Eric. Maybe you should give him a go."

"Blaze?" I asked, as if the thought was preposterous.

"Mm-hmm," Melanie replied, not taking her eyes off of him.

"But he's our boss."

"So what?" Melanie said.

"He's probably not even single," I countered.

Melanie finally tore her eyes away.

"I'll bet he is. Or at least that's what office gossip says."

"Interesting," I acknowledged, giving her my full attention. "What else does office gossip say?"

Melanie moved in real close and spoke in a whisper. "That he's a dom."

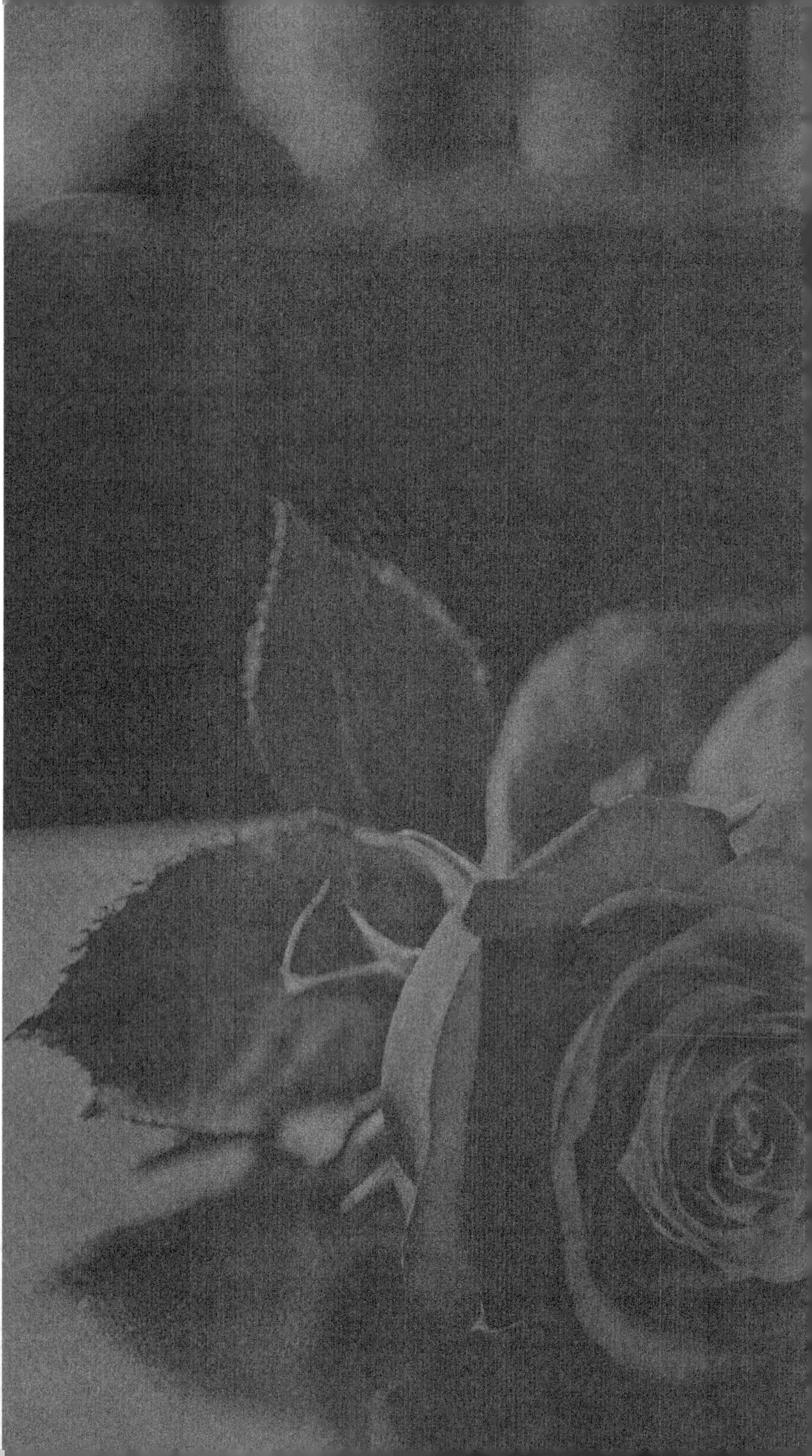

Chapter Three

"I HAVE OTHER WAYS TO ALLEVIATE STRESS."

I averted my eyes, but I don't think Melanie noticed. Her attention had returned to Blaze, and she was busy carrying on a conversation with herself.

"I wonder if it's true? Could he really be a dom? A man that uses chains and whips to spank women when they're naughty?" She gave a little giggle and jerk at the last sentence as if she were imagining someone tapping her on the ass.

Melanie's intense concentration on Blaze was so evident that it was surprising he hadn't turned around, given that she was practically laser-focused on him.

I smiled to myself because for Melanie, Blaze's sexual interests were merely speculation based on office gossip, but I knew for a fact that he was a dom.

I'd never had the guts to ask, but I was smart enough to put two and two together.

My close friend Jocelyn, who got me this job, was engaged to a man named Merrick.

Merrick was not only a long-time friend of Blaze, but thanks to a fun girls' night out, I'd learned that Merrick was a Dom and Jocelyn was his sub.

The drunken confession from my friend instantly clarified what I'd noticed in Blaze.

Both he and Merrick had an energy that demanded respect, attention, and obedience. It was no wonder women lusted after him and men automatically gave him the utmost respect.

Since her slip up, Jocelyn had welcomed my questions about her role as a submissive and I found myself baffled.

I respected Jocelyn, and it seemed Merrick respected her too, and that's why it made no sense.

Jocelyn was a lawyer. A successful one at that. She was also strong, intelligent and independent. It was why we were such good friends.

But on the flip side, I couldn't understand why she would let Merrick degrade her, tie her up, make her do unthinkable things, and then beg for more.

It all seemed so disrespectful, chauvinistic, and just plain wrong. And yet, the idea of being a sub intrigued me.

I shook my head to clear it. The heat must have been getting to me.

"That's only office gossip," I said to Melanie.

We watched Blaze and his team disappear into his office and close the door and my knees ceased from being Jello.

Suddenly, every sound that I'd unconsciously pushed aside flooded in at once. Phone's ringing, people speaking, the clattering of fingers on keyboards, and the distant noise of traffic outside.

"I'm going to get to work," I said, heading back to my desk.

Despite agreeing, Melanie didn't move. I think the trance had paralyzed her. Therefore, I left her there to sort it out.

Two hours later, I had processed four new security jobs and closed out seven.

Only one was so hilarious I had to read it twice.

Security officer, Romeo Hodge, was on assignment for a dinner party at a famous movie star, turned politician's residence and had experienced a very eventful evening according to the notes...

At approximately 2100 hours, I noticed a man across the lawn, inside the guest home, standing in the window watching us. Unable to make out the suspect's face, due to poor lighting and his position, I pulled out a pair of binoculars to further investigate.
It was then that I determined the suspect was wearing a hat, sunglasses, and was clutching the lower half of a rifle.
Following protocol, I notified the security officers on sight and we discreetly made our way to the subject.

Adjusting my fan so that it now blew on my face, I took a sip of water and chewed on a few ice cubes before getting back to the report, certain I was moments away from an awesome kick ass scene.

All I need now is a bowl of popcorn.

Skimming the page, I located where I left off, and in a matter of seconds realized I didn't need popcorn. I'd been had, just like Hodge and his team in the report.

Turns out, the perp was nothing more than a cardboard cutout of a bad guy from one of the actors' movies.

Evidently, one of the waitstaff had gone into the guesthouse to retrieve some extra tables cloths and accidentally left the cutout near the window.

Thankfully, no one got hurt, but anytime weapons are drawn it must be reported.

I processed the report and was moving on to the next when my desk phone rung. Without glancing at the caller ID, I answered and said, "This is Raquel. How may I help you?"

"Just hearing your lovely voice is enough for me."

I couldn't help but smile. It was FBI Agent Michael Swanson. One of the three agents that phoned in the confidential cases for Blaze and his team. These cases were called Red Dot Assignments, but within the office we referred to them as R.D.A.

"Agent Swanson," I said. "How are you?"

"You know me, beautiful, always trying to keep my head low so that the boss doesn't put more on my plate."

I'd only physically met Swanson and the other two agents, Divers and Steele, twice, and both times were at company events for local charities.

Even then Swanson was a nonstop flirt, but I didn't take it personal. He struck me as the type that was overly charming with all the ladies.

"But you are the boss on your team," I reminded him.

Swanson sighed. "Only one of the many, sweetheart. Everyone answers to someone."

"In that case, what can I do for you? Are you calling to submit an R.D.A?"

"No. I actually called to speak to you. I saw the news." He said, letting that suffice as enough prep to dive into a conversation.

My mind flashed back to that night and I blinked multiple times to eliminate the forming images.

"Yeah," I said, hoping to swiftly wrap this up. "It was rough, but I have already begun to put it behind me."

"I'll bet that was scary, though."

I slouched in my chair. This would not be quick.

"It was," I said.

"Did the investigating officers learn anything more about the robbery? Like why the guy hit up the store in the first place? Or who he was?"

I shook my head. Then, realizing he couldn't see me, gave a verbal response.

Prying came with the territory around here. Especially when I was talking to Agent Swanson. He never volunteered much information, but he always had a boatload of questions.

I guess it was because on his end he conducted field interviews and interrogated suspects, which meant he was always giving others the side eye and double checking that everyone else, even if they didn't work for him, did their job.

"You aren't safe anywhere these days," Agent Swanson muttered. "What about the mysterious hero?"

That question perked me up. I assumed he knew it was Blaze. Was he asking to see if I knew as well, or because he didn't?

"I do not know who it was."

Swanson was silent for a long moment, then said, "The other hostages saw nothing, either?"

For the love of God!

I strived to be respectful and patient, but the questioning was overwhelming.

In my calmest voice yet I said, "I'm not sure what they saw, but the police reports would give you more answers than I can."

"Yeah," he said, as if in deep thought. "Either way, I am glad you are okay and you tell Blaze I said to take it easy on you. We don't want..."

I zoned out on Swanson's incessant chatter, getting lost in my thoughts. The comment about Blaze had fired up my imagination. The last thing I wanted was for him to be gentle with me.

Rough me up, pull my hair, give me the orgasm of a lifetime.

"Raquel, are you there?"

I snapped back to the conversation.

"Sorry, got caught up in a work matter."

Swanson chuckled gruffly.

"I guess I have held you up long enough. I'll let you get back to work. If you think of anything at all, please don't hesitate to let me know. If need be, I won't bat an eye to get some of my fellow agents involved."

"Thank you. You're too kind."

"No need to thank me. You may not be an agent or work for me directly, but I consider you one of our own. And we take care of our own."

After thanking Swanson yet again, we ended the call, and I decided it was time for a break.

Entering the restroom, I wet a few napkins and took them into a stall with me. As I closed the door, I couldn't wait to escape the suffocating warmth of my red suit jacket.

It had felt like a heated blanket trapping me and making me feel constricted. The moment I slipped it off, a rush of air brushed against my skin, causing an instant wave of relief to wash over me.

The sensation was so refreshing that I couldn't help but let out a sigh of relief, feeling the tension in my muscles gradually melt away.

I rubbed the damp napkin on the back of my neck and upper shoulders and moaned.

This feels amazing.

A few droplets of water trickled down my back, disappearing all together midway down my spine, mixing in with the sweat.

Yuck!

Thank God the AC was being fixed tomorrow. I felt gross.

As soon as I got home, I was going to stand in a cold shower for an hour.

I remained in the stall for a few more minutes, relishing in the small comfort of coolness, before I eventually pulled my jacket back on and left the bathroom to return to my desk.

"Hey chica," came a voice from behind me not less than a minute after I sat down.

I didn't need to turn around to know it was Hannah. Her Colombian accent was unmistakable, and she was the only one that called me chica.

"What's up, Han — "

I broke off once I saw her hand. Hannah was leaning against the side of my cubicle, the injured hand dangling over the edge. It was swollen, red, and had multiple cuts.

"Rough day?" I asked.

"My day was great," Hannah replied nonchalantly.

If I wasn't looking at proof that indicated otherwise, I would have believed her.

Hannah stood there, appearing perfectly normal. She was wearing her black cargo pants and tank top, displaying the same "I crave chaos" tattoo that Blaze and all the other team members had.

She had a gun securely strapped to her thigh, and her hair was neatly pulled back into a ponytail.

Nope. Hannah didn't look bothered at all and every time I saw her, I thought about the character from the video game, Tomb Raider.

"And that?" I added, motioning at her hand.

"Well, this is evidence that the asshole that attempted to kiss me while I was taking him down isn't having such a great day."

I winced, remembering the after photos of a few aggressors that tried and miserably failed at taking her on.

"Anyway," Hannah said, cradling her bruised hand with the other. "Blaze is forcing me to go get this looked at, so I've got to go, but he said he wants to see you."

She walked away, and my nerves shot up several notches. Obviously, he, too, wanted to talk about the incident.

Mentally preparing for the exchange I'd been dreading all morning, I walked the short distance to Blaze's corner office.

Normally, I would welcome time around Blaze. He was not just great eye candy, but a host of other things which often included funny, kind and very down to earth.

I knocked on the already open office door and Blaze

motioned for me to come in, then held up a finger to let me know he would be with me shortly.

He was on the phone, attentively listening to what the caller had to say.

Therefore, I quietly closed the door behind me and took a seat, busying myself with a visual tour of his office.

It was standard size. Nothing fancy.

Pictures of him with his team members and political figures lined one wall, and a bookshelf filled with books on psychology, tactical training, and the law stood against the other.

The overall atmosphere exuded professionalism and a sense of purpose, reflecting the importance of the work that took place within these walls.

My eyes shifted back to him, sitting in his comfortable black leather chair.

I couldn't help but notice he'd removed the vest, and now, I could see the defined outline of the chest I desperately wanted to be my pillow.

"I heard you," Blaze suddenly said, "And you and Swanson can kiss my ass if you think I'm going to send my team into anything prematurely."

He was quiet again, and I avoided eye contact, feeling embarrassed for whomever was on the other end of that call.

A couple of other things Blaze could be besides down to earth, kind and funny was unabashed, direct and a smart-ass.

He named his company Vex for goodness' sake. A word that meant to cause stress, worry, or frustration.

When I asked him why he'd chosen that name, Blaze smirked and said, "Because I hope to cause all criminals stress and worry when they know I'm on the job."

A true Blaze response if I ever heard one. The point was, the man took no shit, and while it was very beneficial for his line of work, I assumed it could be offensive to those that weren't used to it.

"Smart choice," Blaze said into the receiver. "I'll be in touch."

After hanging up, he smiled at me. It was innocent, I'm sure, but it gave me goosebumps.

I returned his expression with the easy, breezy smile I'd been perfecting all morning.

I knew what was coming next. Some version of "Are you okay, Raquel?" and in response I would satisfy his concernment with assurances that I was.

However, my fake smile turned into genuine laughter when he said, "Batteries for your vibrator, huh?"

"Oh, you heard that?"

"I think the entire store heard it. But that was undoubtedly a good save and very creative too."

Instead of enlightening him to the fact that what he took for creativity was literally a full-blown confession blurted out to save my life, I said, "Yeah, creative, that's it. Hey, why were you there anyway? That couldn't have been just coincidence."

Blaze ran a hand over his low cut beard. The action placed enticing emphasis on his massive biceps and the burning skull tattoo with the words "I crave chaos" scribbled across its forehead.

"That's confidential, Ms. Ash."

Dammit!

Now I had no hope of learning what the hell was going on.

I gave a slow nod of understanding.

"Good thing I didn't reveal you as the mysterious hero."

"Yes it is," Blaze responded. "Thank you for not blowing my cover. Unfortunately, this job sometimes requires total anonymity."

I didn't know why he was thanking me. He knew I was

under an obligation to not say anything once I found out he was involved.

"It's no big deal," I fibbed.

When, in fact, it was an enormous deal. I wanted to know what the hell was going on. Not being able to ask questions only filled my head with more of them.

Was this about Lenny? The robber? Or was criminal activity going on in the area?

Then suddenly, a particularly important thought occurred to me. Just because I didn't give the cops a description of Blaze doesn't mean Lenny or the other hostage didn't.

"Did anyone else provide the police with a sketch of you?"

"No, luckily they didn't get a good look at my face and even if they had, I've already sat down with the lead detective on the case. My involvement will not be made public."

"That's good," I replied.

A long silence engulfed the room and I could feel the mood shift from casual to serious and I instantly felt out of place.

Blaze felt sorry for me.

I could see it in his eyes, and because I needed to escape that empathetic gaze, I pulled at an imaginary thread on my dress.

Ever since I was a little girl, I'd been tough. Protecting not only myself but my little brother Des from bullies and overall negativity.

Now, I'd found myself at a stage in my life where I felt helpless. Stripped of all power, some small version of myself cowered in a corner, fearing the unknown.

"Ms. Ash," Blaze said, waiting until I made eye contact before continuing. "You know what I'm going to ask."

"Yes, I do and I assure you I'm —" I was about to say fine, but when Blaze's eyes narrowed on me, the lie faded from my lips. "I have my moments," I said instead.

"Needing time is nothing to be embarrassed about. Do you want to take a few days off?"

He said it so gently, like he was trying not to scare a puppy, and it revealed a side of him that I'd never seen before.

Briefly, I considered his question, but ultimately declined his offer. I needed to work.

Work kept me busy and right now, busy was the best solution for my life.

Blaze studied me, as if trying to decide if taking some time off would be a decision he was better suited to make for me.

Hell no.

I would stand my ground. Yes, as my boss he could order me to go home, however I wouldn't do so without a fight.

Getting up from the chair, I placed my hands on my hips, straightened my shoulders and utilized my full five feet ten inches to stare him down.

His lips curved into a slow smile.

"Will I see you Saturday?" he said.

"Saturday?" I asked, puzzled.

I was prepared for a fight, a reason to dig my heels in, not an inquiry about my future plans.

"You know Merrick and Jocelyn's wedding? If you have forgotten, don't call my team for back up when Jocelyn loses it on you."

I couldn't help it. I laughed again. He was right, Jocelyn would lose it.

She had worked her bridesmaids endlessly to ensure that every single detail was up to fairytale standards and we would deliver, because no matter how much of a Bridezilla Jocelyn was, she deserved the very best.

My hands dropped from my hips.

"Yeah. I'm ready," I said. I'd passed the test and now I could get back to work. "You will be there too, right?"

"I wouldn't miss it," Blaze replied.

"Well, I guess I'll see you there."

I turned to leave, just as Blaze pulled something from his desk drawer.

"Think fast," he said.

I spun around in time to catch a small squishy football. Turning it over, I noticed his name, Blaze, was printed above the white line that represented laces, but they always made me think of cartoon stitches.

"What's this?" I asked.

Blaze got to his feet and came to stand next to me by the door.

"It's your stress reliever. I think after all you have been through, you should at least allow yourself this."

He smelled amazing and I looked up at him, yearning to kiss those lips.

"Oh," I said, trying to keep my voice even. "And if you give me this, what will you use?"

Blaze grinned. "I have other ways to alleviate stress, Ms. Ash."

His voice was so seductive I swallowed hard to fight back a moan.

And then, as if he hadn't just started a fire inside me that only he could put out, Blaze reached around me, opened the door and with one last flirtatious smile said, "You can get back to work now."

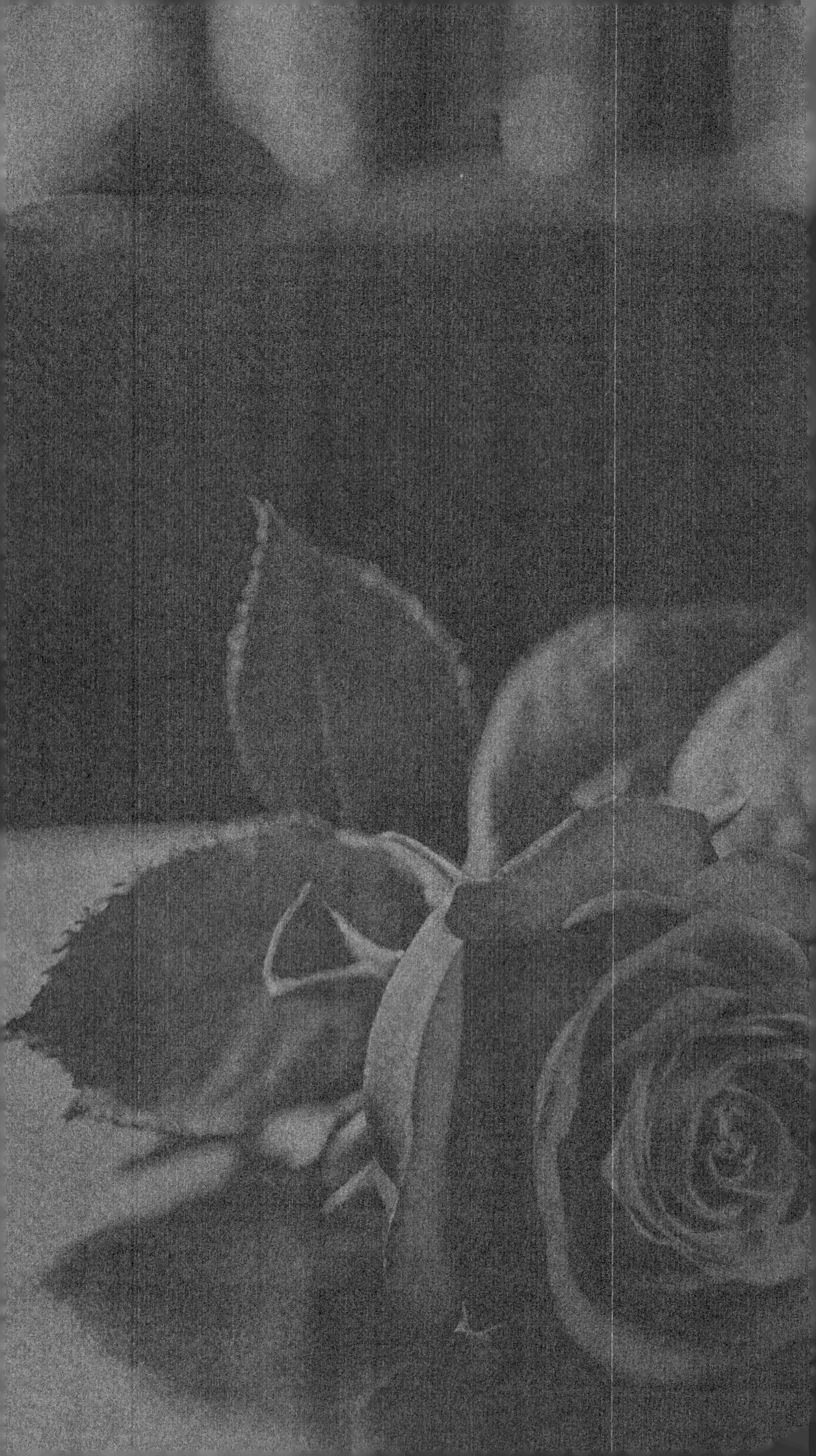

Chapter Four

"Pussy scorcher?"

"Loni watch out!" I screamed, bolting upright in bed, but it was too late.

The guy with the black mask and the snake tattoo had shot her, and she was gone.

There was blood everywhere.

I stared down, seeing her body. Just like that night. Limp, unresponsive... dead.

Slowly, my surroundings materialized in front of me. I wasn't at the store, looking down at Loni's body. I was at home in bed.

The only light coming from a crown shaped nightlight in the corner of my room.

I checked the time.

The clock on my nightstand read 5:21 am and the low hum of my diffuser was still going strong, with an essential oil blend that promised peaceful sleep and sweet dreams.

So much for that promise.

My eyes welled with tears, and I inhaled deeply before squeezing them shut.

Loni was dead, but not from a gunshot wound, from a car accident.

Gasping for air while my heart pounded in my chest, I wiped the sweat from my forehead with the back of my hand. In a cruel twist of fate, I understood what had happened.

The two most tragic events of my life had merged into one gigantic nightmare, and I was left grappling with the grief.

Yanking the covers off, I threw my legs over the side of the bed and sat there for several minutes before sliding my fingers down my neck and across the top of my shoulders.

The familiar raised scars were still there, my permanent reminder of that night. Disgusting.

But you made it, Loni didn't.

The thought was the opposite of settling. Especially since it was all my fault Loni had died.

I rose from the bed to prepare for my morning run. It was an hour earlier than my usual time, but clearing my head would do some good.

After pulling on my sportswear, I slipped into my running shoes and stretched my tired muscles.

The air was refreshing as I stepped out onto the quiet street. It took no time at all for the stillness of the morning to envelop me in a sense of tranquility that I desperately needed.

I started the familiar two-mile trail I ran every morning and the rhythmic sound of my footsteps echoed in my ears, creating a soothing melody that drowned out any lingering thoughts.

When I first began these early morning workouts, they were to benefit my health. Nowadays, it was less about my physical health and more about my mental health.

Running was therapeutic. It lifted my spirits, untangled my nerves, and provided me with a sense of clarity.

Breezing through the first mile, I pushed hard as I approached the second, stretching my legs further, pushing my body to move faster as I rounded a curve, passing another early morning jogger.

Today was Jocelyn's wedding, and I needed to be focused.

There was no room for destructive memories that tore

away at my very soul. Today was a happy day and I would make it the best day possible for my friend.

"Wow!" I said to myself as I stared out the window at the massive royal looking building.

I'd driven by this place a few times in the late afternoon in order to know the venue for the wedding, but seeing it this close and in the light of day was breathtaking.

The Palace, as it was called, was an elite hotel and an extremely popular location for weddings. It sat on twenty acres of land, giving guests the options of making their dreams come true inside the mansion style building or outside in the most extravagant vineyard I had ever seen.

"Do you need help with your things, ma'am?" The driver, Diego, asked.

I considered my small luggage bag and the bridesmaids dress carefully placed across the seat, then shook my head.

"No, thank you. I am good from here."

After exiting the vehicle with my bridesmaid dress over one arm and my bag of accessories in my hand, I waved goodbye and proceeded toward the building's stairs.

I would have tipped him, but Diego insisted I didn't need to, stating that everything was already taken care of, and if I knew Jocelyn, it was.

As part of a thank you, she had hired personal drivers to bring us to and from the event.

As soon as I entered the building, I was graced with the subtle fragrance of freshly cut flowers and warm vanilla, and that was enough to make me pause and admire the lavish interior laid out before me.

Twin stairways, designed with black iron rails, ascended to a spacious landing that featured 3 elevators. The walls were adorned with ornate tapestries depicting scenes from mythological tales, adding an air of timeless elegance, and the ceiling boasted a vast chandelier that sparkled majestically.

Even the floor was a statement piece, covered in a lovely design of rose petals and gold flecks, spread out across the glossy floor.

"Coming through! Coming through!" a guy shouted, pushing a giant ice structure on a cart through the lobby.

Several of the staff members avoided the collision at the last second, but if the cart driver didn't slow down, that work of art was going to become a million ice cubes on the floor.

Everyone in the building seemed to move at full speed. Rushing this way and that, shouting orders and checking in guests.

I naively believed that things would become less hectic once I reached room five for prep. I was mistaken. If anything, the pace quickened.

After knocking on the door once, it was yanked open, and a short woman with a pencil behind her ear and a clipboard swiftly ushered me into the room.

"Finally!" she said. "I am Ms. Loosh. You are Raquel, right?"

My mind immediately associated her name with the word whoosh, because not only did it rhyme, it was pretty spot on for how the Loosh-Whoosh was behaving.

"Yes, am I late?" I said, increasing my movements to keep up. Her brisk pace matched her efficient demeanor. "I thought I was on time."

"On time is late, dear. You should have arrived an hour ago."

"My apologies," I said, old habits instantly rearing their heads from my modeling days. I had several designers that said the same thing. While others took showing up early as a blatant disregard to their schedules.

Can't win them all.

However, I don't think Ms. Loosh even heard me. She stopped abruptly and snapped her fingers in the air. "Valencia, the last one is here. Get her setup please."

Valencia, I presumed, rushed over, giving me a quick bow and a warm smile before leading me to the area where I spotted the other women.

Tamika and Kelly, the other bridesmaids, were in chairs near the door getting their hair done.

Jada, the maid of honor, was getting a pedicure, and Jocelyn, the beautiful bride-to-be, had three people working on her hair, nails and feet as she rested in a throne-like chair, being spoiled like a queen.

Quietly, I greeted all four women while Valencia pushed me into the chair, her hands in my hair, tossing it side-to-side.

They smiled and waved hello with an unmistakable energy and excitement, but they didn't dare move too much or speak too loud, likely afraid that Loosh would whoosh them away to time out.

I chuckled at my silly thoughts. I hadn't even started drinking yet, and the reception was hours away, but that didn't stop how giddy I felt.

Today was going to be a great day. Where the night would take me after several drinks was anyone's guess.

I was hammered.

After shots with the entire wedding party, the bride and a few persistent guests that recognized me from some of my modeling work, double vision had become my norm for the night.

Yet, I was having the best time I'd had in a long time. The evening was filled with drinks, laughter, love and the tiny annoyance of the non-stop camera light flashing to document the special celebration.

Which made me so appreciative of Loosh and her team, because even though I was too tipsy to stand up straight for long periods of time, I still looked pretty.

My makeup was flawlessly intact, the gorgeous rhinestone leaf that held my hair in the most extravagant updo known to man hadn't moved an inch, and the sexy dress that elegantly covered my back, while accentuating my figure, fit like a glove.

I felt invincible.

All traces of the nightmare that had jarred me from sleep were gone, replaced with exhilaration and a renewed energy, and I would use all that energy for one goal, to get Blaze into bed.

"Want another shot?" Kelly screamed from beside me.

I wasn't sure why she was yelling. True, the music was loud, but we were shoulder to shoulder and I could hear her just fine. Obviously, she was riding the same inebriated wave I was.

Instead of waiting for an answer, Kelly slid a bronze-colored shot glass filled with a dark liquid in front of me.

"This one is for the beautiful couple!" She cheered, lifting her own glass and toppling sideways.

I caught her at the last second, and we burst into laughter.

"We have already drank to that!" I said. "And I don't think you can handle any more drinks."

"Neither can you," she accused, aiming a finger at me.

However, the finger was actually pointing over my head at the group of people behind me.

Pushing her hand down, I said, "They do say friends shouldn't let friends drink alone or something like that."

We threw the shots back, and I promised myself that the next thing I drank would be a glass of water because my vision had upgraded Kelly from a twin to a triplet. I was clearly dehydrated.

"Now, all I need is to get laid," she announced.

"Ha! You and me both."

Kelly surveyed the room.

"Merrick has so many sexy friends. I found out which ones were single earlier and any of those fine specimens will do. Hmm," she said, her eyes scanning the room. "Where's the tall one?"

I coughed a few times and swallowed the disgusting regurgitated taste of alcohol.

"What tall one?" I asked, feigning ignorance.

I wasn't that damn drunk. I knew exactly who she was referring to.

"You know," she said, placing one hand high above her head, then snapping her fingers. "Dammit, what is his name? Fire…Heat… Pussy scorcher… oh yeah, Blaze," Kelly finally recalled, a naughty grin forming on her lips.

"Pussy scorcher?" I questioned.

"Hey, he sets mine on fire. Anyway, where's Blaze? That man is sinfully sexy!"

I shrugged.

The response wasn't a complete lie. I hadn't seen him for the last ten minutes, anyway.

Besides, if I added that the last time I saw Blaze he was two steps left of the punch bowl, facing east, with his jacket off, talking to a couple, and I noticed he'd loosened his tie several notches, I'd sound like a stalker.

"Haven't seen him," I said verbally, solidifying my version of truth.

Blaze and I had known each other for almost a year, and I was tired of fantasizing about him day and night. I yearned for the real deal.

"What are we talking about?" Tamika asked, moving her hips to the music as she approached the table and slid into the conversation.

"Which of Merrick's single friends we plan to screw," Kelly stated.

"Ooooh the tall one!" Tamika said.

Okay, I'd remained composed when Kelly said it, and although Blaze wasn't mine, territorial instincts were taking over.

No one is fucking him, but me!

"Can't find him," Kelly said sadly. "But I see some more potential."

Kelly nodded toward Xavier, the professional ice hockey player, and the two men he was talking to.

"Is that Xavier?!" Tamika exclaimed. "I heard he was coming, but I didn't believe it."

Kelly stood. "Yes, it is him, and I am about to get better acquainted."

Both of the ladies put down their drinks and prepared to leave.

"Are you coming, Raquel?" Tamika asked, straightening her dress and smoothing down her hair. "There are three of them."

I shook my head. Settling for the player wasn't in my plans. They could fight over him. I wanted the captain, and that was Blaze.

Besides, I knew something they didn't.

The first night they all met, Jocelyn had a one nightstand with Merrick and Xavier, and according to her, Xavier's abilities were only impressive when it came to his performance on the ice.

"No, you guys go ahead. I'm going to sit here a little longer."

As Kelly and Tamika headed toward a night of rude sexual awakening, at least as far as Xavier was concerned, I sipped on a glass of water, searching the crowd for the man of my dreams.

To my delight, I was rewarded shortly thereafter when I caught sight of Blaze on the other side of the room, posing for pictures with Merrick and Ashton, Jada's boyfriend.

Once the photographer finished up, the men chatted for several more minutes before going their separate ways, presumably to mingle with other guests.

Now's my chance, I thought, getting to my feet.

Drinking the water must have helped with my dehydration because I could now walk straighter, but thankfully the alcohol was still pumping strongly through my veins, making me feel fearless — a required side effect for the mission at hand.

Entering the crowd, I weaved through the sea of guests in the direction of where I'd last seen Blaze.

Suddenly, the beat to the song increased and an older lady, standing near her table, clearly enjoying herself, swung her hips hard to the left and it collided with my right side, knocking me over.

As I was about to hit the floor, someone caught me, and my heart skipped several beats when I looked up into the eyes of Blaze.

"I was coming over to ask you to dance, but seeing as how you're already in my arms, I'll take that as a yes."

After apologizing for almost knocking me on mine, the woman with the weaponized ass took a seat.

Blaze led me out to the dance floor just as a slow song was beginning. Luck was surely in my corner tonight, because I'd much preferred lying against his chest over shaking everything I had to the beat.

"You look lovely tonight," Blaze said, pulling me close.

I echoed his compliment instantly. "So do you."

As we swayed to the rhythm of the music, I could feel the warmth of his hand on the small of my back, guiding me effortlessly across the dance floor. His touch, his calming breaths, and the alluring aroma of his cologne were all sensations that I was thoroughly enjoying.

I don't think I'd ever been this close to him for this long. It was nice and soothing, almost surreal, as it felt more natural than I'd imagined.

Catching sight of Merrick and Jocelyn, my heart swelled with love.

"I'm so happy for them," I said, nodding toward the beautiful couple.

Blaze followed my line of vision.

"Yeah, they are perfect for each other."

"Do you ever think about getting married?" I asked.

Blaze considered the question.

"It would be hard to get married when I don't seriously date."

I laughed to myself.

"Stop playing around. You know you date. I've seen you with women at different events."

"That's only casual, sweetheart," he said before taking my hand, spinning me around and then pulling me back into him.

Look at that, Blaze had moves.

I prayed his smooth skills transferred over to the bedroom because I didn't just want sex. I wanted phenomenal sex.

"Alright," I said, looking up at him. "Let me guess, you never want to be tied down to someone, and that's why you won't consider anything serious?"

Blaze laughed.

"Are you judging me, Ms. Ash?"

"A little," I said. "But it's your preference. I understand that."

"Then you don't understand at all," Blaze replied. "I don't hold some torch for bachelorhood. It's because of my job. It is really dangerous and I don't think it's fair to pull a woman into a world that she likely can't handle."

"That's fair," I responded, stepping left, then slightly to the right, following his lead.

We were close, much closer than necessary for slow dancing, and I couldn't help but notice how easily our bodies meshed together.

Blaze spun me around again, but this time, dipped me. His arm stretched across my upper back, providing support but also pressing into my scars. It didn't hurt, but it triggered my self consciousness.

"Your back is tight," Blaze said, steadying me on my feet.

Still in my thoughts, I heard the words, but they made little sense.

"Huh?"

"Your back," he repeated. "It's tight. Most people carry stress there and with everything you have gone through lately, it makes sense."

"Oh, that!" I smiled, his gorgeous face reminding me of my mission for the night. "Nothing a good night's sleep won't fix."

"Uh huh," Blaze said, his gaze unwavering.

Stop being a human lie detector! I mentally screamed.

"How was your day?" I asked, getting the attention off of me. "Before the wedding, I mean."

Blaze sighed. "Stressful and long. We had drills and attack dog training at 3am."

"Attack dog training? That sounds intense. Did anyone get hurt?"

"Only our pride. None of us met the goal time Lucas wanted. Which means we will have to do it again next week."

"What time did he expect?"

"He wanted us in and out of the course within two minutes."

"That's hardly any time at all!"

"That's actually generous," Blaze said.

I was astonished.

"Two minutes is generous? To escape attack dogs!"

Blaze gave me a simple nod.

"You have to be quick. The bad guys aren't going to give you time to figure it out. And a lot of them use dogs to help buy time for their escape."

"That's logical, but I must know, how is this training even set up."

Blaze cleared his throat, and my eyes shifted to his neck. Even his Adam's apple was sexy. I needed to move this conversation to sex because drooling over the man's Adam's apple signaled thirst and desperation.

"Alright," Blaze began. "Lucas sends us into a large area where he can watch us overhead. There is only one way in and one way out. We are given a ten second head start to locate the exit before he lets the first dog in, and thirty seconds later he releases another."

My eyes widened. "And all this is within your two-minute escape expectancy."

"It is."

"Sheesh, Lucas is harsh."

"To some, but he is the best, and that's why I hired him."

"And your team is practically legendary, from what I hear, so it makes sense. But you said you didn't meet the two-minute deadline this go round. How did you do?"

"Five minutes."

"Not bad," I said, impressed. "What about the rest of the team?"

"It took Vadim eight minutes because one dog got stuck to the padding on his ass and wouldn't let go. Jolli, eleven minutes because he kept laughing through the course every time Lucas warned him he would end up like Vadim. Hannah, ten and Axel got disqualified for bringing a knife inside."

I giggled. "Seems like a good experience."

"Yeah, we like to have fun with it. This is our first time with this exercise though, but like everything else, we will train hard and tighten up our times."

The song ended, and Blaze released me. I scrambled for something to say to keep us chatting. It was taking me way too long to seduce him.

How did people do this so effortlessly? I'd never asked a guy out before, so asking one to sleep with me was a daunting task.

"Want to grab a drink and continue this conversation at a table?" I asked.

Blaze looked around, as if he were searching for someone, and I thought he would say no.

"Uh, sure," he eventually answered, still glancing around. "I can go for another drink."

Oh shit!

I felt stupid. I was so wrapped up in making my move on him I didn't even consider that he might have someone else he wanted to talk to, or that he'd brought a date and I was the woman pushing up on someone else's man.

"You sure? I don't want to keep you from anything," *or anyone,* I mentally added.

Blaze's gaze shifted down to me. "I'm sure, beautiful. Ashton wanted me to help with setting something up for Merrick, that's all. I'm sure he will find me when he's ready."

After we got our drinks, Blaze lead us to a bar table far off in a corner so we could hear each other easily over the music.

"What's that you're drinking?" I asked.

Blaze's eyes dropped to the dark liquid filled with ice cubes. "It's bourbon. My favorite drink to unwind with. What about you?" He said, motioning to my glass.

"A cosmopolitan," I answered. "It doesn't taste as good as I thought it would, but it sure makes me feel lovely."

"You're lovely without the drink," Blaze commented, giving me a wink.

I blushed, and we made small chit chat about work, shared general stories about my friendship with Jocelyn and his with Merrick, but I could tell all of it was merely a way of avoiding the obvious.

Blaze wanted the same thing I did. Sex.

I saw it in his eyes and if I were being honest with myself, it probably didn't matter to him if he slept with me or some other woman tonight, as long as he got what he needed, but I didn't care.

Let the regrets of tomorrow wait until tomorrow. I was sleeping with him tonight, repercussions and consequences be damned.

But how do I broach the subject?

Dive in and demand he satisfy my carnal cravings? Use a tacky pick up line? Or what? Blaze was nice, but he was intimidating as hell. Even the way he held his glass looked like a threat to the ice cubes to not clatter too loud.

Just be smooth.

I opened my mouth, preparing to say something that would properly lay the groundwork and not make me look like the horny bundle of nerves I was, but my mouth abandoned the mission at the last second.

"Are you a dom?" I asked.

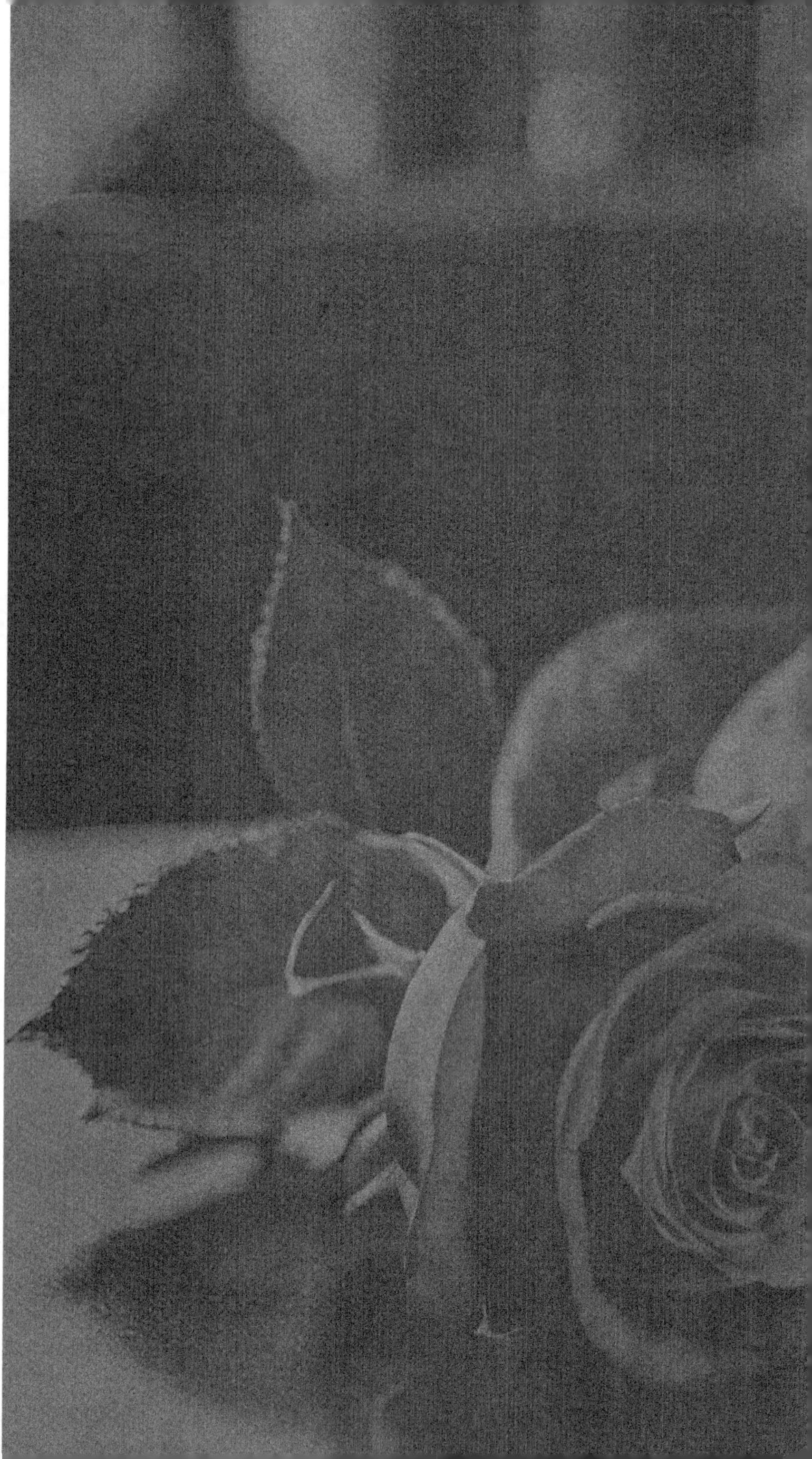

Chapter Five

"Would you like to make a friendly bet?"

It was the alcohol, had to be the alcohol, because that was definitely not smooth! However, it also wasn't a mood killer. In fact, I think I piqued his interest.

Blaze lifted a brow and his eyes shifted from my face down to the cup attached to my hand, then back at me again.

"What number does that make for you?" Blaze asked with a narrowed gaze.

Abort mission! Abort Mission!

I'd read this all wrong. Blaze didn't want me; he was just being nice and now I had crossed the line. Coming on to your boss was an idiot move. I knew that! It's business etiquette 101. I could get fired over this.

"I've lost track," I said, embarrassment creeping in.

I took another long sip of my drink to avoid eye contact.

"You know," Blaze said. "Of all the times I have been around you. You have never been this outspoken."

I gripped my glass tighter. "Yeah, sorry about that. I was out of line. That was a rude thing to ask."

"Don't apologize," Blaze replied. "I enjoy seeing you open up. It's very sexy."

Hey now!

Maybe I hadn't misread the signals. He wanted me as much as I wanted him, and since he'd just called me sexy and opened the door to a less professional conversation; I gathered my courage and walked inside.

"Well, in the spirit of full transparency, I've had a crush on you ever since you hired me."

"Have you now?" Blaze asked, genuine surprise in his tone. I wasn't sure if his reaction was because he didn't believe me or because it shocked him that I would admit it. Regardless, when he spoke again, I was the one shocked. "That's funny, because I have felt the same way about you."

Blaze was lying. He had to be.

There was no way he had a thing for me all this time. He showed no signs of having an interest in me.

This was all his way of trying to stroke my ego, some weak attempt to pacify the woman that was throwing herself at him, which was unnecessary.

I knew for him this would be nothing more than an emotionless sexual encounter.

I narrowed my eyes.

"I don't believe you. If you had a thing for me, why have you never said anything?"

"Because as much as I'd like to be, I am not the guy for you."

"Good thing I'm not looking for forever," I responded suggestively. "I'm only worried about tonight."

It was a partial truth.

In a perfect world, I would love more than a steamy night, but if I wanted him to get on board, I had to show myself to be as nonchalant about sex as I was certain he was.

"The answer is still the same. I am not the guy for you."

Now I was confused. Blaze apparently wanted me, but he wasn't going to go for it? Even though I was all but throwing myself at him?

If any of my common sense brain cells were working, I would take his answer as the rejection it was, but I was intrigued, which only made me more assertive.

"Why don't you let me be the judge of who is, and who

isn't, the guy for me, and you can start by answering my question. Are you a dom?"

Blaze ignored my expectant tone. Instead, he once again answered my question with a question.

"Where'd you hear that?"

"Office gossip," I answered, not wanting to divulge my source. "It reveals some pretty interesting things."

"I'll bet it does, and what do you think? Is it true?"

He was messing with me and the more I pushed, the more he would dodge, but I had patience.

Plus, this was fun. Taking control, flirting with him and finally shooting my shot.

Not to mention I could see him wavering. Saying no to me was difficult for him, yet for some reason he was holding back. I wanted to find out why.

"Yes, I think you are a dom," I said, lightly touching his hand. "And I'd love for you to dominate me."

That got the reaction I wanted. Blaze's eyes darkened, and those broad shoulders of his tensed as he glanced down at my hand on his.

"You are playing with fire, Ms. Ash."

"So burn me," I taunted, meaning every word. "Come on, Blaze, show me what you got. Stop playing hard to get."

He moaned deep in his throat.

"I'm not playing hard to get, but I am getting hard." He turned his hand over so that mine now rested in his large palm and gently stroked it. Shivers ran through my body. "I warn you again. This isn't what you want. You can't handle me."

I may not have had a long sexual history, but that right there was every guy's motto.

"I'll be the best you ever had.", "You won't be able to remember your name.", "I'll make you cum so many times." Blah blah blah.

"You don't know what I can handle," I said. "But since you claim you do, how about you tell me why?"

Blaze released my hand and walked around the table to stand directly in front of me, forcing me to look up and absorb all the masculine energy he was emitting.

An intense yearning surged through me as he reached out and touched the rhinestone leaf wrapped around my head. From there, his fingers delicately traced the side of my face.

"Because besides being the most beautiful woman I have ever seen," he complimented. "You are a dainty little princess standing right in the middle of a danger zone and you don't even know it."

I got chills.

Perhaps I had underestimated him because, liquid courage or not, the sexually bold woman in me was waning.

"I see," I said, my voice not as daring as it had been. "If I'm a dainty princess, then who are you?"

"I," he replied, staring at me so intently, I swore he could see all of my insecurities, secrets, and flaws. "Am not the man you can casually fuck. Sex with me will shatter your world and push you so far past your limits you won't even recognize yourself, because to answer your question I am not only a dom, I am a sadist and I will ruin you."

Well, shit!

I opened my mouth, but Blaze's lewd response had my voice caught in my throat. If his uncensored warning was meant to deter me, it worked.

With his lips so close to mine I thought he would kiss me, Blaze said, "Where's that confidence now, Raquel?"

The name change indicated just how personal this encounter had become. Blaze never addressed me by my first name, and the way he said it almost made me melt.

"It..." I cleared my throat and started again. "It's still there."

Blaze smirked and walked back to his side of the table. The whole time, his eyes were on me.

The room buzzed as music reverberated through the air. Groups of people at other tables drank and sang their inebriated hearts out or carried on in animated conversations that blended into a symphony of joy.

Yet, amidst the lively atmosphere, it was as if a bubble had formed around us. Time stood still, and all that mattered was the connection we shared.

Blaze downed the rest of his drink and I licked my lips as if I could taste the rich alcohol on his.

"Would you like to make a friendly bet with me?" he said decisively.

"A bet?" I asked, confused.

"Yeah, you know, if you lose, you give me something. If I lose, I give you something."

"I know how a bet works. I just don't know why you want to do one."

"Consider it a test. Are you in or out?"

I pushed my glass aside and leaned closer.

"Oh, I'm in. What's the bet?"

Glancing around the room, Blaze suddenly stopped when he saw a group of guys holding up drinks in full on party mode. Dancing and shouting something at the top of their lungs that was drowned out by the music.

"I'll bet that the next song is a slow one," he said.

Immediate joy filled my heart. This was going to be a very simple wager to win. I'd helped Jocelyn pick the playlist and fast songs significantly outweighed the slower ones. Odds were against there being a slow one up next.

"You know I helped plan this reception, right?"

I didn't feel it would be fair to agree to a bet without disclosing the fact that I had insider information.

"I do indeed," Blaze said.

"And you still want to do this bet?"

Blaze shrugged. "What can I say? I enjoy taking risks."

I'll bet you do, I thought, remembering his chaos tattoo.

"You've got yourself a deal," I said, rubbing my hands together like a villain that had just done a wicked deed. "What do I get if I win?"

"Anything you want," Blaze said.

"Anything?" I repeated, as if I had something diabolical in mind. I didn't.

Blaze nodded. "Nothing is off limits, no matter the cost or how farfetched it is."

I tapped my chin.

The first thing that came to mind was sex, but I pushed that aside because that would benefit us both. If I were going to win a bet, then my prize should be self serving.

Instinctually, my mind went to the one thing I knew best. Fashion.

"See these?" I said, pointing at my shoes. "They are by my favorite Italian designer René Caovilla."

Blaze glanced down at my stylish, shiny heels.

"Fancy," he said.

"And very expensive," I added. "If I win, I would like a pair of heels from his new collection."

Blaze nodded in agreement. "I can do that."

"Great!" I responded cheerfully. "What do you want?"

He wasted no time.

"I want you to follow me to that backroom over there, wrap those long legs around my neck and let me use my tongue to work all of that tension and stress out of your body."

Hiding my initial shock was impossible and words escaped me for the second time that night, but I quickly recovered.

"Umm sure! Why not?" I said, much too lively.

Gone was the courageous woman from earlier. That

request crushed me, and if Blaze knew he'd just tapped into one of my sensitive issues, he didn't let on.

Of all the things he could ask for, why would he ask for that?

Wouldn't a nice blow job suffice? Or maybe a provocative lap dance? No! He had to want the one thing that even alcohol couldn't prep me for.

Trepidation filled me as I prayed that another upbeat tune would come blasting out from the speakers within the next sixty seconds.

That didn't happen.

Not only was the song slow, it had the audacity to have micro second pauses within the song were there were no instruments playing at all!

My stomach was doing somersaults as though a swarm of butterflies had taken up residence inside me, their wings fluttering with nervous anticipation.

I could feel the weight of Blaze's gaze, his intense brown eyes piercing through me as he awaited my reaction. The door to the back room sat in a corner just beyond fifteen tables.

If I did this, I could have an experience of secrecy and adventure with the man of my dreams. All I had to do was take that first step.

I turned back to Blaze. I couldn't do this.

"Here's the thing," I said, apologetically. "I completely forgot my period is on. I'll have to take a rain check."

"And you didn't think to say this before?"

"Honestly," I admitted. "I didn't think you would win."

"Well, I did, and now you suddenly remember you have your period?"

The way he restated my excuse sounded laughable, even to me.

I lifted my hands in surrender. "Yeah, sorry."

Blaze crossed his arms, reminding me of the way he looked

in his gear the last time I saw him. Bold, direct and not in the mood for bullshit.

"Show me," he said.

"Ex... excuse me," I stammered, blinking rapidly, as if that would somehow help me hear better. "What do you mean, 'show you'?"

"You heard me. Take me to the backroom and show me."

"I can't do that."

"Why not?" he challenged.

I had tons of reasons, but the shock of his request took my mind to one place, the first and only time a guy went down on me. His name was Jamie Hall, and it was my first year in college.

Neither of us had ever had oral sex before, but me being a trooper, I went down on him first, and he loved every minute of it and, to be honest, so did I.

However, once it was my turn, Jamie was only down there for a few minutes before he came back up gagging and spitting. Some of the spittle actually landed on my legs and thighs.

He said it was the most disgusting thing he had ever done, and that I needed to learn how to not get so wet.

To say I felt embarrassed was an understatement. What do you say when a person reacts like that? Well, I was speechless and the experience completely turned me off from wanting oral. Ever since, I refused to let another guy's mouth anywhere near that area.

"That's private," I said to Blaze. "Not to mention gross. No one wants to see that. I don't even want to see it."

"Have you forgotten what I do for a living? The sight of blood doesn't bother me. Try again."

"But I..." My brain wasn't developing excuses fast enough.

"You lost," Blaze said, halting any further dispute. "And I won. So let's go."

My eyes darted around the room, noticing all the cheerful

faces. Not one of them was sweating bullets like I was over here.

No! Hell No! I wasn't showing him anything. Besides, I wasn't even on my period.

"Let's change the bet," I said in a rushed tone. "It's like you said I lost, so why don't you pick something else? *Anything* else," I said with emphasis, "and I'll do it."

Blaze's serious expression vanished.

"So it's true what they say about you? You don't like oral?"

"I have no idea what you are talking about," I said, gaining a sudden fascination in my nails.

"Office gossip works both ways," Blaze informed me. "I hear things too."

I am going to kill Eric.

"It's not that I don't like it. It's just not my thing."

"Not your thing, huh?"

"Yup."

"I don't believe that," Blaze said bluntly. "I think you had an unpleasant experience and now you want nothing to do with it."

And the human lie detector strikes again.

Blaze may have hit the nail on the head, but I was sticking to my guns.

"Well, you'd be wrong. Like I said, it's just not my thing."

"It's nothing to be ashamed of," Blaze replied, continuing on as if I hadn't just denied his accurate guess. "It's more common than you think."

The sincerity in his eyes made me avert my own. I wanted to feel sexy, not self conscious.

I would not confirm his suspicions, but I wholeheartedly appreciated him putting me at ease about something that had always felt so devastatingly embarrassing.

"I'm curious, though," he said. "When was the last time you had sex?"

I didn't even need to think about it. "Eight months ago."

Blazed let out a low whistle. "That's a long time in my world."

"That's a long time in anyone's world, if you ask me. Which is why I was hoping a sexy friend would help me end my dry streak tonight."

That last part I didn't mean to say out loud.

Blaze laughed. "Trust me gorgeous, there is nothing friendly about what I want to do to you. But unfortunately, since you aren't ready, you won't be getting fucked tonight, and if you do, it won't be by me."

I gaped and lightly swatted his arm. "Oh, that's cold."

We both laughed, and I was once again reminded of how easy he was to talk to.

"If it makes you feel any better," Blaze said. "I'm devastated, too. I wasn't lying when I said I've had a thing for you for a while." His eyes raked over me again. "You would make an excellent submissive."

"Well, maybe we could work something out."

Blaze pinned me with a stare. This was not up for debate.

"I gave you a chance to prove you weren't a dainty princess, remember? But you aren't ready to get dirty." He touched my face again in that delicate way that sparked to life every erogenous zone I had.

My pussy tingled. He had no idea how much I wanted him. How much I wanted to be his submissive, to be dirty. Hell, fuck me face down in the dirt even. I wanted to experience it all.

All except that one tiny sex act that made me feel way too exposed. I didn't even understand why it was such a big deal, but Blaze wasn't budging and I couldn't lie, I was disappointed.

"So it's really all or nothing with you, huh?" I said finally.

"Hey Blaze," Ashton called out, approaching. He suddenly stopped, taking in the scene; Blaze and I huddled close, hands touching, speaking in hushed tones and the sexual energy emitting from both of us.

"Did I interrupt something?" Ashton said.

Nope buddy, that ship has sailed.

"You're not interrupting," Blaze answered. "I'll be right there."

Ashton reentered the crowd and Blaze faced me. "Thank you for keeping me company this evening. I enjoyed talking to you."

"So did I," I replied.

Blaze leaned down and whispered into my ear, "Never try to seduce me again unless you are ready to let me have every inch of you. Because when you're mine, I am going to treat you like the whore I expect you to be and not like the lady that you are." Then he kissed my cheek and walked away.

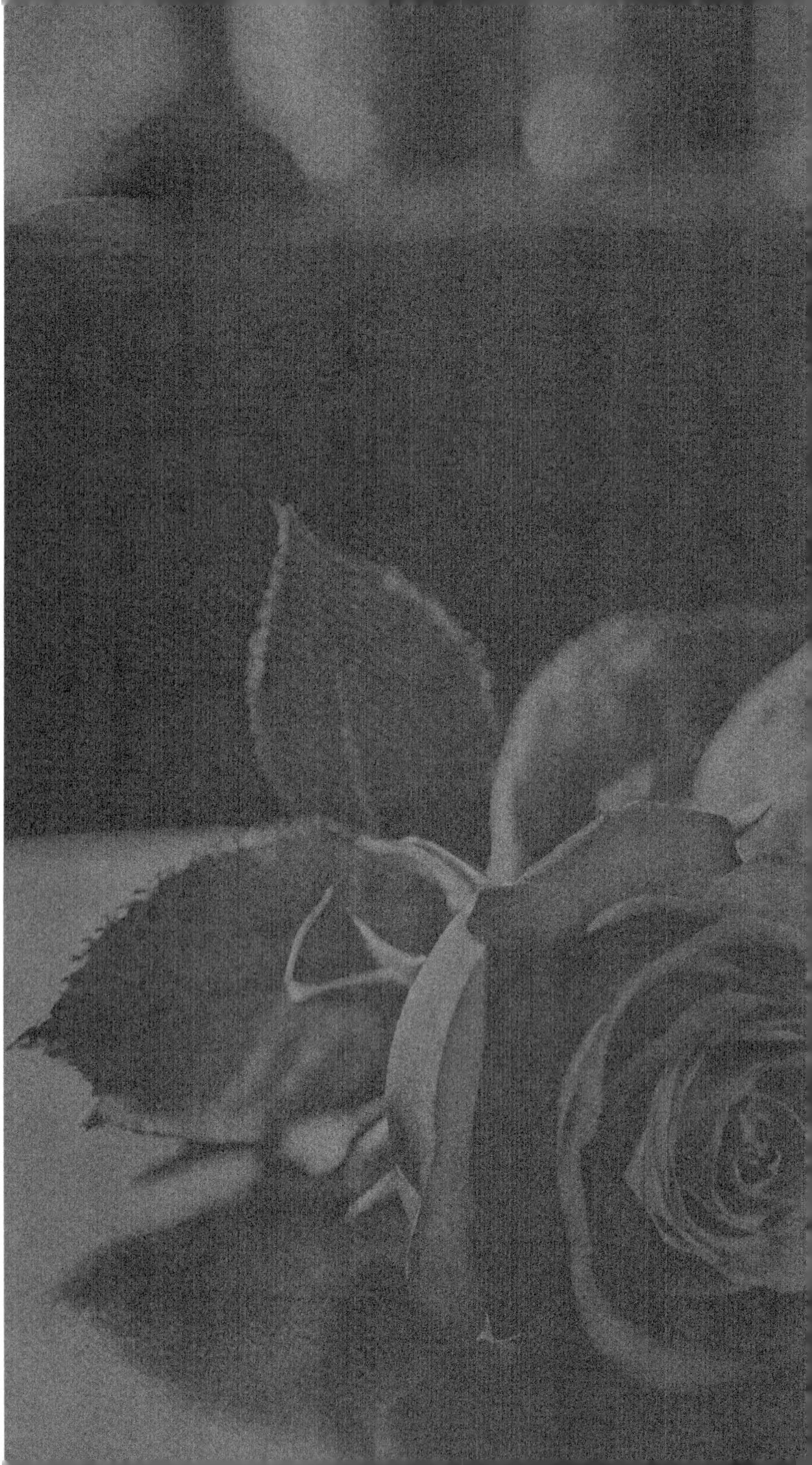

Chapter Six

"Someone is trying to kill me."

"Come on Des, keep up," I said, running backward and egging him on.

Des flipped me off before wiping sweat from his forehead, but he kept running. Or I guess it could be considered running. He was putting one foot in front of the other at a snail's pace.

He was trying to match my speed, and he did well the first two miles, but now we were on mile three and my poor little brother was struggling.

In between ragged breaths he said, "I may be … in shape… but this is insanity. Who runs two miles a day… and doesn't take a break?"

An extremely sexually frustrated woman, that's who.

"And also," he said, sucking in a giant gulp of air, "I thought you said it would be two miles. Why do I feel… like we've run more than that?"

I gave him my most angelic smile before confessing.

"Because we're on mile three and a half," I said, glancing at a distance marker that was slightly hidden by a small bush.

All the markers were obstructed in some type of way. You simply had to know where to look and unfortunately Des did not.

Des stopped. "You evil woman… I'm taking a break."

He huffed and puffed his way to a brown wooden bench,

and I followed. Once he got there, he collapsed onto it, tilted his head back, and closed his eyes.

"Yes, she tried to kill us, but I'm done with her, I swear," Des said.

"What are you talking about, old man?" I teased. Even though he was a year younger than me.

"I'm trying to convince my heart that I'm actually on its side so it won't quit on me."

"Seriously!" I laughed. "We are only running. What are you doing in the gym all the time if you can't handle running a few easy miles?"

"I run," he said, "but not three miles. In addition to that, I do other things which include lifting weights." He tilted his head slightly toward me. "How about you come to the gym and lift the 350 pounds I do every day?"

I couldn't argue with that. I was a runner, not a weight lifter.

"Point taken, but I'm glad you're here," I said, poking his leg.

"Yeah, well, I would have cancelled if I knew you had plans to end my life. What will Regina or Donovan do without me to babysit their kids?"

Scooting closer, I laid my head down on his shoulder and smiled. Regina and Donovan were our other siblings. There were eight of us in total and we were all pretty close, but Desmond and I were the closest.

We shared a special bond that likely started in grade school when I used to protect my then scrawny little brother from all the bullies.

Nowadays, though, Des didn't need protecting. He was much taller than me, built like a truck, and married to an amazing woman. I was so proud of him.

"Have you spoken to mom today?" Des asked.

"About an hour before you showed up. When she isn't out

with dad or helping with her grandkids, then she is calling to check in on me."

"You know mom worries about us," Des said.

"Yeah, but she should slow down. We are all grown and living productive lives, so she doesn't need to stress so much."

"From your mouth to God's ears. I think being a mom is mom's joy in life. And I will not complain," Des announced. "She sends me pies."

"Hey, I didn't get any pies," I pouted, abandoning his shoulder like he'd betrayed me.

My brother's solution was simple. "Get married. Ever since I did, she has been sending Piper and I delicious treats."

I crossed my arms. "Guess I won't be getting any pie then. I'm more likely to get mugged before I get married."

I was only kidding, but from Des' expression he was about to go all protective mode on me.

"Are you sure you're good? First you lose Loni and now someone holds you at gunpoint. If you need Piper and I to come and stay with you for a little while, we will."

"No, Des, I don't need you and Piper to disrupt your lives for me. Besides, you two have only been married a little over a year. You're practically newlyweds!"

He waved me off.

"We don't care about that,"

"You are speaking on your behalf. You can't speak for Piper." Des opened his mouth to respond, and I held up a hand. "And even if you could. The answer is still no."

As if I'd summoned her, Des's phone rung. He retrieved it from his pocket and showed me the screen.

"Hmm, how do you like that? Let's see what my wife has to say."

Turning on the phone's speaker and laying the lovey-dovey on extra thick, he said, "Hello love of my life."

"Oh no," Piper said, "What did you do?"

"I didn't do anything," Des said. "I told Raquel that you don't mind us moving in with her for a little while to help her through this tough time in her life."

"Of course, we don't mind," Piper said sympathetically.

Des stuck out his tongue at me, and I rolled my eyes.

"But she said no," Des continued. "Help me change her mind."

"Desmond Ash!" Piper shouted. "I will not help you! Respect the boundaries that Legs has established."

I smiled when Piper called me Legs. It was the cute nickname she had given me based on my height, even before we officially met.

Turning to my little brother, I stuck out my tongue in victory and snatched the phone from his hand.

"Thank you, Piper," I said. "That's why you are my favorite sister-in-law."

"I know I am. Even though I called you last week to ask the same thing!" Piper said, suddenly turning on me.

I passed the phone back to Des.

"I thought you were on my team, Piper."

"I am, which is why I am going to reluctantly respect your wishes. I know after Scott attacked me, recovery wasn't easy. We all heal in our own way."

Damn. I had forgotten about what Piper went through. Her ex, Scott, was a horrible man who not only tried to kill his own wife, but Piper, too.

There was a voice in the background on the phone.

"Time for me to go to my appointment," Piper said. "I love you so much, Legs. Call me if you need me. And I'll see you later, hubby," she added seductively and hung up.

"Ready to finish this last lap?" I asked.

Des got to his feet and stretched. "I don't have a choice. It's the only way I can get back to my car."

Then he shoved me aside and sped off. "Last one buys breakfast!" he yelled over his shoulder.

My stomach was growling. That breakfast I won from beating Des in the race was long gone.

Before heading to lunch, I wanted to complete enough reports to get halfway through those in my virtual pile, but I was going to have to tap out.

I heard someone laughing and talking over to the left of me. Before I could even consciously comprehend it, my body instinctively recognized Blaze's presence, primarily due to the captivating and alluring way he spoke, with a deep and velvety octave that never failed to excite me.

Rolling my chair back so that I could get a better look, I spotted him and bit my lip. He looked so good. I hadn't seen him since the wedding, which was almost a week ago.

Blaze worked mostly in the field, so coming into the office for paperwork and meetings wasn't top priority, but it was always a special treat for my eyes when I saw him.

Fantasies about him had been at an all-time high ever since we'd talked that night. I imagined allowing him to do so many of the things Jocelyn had told me she'd done with Merrick.

For instance, letting Blaze tie me up and fuck me into a state of mindlessness, sucking him off for hours, or even the thought of him spanking me lured me in and I was ready to surrender.

There were a few instances where I almost called him to say just that, but every single time, two things gave me pause.

The first was the comment he made about wanting

complete access to my body. That would include him eating me out.

Despite all my attempts to convince myself otherwise, the idea of Blaze going down on me and then expressing his disgust was petrifying. Blaze was way more straightforward and unapologetic about things than Jamie was. I didn't think my ego could take a hit like that.

The second was the fact that he was a sadist. I didn't mind testing out a little pain, but how far did Blaze want to go? Cutting? Severe beatings?

Jocelyn had told me she'd seen so many extreme things at the BDSM club, as everyone has their kinks, and I wasn't sure if I could handle Blaze's.

My computer chimed, drawing my attention back to work. I hit the enter button once, twice and then in quick succession to submit the file, but it wasn't clearing.

I didn't understand what I was doing wrong.

Picking up the palm sized squishy ball Blaze had given me, I squeezed it until it was the size of a chicken nugget and studied the screen.

Goodness, I was starving.

"Melanie," I called. "Do you know why this security assignment won't submit?"

Melanie's head popped up over the divider, her eyes shifting to my screen.

"Oh yeah, remember I told you about those rare occasions where the system will require a green light before processing the file?"

I glanced at the lower right-hand corner of my screen and noticed a small yellow banner had emerged, requesting that I forward the report to management for further review.

Squeezing the stress ball even tighter, and turning my hypothetical chicken nugget into crumbs before allowing it to fully inflate again, I gave up.

"Sorry Melanie. I need to eat. I completely forgot about those."

"It's no big deal. It took me years to remember all those little small steps and you're catching on way faster than me. Anyway, the prompt means that a particular officer has worked more jobs than he should have and management needs to clear him for more." Melanie walked around to my desk to investigate for herself. "Who is it?"

I scanned the screen for the name.

"Trenton Rogers," I stated, reading it aloud. "I didn't know he worked security jobs, too. I thought he only worked downstairs."

"No, he does a lot of night assignments after we close up here. Too many it appears," she said, looking at the jobs tallied for the month. "Anyway, hit that little round icon at the top and press send."

"Thanks."

Melanie patted me on my shoulder and was about to leave when she noticed the ball in my hand.

"Did you steal that?" she asked in astonishment.

I looked down at the stress ball.

"No, Blaze gave it to me."

"What?! He gave you *the* ball?"

"What do you mean, *the* ball?" I asked, echoing her curiosity.

She took it from my hand. And held it up like it was some prized possession. Then squeezed it a few times.

"This is so awesome."

"Please clue me in," I said.

"I'm sorry, I'm sorry," she said. Pulling up a chair and sitting down next to me. "I just can't believe he gave it to you."

"Borrowed," I corrected. "He let me borrow it. I don't think he was giving me anything."

"Still!" she exclaimed. "Either way, like three years ago, the team worked this major assignment for a football player's son that was kidnapped."

"What? I didn't hear anything about that on the news."

"You know how these things go. It was highly classified, but as you would expect, the team got the boy back safely and as part of their thank you, Agent Divers told me the football player gave Blaze and each member of his team one of those balls."

I understood the sentiment, but not why Melanie was so taken with it.

"That's nice," I said.

"Yeah, it is because this ball is some type of limited edition and worth $25,000."

"Whoa," I said, looking at the ball with a whole new respect.

It was definitely more valuable than a chicken nugget. I felt honored that Blaze trusted me with it, but also a little undeserving. Why give it to me?

"So he really didn't tell you anything about it? He just handed it over?" Melanie questioned.

"Yeah," I said with a shrug.

Melanie grinned. "I bet he did just give it to you. I'll also bet there is something else he wants to give you."

"Do not start," I warned.

"Fine," she said, tossing the ball back to me. "I am going out for lunch? You want anything?"

"God yes!" I exclaimed. "Bring me whatever you are having. My card is where it always is," I said, facing my computer again.

Melanie retrieved my debit card from my purse in the side desk drawer and went about her merry way.

An hour later, I was full but hadn't made enough headway in my workload to leave on time.

The pile of unfinished tasks mocked me from the virtual

basket. In addition, urgent deadlines loomed, threatening to derail any chance of a timely departure, so I promised myself I wouldn't leave until I'd made a significant dent in my stack.

Turns out I didn't meet my goal until 6:30 pm. Two hours after my normal clock out time.

Gathering my things, I walked past the empty stations and offices towards the elevator. It seemed I was the only one left on this floor, possibly even in the building.

"Hold the elevator," Blaze called out seconds before he appeared.

Pressing the hold button, I waited for him to step inside before releasing it.

"Hi there," I said. "I thought I was here alone."

"So did I," Blaze responded. Short and to the point. With his jaw firmly set, he didn't even bother to glance in my direction.

Adjusting my purse strap on my shoulder, I stood back, allowing him to press the button for the bottom floor. I would have done it, but he seemed like he was in a rush.

The silence as we waited to be delivered to our desired floor was weird. He kept tapping the envelope he held in one hand against the other, and staring at the elevator doors like he could use sheer willpower to open them.

"Did you have a good day?" I asked.

"It was fine, Ms. Ash," he responded.

Still, Blaze didn't look at me or elaborate and I couldn't help but notice we were back on professional terms. I knew it would happen, but somehow I felt like I'd done something wrong.

He could be upset about anything. Stop thinking it's you.

The logical part of my brain recognized that, but the emotional part didn't. He seemed irritated and preoccupied.

Was he upset because he felt I led him on at the wedding? Saying I wanted him, but then refusing his request?

I faced him. "Blaze, is everything alright?"

The elevator finally stopped, and the doors parted.

Blaze looked at me, an unfriendly edge to his voice. "I've already said everything was fine. No need to ask again."

What crawled up his ass?

He exited the elevator, and I followed.

It actually surprised me when he held the front door open. Initially, I thought he was going to let it close in my face, so I had freed up one hand to catch it for myself.

We walked towards our parked vehicles, mine further to the right than his. Despite my concern about what was on Blaze's mind, I respected his silence and refrained from pressing him for answers.

Maybe the next time I saw him, he would be in a better mood.

I was about to tell him goodnight. Even if he didn't respond, that was fine. It felt disrespectful to not at least say goodbye, but that's when I noticed something peculiar.

There was a third car in the parking lot. One that I hadn't seen before.

It was an all black SUV, no major identifying features or noticeable marks. The windows were heavily tinted, concealing whoever was inside, and I could hear the quiet purr of the engine.

Suddenly, the vehicle shot forward, fast and loud. I froze, like a damn moron, comprehending that danger was amidst, but unsure how to react.

"GET DOWN!" Blaze yelled, not even giving me a chance to move before he was on top of me, shielding my body with his.

The deafening sound of gunshots echoed around us as adrenaline surged through my veins, and my heart pounded in my chest.

Bullets whizzed past, and the sound of metal piercing the

air forced an involuntary scream out of me. I covered my head with my hands, praying I could simply disappear.

Blaze must have retrieved his weapon because he was now firing back at the gunmen.

My face was pressed firmly against the ground for protection, causing dust from the asphalt to fill my nostrils and the rough concrete to dig into my forehead. It hurt, but I'd welcome this minor inconvenience to the alternative.

I couldn't see the SUV closing in on us but I could hear it, as the engine grew louder, and then, *was that quieter?* As it sped away, leaving the scent of burning rubber in its wake.

"Stay here," Blaze instructed, the weight of his body lifting off of me.

He didn't have to worry, I wasn't going anywhere. I didn't even uncurl from my ball of protection until he returned sometime later, placing his hand on my back.

"It's alright, they're gone," he said gently, helping me to my feet.

I looked around the parking lot and sure enough, no sign of an SUV intending to obliterate us, but my car was destroyed. Broken windows had left heaps of glass strewn randomly on the ground, and my passenger side doors were riddled with tiny bullet holes.

"What..." I licked my lips to start again, my voice trembling. "What just happened?"

Blaze pulled me close and wrapped his arms around me. He spoke barely above a whisper, but I heard him loud and clear.

"Someone is trying to kill me."

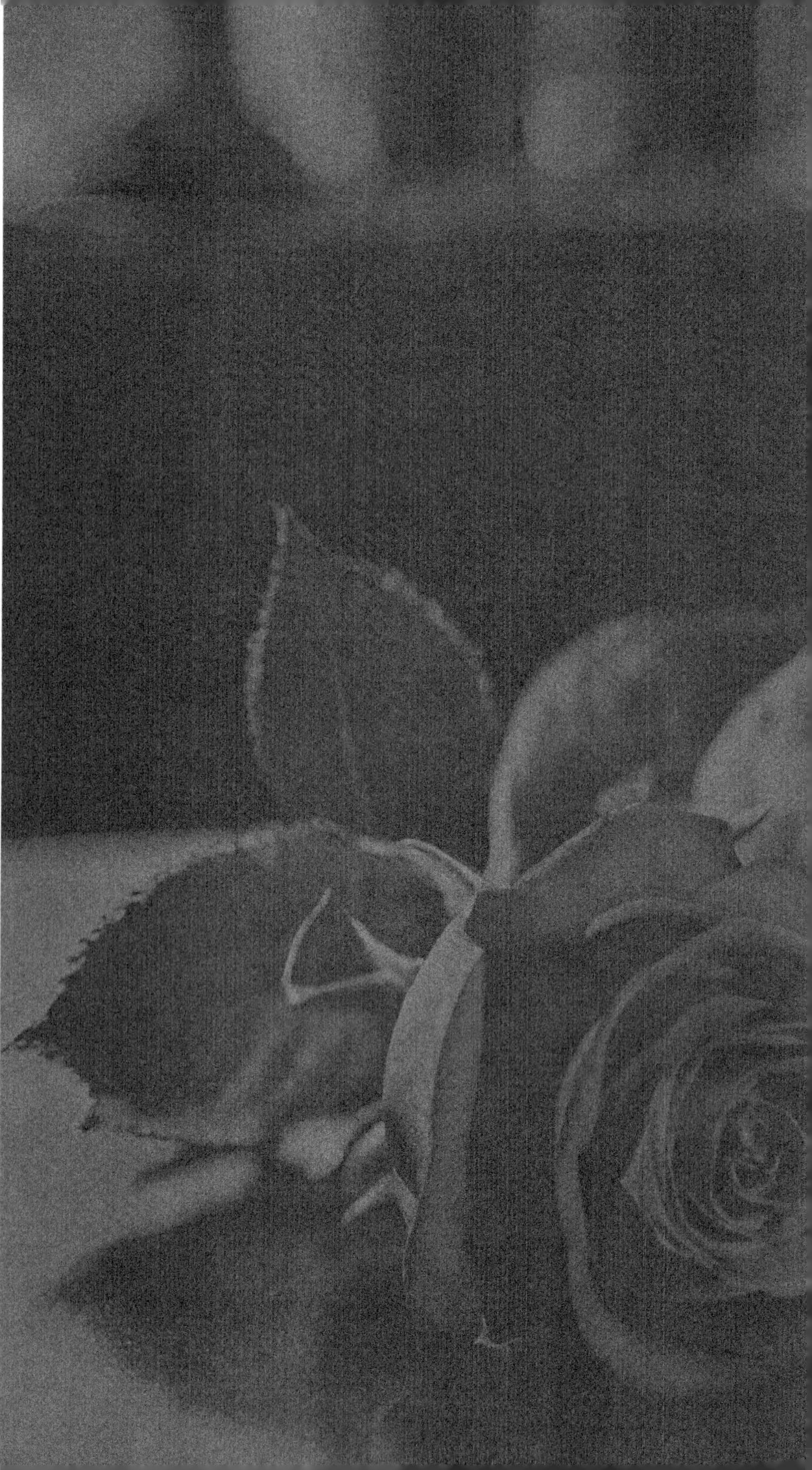

Chapter Seven

"Why doesn't anyone call you Adrian?"

Blaze insisted on bringing me home, despite my assurances that I was fine.

The man had done enough to make up for something that wasn't even his fault. I blamed the gun happy criminals, not him. Already Blaze had gotten my car towed and instructed them to deliver the bill to him.

Then, to spare me any additional hassle, the arrangement for a rental under his account would be delivered to me tomorrow.

As per usual, all I wanted was answers, but Blaze wasn't being forthcoming.

Why is someone trying to kill him?

The question bounced around in my head like an animated computer screensaver. We sat, not uttering a word, in my living room, taking small, barely noticeable bites from the pizza I'd ordered.

Blaze put his slice down and took a sip of water.

"I'm sorry about earlier in the elevator," he said.

I shook my head, putting my pizza down as well.

"You've saved my life two and a half times now. You owe me no apology."

"Two and a half?" Blaze asked. "I know about two, but where'd the half come from?"

"At the wedding, remember? When granny almost

knocked me on my ass. That could have been dangerous if you hadn't caught me."

Blaze laughed. It wasn't a big laugh, but it was all I needed. Something bad was happening and my heart ached to see that level of worry on his face.

"Regardless, I'm sorry. There was no reason for me to be rude to you."

If I needed an opening, here it was.

"What was that about?" I asked, shifting on the couch to face him.

Reaching into his jacket pocket, Blaze pulled out the envelope he was holding earlier. He offered it to me, and I opened it, pulling out a paper with four chilling words on it:

Stop digging or else.

My eyes darted up to his.

"This was connected to what happened in the parking lot?"

Blaze nodded.

"It was delivered today, and I was at the office late because I was doing some investigating. When I ran into you, I had switched to field mode, which usually results in complete focus and no chit chat because I have to stay on high alert. It's like second nature to me and I've been doing it for so long, I don't even realize when it happens."

"I get it, and I didn't hold it against you." I glanced at the letter again. "This is scary. I'm so sorry Blaze." I wanted to hug him, but I wasn't sure what was appropriate, so I settled for resting a hand on his leg. "What are you going to do? Disappear for a while?"

Blaze gave me a perplexed look.

"Hell no."

"But someone is trying to kill you!"

"Someone is always trying to kill me," Blaze said like it was no big deal. "It's part of the job."

"Oh, right," I mumbled.

In moments like this, where it was just us and he seemed so normal, so respectful, so tender, I often forgot that he was an assassin. Death was as common for his workday as security reports were for mine.

"Okay," I said slowly, accepting his response. "Well, if this isn't out of the ordinary, why do you seem so distraught?"

"They almost..." His voice trailed off, but I waited, not wanting to interrupt if he was in the mood to share. "Hurt *you*," he said, finally looking over at me.

I blinked rapidly, shocked by his admission.

Is that what this was about? He was beating himself up over me, almost being hurt? Or worse?

This raised the question: Did Blaze care for me as much as I cared for him?

Acknowledging my feelings toward Blaze felt stupid and reckless. There was no basis for it. We hadn't had sex or even dated, yet he already held a special place in my heart. I was inexplicably drawn to him and deep down; I wondered if he felt the same.

"Blaze," I began. "I'm still alive because of you. There is no need to feel you failed yourself, or me."

"No one gets hurt on my watch," he said.

If I thought this was about his concern for me personally, that statement clarified it. He was a team leader, a civilian protector. It was his job to keep everyone safe, and he took anyone getting injured or killed as a personal discredit.

I buried my feelings of hope that he could feel the same way about me and focused on what mattered. I was alive.

"Thank you again for saving me, Blaze. Do you have any leads on who could be behind it?"

Blaze sighed and leaned back on the couch. "I do. And

once I uncover who is running this giant operation we are working on, I suspect I'll get the answers I seek."

"And let me guess, I should stop asking questions because the information is confidential, and you are done sharing."

He smiled at me then. A genuine smile that lifted my spirits.

"Your intelligence is exactly the reason I hired you," Blaze said.

"Say no more," I replied, grateful that he'd even shown me the letter. "I'll leave it alone." Noticing his bottle of water was almost empty, I asked, "Would you like something else to drink?"

Blaze's attention was drawn to something in the vicinity of my fireplace.

"Nothing more to drink, but I would like for you to tell me about those people on your mantle."

I glanced up to see the four pictures I'd placed there when I moved in. Getting off the couch, I walked over to the photos, and Blaze joined me.

"These are my grandparents," I said, pointing at the first picture of an older couple holding up a giant fish and grinning from ear to ear. "They have been married for 52 years and they live on a farm in Alabama."

"Beautiful couple," Blaze said. "They look like lots of fun."

"Oh, they are," I replied, moving on to the second photo. "These are my parents. As you can see from this striking pose she is making, I got my gorgeous legs and looks from my mom and my eyes from my dad."

Blaze leaned in closer. "I can see that. You and your mother are definitely twins."

"Thanks, I am so grateful for them. They taught me the three Rs," I said confidently.

"Reduce, reuse and recycle?" Blaze asked.

I thought about it. "Those are the 3 Rs, aren't they?"

"Pretty sure they are," he said.

"Well, in this case, I am talking about respect, resilience and reflection," I stated, wiggling three fingers at him. "All important aspects that built me into the well-rounded individual you see before you today."

I did a little bow, and that earned me another genuine smile from Blaze. He touched my lower back affectionately, gazing down at me.

"They did a lovely job because you are perfect."

The room grew warmer. Okay, that was just me, but he was looking at me in that way that made me want to melt.

However, before I read too much into his compliment or ended up in a puddle on the floor, I moved on to the next photo.

"This wild bunch is my siblings and their kids."

Blaze picked up the photo, the 4x6 crystal glass frame fitting in his palm.

"Wow, this is an entire basketball team," he said.

I smiled with pride. There were seventeen people in the photo and that was without counting my sweet little niece, Riley, that my sister was pregnant with in the picture.

"Certainly is. Lots of fights over space and privacy growing up, but fun nonetheless. Do you have any siblings?"

"Nope, just me," Blaze responded, his eyes taking in all the love and laughter captured in the image. "When I was younger, I wanted some, though."

"And now?" I asked.

His tone was flat. "Now I am used to being alone."

Not knowing what to say kept me from saying anything at all. Blaze placed the photo back on the mantle, and it was me who picked up the next frame. My heart filled with sadness and affection.

"This is Loni. My best friend and the sweetest woman in

the world." I rubbed a finger over the glass, tracing the image of her face. "I lost her in an accident," I said quietly, my voice cracking slightly with emotion.

"I heard about that," Blaze said.

It came as no shock. Many people had. Bad news traveled fast, it seemed.

"I am so sorry for your loss."

Thanking him for his caring words. I took another minute to admire Loni's happy face and then tried to perk up.

"Bad things happen, right? Anyway, we raised a lot of money for Loni's favorite charity dedicated to international needs. That would have had her jumping for joy."

"Concentrating on the good things is always beneficial when we lose someone. It helped me through the worst times right after I lost my parents."

Now, I was the one expressing condolences. "How long ago was that?"

"About ten years."

"Does it get easier?"

"No." Was all he said.

Blaze was such a complex man to me. He was beautiful, but brutal, honest, but secretive and welcoming, but withdrawn.

"May I ask you something?"

"As long as it isn't about the case, then I am an open book."

"Of course not," I said politely. "It is actually more personal. I wanted to know why no one calls you Adrian?"

Blaze looked at me strangely, as if the questioned conjured up some distant memory and from his expression, I couldn't determine if it was hurtful or happy.

"No one has called me Adrian for a very long time, and even before Blaze, everyone called me Shaw," he said, referencing his last name.

"Really? Not even other family members, or friends you knew since grade school?"

Blaze shook his head.

"The last person to call me Adrian was a woman I was in love with over eight years ago."

Blaze in love?

That was hard to imagine. He seemed so tough and untouchable on so many levels.

"What happened between you two?"

"My work," he said. "She couldn't handle the constant danger and it drove us apart."

"That's kind of sad."

"It was for the best, plus she was right. No one should have to be a part of this world that doesn't choose it."

That's lonely, I thought, but surely wouldn't say.

It was his life and his decision, but wanting to save the world shouldn't condemn him to solitude.

"So, to answer your question," Blaze continued. "I guess the usage of that name died with the relationship."

Translation, Blaze had chosen to guard his heart.

He didn't have to tell me that calling him Adrian was much too intimate, or that its usage symbolized a risk he was no longer willing to take. The matter-of-fact tone he used said it all, and even though I understood his stance, it was a letdown.

"How did you get the name Blaze?" I asked, shifting to a less complex topic.

"A very nasty takedown," he said.

I waited, but he didn't elaborate.

"Office gossip says you were on a classified mission and tore through a warehouse in a full on rage, killing ten bad guys in the process."

He cocked his head. "You and office gossip have become quite cozy, haven't you?"

"It's the only way to stay up to date on everything about you," I admitted, sliding my hands into the back pocket of my jeans.

"Or you could simply ask me, beautiful," he said.

I grinned like a schoolgirl with a crush.

Ugh! Get it together, Raquel.

I was like putty in his strong, large, and I'd bet skilled, hands.

"I'll keep that in mind," I responded.

"Please do. In the meantime, don't believe everything you hear." Placing his arms around my waist, Blaze pulled me close. "It was only four men."

I licked my lips, trying to remain aloof, but he was reeling me in with the way he was massaging my lower back.

"Does killing people bother you?" I asked in a whisper.

"Not even a little," he said. "I will always do what needs to be done."

I need to be done, I thought mischievously.

There was a sudden spark between us, and that's when I knew that resisting him was no longer an option.

"Blaze I—"

His phoned beeped, interrupting the conversation and Blaze released me to check it.

He exhaled audibly. "It's time for me to go."

I took a step back from him. "Yes, yes, of course. I'll walk you to the door."

Before leaving, Blaze turned to me.

"What was it you were going to say?" he asked.

The confession that I wanted to be his was right on the tip of my tongue, but I held back. What if opening the door to his sexual world was a big mistake?

"Umm, it was nothing," I said.

"You sure?"

I smiled and nodded. "I'm sure."

"Because I thought," he replied stepping close to me, "That it was this."

And he kissed me. And I am not talking about a quick, soft, innocent peck. It was passionate, consuming and gave me a full on taste of what I could expect if I were to submit to him, and that sealed it.

I no longer gave a damn about my insecurities, that he was my boss or a sadist. It was time to take a walk on the wild side.

"Goodnight, Ms. Ash," he said, ending the kiss. "Thank you for a lovely—."

"I'm ready," I said, blurting it out with confidence.

Blaze regarded me and gave a slight shake of his head. "That is the adrenaline of the incident talking."

"You're wrong. I know what I want."

"I don't think you do."

His skepticism was valid. I cowered the first time, however, I would not make the same mistake. I knew what Blaze wanted, expected, and demanded. Complete submission.

Keeping eye contact and trailing a hand down his chest, I said, "You told me that the next time I seduce you, I better be ready to let you have every inch of me, and I am."

For a moment, I wasn't sure he would take me seriously, but then he said, "Take the rest of the week off."

I opened my mouth to protest, but he cut me off.

"There will be no challenge on this. Get some rest and I will come by Friday and then you. Are. Mine."

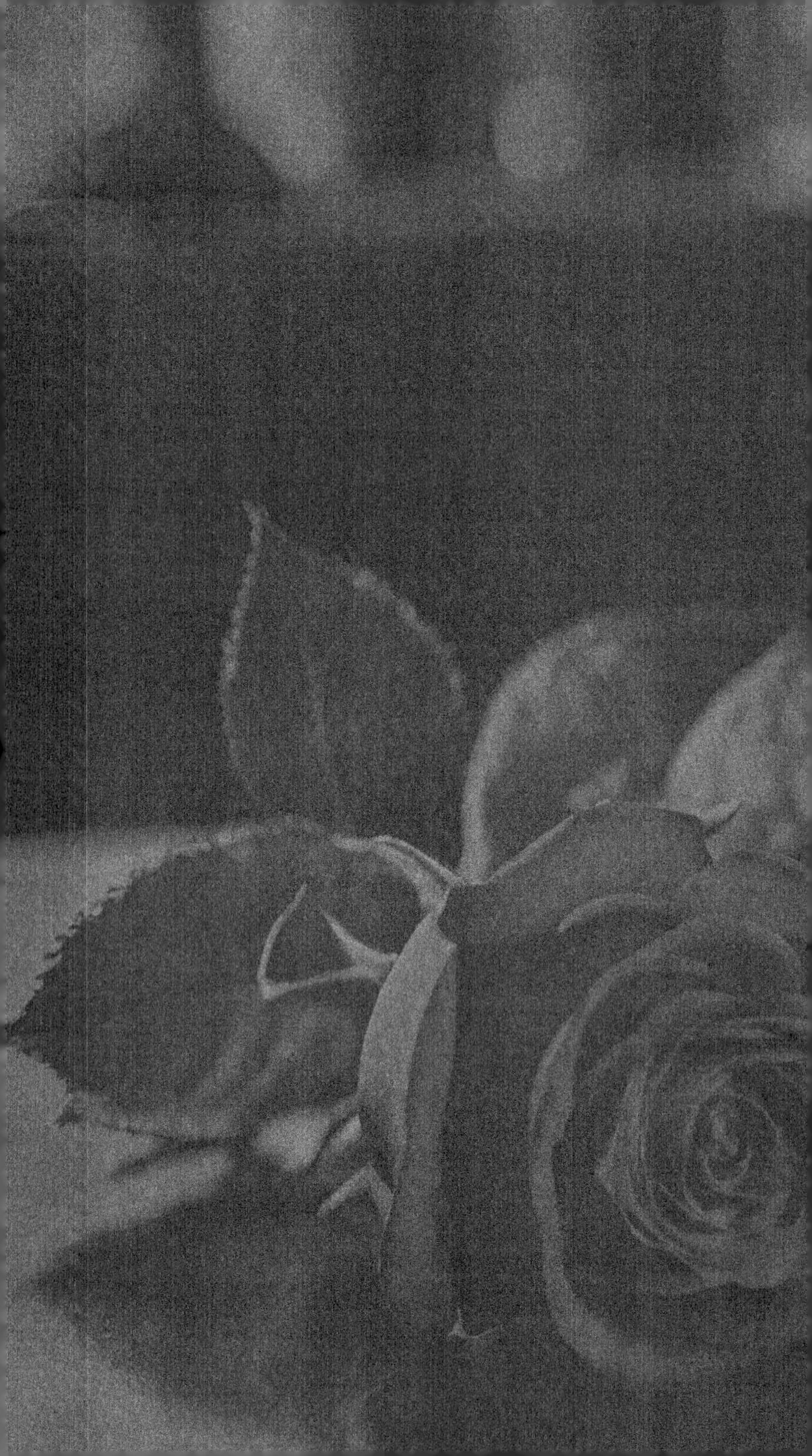

Chapter Eight

❖

"I'VE SEEN HORROR MOVIES. I KNOW WHAT A SCREAM OF TERROR SOUNDS LIKE."

Using a small table top mirror and brush, I applied a thin layer of the lavender and mint clay mask to my face.

"Why didn't you tell me Blaze was a dom?" I asked Jocelyn, rolling my lips inward to avoid getting any on my mouth.

Jocelyn scooped up a spoonful of her bourbon and brown butter mangomisu. It was her second piece and I could smell the alcohol baked into it from here.

"Because you never asked," she said simply, then with a half shrug added, "Besides, you knew."

"I agree," Jada chimed in, walking into the living room with a glass of white wine in one hand and a clear basket of nail polishes in every color of the rainbow in the other. "Even I knew and I'm not a member of the club."

"Fine, I knew," I admitted, eyeing a pastel pink polish sticking out of Jada's basket.

She and Jocelyn had been doing these girls' night pampering parties for years, deeming it a must for not only their appearance but their sanity.

Given their demanding professions as outstanding lawyers, they used these occasions to detach from their cases and reconnect with each other over wine, junk food and sweets.

I was grateful that ever since I'd moved here, they'd welcomed me into the mix.

"Now what did I miss?" Jada asked, sitting down. "What

happened after Blaze left?"

I finished covering my face with the mask and said, "I took a cold shower."

We all laughed, and Jocelyn put her spoon down and clapped her hands together with excitement. "This is fantastic," she said. "You and Blaze are finally going to happen."

"What do you mean, finally? You didn't know I liked him. I specifically avoided telling you because I know you like to play matchmaker," I said.

Jada's head shot up, about to agree with me that Jocelyn's side hobby was playing cupid, but Jocelyn silenced her by threatening to hide her beloved nail polishes.

"Ignore the reaction of my delusional friend," Jocelyn said. "Jada's annoyed that I knew she and Ashton would wind up together before she did. Anyway, I saw the way you looked at Blaze whenever he was around."

"And I thought I was being discreet," I muttered.

"Maybe to people that don't know you," Jocelyn said. "But to me you were practically swooning like one of those cartoon characters with their hands on their chests and hearts bulging out of their eyes."

"Well, gee thanks," I said unenthusiastically.

"At least you have him now," Jada commented. "Even if it's only for sex."

"Trust me, sex is all I need from him. Blaze isn't open to anything else and the last thing I want is to push for a relationship with a man that truly doesn't want one. I will take my sexual adventures and be happy. Thank you very much!"

"Good for you!" Jocelyn and Jada cheered in unison.

"Speaking of sexual adventures," Jocelyn said. "You're going to be having quite the experience. You know Blaze shares his subs, right?"

I was grabbing a polish from Jada's basket, but that comment made me freeze.

"What the hell do you mean, share? And how would I know that? I get most of my submissive insight from you, Jada, and bad porn."

"Calm down, calm down," Jocelyn said with a giggle. "Sharing just means that sometimes he will let others enjoy you. Maybe as being part of a threesome, orgy or some other form of sexual gratification."

I let that sink in. I never imagined that being with Blaze could also mean that I would have sex with other people. *Was I ready for that?*

The answer came to me almost instantly. I would have to be, because I wasn't backing out this time.

My whole adult life, I'd stayed on the straight and narrow, too afraid to open up about my sexual fantasies. It was time for me to explore, experience, and find out exactly what I liked, without shame or fear, about what others thought.

Walking away was always an option if I didn't like it.

Jocelyn must have noticed my contemplative expression. "I think you're going to love being a sub," she said. "It is a great mental escape."

"To be honest, I agree and I'm thrilled, but my anxiety is off the charts. How did you handle the first day you were Ashton's sub?" I asked Jada. "Were you nervous?"

"Yes, and at the time, Ashton was very hard to read. He didn't like for me to ask him personal questions or talk back. I could respect the personal questions part, but my smart mouth got me lots of punishments." Then she smiled. "Turns out I liked to be punished."

"So do I," Jocelyn muttered, biting her lower lip. She was obviously thinking about something raunchy. "And why have you never asked me if I was nervous with Merrick my first time?"

"Umm, because you instigated a threesome with two men," I reminded her.

"Oh, right!" Jocelyn replied, clearly needing to let the cake be her last bit of alcohol for the night. "Shutting up now."

Pulling a few loose strands of hair free that had gotten stuck to my drying face mask, I grabbed my glass of wine from the table to take a sip, however I put it back when pieces of my mask crumbled to the floor.

Looks like there would be no drinking until I rinsed this off.

I shook my head. "I can't believe you like punishments, Jada. I mean, I know Jocelyn does, but you too?"

Jada nodded. "I know, with Jocelyn being a certified slut, it's hard to believe anyone else can be so kinky, but it's true."

"I'm sitting right here!" Jocelyn exclaimed, shoving my shoulder for laughing and giving Jada an icy glare, before taking another bite of her dessert. "And that's Mrs. Slut to you. Merrick made it official."

Jocelyn wiggled her fingers to showcase her wedding ring, then recalled she took it off for the night's festivities, not wanting to get any wax or product gunk in it.

I loved their sense of humor.

"So what's the deal with punishments? I thought punishments were bad."

Jada answered. "Yeah, punishments can be challenging, but they can also be erotically fulfilling. I remember this one time, Ashton used a vibrator on me and made me cum so many times, I couldn't walk. He had to carry me out of the office."

My mouth fell open. "Wow!"

"It was so good," Jada said.

Jocelyn squealed and held up a finger, signaling that she had something important to say, but couldn't because her mouth was full.

Jada and I waited, impatiently might I add, until she swallowed before we could find out what was so important.

"Speaking of punishments," Jocelyn announced, dabbing at her mouth with a napkin. "Did I tell you the first time I unofficially met Blaze?"

"Unofficially?" I asked, confused.

Jocelyn nodded, and she only got two words out before Jada interrupted.

"Wait! I haven't heard this one. Let me pour some more wine."

"I'm going to shake you both," I said. "Stop playing with my emotions! What happened?"

Jada finished pouring her wine, and I scooted closer as if the few inches would really make a difference, and Jocelyn started again.

"It was my first time at the club and I heard this woman scream like she was being murdered."

My irrational mind went into overdrive with only that limited information.

Blaze is going to kill me. Obviously, he was killing the screaming woman, and I had just signed up to be next. Great! I'm going to get fucked and end up at my own funeral on the same day.

"What did you do?" Jada asked.

"I tried to run, but Merrick caught my arm and assured me that everything was alright."

"Did you believe him?" I asked, reaching for a chip and shoving it into my mouth. Dried pieces of my mask hitting the floor every time my jaw moved.

"Hell no," Jocelyn said. "He tried to tell me some woman was having a spanking session with Blaze and enjoying it. I've seen horror movies. I know what a scream of terror sounds like. That woman was not happy."

Jocelyn faced away from us and resumed eating, as if the story was over. Jada and I looked at each other and then at the back of Jocelyn's head.

"Umm, hello, what happened to the woman?" I asked.

"Yeah," Jada said. "Did it end up on the news that he harmed her?"

"No," Jocelyn said nonchalantly. "Merrick was telling the truth. She was enjoying being spanked. A few seconds later, I heard her begging for more and saying how much she loved it."

Jada and I exchanged another glance, then grabbed pillows from the couch and hit Jocelyn with them.

"Alright," I said after we all got our laughter under control. "So besides instigating punishments and hoping to get a good one, do you have any recommendations for my anxiousness?"

Jada paused before painting her next toenail. "Don't think too hard. Allow yourself to enjoy how everything feels and learn your body."

"I agree," Jocelyn joined in. "Women especially spend too much time worrying about if our behavior is acceptable or not. I say, as long as you are safe and feel comfortable, dive in, take control of your sexuality, and have a good time."

I looked from Jocelyn to Jada. "You guys are the best. Thanks for everything."

"No problem," they both said.

After glancing into the mirror to ensure my mask was fully dry, I got to my feet. "I am going to go wash this off my face and then you, Mrs. Alexander, can tell me more about your honeymoon."

Hurriedly, I tidied up my apartment by putting a shirt in the hamper and organizing papers in my desk drawer. I needed to keep myself busy, even though the place wasn't really messy.

Blaze was on his way, and when he called thirty minutes ago, the only instructions he gave were for me to wear a dress with no underwear. He didn't say why. And when I asked if there was a specific style of dress he preferred, he answered with, *"Surprise me."*

My nerves were shot.

I could only imagine that his first order of business as my Dom was to cash in on his winnings from our bet. However, I didn't have time to stress about him going down on me because now I had a new worry, my performance.

It was a pretty fair assumption that Blaze had slept with enough talented women that my basic sexual skills would stick out like a sore thumb.

I blew out a long breath and hurried to my bedroom to check my reflection in the mirror.

I'd decided to go with a medium length blue dress that was fitted enough to highlight my shape, but flexible enough too easily slide up my waist. As I glanced down at my bare feet with a fresh pedicure, I noticed a piece of lint on the floor.

Oh no! I didn't sweep.

Taking off in the direction of my utility closet, I stopped when I heard a knock at the door. Too late, Blaze was here.

I took a deep breath, put on a confident face, and opened the door.

"Hi," I said to the most handsome man I had ever seen.

He was in uniform, minus his tactical gear which was a slight surprise. I assumed we were spending the evening together.

Blaze greeted me with a tender, comforting kiss on the cheek.

"You're still wearing your uniform. Do you have to go back to work soon?" I asked, closing the door.

I wasn't complaining. I loved how authoritative and sexy

Blaze looked in his gear. My eyes traveled the length of his body, taking in every curve and muscle of his arms and chest.

However, when I reached his waist and spotted his gun, I paused, a weird, uneasy feeling engulfing me.

If I weren't mistaken, a twinge of fear was present, which was odd because I'd never feared guns. Many men in my family owned them and I'd fired my first one when I was five, so what was the deal?

They weren't aimed at your head before.

The intrusive thought was unsettling and frustrating. This better not be a new fear unlocked sort of reaction, because I have enough damn problems.

I realized Blaze hadn't answered my question and glanced up. He was observing me, no doubt reading me like the people he interrogates.

"So work soon?" I repeated.

"Yeah, I won't be staying long, but I felt it was time to come see you. How are you feeling?"

"Much better. Thanks for the days off."

"No problem," he said.

Blaze left the entryway and grabbed a chair from my table, placing it in the middle of my living room floor. I watched, questioning his actions only in my head.

Curiosity piqued, I hesitantly took a seat once he motioned me over, unsure of what was about to unfold.

"Good choice with the dress. It suits you well."

I looked down at myself. "Thanks. You gave little to go on. I was hoping I didn't overdo it."

Blaze took my hand and kissed it.

"As always, beautiful, you are perfect and soon we will be ready to get started." He walked back to the spot at the table that was now missing a chair, and leaned against it, crossing his arms. "We need to talk first."

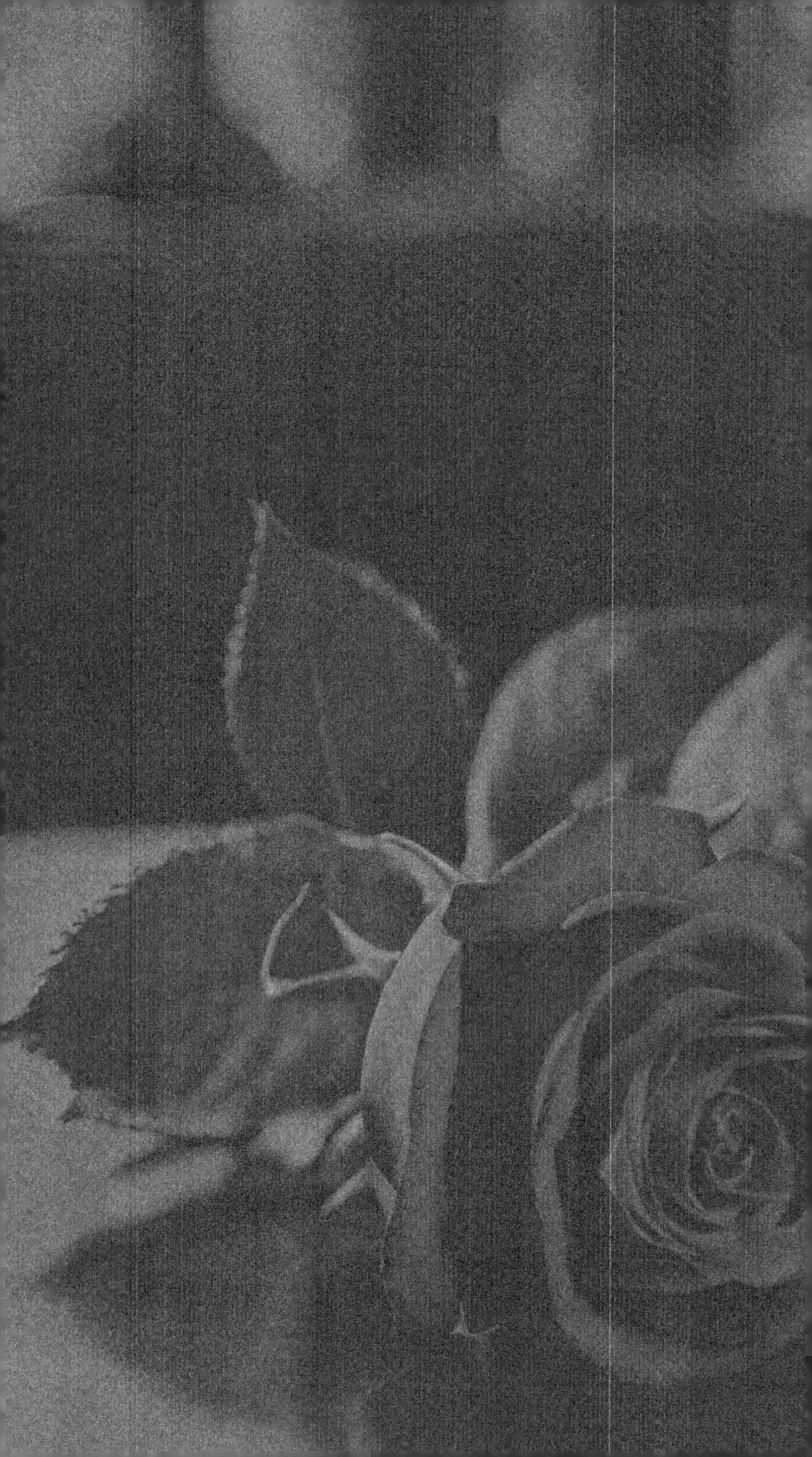

Chapter Nine

"I DO NOT RESPECT YOU. I OWN YOU."

He wanted to talk. It was never a good thing when a guy said that.

Repositioning myself in the chair, I tucked my hands beneath me. "Okay, what's up?" I asked.

Blaze got right to the heart of the matter. "Why do you want to be my submissive?"

I laughed, slightly taken aback. "I want to venture into new sexual territories with someone I trust."

"Uh huh, and you understand that this is *only* sex, right? We are not going to fall in love or anything."

"Yes, of course," I said, as if his clarification was unnecessary. "You told me before that relationships are too risky for you."

Blaze studied me in his usual manner.

"I want to make sure I'm upfront and clear about that. We currently have a good friendship and I don't want to lead you on. All I want," he said pointedly. "Is to use you sexually in every way possible, but nothing more."

There was that outspoken Blaze I'd grown accustomed to over this year.

"We're good," I reassured him. "I want the same thing you do."

"Alright," Blaze said, moving on. "What do you know about being a sub?"

"Only what Jocelyn and Jada tell me. They are pretty open."

"I get that, but every Dom is different and duties of a sub vary significantly. Being my sub can be enjoyable, but it is not easy."

"I know, and that doesn't bother me."

Blazed fired off his next question. "Are you on birth control?"

"I am."

He smirked. "You're feeling very comfortable with the idea of submitting to me right now, aren't you?"

"There's no reason I shouldn't be," I retorted.

He looked at his watch. "In about five minutes, you're not going to feel that way."

What insane idea did he have up his sleeve?

"Your safe word will be stop," Blaze informed me.

"Stop?" I was disappointed. "Isn't that a little elementary? Shouldn't it be something unique like pepper jack or jellybeans?"

Blaze laughed.

"Trust me, for you, stop will be sufficient. You're new to this and I don't want you panicking while trying to recall your safe word. For newbies, saying stop is a knee-jerk reaction, and it works. Once you become more familiar with your role as a sub, I may allow you to choose your own safe word."

I gave a curt nod. "Fair enough. So you are giving me another test today?"

"Yes, and I don't want any more random excuses like the last time."

I groaned. "You will not let me live that down, will you?"

"Not on your life, princess."

I detested when he called me princess. Honestly, I didn't like for anyone to call me that. It felt like an insult, suggesting that I was fragile or had no substance beyond my appearance.

I rolled my eyes. "I hate when you use that name."

"I know," Blaze confessed. "And if you roll your eyes at me one more time, you're going to hate my response to that, too. You're familiar with general sub expectations, so you know that respect is a big deal."

I paused before countering to ensure that I didn't roll my eyes again. That habit was sometimes automatic.

"Can you call me something else?" I asked.

Blaze uncrossed his arms.

"I could call you a whore, but that is a reward and you haven't earned it yet."

I gave him a tight smile. "Well, I guess I better up my game then."

Blaze tapped his watch. "Time is ticking. You are welcome to ask me any questions you like."

I, too, jumped right in. "Let's talk about this sadist thing. It means you like to incorporate pain with sex, right?"

"Correct."

"How much pain?" I asked.

"How much can you handle?" he fired back, answering my question with one of his own.

"I don't know. I guess I'm going to find out. What do you plan to do to me?"

"Tonight? Or overall?"

I went with the latter. I already figured I knew what he had planned for tonight.

Blaze leaned off the table. "I haven't decided yet. My urges come to me in the moment and I take my cues from the energy and desires of my submissive."

"In short, I just have to roll with it?"

"Basically," he replied. "I could explain scenarios to you all day and still wouldn't cover everything. The bottom line is that you have to trust me, and if that is ever not enough for you, all you have to say is…" he paused, urging me to fill in the blank.

"Stop," I said. "I can always say stop."

"And I will immediately," he assured me.

There was a knock at the door, and I glanced toward it. I wasn't expecting anyone, but Blaze must have been, because he went to answer it. Before he turned the knob, he said, "By the way, when you are active as my sub, do not call me Blaze. Only refer to me as sir."

"Why not?" I asked.

"Blaze is reserved for friends and people I respect. During our scenes, I do not respect you. I own you."

He opened the door, and Hannah strode inside, cool and composed, wearing her uniform as well.

The only difference was Blaze was wearing a long sleeve black shirt, and Hannah was wearing her usual tank top, once again reminding me of a tough video game chick ready to take on any challenge that came her way.

Greeting us both, she said, "Hi, Blaze. What's up chica?"

"Hey Hannah," I said absently.

What was going on?

Yet, I was afraid I already knew. This was that sharing thing Jocelyn had mentioned. I was about to have my first threesome and the realization caused my mouth to go dry and my heartbeat to quicken.

Blaze came toward me and I merely sat there, my eyes shifting from him to her, mentally orchestrating how all this would play out. I barely knew what to do with Blaze. What the hell was I supposed to do with her?

Then again, Hannah had an edginess about herself as well. Would they both be bossing me around?

He stopped beside my chair, and I looked up at him.

"It's time to see what you're made of," Blaze said.

Determined that he would not make me go back on my

word, I said, "If you thought a threesome would scare me away, then you're wrong. I'm game for anything."

"Oh princess," he said smoothly. "She's not here for me."

Blaze stepped behind my chair, and my eyes darted to Hannah.

OH. SHIT.

He wouldn't. He couldn't.

"Put your hands behind your back," Blaze ordered.

He was going to!

I complied, and seconds later, I felt the hard metal handcuffs close around each wrist, securing me to the chair.

"She's all yours," Blaze said to Hannah, walking back across the room.

Hannah pulled off her tactical fingerless gloves and unfastened her duty belt from around her waist, depositing them onto the table.

My shoulders stiffened as she came toward me. I didn't want to appear like I wasn't game for anything, like I'd just said, but I was kind of freaking out here.

"Aren't you forgetting something?" Blaze said.

"Sorry, sir," Hannah replied.

She removed the band that was holding up her ponytail and shook out her hair. Full, loose waves framed her face and only added to her usual attractiveness, and that's when I noticed her entire demeanor had changed.

Her usual edginess was gone, replaced by a docile, flirtatious woman.

Was Hannah a sub? No way.

She was now down on her knees in front of me. Once she placed her hands on my legs, I wasn't sure they would open, but they did with surprising ease as I stared at her.

"Demuéstrame que no has olvidado tu entrenamiento y hazlo bien," Blaze said to Hannah.

And although I had no idea what Blaze said, hearing the

seductive familiarity with which the words flowed from his lips had me mesmerized.

Could he get any sexier?

"No te fallaré," Hannah said in response.

Could she?

Then looking up at me, Hannah added, with a flirtatious wink, "I promise this won't hurt a bit."

Hannah's hands caressed the inside of my thighs and I didn't know if I should look down at her, or straight ahead at Blaze. Neither option seemed safe, so I decided not to look at anyone and closed my eyes.

"Don't even try it," Blaze said firmly. "Eyes on me."

My eyes fluttered open, and I looked across the room at Blaze, immediately noticing the smile on his face. He was enjoying this.

The confusion, anxiousness and downright struggle as I fought to hold myself together when I was so evidently falling apart was highly entertaining to him.

Hannah touched me softly, and I remained still. This was so foreign and unlike any situation I ever expected to be in. How in the hell was I supposed to take this?

Hannah was gorgeous and dangerous, watching me carefully while she ran her fingers over my freshly waxed pussy, exploring and quickly uncovering what I liked, no doubt using my slight uptick in breathing and how often I blinked as a compass.

Her thumb found my clit, and she massaged it.

It felt incredible. Nevertheless, I was still determined to keep my composure, so I stared harder at Blaze's smirking face.

My plan was to conceal my reaction, but when she gave me an extremely sexy smile and said, "You can stop your internal struggle, chica. I know this feels good, so just relax and enjoy it." I squirmed in my seat.

Why did I even think she would be easy to fool?

Hannah was also an assassin and trained alongside Blaze. Of course, she would have great interrogation skills and know how to pick up on micro-expressions.

Using her free hand to caress my inner thigh, Hannah leaned forward. "Time to see if you taste as good as you look."

Then she replaced her thumb with her tongue, slowly sweeping it across my clit several times. The sensation felt weird.

This was the first time someone had gone down on me for longer than a few minutes, and embarrassment from my initial experience kept mentally springing forth. At any second, I expected Hannah to stop and say, "I can't do this anymore. It's too disgusting."

But she didn't. In fact, she seemed to be enjoying this, but *I* shouldn't enjoy this, *should I?*

Hannah's dark hair fell against my skin, tickling my inner thigh, adding a new sensation to the mix. Her tongue gradually dragged up my center, returning once again to my clit, but this time instead of flicking her tongue over it, she closed her lips around it and sucked.

My breath caught in my chest, my hands tightened into fists behind my back and a half moan escaped. I swallowed it down, striving to be poised and unaffected while Blaze's gaze bore into mine.

It was hard, because Hannah was doing an excellent job.

Blaze pushed off the table and walked over to us, stopping in front of me. *Was I sweating?* I had to be sweating. Damn, this girl knew what she was doing.

"Remind me of what you said that night about oral?" he said.

Between the pleasurable sensations Hannah was providing, I scrambled to locate which lie I'd formulated and when I did, restated it to him.

"I said it wasn't my thing."

How I got that entire sentence out without my voice cracking. I had no idea.

"Right, that's it," Blaze said. "It's not your thing."

He looked down at Hannah, or rather at the back of her head, and spoke, his voice like a drill sergeant.

"Come on, Hannah. My new sub is trying to keep it together, and that is fucking unacceptable."

Blaze walked a slow, steady circle around us and I was thankful to have a minute to close my eyes and completely lose myself in how divine her tongue felt on my pussy.

However, I was still keeping it together... I think.

If these slight quivers didn't give me away, then my lie about not caring for oral might remain convincing. I didn't want Blaze to know I straight up lied to him, although I think that ship had sailed.

"You are embarrassing me, Hannah, do better."

No, he had it wrong. Hannah was embarrassing me. She was doing such a good job I'd drench this chair and likely her face.

I was shocked, unsure of whether to concentrate on my own sensations or on the way he was speaking to her.

Blaze had never addressed Hannah with anything but respect as far as I'd seen, and I knew she had a temper, but the only reaction Hannah had to his insults was to do exactly what he ordered. Better.

Changing it up, Hannah slid her tongue inside me, alternating between fucking me with it and then hungrily sucking and licking my most sensitive spot.

I moaned. I couldn't help it. This felt phenomenal, and if I thought that was as good as it could get, I was wrong.

Blaze grabbed the back of Hannah's head, pushed her hard against my pussy, and held her there. The action forced her tongue further inside me, and I cried out in ecstasy.

My head fell back on the chair as I was no longer able to contain my reaction.

"Grind your pussy against her mouth," he told me.

I moved carefully, not wanting to add too much pressure to her face, but even this up'd the heat of this exchange.

The more I moved, the more the cuffs dug into my wrist, yet I ignored the pain, too preoccupied with pleasure. I was getting close.

"Harder," Blaze ordered. "Don't worry about suffocating her. She's a whore, she's used to it."

Moaning louder now, I sped up. "Oh yes, that's it," I cried.

Blaze released Hannah, but she kept going, and so did I. Blaze stepped to stand beside me, sliding his fingers into my hair, then with a hard yank, he forced my gaze straight up at him.

"I thought you said you didn't like oral. That it's not your thing. Sure, looks like you're enjoying it to me."

"I am, sir," I said between ragged breaths. "I am."

Blaze's grip on my hair was rough, but I liked the way it intensified the sensations. Until now, I never truly believed pain and pleasure could go hand in hand.

"The next time you lie to me," Blaze warned. "You will be punished."

"I understand, sir," I replied.

"Good girl," Blaze said. "Now, I want you to keep moving those hips and cum all over her face for me. Use her to get yourself off. Can you do that?"

Blaze didn't let go of my hair, but he did loosen his grip and I nodded, maintaining eye contact with him while I found a speed that would get me my release.

Right before I came, Blaze leaned down and kissed me long and deep.

My body exploded, and I jerked, kicked my legs, and squeezed my fists tighter behind me. Blaze was an excellent kisser, and just having contact with him made my climax that much sweeter.

As my moans, cries and whimpers spilled into his mouth, our lips almost broke contact several times because I was shaking so hard, but Blaze held me in place, by re-tightening his grip on my hair and sliding his free hand around my neck.

"Swallow every drop," Blaze said to Hannah when he ended the kiss.

And she obeyed, kissing, licking, and sucking my pussy as I came down from my orgasmic high.

"Mmm," Hannah moaned. She licked her lips slowly and seductively before wiping her mouth with the back of her hand. "You didn't disappoint, chica. You taste amazing."

I couldn't muster up any words. I was drained, and I didn't notice it at the time, but now that I was back in reality, my right arm had a massive cramp from being in that position too long.

After unfastening the handcuffs, Blaze reached down and rubbed my shoulders, arms, and wrists. It was exactly what I needed. I watched Hannah across the room, pulling her hair back into a tight ponytail and reattaching her belt.

"Damn Hannah," Blaze said. "If you can show that much enthusiasm when you are running those drills, we might have something."

Hannah laughed. "Don't fucking start with me, Blaze. I got myself covered, you just bring your A game."

And just like that, they were back to being teammates. Hannah's edginess had returned, and I was in awe of both of them.

Using one finger, Blaze lifted my chin. "You did good. Are you okay?"

I blinked a few times. Hell, I was more than okay, thanks to him and Hannah.

"I feel good," I said honestly.

Blaze gave me a smug look, and I thought he was going to rub it in my face about being so scary to open up in the first place, but he didn't. Instead, he said, "I have to go now."

He headed toward the door, then opened it for Hannah. She blew me a kiss and exited. Right before Blaze disappeared behind her, I called out, "Will you be back later?"

I wasn't sure why I asked. Maybe I was already missing him, or maybe I wanted to make sure I would have the rest of the evening free to freak the fuck out about what had just happened.

"Not tonight," Blaze said. "But I suggest you get some rest because once I get my hands on you, your whole body is going to be sore."

And then he left. *Freak the fuck out it is.*

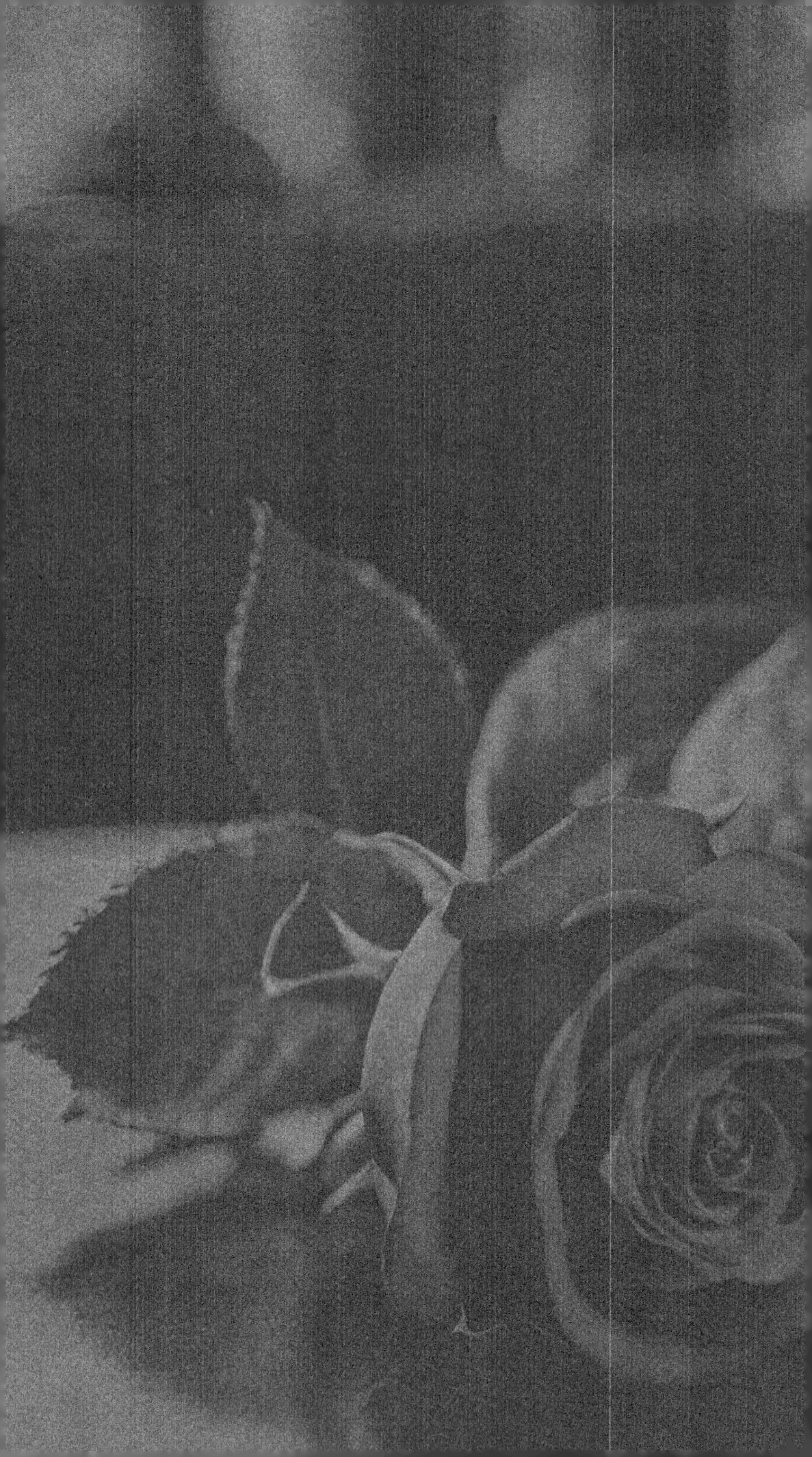

Chapter Ten

"Did I just bite his dick?"

I was clutching my small purse in one hand and my keys in the other. After getting out of the car, I didn't even waste the few seconds it would take to shove them into my purse.

Because of a road closure on my regular route, I had to take multiple detours to bypass traffic, but unfortunately, it only led me further into the congestion, resulting in a delay of forty minutes.

I was never late, and the last thing I wanted Blaze to think was that our sexual arrangement had affected my professional responsibilities.

Pulling the door open, I stepped inside, Trenton watching me, likely wondering why I was moving so quickly.

"Hi Trenton," I said, already dumping my purse and keys into the bin.

"Hey Raquel, are you alright?"

"Yeah, just really late."

"Oh," he said with understanding. "The construction on fifth avenue slowed you down?"

"Is that what that was, construction?" I asked, exasperated. "I never got the chance to see anything but a long line of cars and a man directing us to follow the signs. Thank God it wasn't an accident. Did you get caught in it, too?"

"No, a friend called and told me to avoid the route."

"Lucky you," I said. Then realized my phone was still in the car.

"Darn it," I said, looking up at him. "Can I leave my stuff here? I have to go get my phone."

"Of course, it's no problem. I'll keep it all safe for you."

"Thank you," I said, relieved.

It was rare for me to forget my phone, but my mind had been on the fritz all weekend. Replaying the erotic scene, replacing Hannah with Blaze, back to Hannah and then, in a shocking twist, both of them.

Blaze had me in the doggy style position, while Hannah lie underneath between my legs, eating me out.

My mind was a wild place, and vivid dreams were not new to me.

When I was younger, my mom told me it was a special gift because not only were my dreams lively and usually happy, they often helped me recall things I'd forgotten, such as where I'd left my favorite teddy bear or the answers to the study questions I'd been working on for weeks.

However, it wasn't until the death of Loni and these recent attacks that my "special gift" backfired. No one wants to go to sleep and have clear recollections of bullets flying, bloody scenes, or crying a sea of sad tears.

After grabbing my phone, I went back inside, checked in, and started my work day. Blaze wasn't in the office, which meant I spent more time working and less time wondering what wild things he would do to me the next time we were together.

When my phone beeped around noon, I assumed it was Des or Jocelyn. Turns out, it was Blaze. The smile that spread across my face was embarrassing. I was way too thirsty for this man.

Blaze: Hey love. What are you doing?

> Me: Processing reports and trying not to fantasize about my Dom.

> Blaze: You're a smart and talented woman. Do both.

I gripped the phone tighter, trying to figure out the best response.

> Me: Yes, sir, anything you want.

I got hot even saying that to him. It seems this submission thing came naturally to me. I stared at my phone, awaiting his response, but nothing. Eventually I put my phone down and started back working, certain he'd gotten caught up in the field.

At 3pm, he finally responded, and it was enough to spike my nerves and excitement.

> Blaze: I think I'd rather hear that in person. I'll pick you up at your place at 7.

Guess there was no need to wonder anymore about what he would do to me because tonight, I would find out.

I wanted to look sexy for Blaze, but my curls weren't curling correctly. This morning before work, I'd flat ironed my hair to get a smooth, sophisticated look that went well with my suit.

Now, I wanted my curls back. I wanted to give Blaze the version of myself that screamed I was a carefree, sexually dangerous woman. Unfortunately, this look was giving off a deranged woman instead.

There were sections that remained straight no matter what I did, and the parts that did curl were limp and frizzy. The only solution was to wash my hair and start over.

I didn't have time for that. Therefore, I combed it back into a sleek ponytail and hoped the fitted jeans and sheer blouse would do the trick.

When Blaze arrived, I was already outside waiting for him. If I spent a second longer inside my place, I would have changed outfits again and attempted round two on my hair.

We traveled the almost hour drive to his house in mostly comfortable silence. We discussed our days, more me than him since he was working a case, but mostly, I enjoyed the scenery.

Blaze stopped in front of a wrought-iron gate and rolled down his window. A digital screen that emitted a soft blue glow awaited his credentials.

Before entering the required five-digit code, Blaze placed his hand on the screen to be scanned.

"Wow, that is a lot of security," I said and diverted my eyes to give him the opportunity to input his code.

It reminded me of the scanner at work, but this one appeared a lot more advanced.

"With the life I live, I can never be too careful. Few people know where I live and all personal info about me is scrambled in all search databases."

"Scrambled?"

"It's a perk of working with the FBI. The only public information listed about me is that my name is Adrian Shaw and I own Vex security. Digging any deeper results in error messages and dead ends."

We entered the gate, but drove at least another two minutes before we got to the house. Off in the distance, I spotted glimpses of what looked to be metal poles in the ground that glowed a greenish color near the top every few seconds.

"What are those poles that glow?" I asked.

"They secure the perimeter. If anyone or anything approaches the property within a certain distance, even if it's in the air, I get alerted."

"Very high tech," I said, more to myself than him.

My attention was still out the window, looking at the vast land and the tall, majestic trees.

It reminded me of my grandparents farm, minus the animals, of course, and evoked a sense of warmth and contentment.

Blaze pulled into a parking spot next to two SUVs; one black and one blue. The blue one I'd seen him in leaving from work a few times, but the black one I'd never seen before.

It looked high end, leading me to believe that he purposely kept it away from the perils of his job to prevent it from possibly being riddled with bullet holes.

The house wasn't huge, and it would have surprised me if it was. There was no doubt Blaze had a lot of money, but he didn't strike me as a materialistic man.

A nice item here and there like that gorgeous black SUV, sure, but other than that, he wasn't obsessed with material things.

When we walked through the front door, I noticed immediately, how high all the ceilings and door frames were. They had to be at least twelve feet tall, if not more.

The open floor plan seamlessly connected the living room to the dining area and kitchen, making it perfect for entertaining guests, or in Blaze's case, easier to spot anyone or anything that didn't belong.

"I love your place," I said, tearing my eyes away from the rack of guns that were hanging in a far corner. "So quiet and discreet."

"Thanks."

I took a seat on the couch and watched Blaze walk into the kitchen. No uniform today. Just grey sweats that made me sweat, and a dark blue shirt that emphasized his perfect chest.

I could not wait for him to fuck me.

Blaze closed a few folders on the kitchen counter, before turning to the refrigerator, pulling out a bottle of water.

"Do you want something to drink?" Blaze asked.

"Sure. A bottle of water would be fine."

He came over and offered me the water. I took it, my fingers brushing across his hand, and my body tingled.

Since Blaze was still standing, I took a quick sip, then put the bottle on the coffee table and got to my feet. Blaze finished his water completely, before putting it on the table next to mine.

"Say it," he said, staring down at me.

I didn't understand. "Say... what?"

"What you sent me in the text message?"

"Oh, you mean," I made my voice extra seductive. "Yes, sir. Anything you want."

Blaze closed his eyes and hummed deep in his throat. "That's it. I like hearing that. Do you need anything before we get started?"

"No, I'm ready."

I licked my lips, mentally urging him to kiss me, but he didn't. Instead, he took my hand and gently lead me out the living room and down a short hallway.

This is it. He is leading me to the kinky room, or maybe a dungeon, where there will be paddles, chains and interesting devices.

"If you squeeze my hand any tighter, you're going to cut off my circulation," Blaze said without looking back at me.

I released a nervous laugh.

"That obvious, huh?"

"Yup," Blaze responded, offering me nothing more.

We arrived in front of a closed door and he let go of my hand and faced me.

I nibbled at my lower lip. "Got any advice for a newbie?"

Blaze tilted his head slightly, and thought about it. Eventually, he said, "You have one job, and that is to please me. If you find yourself at a crossroads, don't think, just obey."

"Somehow, that makes me even more nervous."

Blaze's eyes traveled from my head to my toes, then back up again. "You should be nervous, Raquel. I can be harsh, and demanding, and tonight I plan to tear you apart."

He said that with a straight face, right before opening the door, and I questioned my sanity.

Blaze extended a hand into the room in an "after you" motion, and because I didn't want him to see me falter, I strode past him with my head held high.

He laughed to himself and shook his head.

Once inside the room, I was shocked at what I found. There were no torture devices, no chains or paddles, just a simple room with tall ceilings and minimal decor that maintained the comfy feel akin to the rest of the house.

Against the wall facing the doorway was a massive bed with a four-poster frame made of solid wood, and two nightstands.

On the right wall was a couch with a square glass table next to it.

And on the left wall were abstract paintings in between two doors, leading to what I assumed were the bathroom and closet.

"I thought this would be more of a kinky room," I said. "Where are the tools of sexual destruction?"

"Through that door over there," Blaze said. Nodding at the door that I thought was a closet. "I call it the dark room."

"Oh," I murmured. Nothing else seemed to suffice.

"But we won't be going to that room yet," Blaze said, pulling his shirt over his head, tossing it to the floor. "Tonight, we will start with the basics."

At the sight of his bare chest, I almost fainted.

The last time I saw him shirtless was six months ago, when they were doing drills in the parking lot. I remember because I was having the worst time locating the button to unlock my car.

It probably would have helped if I actually looked down at the controller in my hand, but I was experiencing technical difficulties tearing my eyes away from Blaze.

Now, with him standing within touching distance, I was in a trance, just like Melanie that day at work.

Oh, she would die if she knew I was here.

Blaze's chest appeared sculpted, smooth, and strong. So very strong. Ripples of tight muscles covered his chest and abdomen as if an artist had meticulously chiseled every detail.

It was now evident that the tattoo from his arm was a smaller part of an intricate design that zigged and zagged across his pecs, connecting at various points, forming a shield-like pattern over his chest.

"No need to only stare," Blaze said. "You can touch."

He didn't have to tell me twice. What did Jocelyn always say? "*Don't threaten me with a good time.*"

I walked over, placing my palms on his chest, first carefully and then more consuming, feeling the warmth of his body beneath my hands.

I traced the complex art inked on his skin with one hand, while the other dipped lower and lower.

Blaze caught it right before I slid it into his sweats and backed away from me, taking a seat on the couch. I was left standing there, yearning for more.

"Do you remember that day in my office, when I suggested

you might need some time off and you put your hands on your hips and stared me down like you could intimidate me?"

"Yeah," I said slowly.

"I'd always had a thing for you, but it was in that moment that I wanted to see you naked."

"All you had to do was ask," I said.

"I don't ask, I tell," Blaze said. "Take off your clothes and assume that position."

I did so without hesitation, giving him a little teasing dance in the process. After all, getting naked didn't bother me. I was comfortable with my body, unless you counted my scars.

Regardless, I stood there, hands on my hips, posing for him to admire.

Starting at my face, Blaze's eyes traveled downward, their pace unhurried as they took in every detail along the way. I noticed his pauses at my breasts, my pussy and then my legs.

I was definitely more blessed in the legs department than I was with my breasts. I was only a C cup, so not too big, but it fit well with my tall, slender frame.

"Your body is stunning," Blaze said. "Exactly what I imagined."

"Glad to know I didn't disappoint, sir," I said.

"Impossible," he said. "Come over here and get on your knees."

I went over to the couch and did as he'd instructed. Blaze reached behind my head and removed the band that had been restraining my unruly hair. Instantly, I felt my wild wannabe curls spring out.

"Always wear your hair down when you're servicing me, or anyone else," he said.

Anyone else?

I sincerely hoped I was successful in concealing my emotions when he said that.

Blaze removed his sweats, and my eyes dropped to his manhood.

Wow!

He was definitely well endowed. Not to a point that it was freakish, but nothing like any of the guys I had ever slept with. It was nice, long, thick, and enticing.

I wanted to make this good for him, but suddenly I am reminded of my inexperience. My oral skills were pretty good, but the type of women Blaze had likely been with could probably suck a guy's dick while doing hand stands.

I glanced back up at him.

"What's wrong?" he asked. Now running his fingers through my hair.

Deciding to only reveal my hesitation as it pertained to his impressive size, and keep quiet about my feelings of intimidation over my minimal skills, I said, "You're just, umm... big."

It was the most simplistic and spot on word I could conjure up.

"Were you expecting something else?"

"I don't know. Average maybe?"

He looked at me, puzzled. "I am 6 foot 6 inches, speak five languages, and kill people for a living. Raquel, nothing about me is average."

My eyes shifted from his face back down to his dick, that I'd already begun lightly stroking.

"Now, when you put it that way, I guess that's true."

"I'm ready whenever you are," Blaze said.

No doubt that was his way of saying get to sucking. And I wanted to. I wanted to hear him moan and I couldn't wait to taste him... I just had to get out of my own head first.

Alright, Raquel, I thought to myself. *You got this!*

I cleared my throat and got up higher on my knees.

Blaze was watching me, like a judge holding a clipboard, ready to rate me. Talk about unnerving.

Running my tongue over the tip, I teased and tasted his dick for several long seconds before taking him in further.

Blaze eventually laid his head back on the couch and closed his eyes.

I wasn't sure if he was enjoying it, or getting bored, because my technique wasn't exactly going smoothly.

Every time I went down too far, I gagged and withdrew. Only to repeat the process again, with little to no hand action as I tried to use my mouth to do all the work.

Blaze said nothing, but I could feel the judgement in his silence.

Things were not going well and once my teeth scraped down his dick, things got worse.

Oh, shit! Did I just bite his dick?

I glanced up at Blaze, still leaning back on the couch. He didn't say anything, but now his eyes were open, staring up at the ceiling.

He released a slow breath, and I figured I should try again, which I was about to do when Blaze halted me.

"Stop," he said before I could get going. "Maybe you're confused. I told you that I was a sadist, not a masochist. There is a difference that I assume you are aware of."

His eyes bore into mine and his tone indicated I was expected to listen. Blaze was not asking a question. He was making a point. A point that outlined how unimpressed he was.

From his expression, I couldn't tell if he was upset, neutral, or intrigued by my inexperience.

Regardless, I didn't say anything and, after ensuring his words had sunk in, Blaze finally asked, "Have you ever sucked dick before?"

"Yes," I replied, sitting back a little, "And contrary to what just happened, I actually know how to give a blow job."

Blaze only stared at me. I couldn't blame him. I did just, in essence, bite the man.

"I'm serious," I said, trying to plead my case. "I'm really not this bad."

Blaze tapped his fingers on the arm of the couch. "Tell me this, did the men enjoy it? Or did they just enjoy *you*?"

I didn't like his emphasis on the word you.

"What exactly does that mean?" I asked.

"Come on, Raquel. You are an actual model. Some men can get off by the mere thought of you. Which, in turn, requires no actual skills on your part," he said blatantly.

I snorted a laugh. "Instead of saying you were harsh earlier, you should have simply said you were an asshole."

I knew it was a mistake as soon as it left my mouth.

It wasn't that his brazen assessment hurt my feelings. It was true, I'd fumbled my oral performance, but his slick way of telling me I was all looks and nothing more didn't go unnoticed. I wasn't used to a man belittling me.

Nevertheless, rule number one was do not insult your dom, but it was too late to retract.

Blaze leaned forward and gripped my chin, holding it firmly in his large hand. His gaze fixated on my mouth before returning to my eyes.

"Thank you," he finally said.

It was his composed demeanor and the absence of any hint of anger, irritation, or impatience that alerted me to the fact that I was in trouble.

I wasn't sure I wanted to hear the answer, but I asked anyway. "For what?"

"Earning your first punishment."

Chapter Eleven

"I WAS PEEING ALL OVER HIS BED!"

My mouth remained shut as I stared up at this gorgeous, intense, unwavering man. It would not get me in trouble again.

"What is your job?" he asked.

"To please you, sir," I answered respectfully.

"Exactly, so let me be clear," Blaze began, his hand still cupping my face. "I am training you to be a whore, not wholesome. Therefore, I suggest you leave your moral compass at the door. As your dom, if I want to question you I will, if I want to use you, I will and if I want to degrade you, I most definitely will. Learn to appreciate it, because disrespect from you will not be tolerated. Do you understand?"

This time, I held back my knee jerk reaction to get defensive about being spoken to in such a way because if I were being honest, I kind of liked it.

Usually men treated me with kid gloves too afraid that I would break, or possibly retaliate and dump them.

But Blaze didn't care that I was beautiful or had a long line of men begging to date me. He treated me exactly the way he wanted to, like a woman that he expected to obey his commands with no negotiations and no apologies.

In conclusion, I was embarrassingly wet.

"I understand," I said.

I heard myself say the words, but I still couldn't believe it.

This was strange as hell. I felt like I was in the twilight zone or something.

After giving me a nod of approval, Blaze settled back into his seat.

"Now, tell me. How many guys have you gone down on?"

I calculated three guys in my mind: Avery, Chaz and Eric.

"Only a few," I said. When he didn't respond, I felt the need to fill the silence and rushed to add jokingly, "I mean, it's not like I made a habit of going around and giving blowjobs for sport."

Blaze lifted a brow. "Not yet."

And there it was again, that not-so-subtle reminder that I would be shared.

My stomach tightened and my mind split into two conflicting reactions concerning sex with other people: *Let the fun begin,* and *I'm going to have a panic attack.*

I gave voice to neither because I was likely to say the wrong thing and earn myself another punishment.

"Do you like the flavor strawberry?" Blaze asked.

Baffled at how the conversation turned from oral gratification to strawberries, I said, "Uh, yeah, why?"

Blaze opened the small wooden treasure chest on the table next to him and pulled out a tiny box. Flipping back the lid, he retrieved a thin, red, rectangular shaped strip.

"Open your mouth," Blaze instructed.

When I did, he placed the thin strip near the back of my tongue. It dissolved almost immediately, tasting like strawberry candy.

"What was that?" I asked.

"Something that's going to help you suck my dick easier. Are you ready to try again?"

I looked at his length, so hard and big. I wanted to please him.

"Yes, sir," I said.

He removed the hair that had fallen in my face by tucking it behind my ear. "Alright then, slut, show me what you got."

And I did.

Thanks to his assertiveness, my initial jitters had disappeared, and I was eager to prove that I was more than just a pretty face. I may not be an expert, but I knew how to make a man feel good.

This time, I took my sweet time kissing and licking his entire length. Making my kisses seductive and passionate.

Once I locked my lips around his dick, I was more relaxed and easily found a rhythm to jacking him off while sucking him at the same time.

By the time I got him halfway down my throat, I understood what he meant about the strip. It had numbed the back of my throat and I could take him a whole lot deeper.

Finally, Blaze moaned, and it sounded so good I felt my pussy twitch. It was the titillating boost I needed to repeat the deep throat motion over and over again.

I slid my free hand between my legs and began rubbing my clit. It was a habit I'd formed when I went down on guys, because often enough, it was the only way I could get mine too.

Suddenly, Blaze lean forward and grabbed my wrist.

"Don't touch yourself," he said. "I'm going to take care of that. Put your hands behind your back until I allow you to move them."

Following orders, I folded my arms behind me, and Blaze gripped my shoulders. I was vaguely aware of his fingers grazing across my scars, but I was too engrossed in the moment to care.

His hands slid up my neck and into my hair, and he began shoving my head down hard and fast, stretching my mouth wide with his dick.

"That's it," he encouraged. "Take me all the way in."

He repeated the process, stopping every so often to let me catch my breath, before guiding me back down again.

I don't know how long he fucked my mouth, but eventually he allowed me to use my hands again to create the perfect hand and mouth combo to get him closer to his climax.

I had to stop yet again to catch my breath. During those few seconds that my mouth wasn't sucking him dry, I continued jacking him off. Finally, I must have gotten it right because before I could swallow him again, he came.

"Damn," he moaned. His eyes closed, his breaths coming in heavy, as were mine.

It had taken forever to get him to cum, and his release landed on his chest and abs. It was silly, but I really felt like I had accomplished something, and when our eyes met, something had changed. We had changed.

It felt as though this act solidified our connection to a point where it was impossible to deny that I was his. All of my limits and fears melted away, and even before he spoke, I knew what he wanted and I was ready to appease.

"Clean it up," he ordered.

"My pleasure," I said.

Gone was the timid girl I was when I first entered this room. For the first time in my life, I'd officially set free the licentious woman that I'd always kept buried deep inside.

I liked how cocky Blaze was, loved that he was unapologetic about wanting to use me as a sex object and then toss me aside when he was done.

It was part of the thrill, and now that I was being totally honest with myself, it was one of my biggest fantasies come true.

My nipples brushed against his knees as I shifted forward, dipping my head low to lick up the first few drops of cum. Although I could still taste the strawberry numbing strip, it was easy to differentiate between that and Blaze.

His release was salty with undertones of his own unique sweetness that I couldn't get enough of.

I took my time with this, my ass high in the air, teasing him, kissing the areas after I cleaned them, and never breaking eye contact.

Once I was done, I sat back and sucked on my lower lip, still tasting him.

"That was good, sir. What else do you want me to do?"

Blaze snatched me up onto his lap, snaked his arms around my waist and stood, carrying me over to the bed, kissing me the entire way.

"I like you naughty," he said, tossing me onto the bed. I bounced a little and grinned, ready to play.

Blaze motioned for me to reposition myself so that I was lying on a pillow against the headboard. After stretching his body out over mine, he covered my neck and chest with kisses that randomly turn into love bites.

When his mouth reached my breast, he bit gently and then harder as he took in one tight, sensitive nipple.

I gasped, momentarily flustered. It stung, but I liked it, and before I could meditate on the pain too long, Blaze repeatedly ran his tongue over my nipple until the discomfort subsided.

What I was feeling was otherworldly, and a fiery excitement surged through me as he continued his pleasurable torment, exploring my body.

His technique wasn't rushed, clumsy or unbalanced. Everything he did blended pleasure and pain in a skilled eroticism that only he could master.

Blaze knew how hard to inflict pain and where.

I couldn't help but think of all the passionate scenes in vampire movies where the main character is aroused by the biting and begging for more.

The need for it to hurt, because it felt good, now made sense to me.

By the time Blaze reached my belly button, I was sure he would go down on me and I tensed, but I didn't stop him. However, instead of going further south, he worked his way back up, seizing my neck with more of those vampiric kisses.

Gradually, Blaze slides into me and I whimper, wrapping my arms and legs around him, digging my nails into his back.

"The deeper you dig into me, the deeper I dig into you," Blaze warned in my ear, switching to an angle that allowed him to penetrate my very depths, proving that he was serious.

My body clung to his, and I understood that my fantasy of Blaze was nothing compared to the reality. He had skills on top of skills.

"You're soaking my dick now, princess," he groans into my ear, and my pussy clenches around him.

Great! Why'd he have to say that? Now I was going to ruin his sheets and drown us both.

"I think you're about ready?"

"Huh?" I say absently. Only coming back to reality, because he pulled out of me, yanking me from my paradise of euphoria.

"Warm-ups over. Get on your knees and face the edge of the bed."

Enthusiastically, getting on all fours and facing the foot of the bed, I wiggled my ass, glanced over my shoulder and said, "Is this where you ruin me?"

Blaze gave me a lascivious wink, and I knew then that it was over for me.

He took hold of my waist, roughly pulling me back toward him before impaling my pussy.

It knocked the wind out of me and a weird squeal type cry escaped as he sped up. I had never, and I mean never, had sex like this before. His dick was touching places I didn't know I had.

Who knew there was a spot that every time it was tapped, your eyes twitched and your inner thighs shook? I didn't!

I clutched the sheets, searching for an anchor as they twisted and tangled around my fingers. But I was too slow, and he was much too fast. Blaze slammed into me relentlessly, seizing my soul with a pleasure so strong it felt insurmountable.

He was doing more than dominating me. He was igniting a fire inside that burned hotter with every stroke and I could barely stand it.

This was the best and only rough fucking I had ever experienced, and as I tried to pull free for the thousandth time, I realized that was the problem.

If I couldn't handle my vibrator, being turned up to anything past a three in a ten-level setting, I could not handle this!

Already my legs had become ineffective, my wild hair was hanging down all around my face, making me sweat and boxing me in like someone had tossed a pillowcase over my head, and my mouth was a permanent O.

Desperately, I tried to ease forward, to relieve some of the pressure while Blaze continued drilling into me, making my toes curl.

"Wait... Wait. I just need... a second," I pleaded.

But Blaze ignored me, and I knew why.

Wait was not my safe word, stop was, and if I wouldn't use it, he didn't have to adhere to it.

Silly me, I didn't want him to stop, only slow down, or not go so deep.

"Please... it's too much." I begged, trying to appeal to him in another way.

"Too late for that now," Blaze said sternly, his hands on my shoulders, cementing me in place. "You said you wanted to be my whore, and now you are."

Then the bastard kicked it up a notch, by grabbing a hand full of my hair, pulling my head back, forcing the arch in my back to deepen. The vigor of his thrusts felt so good I was on the verge of tears.

I shifted forward again, slipping from his hold.

"Stop running from me," Blaze cautioned. "Or I will make it more intense."

More intense! He was going to kill me.

He was already rearranging my insides and my hands now gripped at thin air because he was pulling me back so hard.

Instinctually, I tried to slow him down again, reaching back and planting my hands on his legs.

Bad move.

Blaze stopped and leaned away, his dick withdrawing from me, and I was so grateful for the break. I should have known something was wrong when I heard him open the nightstand drawer, but I paid it no mind.

Suddenly, something soft and flexible wrapped around my neck and I felt Blaze's fingers lock it in place.

I was in such a delirious state, my dumb ass thought it was a necklace and that the gesture was both sweet and odd that Blaze would pause during sex to give me jewelry.

However, after leaning forward to readjust my position, panic seized me when I realized I couldn't breathe!

I coughed, fought, and blindly scraped at my neck for the object restricting my air supply.

"Hands off," Blaze ordered in an authoritative voice.

And with a strong jerk, he pulled me backwards towards him and, of course; I lost my shit again.

"You will not win this. Calm down," he said.

This time, it was easier to follow instructions because I could breathe. Regaining access to oxygen, combined with

Blaze's gentle kisses on the back of my neck and shoulders, gave me some much needed clarity.

I was wearing a collar attached to a leash and its pressure around my throat reminded me of my submissive position.

We were now both up on our knees in bed, my back nestled against his chest and his arm possessively holding me immobile. I could feel the slow rise and fall of his breathing, much steadier than my own.

I was safe.

Breathing easier, I unhooked my fingers from the collar, relinquishing my control.

With the hand that wasn't holding the leash, Blaze caressed one breast and then the other, taking each nipple between his fingers, twisting and rolling it, transforming any apprehension I had left into arousal.

I moaned quietly, my eyes closed and my desire reignited. Strong fingers moved down my belly and stopped right at the entrance of my pussy.

He tightened the collar so that I had to concentrate hard in order to get in enough air, then said, "Pull away from me and I will make it hard for you to breathe. Take this dick like a good girl and you will be fine. If you need to tap out, use your safe word and if you cannot speak, lift one hand in the air."

A strangled "Yes" fell from my lips, but I wasn't tapping out of anything. Now that I'd adjusted to what was happening, I wanted the experience.

Blaze pressed two fingers into me, and I rocked my hips steadily against his hand, urging him to speed up.

"Are you better?" he asked.

I was beyond better. It was as if I had returned to my own personal paradise of pleasure. The way Blaze put my mind and body at ease spoke volumes about his talents.

He withdrew his fingers from inside me and inserted them

into my open mouth. I sucked hungrily, cleaning my juices from his hand until he pulled it away.

"Good girl. Ready to try again?"

"Yes, sir," I said, a nod accompanying my words.

He loosened his hold on the leash and placed a hand on my upper back so that I could re-assume the position.

Back on my hands and knees, I braced myself for what I knew would be another round of hardcore fucking, and Blaze delivered beyond my wildest expectations.

Within seconds, I was once again clawing at the sheets, swearing and spitting out strands of my damp, sweaty hair that clung to my lips.

Blaze pounded into me like a jackhammer doing construction, and I hung in there like a champ. Taking the blows, the biting and the bruises I knew he had to have been leaving all over my lower back and arms.

He was rough, then merciful, aggressive, then affectionate. Making my head spin with a merry-go-round of passion.

Just lean into it. Just lean into it.

The mental reminder, along with the verbal ones Blaze had given, went well for a while.

However, when continuous spikes of pleasure ripped into me like a tsunami, I got choked with that leash several times because I couldn't resist attempting to escape.

I was on the verge of the biggest orgasm of my life, and what did Blaze do?

Reached around and isolated my clit with his pointer finger and thumb and expertly manipulated every feel good nerve it possessed.

I screamed.

Blaze no longer had to pull the leash because the uncontrollable shaking made me too uncoordinated to get away.

His warning before we entered this room was right, he was going to tear me apart.

My orgasm swelled inside of me until it was too large to contain and suddenly when it exploded out of me, so did a massive stream of pee!

NOOOOOO.

My mind was shrieking in embarrassment, but my body had succumbed to how unbelievably incredible this felt.

I had to stop this! I could not continue peeing all over Blaze's bed, but I had no choice. He was not slowing down!

Blaze ravaged me with his manhood, while his hand remained fixed between my legs, encouraging the spraying and gushing.

Despite my weakened state, I persisted with futile attempts to wriggle free and put an end to the most humiliating and pleasurable experience of my life, but when Blaze tightened the leash around my neck and said, "Am I being enough of an asshole for you now, princess?" I accepted my fate.

Absolutely mortified, I sat on Blaze's couch with my hands covering my face. He'd already stripped the sheets and the mattress protector from the bed and went to put it in the wash, while I tried to find the silver lining in all this.

Alright, I had just had the biggest orgasm of my life and survived my first punishment... even though Blaze's bedding didn't.

Oh, the shame!

I groaned into my hands, unable to get it out of my head.

My body had been dickmatized, hypnotized and, after all these bruises and bite marks, vandalized, and I was good with all of that, but the peeing. That took the cake.

I could hear approaching footsteps, and I knew at the exact moment Blaze entered.

"Why are you covering your face?" Blaze asked, as if he didn't know.

"After peeing all over your bed, I'm a little embarrassed at the moment. Could you come back later?" I pleaded.

"For the third time, you didn't pee, you squirted, and it was natural and sexy."

I peeked up over my hands.

"Sexy?" I asked bewildered. "Who are you? That was not sexy."

"Everything a woman's body does is sexy to me," he said. "Now uncover that beautiful face and let me check you."

Begrudgingly, I moved my hands and Blaze told me to stretch out on the couch, first on my back and then on my stomach, while he applied a silky, fresh smelling oil to my skin that had a cooling sensation.

"How do you feel?" Blaze asked, his hands moving in small circular motions.

My eyes felt heavy and I was exhausted.

"Sore like you said I would be," I admitted. "But overall, I'm wonderful. What is that? The smell is calming, and it feels wonderful."

"It's an after care oil used to relieve aches and pains. It also helps promote sleep."

The infamous aftercare. I'd heard it was a must after intense scenes and can be very therapeutic, often including massages, snacks and cuddling.

After destroying his sheets, I was surprised he didn't toss me out his bed and his home. However, the only person who seemed bothered by it was me. Maybe he was right. I was dainty.

"So my punishment was utter, absolute embarrassment?" I asked.

"Yes, it was, but I am a fair man and this was your first offense. I took it easy on you."

Easy? Ha!

Blaze knew exactly what he was doing, and he knew the reaction I would have. Making me pee, okay squirt, all over his bed may have been a welcomed experience for someone else, but for me, I was much too new to this and still wanted to crawl under a rock and die.

"The question is," Blaze said. "Did you learn your lesson?"

"Oh yeah, I won't ever call you an as..." he stopped rubbing my back, and I took the hint. "A disrespectful word again."

He resumed my sensual massage.

"I figured you'd see things my way. And if you ever need to be reminded, I can and will do much worse."

I believed him and had already decided that I wouldn't be willingly seeking any more punishments from Blaze. Something told me that his normal scenes would be wild enough for me.

Blaze applied another thin layer of the oil to my lower back.

"You respond well to breath play," he said. "I like that."

I yawned. "Breath play?"

"In layman's terms, me choking the shit out of you."

I giggled.

"Yeah, that was nice."

After finishing the massage, Blaze carried me over to the bed, where I melted into his arms, the back of my head resting against his chest.

In all my dramatics, I hadn't noticed he'd already put on fresh sheets.

"Did you enjoy yourself, Princess?"

I shook my head and reminded him of what he said to me the day I officially became his sub. "No, no, no. You called me a whore earlier, which meant I earned my title. No more princess."

Blaze laughed. "So you did."

Fighting to keep my eyes open, just a little longer as a cloud of bliss threatened to overtake me, I held up both of my hands.

On the left hand, I only lifted my pointer finger and with my right hand, I formed a zero.

"What's that?" Blaze asked.

"Your score. You asked me if I enjoyed myself and that dick was a ten out of ten!"

Blaze cracked up and then kissed me on the forehead.

"Get some rest, my little whore."

I snuggled closer, smiling to myself. Blaze had met and exceeded every expectation I had formed that night I propositioned him, but one statement was no longer accurate.

He wasn't *going to* ruin me, because after what I'd just experienced, I *was* officially ruined.

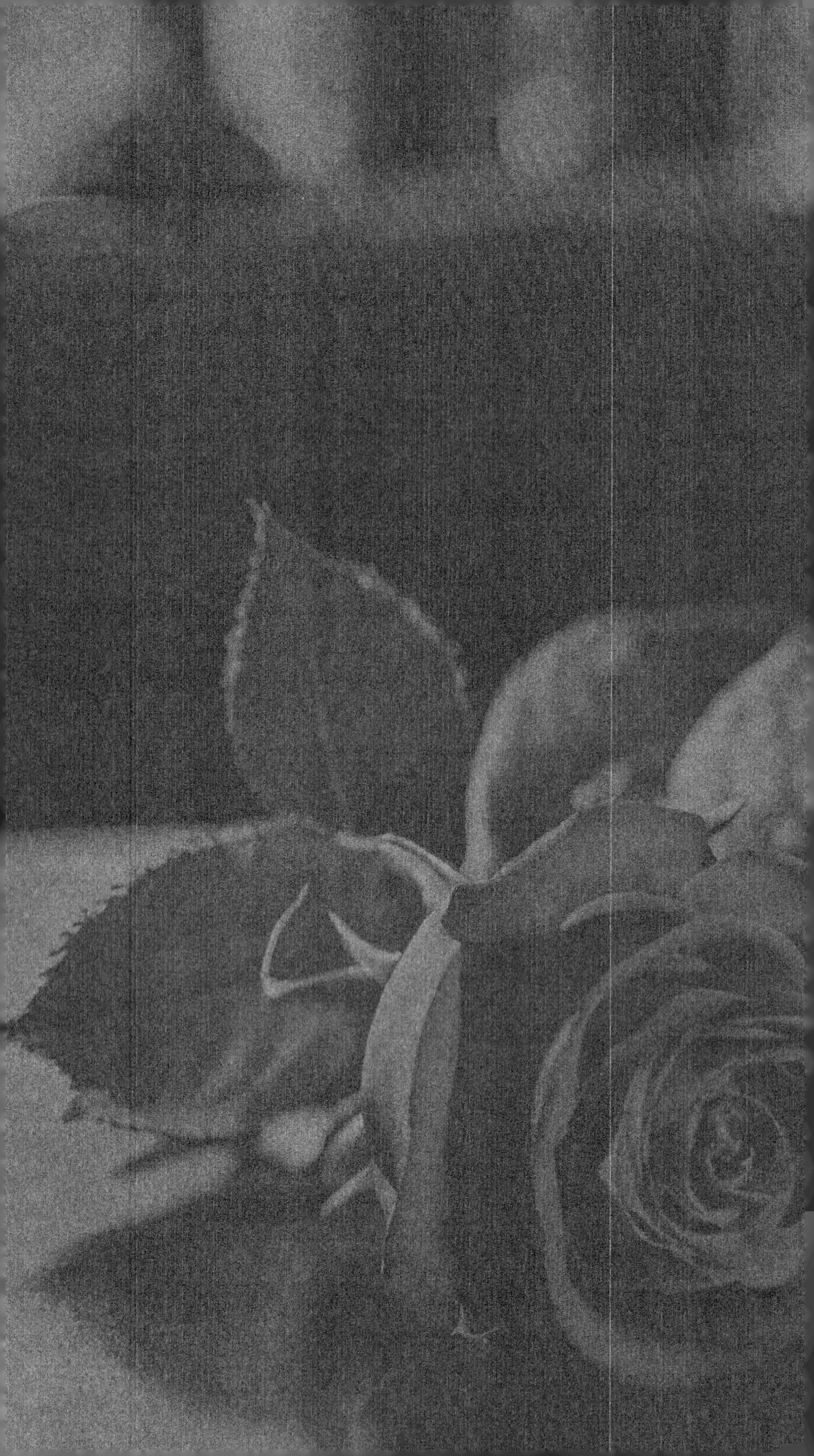

Chapter Twelve

"He was wearing a mask."

I turned off the shower, pulling my towel down from the rack and wrapping it around my body as I stepped out.

The sweet smelling body wash that I'd become addicted to a few months ago had scented the entire bathroom like a fragrant candle.

Wiping the condensation from the mirror, I stared at my reflection. My face was familiar, but the woman I'd become wasn't.

Officially, I'd been Blaze's sub for two weeks and the interactions we had still made me blush.

His goal was to get me used to his appetite, which equated to constant sex. Therefore whether it was day or night, his place or mine, Blaze had me every day in every way: bent over tables, kneeling in a chair, riding him, even hanging from his swing.

If he thought about it, we did it, and I'd been bent into so many positions, I felt like I was auditioning to be a contortionist.

Nevertheless, Blaze gave me remarkably powerful orgasms and when I tried to get away, a habit I still hadn't broken, he punished me.

Sometimes he wouldn't allow me to climax for the rest of the session, which was cruel because he evoked orgasms out of me so easily. Or he would make me edge myself with a vibrator and then take it away at the last second.

The man was sexually ruthless and true to his word, not an easy Dom.

Blaze enforced the same level of strictness when it came to me performing oral sex on him. He liked to be deep throated, slow and sensual and that really took some getting used to. I'd gone through an entire pack of those little throat numbing strips.

In the end he would cum in my mouth, or on my face and since I couldn't figure out what made him choose one over the other, I asked, *"What do I have to do to get you to cum in my mouth every time, sir?"*

"A better job," he said flatly.

See, ruthless.

Yet, his tactics were effective because I craved the taste of his release and actually felt disappointed when I failed.

One questionable thing though, Blaze had yet to go down on me and that had me confused.

Yes, in the beginning the idea gave me dread, but now it spiked my desire. What would it feel like to have a man as powerful, confident, and sexually talented as Blaze to feast on me? My guess, spectacular.

Which led to the question, why hadn't he done it? Had he changed his mind? Decided it wasn't worth dealing with me and my illogical apprehension over it?

I sure hoped not, because that would be a pity.

I stared in the mirror at the slight bruises that covered my golden brown skin and smiled.

Instead of being disgusted. I was turned on all over again. The marks were a reminder of how free and alive I felt when I was with him.

My hand traveled to my neck and although nothing was there, I could still feel the grip of the various collars I'd worn this week. Could even hear the quiet jingle of the small charms that hung on the loops as Blaze pounded into me.

Pushing thoughts of my blissful sub life aside, I went into my closet in search of what I was going to wear for the day, which is when I remembered Melanie asked me if she could borrow one of my diamond necklaces.

Retrieving it from my jewelry box, I placed it near the suit I was wearing tomorrow to work so that I wouldn't forget it.

I had tons of clothes, shoes and jewelry left over from my modeling days, so my friends were always raiding my closet.

Today I was in an extra good mood. Caovilla, the famous Italian designer I'd told Blaze about at the wedding, was releasing limited edition designer heels and I was going to buy a pair today.

I had an unhealthy obsession with clothes and shoes my entire modeling career, but ever since I moved here, I'd tried to keep it under control, and for the most part, I did. Only buying new items every other month.

As I got dressed in jeans and a light purple cashmere sweater, my joy turned to sadness. Loni always went with me to buy new shoes. We'd even plan an entire night out on the town just so that we could show them off.

God, I missed her.

The moment I pulled my sweater over my head, I heard a soft creak.

Assuming it was the neighbors moving around above me, I continued to get dressed, but suddenly there it was again.

The hairs on the back of my neck stood. I didn't like this feeling. I didn't know why, but somehow it felt like I wasn't alone.

Since I was inside of my bedroom closet, I would first have to exit this room and then the bedroom before I could go investigate the rest of the house. I wasn't too thrilled about that.

Silently and cautiously, I advanced towards my bedroom, methodically placing one foot in front of the other. In my quest for self-defense I rummaged around the closet for a weapon, but unfortunately, hangers, heels, and sweaters would not save me.

I needed a gun, which I didn't own, or at least a knife or bat, both of which were in or near the kitchen.

Peeking out of the closet and into my bedroom, I saw no one, but I didn't relax because the creak from a minute ago had now become clearly audible footsteps moving across my hardwood floor.

My heart relocated from my chest to my throat as I entered my bedroom and glanced at my nightstand.

Dammit! My phone was out on the kitchen table. I considered my options.

Should I stay hidden in the bedroom, hoping that whoever it was would find what they wanted out there and leave without causing harm? Or gather my courage and confront the intruder head-on, ready to defend myself if necessary?

Option two was the best choice.

My apartment was on the fourth floor. If someone was in here, they didn't want to steal a TV or a designer bag. They were likely here for me, and cowering in my room wishing and hoping they suddenly left would only end with me being slaughtered.

"Fuck," I muttered under my breath.

It wasn't like I could simply run out there empty-handed and yell, "Surprise!" I'd end up in a body bag. I needed something, anything.

Unplugging the giant lamp that sat on my nightstand, I wrapped the cord around it and went to stand behind my bedroom door. My plan was to wait until my unwanted guest opened it, hit them as hard as I could with the lamp, and run like hell.

Not the best plan, but better than nothing.

It felt like I was standing behind my door forever, listening to the sound of my heartbeat, as my hands trembled, but in reality, it was only seconds before the doorknob turned.

As the door slowly opened, the first thing I spotted was a black boot at the base of the door. Tightening my grip on the lamp, I held my breath and lifted it above my head.

Now, with half the intruder's body in the room and their back towards me, I had the advantage.

Using all the force I could muster, I slammed the lamp down as hard as I could onto the person's head.

It connected with a resounding thud, followed by a loud grunt as the man stumbled forward. Wasting no time, I dropped the lamp and ran as fast as I could out the bedroom door.

Regrettably, my attempt to flee was in vain because the guy, who was incredibly quick, caught up to me. He shoved me hard, and I fell into a small table that toppled over, taking me with it.

I tried to get up, but he forced me onto my back, slapping me so hard I saw stars. Fighting through the disorientation, I kicked my legs and swung my arms, trying to throw him off, but the bastard was way too strong.

He held me down with one hand, removing something silver and shiny from his pocket with the other.

A knife!

My eyes locked onto his, and a chill ran down my spine. One was pale blue, and the other was dull, shrunken, and unfocused. He was wearing a black ski mask, and the dark contrast against those murderous eyes was unforgettable.

The glint from the knife he was holding drew my attention away from those evil eyes. He would kill me unless I got out of this.

I went into autopilot; kicking, punching and screaming in the fight for my life. Nothing was landing until my knee connected between his legs. That slowed him down enough for me to roll to my side.

He caught my ankle, sliding me back toward him, but this time I was the one moving too fast. My barefoot connected with something hard enough to be his head.

The man grunted again, this time staying down long enough for me to move across the floor on my hands and knees toward the fireplace.

My fingers locked around the fire poker just as the man with the vicious eyes grabbed the back of my shirt. I twisted hard out of his grasp, rolled over, and blindly stabbed the poker upward.

It dug into his arm, and he screamed. In my hysteria, I jumped up, running like a madwoman out of my front door.

Rather than wasting time trying to catch the elevator, I hurried down the four flights of stairs, out of the building, and didn't stop until I got across the street to Zen's, where I called the police.

"Ma'am, are you sure you didn't see his face?"

I stared into my living room. The items from my fireplace tool kit were strewn across the floor, but the poker was gone. Drops of blood formed a trail from the area where we struggled straight out the front door.

I think the officers told me that the blood led to the stairwell and then disappeared, but I wasn't sure. I wasn't sure about anything. My place was a mess, my life was a mess. I was a mess.

Officer Graham sat beside me at my kitchen table, waiting patiently for a response. Clutching the blanket she'd given me closer to my trembling body, I looked at her.

"I'm sorry. What did you say?" I asked.

"I asked if you were sure you didn't see his face?" Her voice was gentle and patient. It was clear she was used to this, used to dealing with victims. I was a victim... again.

"No. He was wearing a mask."

She glanced down at her notepad. "But you are sure about his eyes? One blue eye and one," she squinted at the notepad. "Damaged eye?"

I turned my attention back to the fireplace and nodded absently. I would never forget his eyes, just like I would never forget the eyes of the guy that attacked us at Zen's.

Oh no!

This was connected. It had to be. Two evil men, both with crazed killer eyes.

"Any other discerning things? Maybe on his clothing? The way he smelled? Or spoke?" the officer asked.

I shook my head. "He didn't speak, but there was a shape or something on his jacket. It was red and resembled the letter T."

It was weird. Until now, I hadn't realized I saw that. Must have noticed it when he pulled that knife from his pocket.

I shivered again.

Officer Graham asked me more pointless questions, only to circle back and ask them again.

Who was he? And why did he want to kill me?

I couldn't tell her what I didn't know, and ever since they revealed that there were no signs of forced entry, I could barely concentrate on anything else.

This man, this stranger, this killer had a key to my place!

I was going to be sick.

"Is there anyone you can stay with for a few days?" She

asked gently. "Cops will be in and out of here processing the crime scene."

I shook my head. There was no way I was dragging anyone I knew into this.

With a light touch on my shoulder, the officer informed me she would return shortly, leaving me to my own thoughts.

Holding it together was an arduous task. No one wanted a hysterical woman on their hands. I would wait until I was alone and then I would fall apart.

My place was wrecked; broken glass was everywhere, tables flipped over, tears along the edges of the throw rug and small puddles of blood. This was awful.

I heard a deep voice behind me near the door and turned.

My eyes had to be playing tricks on me because that wasn't Blaze. It couldn't be. I hadn't called him.

I watched in disbelief as he flashed an ID at the cop guarding the door, who ultimately stepped aside, letting Blaze in. An odd sensation of warmth and safety came over me.

What was he doing here?

Blaze sat down in the seat in front of me that officer Graham had recently vacated.

For a long moment he did nothing, said nothing, only watched me. Then, gently, oh so gently, his hand caressed the side of my face where the intruder had struck me and I almost broke.

"What happened?" he asked.

"Someone tried to kill me." I replied flatly.

"Do you know who? Or why?"

I shook my head, and my eyes welled up with tears. I couldn't take this. The way he was looking at me, the feeling of my sanity slipping away, as I lived in constant fear of death.

What was going on?

Quickly, I wiped away a fallen tear with my trembling

hand, and Blaze covered both my hands with his own. He glanced around the apartment, then back at me.

"We need to get you out of here."

"I know. The officer told me it was best if I leave for a few days."

"Where will you go?" Blaze asked.

"I don't know. I need a second to think."

"You can stay with me," Blaze offered.

I was refusing the invitation even before I verbally declined it. This would not be a situation where I ran from one problem, only to create another.

Moving in with Blaze, no matter how short-lived, was a mistake. He was my boss and the man I was having a fun, carefree, kinky relationship with. The last thing he needed was to have to take care of me. My protection was not his job.

"No," I said firmly.

"Raquel," he replied insistently.

I could sense his frustration, but this was the right decision for me.

"Blaze, I can't. I won't. I'll just...," I thought about it, hurrying to find an answer. "Stay at a hotel. That's it. I will stay at a hotel."

He silenced his buzzing phone and spared another glance at all the police and evidence technicians.

"I choose the hotel," he said.

With a heavy sigh, I nodded in agreement. I had to give him something.

Blaze got up and went to talk to the officer in charge. A few minutes later, he returned, helped me pack some of my things, and then I was saying goodbye to the place that I no longer saw as my home, but as a terrifying crime scene.

"How did you even know about this?" I asked, as Blaze made the third left turn of the night.

I felt like we were going in a circle, but I could just be losing it. Lord knows it would fit with the current theme of my life.

"Ever since the incident at Zen's, I've had an officer keep me in the loop if your address or anything in the vicinity comes through the system."

I turned from the window to stare at him, my eyes narrowing.

"Is that your way of trying to keep me safe? Or is something else going on?"

"Both."

I knew it! This was about that damn case, and Blaze knew more than he was willing to reveal.

"What's going on?" I questioned.

"Nothing I can share."

"Nothing you can share!" I almost screamed. "Someone just tried to kill me for the second time in a matter of weeks and there is nothing you can share!"

I was angry. Someone was playing with my life, plotting to end me, and I needed answers.

Blaze didn't even take his eyes off the road when he said, "The third time."

"What do you mean, the third time?" I asked, worried.

"That is the third time that someone has tried to kill you. At this point, I am assuming the parking lot incident was about me *and* you."

His response left me deflated and speechless. I never asked

for any of this, and now my life was in danger for reasons I couldn't comprehend.

"Why is this happening?" I whispered.

Blaze pulled the SUV to the side of the road and put it in park. Reaching over, he took my hand, his touch providing some much-needed comfort in this moment of vulnerability.

"I can't tell you what's going on," he said.

"Because it's classified, I know," I said, no longer caring. Facts wouldn't save me.

"Not just that. It's also because I am not entirely sure right now. What I do know is that you have somehow gotten the attention of a very dangerous man."

Overcome with terror, my eyes grew wide and I began frantically glancing around as if I could spot the dangerous man Blaze was speaking of. "Why? How?"

"Raquel," Blaze said, reading the alarm written all over my face. "I won't let anyone hurt you."

"But you can't promise that."

"I can and I will." He shifted closer. "No one is going to hurt you. Do you understand me?"

I didn't respond right away. This was an impossible situation and as magnificent as Blaze was at his job, I feared this was one promise he couldn't keep. However, it felt good to pretend, even if I didn't believe him.

"Yes," I said, giving him a weak smile.

"Once you have had some rest. We can go over the details of what happened at your place."

I agreed, and Blaze shifted the vehicle into drive and continued on our way. On the corner, I noticed a store that we had surely passed for the second time.

"Did you drive in a giant circle?" I asked.

"I did," Blaze replied.

"To make sure we aren't being followed."

"Yes."

"Are we good?"

"We are," he assured me.

I closed my eyes. Maybe he couldn't keep me safe forever, but I'd have to trust that he could at least keep me safe tonight.

Blaze checked me into a gorgeous hotel on the outskirts of the city. Instead of getting me a standard room, he had booked me a suite that included a spacious living room and marble floors in the bathroom.

However, considering my current headspace, I was barely aware of my lavish surroundings.

Blaze ordered us dinner, and I hardly touched any of it. My mind was too preoccupied with thoughts of recent events that had unfolded. The weight of the situation and the danger that lurked around every corner made it difficult for me to focus on something as mundane as food.

I didn't have an appetite, but he insisted I should at least try to shove something in.

The silence was deafening as we ate. I felt weird, out of place and disoriented, being forced from my home. I didn't want to talk about the case, but I wanted to talk about something.

As I watched Blaze from across the table look exceptionally good, a fact that hadn't registered all night, I knew exactly what we could discuss.

"So Hannah," I said as a way of breaking the ice.

Blaze was responding to something on his phone and didn't look up. "What about her?"

"Is she your sub, too?"

"No, she used to be. That ended a long time ago."

That answer was unexpected.

"Wait, so she isn't your sub, but you treat her like one?"

He pressed a few more buttons on his phone. "When the situation calls for it."

I tried not to read too much into it, but it seemed Blaze was being quite terse with his answers, suggesting he may not be open to discussing the matter.

"What happened? Did she break a rule or something?"

Blaze put his phone down and pushed his dinner plate to the side.

"Uh, we weren't a good fit."

"Why is that?" I pressed.

He sighed and rubbed his temples, looking weary. "Sometimes these things simply don't work out, Raquel."

He wasn't giving me more, but I wanted more, so I continued to dig.

"I get that, but why?"

Blaze seemed to consider responding, telling me what was obviously a big secret about what ended things between him and Hannah, but I guess he decided against it.

"That is a question best suited for you to ask her."

There was something deep there and I would back off. Besides, she wasn't his sub anymore.

"Do you have other subs?" I asked, instantly realizing this was something I should have inquired about in the beginning.

"Currently, no, I don't," Blaze said.

I was taken aback. "But normally you do?"

"Sometimes I have around five at a time, but that's only when they are experienced submissives. If I am training a new sub, I give her all my attention. The emotional and mental impact this lifestyle can have on some people requires and deserves your full attention as they adjust to their new role."

That was impressive. "Seems pretty levelheaded," I said.

"I agree."

I was curious to delve deeper and learn more about his past submissives, but before I could ask, Blaze flipped the tables on me.

"So Eric, huh?" he said, using the same tone I'd used on him.

I couldn't help but laugh. "Eric was a mistake."

Blaze sat back in his chair and crossed his arms.

"How so?" he asked

"In short, he wasn't you," I said.

Blaze smiled. An alluring, pulse racing smile.

A few hours ago, I wouldn't have thought that anything could turn me on ever again, but apparently, if I am around Blaze long enough, he could make me forget my nightmares and return to my living fantasy.

"I like where this is going," he said. "Please continue."

I released a deep breath and came clean.

"I was new at your company and hadn't dated in a while because modeling full-time always carried a hectic schedule. I'd noticed you, of course, because who hasn't," I admitted, "but I figured it best to steer clear. When Eric asked me out one day, I thought he was a pretty nice guy and said yes. A couple of months later, I accepted my mistake and broke up with him. I should have never gone out with him in the first place because, as I said before, he wasn't you."

Blaze lifted a brow. "Good thing you have me now."

"Do I?" I asked in a playful tone.

Maybe sex was exactly what I needed tonight. It would undoubtedly relieve some of my tension.

Blaze nodded. "All night long."

I thought he meant sex. Turns out he meant something much more intimate. After a nice long shower, Blaze pulled me into his arms and the room filled with a serene silence, only broken by the soothing rhythm of his heartbeat against my ear.

He held me like that until I fell asleep, ensuring that I would have sweet dreams, as he promised to always keep the monsters away.

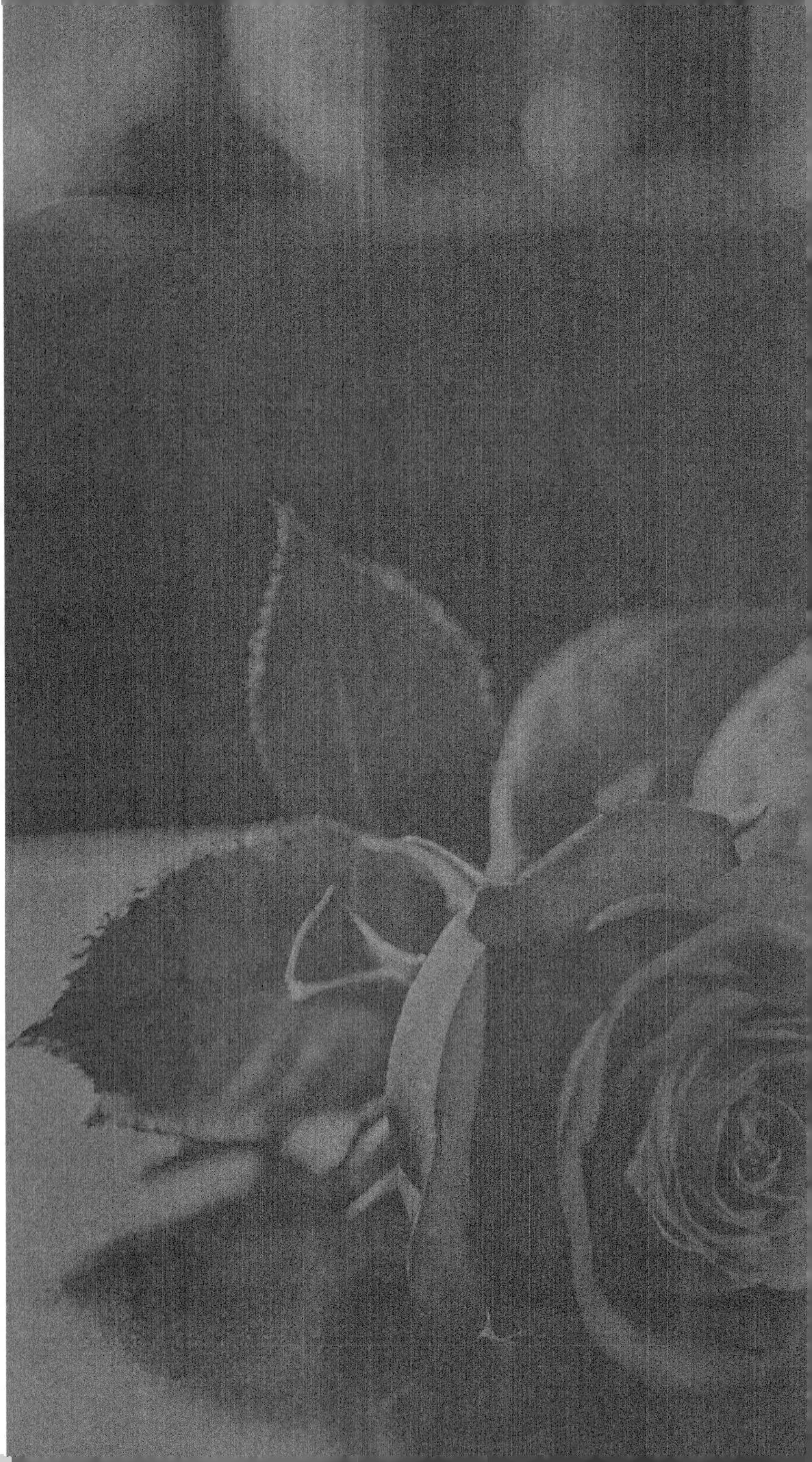

Chapter Thirteen

"Trying to seduce your dom is disrespectful."

Blaze left around 2am, unable to put off the demands of his job any longer. He promised to check on me soon, and as he kissed me goodbye, I couldn't help but wonder if something bigger was developing between us.

I know he told me that this would only be sex, and stupidly I agreed to that, but that's only because I thought it would be simple to keep my romantic feelings aside.

In my defense, I didn't know that his mere presence would draw me in like a moth to a flame, that when he touched me, I would melt, or that he'd have to hold me in his arms to keep me from trembling because I was scared for my life.

Was I the only one feeling this way? Did all the caresses, sweet words, or longing stares mean anything to him? Or was it just Blaze being Blaze, taking care of a wounded woman?

Whatever it was, it was clawing at the barriers that separated lust from what might be love, and that was troubling.

I would not be one of those women that let good sex mess with her head.

Eventually, I fell back asleep, but with Blaze no longer by my side, my peaceful dreams had fled, turning into a horrifying and hilarious replay of events.

During the first dream, I was sitting at a table staring into the eyes of both my attackers.

The weird part was it was only one man, but one eye was grayed out and unresponsive, like the guy in my apartment, and the second eye was keyhole-shaped like the guy from Zen's.

Then, the staring contest became more tortuous, when the two eyes morphed into six, like a creepy spider, carefully following its prey.

Next, I dreamed someone was chasing me with a gun, but when they fired, it only said "Bang" like the guns in cartoons.

In the last one, I was running from a tiger with claws bigger than my face, intent on ripping me to shreds, but once I stole a glance behind me, the vile tiger had become a defenseless kitten.

One thing was certain, these attacks were doing a number on my sanity. If I'd started losing it in my dreams, how long before it affected my reality?

Abandoning the idea of sleep around 5am, I kept myself busy by watching TV and playing games on my phone.

It suddenly hit me that I hadn't spoken to my mom in a few days. She did not know about this latest attack and if I had anything to do with it, she never would.

Therefore, I sent her a message stating that life was great, but I wouldn't be in touch for a few days due to an out-of-town work assignment.

It was sort of true, if out-of-town was equivalent to a fancy hotel and the work assignment was "Can you stay alive?"

After that, I spent close to an hour doing stretches, wishing I could leave this hotel and go on a nice long run.

With my hands resting on my legs, back straight, and head and neck aligned over the spine, I took in several deep breaths and concentrated on all the good things in my life.

Family, health, friends, my Dom.

The last thought brought a smile to my lips, but I didn't linger on it.

I wasn't trying to get aroused. I only wanted to clear my mind, which I eventually did, and for a short while my anxiety abated and everything felt serene, but then I heard a woman shout out in the hallway.

"Stop running Brandon or else mommy will not take you to the pool."

And the serenity was broken.

Also, based upon the heavy footsteps I heard, Brandon was not heeding the warning, so he wouldn't be earning swimming privileges anytime soon.

Getting to my feet, I got cleaned up and chose a long silk shirt as my outfit for the day. If I was lucky, I could entice Blaze to pull me out of my head for a few hours when he stopped by.

Once I was done, I glanced at my phone. There was a "Be safe, I love you" message from my mom, along with two others. One from Melanie, the other from Blaze.

I'd had my phone on silent to help with my sleep, but for all the good it did, I should have left the ringer on full blast.

After seeing Melanie's name, I was reminded that I had forgotten about the necklace I told her I would give her at work today. Perhaps the lunatic after me would be apprehended and I could give it to her later this week.

Doubt it.

Well, it was nice to know the part of my brain that assumed the worst was working just fine.

I opened Blazes message first, my hand automatically going to my chest as I read it.

> Blaze: Order anything you like from the menu. It is already covered. I will stop by soon.

If he didn't want me to fall in love, he should really ease up on being so perfect. Plopping down on the bed, I opened Melanie's message.

> Melanie: Why aren't you here today? The only excuse I will accept is that a gorgeous guy kidnapped you and is holding you hostage, while tending to your every need, of course.

I shook my head. She had it partly right. I was with a gorgeous guy that was tending to my every need, but I wouldn't confirm that. Instead, I responded to Melanie's message without giving too much away about what happened yesterday.

> Me: No, I have not been kidnapped. I have a lot going on and needed to take a few personal days. I'm sorry about the necklace. Will get it to you soon.

After sending the message, the anxiety from earlier came back with a vengeance. Why did I keep assuming this would only last a few days? I could be on the run for weeks! Months!! Years!!!

Unexpectedly, the phone began vibrating in my hand, startling me so much I nearly threw it across the room. It was Melanie. I resettled my nerves and cleared my throat before answering.

"Hello."

"Forget the necklace," Melanie said. "Are you okay? Why do you need to take personal days?"

She was speaking too fast and too loud. Shifting the phone away from my ear, I got up from the bed and walked through the beautiful suite to go admire the view of the city from the living room window.

"Umm, it's personal," I replied in a lighthearted tone.

I didn't want to be rude, especially since I knew she was likely only worried about me.

"Yeah, but after the incident at Zen's, I have to keep an eye on you. Are you okay?"

"Oh, I'm fine. I'm not feeling well, is all."

I predicted her response even before she said it.

"You're sick? That's horrible! Do you want me to come by after work and bring you something?"

"No, I'm not at home. I came to a hotel, you know, to get some room service and relax."

Staring out at the bustling traffic and the towering skyscrapers, I held my breath, praying that what I said made sense. I wasn't a good liar, especially on the spot.

I required time to construct my lies, so that I could form the layouts, build the scenes and make sure it all sounded believable, because this sure didn't.

No one goes to a hotel when they aren't feeling well.

"Okay," Melanie said slowly. "Where'd you go? If you like it, maybe hubs and I can go there, too."

Melanie was a good friend, but I also felt sometimes like she was a bit of a fan of mine, fascinated with the things I did and the clothes I wore. It wasn't an issue because I occasionally encountered it, but it was something I noticed.

Facing away from the window, I searched the room for a hotel booklet or menu that provided the name. I was in such a daze when I arrived yesterday, I only remember that it began with a V.

On the smooth, thick glass table that Blaze and I had dinner at last night, I located a rectangular shaped card that listed spa services. At the very top was the name of the hotel.

"It's called La Verdure," I said.

I was familiar with that term. It was French and translated to greenery.

Melanie gasped, then coughed, then gasped again. I think she was drinking water.

"Shut up! You are not at La Verdure."

I flipped the card over and read that the hotel also had a rooftop restaurant, and several world class chefs available 24 hours a day to prepare any of your culinary needs.

Sheesh. No wonder Melanie choked.

When I wasn't being chased down, I should circle back around and enjoy some time at La Verdure.

I looked around again, basking in my opulent surroundings. "Yeah, it seems I am here."

"Ugh! I am so jealous. Calvin and I have been saying we will go there for years, but that price tag always makes us rethink it. Is it as gorgeous as the pictures?"

I'd never seen a photo of this place. I went back to the bed and sat down, my back sinking into a firm, but soft, pillow. Being sick was a lie at first, but all these questions were making me nauseous.

"Sure," I blurted out.

"That is a hell of a way to relax when you're sick. Did you pay an arm and a leg?"

My goodness, woman! Stop it with the interrogation.

I didn't know how much this room cost. Blaze had taken care of everything, which reminded me I'd need to pay him back for this.

"I got a discount from an old modeling friend." Before she could ask me anything else, I said, "Sorry Melanie, I have to go."

There was a hint of disappointment in her voice, but she didn't press.

"Okay, you feel better. I'll see you soon and call me if you need me."

I let the phone fall from my hand. It bounced on the bed before settling next to my hip. I laid back and closed my eyes. Not tired, just thinking. There was so much I wanted to ask Blaze.

I picked up my phone to dial his number, my finger

hovering over the screen. Yet as I thought about it, I realized he had a lot on his plate right now. A call from me would only add to his stress.

Reluctantly, I put my cell down and closed my eyes again, intending to think, but I fell asleep.

When I woke up, it was 4pm, and I felt a lot better. It seems I was more tired than I originally thought.

After watching some TV, I realized I hadn't eaten all day, so I ordered some fruit from room service. My appetite was still non-existent, but skipping meals wouldn't help matters.

Around fifteen minutes later, there was a knock at the door. I opened it, expecting to see someone from room service, but to my astonishment, there was Blaze, in his uniform, holding a tray.

"You ordered fruit?" he asked.

"Yeah, I did. Didn't know it came with a sexy dessert," I replied, opening the door wider.

"Dessert?" Blaze scoffed, walking in past me. "I'm the whole damn meal."

"That you are," I said more to myself than him.

He brushed a kiss across my cheek, which set off the "take me now" alarm in my body as usual. I wanted to be fucked, plain and simple. Not to mention, thinking about sex was a welcomed distraction to being afraid.

I actually think I read something about there being a correlation between fear and arousal once. The human brain was definitely a complicated organ.

After placing my fruit tray on the table, Blaze angled a chair towards me and then took a seat. His eyes raked over my body appreciatively. But there was also a hint of something else... suspicion?

"How'd you sleep?" he asked.

"Not so good."

"Bad dreams?" he inquired.

"Tons," I answered.

"Recall anything new?"

I thought about that. Beyond being unable to unsee those murderous eyes every time I closed my own, I had recalled nothing.

"Sadly no," I said. "What about you, any closer to this nightmare being over?"

"I've got several theories, no new developments, though."

I couldn't shake the feeling that there was more to his words, but at least he had some ideas. That was more than he had last night.

Blaze couldn't stop staring at me, and I knew why. This long shirt, with no bra or underwear, was calling out to him. My nipples were hard and likely visible through the thin fabric, and his mind was thinking of ways he could use me.

Bring it on, sir.

"Something on your mind?" I asked, moving closer toward him.

Blaze followed me with his eyes as I lowered myself so that I was on my knees in between his legs.

"I think something is on *your* mind," he responded with emphasis.

"Maybe," I replied, tracing my upper lip with my tongue. "You want to guess what it is?"

A mischievous expression appeared on his face.

"If it ends with the letter X, the answer is no. I have killed too many people today and I don't have time," he said.

I sat back on my heels. "You're kidding right?"

Blaze gave me an oddly seductive, yet dark smile and, as twisted as that was, it stirred up something inside me.

"Doesn't that turn you on, then? Making you want to play after a long... hard...," I placed my hand over his dick, feeling it through his pants, "day."

I looked up at him, not wanting him to leave without

giving me what I wanted. Blaze didn't remove my hand or correct me in my presumption that violence was an aphrodisiac for him.

"Your assumption is correct," Blaze responded. "But killing people equals paperwork, hence not having the time."

"Are you sure we can't play?" I asked, gliding my hand up his lower abdomen to his chest, the hard material of his vest exciting me further. "Not even for a little while?" I teased.

I was so horny. Now that I'd gotten my mind focused on it. I wanted it bad.

"Not even that," Blaze replied.

He stood and looked down at me, still on my knees. "But you look good down there. It's the perfect place for you."

"I agree," I said playfully, pulling my shirt off over my head so that I was now completely naked. "You should get full use out of that."

Blaze was about to say something, but then his phone rang. After answering it, he was quiet for a long moment before saying, "Alright Jolli, I'll be there shortly."

Sliding the phone back into his pocket, Blaze stared down at me.

"Stand up," he ordered.

I complied, picking up my shirt.

"Trying to seduce your Dom when he has already told you no is disrespectful. I know you are aware of that."

"Umm, I forgot," I said, hoping to sound convincing.

"Well, since you want to be naked so bad I want you to remain like this until I return."

I could deal with that.

"I don't plan on returning until Thursday," he continued.

Thursday? It was only Monday!

I calmed my nerves. That was no problem. I could stay naked for three days. Many people never even wore clothes while they were in the privacy of their own home.

Then, of course, he dropped the hammer.

"I have already taken the liberty of ordering you breakfast, lunch and dinner because I know you weren't planning to eat as you should. Therefore, whenever any member of the all male staff that I *will* request for you, by the way, brings your meals, I want you to greet each of them, just like this," he said, taking the shirt from my hand.

I was clutching it a little too tight after that last tidbit of information, so he had to tug harder to get it free.

I swallowed hard. "Yes, sir."

Blaze tossed my shirt aside. "Now turn around."

As soon as I did, everything happened at full speed. Blaze cuffed my hands behind me and bent me at the waist, pressing me down against the table. The sudden impact of the cool glass against my bare skin made me jerk, and I squirmed to get off of it.

Blaze wasn't having it. I heard his belt drop to the floor and his pants unzip.

Agonizing anticipation flooded me. He was about to make this hurt and oh, did I need the mental escape.

Right before he entered me, Blaze said, "I can't resist addressing your disrespect."

I'd never been so happy that I crossed someone's line in my life.

Blaze gave me no mercy as he locked one hand around my neck and the other against my lower back, holding me in place. My flattened cheek was sliding roughly against the table with every thrust, and I squealed, unable to release a proper moan in this position.

His movements began coming in so ferocious and hard that he gripped my waist with both hands and lifted my lower half off the table, the rest of my body still pressed against the glass.

The pleasure from this new position was sublime and unimaginable.

Only a man like Blaze would think to restrain my hands behind my back while ravishing my pussy in mid-air. I felt weightless and completely at his mercy, which only increased the eroticism of my submission and vulnerability.

I was already close, and about to cum all over his dick, when out of nowhere, he cums first and then pulls out of me, leaving my climax dangling right there on the edge.

No! No! No! I wanted to cry.

Blaze removed the cuffs and helped me off the table. All the while I fought to hide my disappointment. I needed a release badly.

Without a word, he tapped me on the shoulder, and I knew what was expected. I got down on my knees and sucked his dick clean.

I loved servicing him in any way I could and he knew that, which was why, as soon as I got too into it, moaning and savoring the taste of his release mixed with my juices, he told me to stop.

Reluctantly, I did.

After zipping him up, I got back to my feet and waited for him to speak. He'd trained me well over these past couple of weeks.

"Go take a shower. Do nothing to get yourself off. You will remain like this, yearning, desperate, and ready to be used until I have a use for you. Are we clear?"

"Yes, sir," I said, my pussy throbbing so hard, I bet if I looked down, I could physically see the pulsating.

I didn't dare look, though. I kept my eyes on Blaze and accepted my punishment.

"Remember, no clothes," he reminded me.

Once I agreed, Blaze let himself out, and I went to shower.

Not even five minutes after I'd dried off and laid across the bed did I hear a knock at the door.

Immediately, I bolted up and stared down at my naked body.

That bastard.

It wasn't even dinnertime yet. Obviously, he'd arranged for someone to come up. Probably told the front desk I needed extra towels or something.

I slid out of bed and went to the door. Checking my hair in one of the wall mirrors before I answered it. If I was going to do this, I needed to look good.

Glancing through the peephole, I was met with total darkness, unable to see the usual limited view of the hallway, and that ignited my anxiety.

Was someone blocking it?

"Who is it?" I asked quietly.

"It's Blaze. Open the door."

Something was wrong. I could hear it in his voice. Without giving it a second thought, I yanked the door open and Blaze rushed inside, dragging a lifeless body with him. "Change of plan, get dressed."

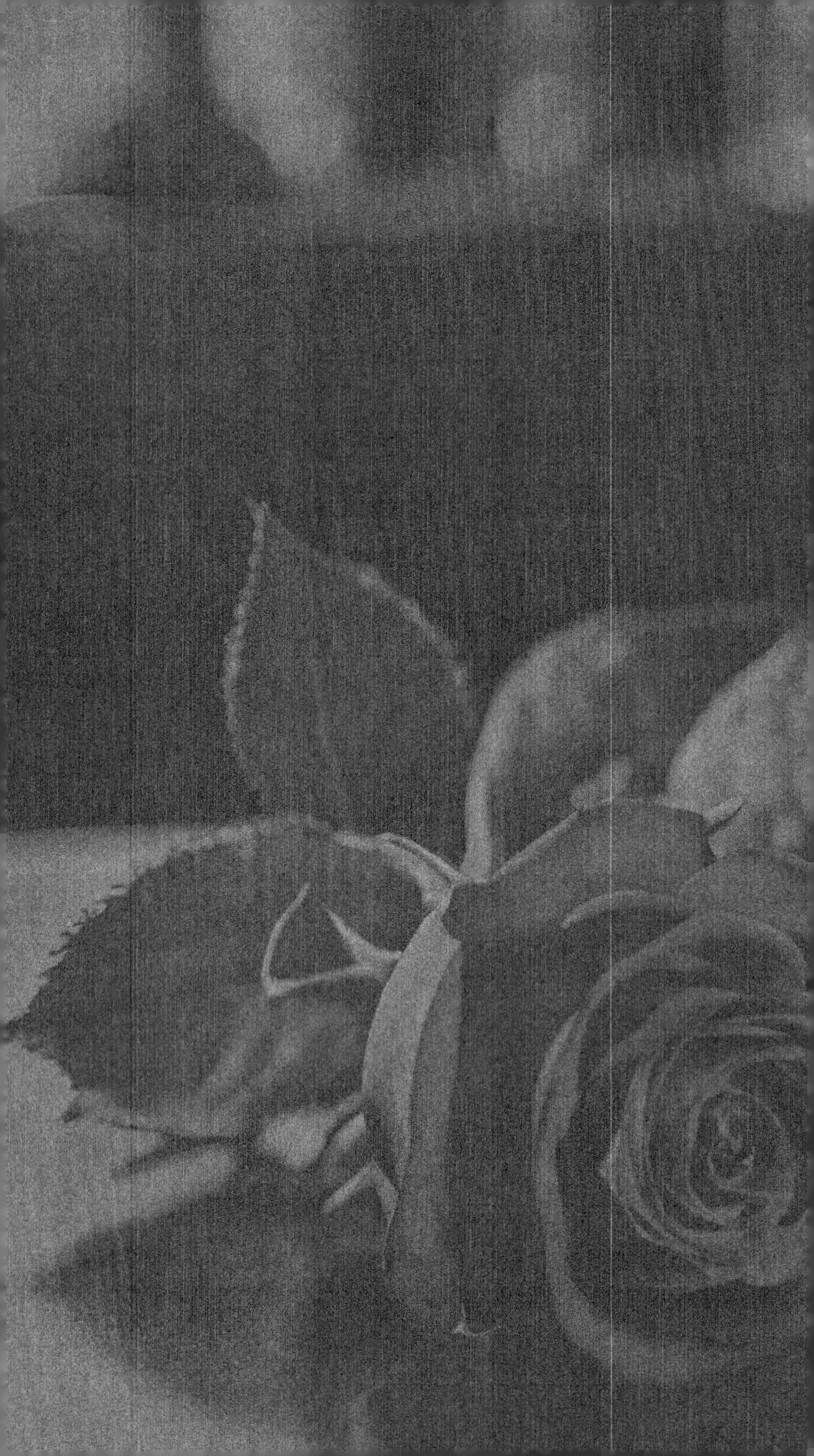

Chapter Fourteen

"This is sex, and nothing more."

"Is he dead!" I asked, panicking, as Blaze dragged the man in.

The guy was huge, although not as big as Blaze, but Blaze was handling him like a rag doll.

"No," Blaze said. "Grab his tool bag and bring it over."

Collecting the bag and then shutting and latching the door, I went to Blaze. He leaned the guy against the wall next to the table we had just screwed on, then secured his wrists to the table's leg with a zip tie.

The man was wearing navy blue, long sleeve coveralls with the hotel's logo stitched on the front.

It said his name was Connor.

Somehow I didn't think this guy with his black wavy hair, tattooed hand that said "La Muerte" and who looked like he belonged in a motorcycle gang, was named Connor.

Which meant the real Connor was probably in the same place this man wanted to send me: the afterlife.

A sudden shiver coursed through my body, bringing to my attention the fact that I was still naked. As I fumbled to get dressed, Blaze maneuvered around the man quickly, searching him and his tool bag, retrieving a cellphone and gun.

After pocketing the items, Blaze tugged up the arm of one of the unconscious guys' sleeves. I didn't know what he was looking for until he pulled up the other sleeve, revealing a long snake tattoo.

Fear gripped me.

I would never in my life forget that tattoo. My mind flashed back to the robbery at Zen's and I shuddered.

"FUCK!" Blaze said.

Activating his earpiece, he instructed it to call Jolli. Once connected, Blaze said, "We have a problem. Bring the truck around back."

Blaze turned around and saw the man fastened to the table beginning to regain consciousness. "We have to go," he said.

Packing faster than I ever had before, I tossed my travel bag over my shoulder and we were out of there. Outside of the suite, Blaze led me down the hall cautiously.

We stayed close to the wall and the whole time he kept one hand on his gun and the other behind him, holding my hand.

The elevator dinged, announcing someone's arrival, and Blaze halted, his tall, broad frame obstructing my view of what was happening ahead of me. I held my breath, not knowing who or what was coming.

Blaze pivoted and gently slid his arm around me, giving the impression that we were a couple in love, patiently waiting for the elevator. I breathed a sigh a relief when I heard a man laughing and a woman say, "I told you the swim trunks were too big."

They acknowledged us with a smile and even though they seemed to not be a threat, Blaze waited, watching them discreetly until they disappeared into a room.

We bypassed the elevator, taking the stairs instead. When we got to the lobby, Blaze slowed our pace.

"Stay close," he said, releasing my hand.

Adjusting the bag on my shoulder, I glanced around as if the bad guy would jump out wearing a big neon sign that read "Here I am."

Of course, that didn't happen, and I realized that this was

the very thing that made it so unsettling. Everyone looked so normal. Like they belonged.

Whoever was out to hurt me could be anyone; A clerk helping guests with their bags, the woman in the floral dress holding the clipboard or the dad bouncing the baby on his knee. Literally anyone.

Instead of keeping straight to exit through the front door, we made a few turns, traveling down the hallways until I spotted a red exit sign hanging above a door.

As soon as we were outside, I noticed Jolli waiting in a standard black SUV. Blaze opened the door for me, helping me into the backseat, casually glancing around before closing the door.

"Drive to station four," Blaze said to Jolli, sliding into the passenger seat.

"Threat Eliminated?" Jolli asked.

Blaze shook his head.

"Yeah," Jolli mumbled, putting the truck in drive. "I hate paperwork, too."

Then he pulled off, blending in with traffic and appearing normal, like the two of them hadn't just agreed that the only reason a man lived was because they couldn't be bothered with more paperwork.

I sat in the back seat, not uttering a word. I wanted to say hello, but the tension was so thick as Jolli drove us to Blaze's requested destination, I kept my greeting to myself.

If this were a typical day, Jolli would likely already be telling me jokes and sharing funny stories, simply because that is what Jolli did.

His nickname was actually comedy in itself. When people heard the name, Jolli, usually a short, fat guy, with a permanent goofy expression, came to mind. However, contrary to the nickname, Jolli was tall, well built, and had a militant edge about himself.

Only those that weren't on his bad side knew that Jolli was the most sweet, kind and funny Texan you'd ever meet.

The further we got away from the hotel, and closer to safety, I presumed, the mood in the truck eased up.

At least for Jolli and I it did, Blaze was assigning codes to small boxes on the screen of a tablet-like device.

Jolli glanced at me in the rearview mirror, giving me a warm smile. "You good back there?" he asked.

"I am."

"Sorry about the absence of pleasantries," he said. "Safety first."

"No need to apologize. How have you been?"

"You know me, kissing asses and taking names."

"Don't you mean kicking asses?"

"Nope. If I don't kiss up to the right people," he nodded subtly at Blaze, who was still much too engrossed in that tablet thingy to notice. "I get stuck doing all the late night stakeouts."

"No way!" I said, pretending to be appalled. "Blaze wouldn't treat you like that."

"He would and he did," Jolli said, clearly looking for pity.

"You got stuck doing the stakeouts because you bet Axel that you could make a Jamaican dish better than he could, even though he is Jamaican," Blaze said without looking up.

I turned my attention back to Jolli for confirmation, and he shrugged. "Guilty."

I laughed, spotting the picture of Sam, Jolli's five-year-old son. He looked just like his dad; the same contagious grin, messy mop of sandy brown curly hair, and mischievous twinkle in his eyes.

Jolli had been a single dad since his wife died four years ago, and Sam meant everything to him.

"Oh my goodness, Sam has gotten so big! The last picture

you showed me of him was the one in your wallet when he was three."

"Yeah and he's a mess too, always kidding and playing around."

"Like his dad?" I offered.

"I guess the apple doesn't fall too far, as they say. Want to hear his current favorite jokes?" Jolli asked, switching lanes and getting onto the highway.

"You know I do," I answered, leaning forward against my seatbelt.

Jolli was such a kid at heart, and his jokes were the best. In a fitting title, everyone around the office referred to them as dad jokes. They were kid friendly, and so silly you usually couldn't help but smile.

"What do you call a fake noodle?"

I threw up my hands. "I already give up."

"An impasta," he said, like he was delivering the punchline to a major joke.

I giggled. Not just because it was so cheesy, but Jolli's silly grin was infectious.

"And one more," Jolli said, starting the joke and finishing it in the same breath, "Can February March? No, but April May!"

I tried to hold back a laugh, but I couldn't. Even Blaze chuckled a little and shook his head.

"See what we have to put up with?" Blaze said.

"You guys are hilarious," I replied, feeling a little better. I loved Blaze's relationship with his team and everyone needed a Jolli in their life.

Close to thirty minutes later, Jolli stopped the truck midway down a dirt path in a deserted area. He got out, leaning against the front, and I knew then that the jovial man was gone.

Jolli was back on duty, ready to defend and on high alert.

Blaze opened my door and guided me through the trees, deeper into the woods.

We only walked a few minutes before coming to a structure that reminded me of an oversized outhouse.

The exterior was weathered and covered in peeling paint, giving it a worn and dilapidated appearance. However, as I stepped inside, it stunned me that the interior was exceptionally well-maintained.

The tiny house was about the size of a standard living room with enough space for a small dining table and a compact kitchenette.

"Did you call or message anyone at the hotel?" Blaze asked once we were inside.

Whoa, he was surely in work mode. I mentally scrambled to find the answer.

"Umm, I messaged my mom and spoke to Melanie. Why?"

"How long did you speak to Melanie?" Blaze said.

I shrugged. "I don't know, maybe five or ten minutes."

"And did you tell her where you were?"

This time I didn't answer as fast. There was an ever-growing tightness in my stomach.

"Yes," I murmured softly under my breath.

Blaze cursed and faced away from me while I let the enormity of his reaction sink in.

He couldn't be saying that Melanie had something to do with wanting me dead, could he? How could she? Why would she?

Shit! I had been so stupid.

I assumed the individual behind all this was some evil, larger than life villain that I had never seen before. The thought never occurred to me that the villain could be someone I know.

I went over to Blaze and touched his arm.

"I'm sorry. I didn't even think about it. Why didn't you tell me not to answer my phone or talk to anyone?"

"It doesn't matter. I've uncovered what I needed to."

"But I messed up and made things worse," I said, feeling guilty.

"No, you didn't. You actually helped me out."

My brows furrowed. I wasn't connecting the dots.

"Well, why do you seem angry at me?"

"I'm not angry at you," Blaze replied. "I'm pissed because it confirms that someone at Vex is a mole."

"A mole! And you think it is Melanie?"

There was a sudden change in his demeanor, and Blaze completely disregarded my question. "You've done your part. Now I need your phone."

I still wasn't following, or... maybe I was. My phone was in my back pocket, but I wasn't giving it to him. I wanted answers.

"What do you mean, done my part?" When he remained quiet, it hit me like a freight train, and I took a step back. "Blaze, did you use me as bait?"

Still nothing.

My eyes widened. "You did! You used me as bait."

"No, I used your obstinance to my advantage."

"You're lying. You did this because I chose the hotel over doing what you wanted. I thought your job was to keep people safe!"

Blaze's reaction suggested that my words were utter nonsense.

"First, I have no reason to lie to you. I did this because I had a suspicion that turned out to be a big break in this case. Second, you were always safe. There is no way I would let anything happen to you."

I laughed without humor. "You have a funny way of showing it. How could you do this?"

"Do what?" he asked, stunned. "My job?"

"Whatever you call it," I said, trying to keep my cool. "I deserved to know."

"That is not how this works," Blaze replied.

"Well, maybe you should change how you handle things because you can't simply assume I want to partake in your dangerous schemes," I said, pointing a finger at him. "You should have checked with me first."

"And exactly when did I start answering to you?" Blaze asked.

"The moment you decided to dangle me in front of a killer," I retorted.

Blaze closed his eyes and exhaled before responding. "Again, you were safe. I know the staff at the hotel and Axel was posted outside of your room all night."

That made me feel a little better, but it still didn't make up for leaving me out in the cold. Wasn't I more to him than some random victim?

"Not good enough," I spat.

"Sounds like a you problem," he said nonchalantly.

I cut my eyes at him.

"Are you kidding me? Do you hear yourself right now? I didn't create the problem, you did. You can't make plans that involve putting me in harm's way and then not say anything about it."

Blaze collected himself before responding. I could tell I was crossing all sorts of lines. Insinuating that he couldn't protect me or that he should have run his plan by me first. I was getting under his skin, but at the moment I didn't give a damn.

"I don't know what the hell is going on here," Blaze finally said, his voice barely above a whisper. "But you need to dial it way back. I owe you protection and nothing else."

I spoke through gritted teeth, digging my heels in. "You can't use someone without their consent."

Blaze crossed his arms and returned my challenge.

"My mission. My call."

"I am not a mission!" I screamed.

He could be such an ass sometimes. I was pissed, and I felt foolish and hurt, but I wasn't exactly sure why. Yes, being used as bait was off-putting, but like Blaze said, I was safe, and I knew that. I trusted him with my life.

Furthermore, if he asked me, I would have agreed to anything to help determine who was behind this.

So why am I so angry?

Blaze didn't say anything. He only silently observed me, no doubt concluding that there was more to this, and he was right.

As the answer came to me, I faced away from him towards the cute little kitchenette area, resting my palm against the counter.

The truth was, his failure to inform me about his plan did not upset me. I was upset because he was treating me like he would everyone else, and I wasn't everyone else. I was the woman that he held all night, the woman that shared his bed, the woman that was falling for him, hard.

"What's going on, Raquel?" Blaze asked from behind me.

I laughed again. This time, it was pitiful and weak, matching the way I felt. "Silly me for thinking I meant more to you?" I said.

Blaze came around to stand in front of me, and I saw the confusion on his face.

"What do you mean, meant more to me?" he asked.

"Nothing," I said, averting my eyes. "It means nothing."

"Raquel, I have a job to do and I will do it. I don't give a damn about hurting feelings if it keeps you alive."

"So it's true," I said. "I *am* just a job to you?"

I know I sounded hurt. Maybe it was all the emotions of the last few days pouring out of me at once, but every time Blaze touched me, it felt so natural, so real. Was I really misreading it?

Blaze sighed again.

"I am going to say this one time and one time only. We are friends and I care a great deal about you. But," he said, taking a long pause, drawing the metaphorical line in the sand, "I am *not* your boyfriend and we are *not* in a relationship. You are my sub and as much as I love the agreement we have, I will end it if you can't get a handle on this, because this is sex, and nothing more."

Well, damn. I asked for it, and he gave it to me, Blaze level straight and he told no lies. Sex was how this started and, for him, sex is all this was. I was the one getting my signals crossed.

"Okay," I said in a chipper tone, laced with a little sass. "Guess you cleared that up."

Blaze wearily rubbed a hand over his face.

"Don't do this," he said. "Don't make this into something it isn't."

I glanced up at him, feeling embarrassed and unable to understand or accept it. I wasn't crazy. There was something between us.

"And what was last night?" I asked. "The way you held me? I couldn't have been the only one that felt that."

"Felt what?" he said, exasperated. "Last night you were falling apart. I couldn't leave you like that."

My eyes shifted to my feet. He was right. I was the woman he had to take care of. Nothing more. Our good chemistry was only that. It would not turn into some beautiful love story.

Blaze lifted my chin and stared into my eyes. "Are you able to handle this?" He asked. "It's okay if you can't."

Even if I couldn't, I did the most damaging thing I could have ever done at that moment. I lied. Because no matter how much it broke my heart, if I couldn't have all of him, I'd settle for some of him.

Is this what people meant by toxic? Being a part of something that you knew wasn't good for you?

I was basically riding shotgun to my own demise. A behavior that was so unlike me. I never thought I could be this woman, but I simply could not let Blaze go.

I nodded, not trusting my voice for several seconds. Then, pulling myself together and clearing my throat, I changed the subject. "So it worked? Your plan to learn more about the case."

"Unfortunately, it did. Someone that works for me is also betraying me."

For the first time, through this entire conversation, I picked up on something I'd overlooked. Blaze was being the protector and the leader because it was what was required of him.

However, in the process, he had revealed something menacing and despicable. Someone that he'd hired, trusted and likely been close to had deceived him. That was like a slap in the face.

"I know finding out about this has to be hard. Are you okay?" I asked gently.

Blaze kept his tough exterior intact. "I'm fine and I will be even better when I learn who is behind all this."

Why did I think he would open up? Blaze was a soldier, through and through. He did the job and was not interested in letting anyone in. He didn't need a metaphorical shoulder to cry on, but I knew it still had to hurt.

"And you think it's Melanie?"

"For her sake, I hope not, but could be." Blaze took both of my hands in his. "Listen, I have protected a lot of people. If you tell them too much, they overthink it and do things out of character to protect themselves, which only makes matters worse. As I have said before, sometimes the less you know, the better."

"I get it. You are going to keep me safe whether I like it or not, and sometimes, whether I know it or not."

Blaze gave me an empathetic look before releasing my hands and holding out one of his expectantly. I knew what he wanted and this time I didn't fight. Reaching into my back pocket, I withdrew my phone and gave it to him.

"What happens from here?" I asked.

"I go back to work and you are moving in with me until this is over."

I opened my mouth to object, though not sure why. I had nowhere else to go and a very good friend may have been trying to destroy me.

"I don't want to hear it," Blaze said, halting any objections I could have formed. "You're coming with me."

"Guess I better listen. The first time I refused to do what you said, you used me as bait. God knows what you will do if I don't listen to you this time," I said sarcastically.

We both laughed and even though my heart ached because I now knew for certain that nothing real would ever happen between us, I was grateful to have a friend like him in my life.

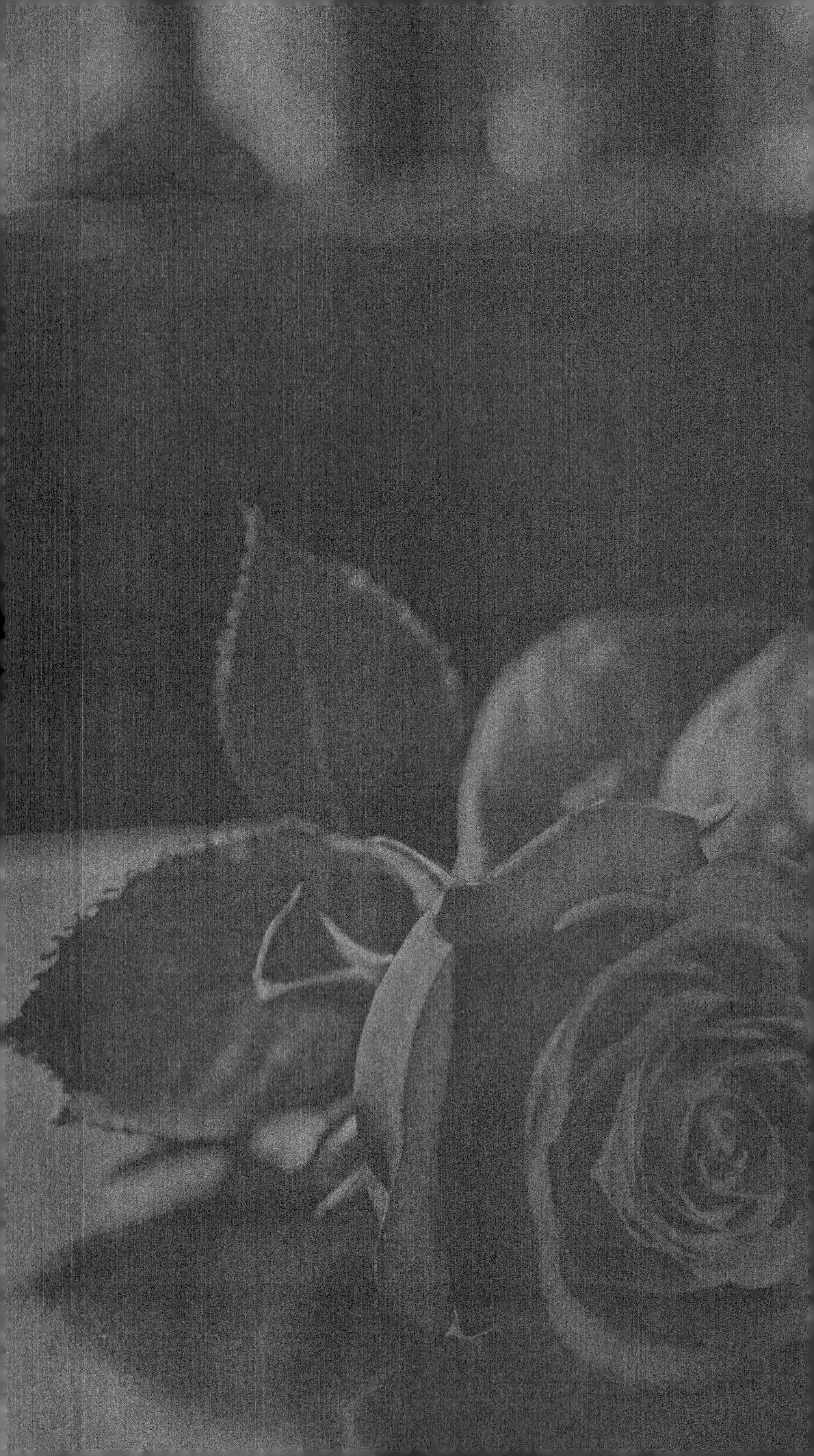

Chapter Fifteen

"Blood gushed out like a waterfall."

We didn't leave station four until the rest of Blaze's team arrived. Axel, Vadim and Hannah greeted me and then the three of them, along with Jolli and Blaze, huddled near the second SUV while I waited inside the backseat of the one we arrived in.

I felt like a spectator on the sidelines, yearning to be part of the action.

I wanted to know what was going on. What information were they exchanging? And what plans were they formulating?

As I strained to eavesdrop on their conversation, I noticed Axel's furrowed brows, indicating the seriousness of their discussion. Vadim listened attentively, occasionally nodding in agreement.

Hannah, with her intense eyes, analyzed every spoken word, with her lips pursed in deep thought, and Jolli was busy examining my cellphone. Maybe his expertise of explosives carried over into other devices.

And then there was Blaze, the fearless leader, his commanding presence holding everyone's attention.

Anxiously shifting closer to the door, I tried to make out their words, but these doors must have been sound and bullet proof.

A fact that was both reassuring and alarming.

Eventually, Blaze and Hannah walked away, coming

toward the vehicle I was in, while Jolli, Vadim and Axel got in the other.

I faced forward, not wanting them to know I'd been attempting to listen in. Blaze got into the driver's seat and Hannah slid into the passenger side.

After riding for several minutes in silence, Hannah said, "I heard you had an eventful couple of days, chica?"

While my gaze remained fixed out the window, taking in the approaching sunset and rapid passing of buildings, trees, and homes, I said, "That's putting it mildly. I have no idea how you guys deal with dangerous people all day."

"It's an addiction," Hannah stated. "One that is only fed by locating and eliminating more bad guys."

Eliminating. That was code for kill, and I noticed how easily and often they used that word. Given their field, it is understandable that they seemed unfazed by the act. I'd bet it would be an unforgettable and insane experience to see all of them in action.

Blaze concentrated on the road, but every so often his eyes met mine in the review mirror. I couldn't tell what he was thinking or if he was watching me or observing surroundings.

"Does work ever become too much for either of you?" I asked.

Hannah and Blaze exchanged glances, and Hannah spoke first.

"Blaze is going to say no because he loves the thrill."

"It's true," Blaze agreed. "I live and breathe the job."

Don't we know it, I thought to myself.

"I love the thrill too," Hannah continued, "But sometimes I wonder if I should try something new."

"Like what?" I asked.

She considered it. "I don't know. Becoming a veterinarian, maybe."

Blaze laughed. "You don't even like dogs."

"Hey," Hannah objected, playfully slapping him on the arm, her Colombian accent heavy. "I could learn to like them and I love a challenge."

Hannah turned in her seat to face me.

"I got bit by a neighbor's dog when I was four and it's been a shaky relationship with me and dogs ever since."

I told her I understood, but honestly, I was more taken with how familiar and at ease she and Blaze were with each other. Come to think of it, the whole team fit together so well.

It gave me a twinge of jealousy because I knew I would always be on the outside, and with each passing day, I wanted more and more to be part of Blaze's world.

"Any cool stories from a day in the life of protecting the world?" I said.

Evidently, that was a great question to ask because it broke the ice even more.

Before I knew it, Blaze and Hannah had me laughing about stories of the time Vadim got into a fight with a sumo wrestler on a mission overseas, the time Axel used a tranquilizer on a man dressed as a clown who'd gotten loose in a psych ward and the incident where not one, but two mice got tangled in Hannah's hair during a fight.

"Oh wow," I said, covering my mouth with shock. "Where were you?"

"So," Hannah began, already animated in her storytelling as she moved her arms, reliving the experience. "I'd chased the guy through the little hole thingy in the street that leads down into the sewer area, and I guess that's how the mice joined the party. I swear I screamed so loud the entire neighborhood heard me. When it comes to people I'm tough, when it comes to mice, I'm terrified."

"How did you get them out?" I asked, literally leaning towards the edge of my seat.

"Timing mostly. They were tangled in there pretty good,

but right after I knocked the guy out, Blaze shows up to find me screaming, turning in circles and pulling at my hair," Hannah said, sticking her tongue out in disgust and wiggling in the seat as if the mice were still on her. "Muy Guácala!"

Blaze laughed and said, "It took everything in me not to snap a picture before helping her out."

Hannah eyed him suspiciously. "I still think you did, and you're hiding it somewhere."

"Guess you'll never know," Blaze replied cooly.

We all laughed, and I turned my attention to Blaze.

"In most of these stories, you do the rescuing. Has anyone ever had to rescue you?" I asked him.

He smiled and shook his head as if he knew what was coming next.

"Hell no!" Hannah answered, annoyed. "Sure, we keep him from getting ganged up on, but in all the years I have worked for him, Blaze has never needed to be rescued. Me and the guys actually have a bet going. Whichever one of us saves Blaze first gets a thousand dollars."

"Sounds like a sweet deal," I said. "I hope you win, Hannah."

I laughed, but no one else did. There was a major mood shift, and the truck filled with an ominous silence. When Blaze spoke, his lax tone was gone.

"Are you seeing this, Hannah?" Blaze asked.

"Yes, I am," Hannah confirmed, seriousness in her voice as well.

"For how long?" he asked.

"Two blocks at least."

"By my count," Blaze countered. "It has been three."

A speaker, built discreetly in the dash, came to life and Axel's voice poured in.

"We have company, boss."

"How many?" Blaze asked.

"Three," he said, his Jamaican accent making it sound as if he said tree, "but there could be a fourth."

Blaze exhaled and hit what I thought was the navigation screen, but the moving dot that represented us vanished and a robotic voice said, "Sending location now, estimated pickup time, twenty-seven minutes."

"We only need to survive until pickup," Hannah said with a grin, pulling on her gloves. "This is about to get ugly."

What did she mean "Survive until pick up time?" What was about to get ugly? And why was she so happy?

This was not good. Not at all.

Hannah pressed a button in front of her and part of the dashboard swiftly descended, revealing a rack of three handguns that quickly emerged.

Blaze started talking again, and for a moment I had forgotten Axel was on the speaker. "There is a stretch of open land coming up within the next minute. If they are going to attack, it will probably be then."

Attack? Wait, what was going on?

When I thought it would be cool to see Blaze's team in action, I didn't mean I wanted to be part of it!

As my heartbeat quickened, I shifted in my seat, desperately trying to comprehend the situation, but I only saw the trailing headlights of the vehicle carrying the rest of the team.

Blaze made a right, and the road stretched out before us, disappearing into the distance. I remembered this road from the first time he drove me to his house.

It seemed to go on forever, and the absence of any signs of civilization made me realize Blaze was right. If anything was going to happen, it would be here.

We drove at a steady speed for less than a mile when Blaze abruptly slammed on the brakes.

Situated directly in our line of sight was an enormous silver truck, positioned diagonally across the road. A man standing in front of it held a gun that was longer than my arm, and it was aimed in our direction.

"Well, shit," Hannah said, tucking two guns into her holsters. "They sure know how to welcome a girl."

Blaze reached under his seat and withdrew a blade and a thin, circular, clear gadget. Inside, tiny wires crisscrossed like a complex spider's web.

"The explosives are always a nice touch," Hannah said, unknowingly letting me in on what the transparent, round thing was.

Wow, those were explosives?

I would have never guessed those small, discreet pieces of what looked like plastic were so deadly.

Blaze pulled out two more and gave them to Hannah. "You can never be too careful."

Hannah took them and turned in her seat. "Looks like today is your lucky day. You get a front-row seat," she said and winked at me.

Fucking winked!

We were all going to die, and she was in a playful mood! She was crazy. They were crazy. This entire situation was crazy.

And then, all hell broke loose.

The guy in front of us began firing what sounded like a thousand bullets per second, and I was thankful that my earlier assumption was right; The vehicle was bulletproof.

Nevertheless, my heart didn't cease its rapid beats, nor did my body stop trembling, as I remained crouched in the back seat, listening to the metallic ping of bullets bouncing off the truck.

"About to light up the sky!" Jolli's voice boomed through the speaker, and in an instant, a powerful explosion reverberated, causing the truck to shudder violently.

The explosion did exactly what Jolli said it would,

momentarily replacing the settling darkness of the night sky with light as bright as the sun.

With my hand clutching the back of Blaze's seat, I turned my attention out the window, unable to see anything, due to the thick cloud of smoke that had formed around us.

However, the good news was, the gunshots had ceased.

Blaze must have thought now was his chance because he turned to Hannah and said, "Stay with her."

Was he seriously about to get out of this vehicle? This was the only safety we had.

Blaze opened the door and slid out, taking his weapons and my voice with him. I wanted to scream, "Stop! Don't go" but I couldn't speak. Hannah relocated to the back seat, forcing me down to take cover.

"Oh shit," Hannah suddenly said. "We're sitting ducks."

With her no longer creating a human fort over me, I glanced up, and through the window I could see figures emerging from the smoke all around us.

A few were stumbling and disoriented, clutching their wounds with dazed expressions, but there were others unaffected and that made my blood run cold.

At least fifteen were closing in on Blaze, Vadim, Axel and Jolli. And another four were heading straight for Hannah and me, one of them holding a weapon that looked an awful lot like the jaws of life, a tool used to open car doors that have been damaged in an accident.

Hannah pulled one gun out of her pocket and shoved it at me. I took it with my now clammy hands.

"This truck is bullet proof and locks automatically," she said. "Normally, nothing can get in, but you see that metal gadget he is holding?"

I wasn't sure how I did it, but I must have acknowledged Hannah in some way, because she continued.

"It will pry this door open with ease, which means I can't

stay here. If they get too close, we're screwed. If I get out, we have a chance. Do you know how to use that?" she said, eyeing the gun.

"Yes," I said, this time speaking and nodding simultaneously. I didn't want her to leave, but I knew she had to go. The guy with the giant can opener was getting closer.

Hannah dove out, firing and running straight toward the four men, but the bullets were bouncing off of them.

Therefore, she abandoned her weapon, picking up speed. I thought she was preparing to punch the man to the far left, but my assumption was off and so was the preparedness of the guy. He immediately took a fighting stance, spreading his legs apart, preparing to block her.

At the last second, Hannah fooled us both.

She swiftly ducked low, almost in a blur, as if defying the laws of physics, and slid between his legs. Her body seemed to glide smoothly while her hand reached out, firmly gripping his leg.

The sudden pull caused him to lose his balance, and he toppled to the ground, falling so clumsily, he knocked down one of his teammates.

Hannah jumped to her feet and rushed toward the first guy in the process of getting up. Her knee landed in the back of his head, slamming it back to the ground so hard I thought I heard the thump through the thick door.

He may have been wearing armor over his chest, but nothing protected his head from the concrete, and with a blow that severe, he was likely dead or at least out cold.

Realizing Hannah was more of a threat than she'd originally seemed, a third guy stopped coming towards the SUV and joined in on the fight. However, the man holding the metallic jaws persisted in moving towards me.

I searched for another tool for defense. If I didn't shoot

him in the right spot, I would need something else to defend myself.

A blood-curdling scream drew my attention and, to my relief, I saw Jolli had come to Hannah's aid. He stabbed the guy holding the gadget in the eye while pulling him backward.

Blaze! Where's Blaze?

In a state of panic, I desperately searched for him and was relieved to find him near Axel and Vadim, who were holding their own quite well.

Three men rushed toward Blaze and my stomach tightened, unsure of how he would escape this, but if I would have blinked I may have missed the entire thing.

Blaze reacted to the first guy that got too close by swinging at him, but his hand didn't actually make contact, so I didn't understand why the guy froze. It wasn't until the man spun around, hand gripping his neck, that I understood his throat had been cut.

The dying man began falling to the ground, but before his knees could connect with the asphalt, Blaze caught him, holding him up and using him as a shield to block the incoming gunfire.

His technique was unmatched, combining a lethal mix of agility, strength, and strategic thinking. Blaze's movements were almost majestic as he ran forward, still holding up the dead guy, and using his free hand to slice through the body of his second adversary.

The sight was incredibly disturbing as blood gushed out like a waterfall, causing me to feel nauseous, especially when I witnessed the guy's internal organs spill onto the ground seconds before he did.

Once Blaze reached the third man, who was holding the gun, he tossed his dead colleague onto him. The man fell, trying to shove the deceased guy off, and by the time he did,

Blaze was on top of him, punching him hard several times before snapping his neck and pulling the gun from his hands.

The entire team was effortlessly destroying their opponents. Proving that they were masters of combat, executing a coordinated onslaught to their foes that was positively incomparable.

It was a sight to behold, witnessing their skills in action and I knew in that instant that if Hannah ever tried to quit ridding the world of bad guys, I'd drag her back to the field myself.

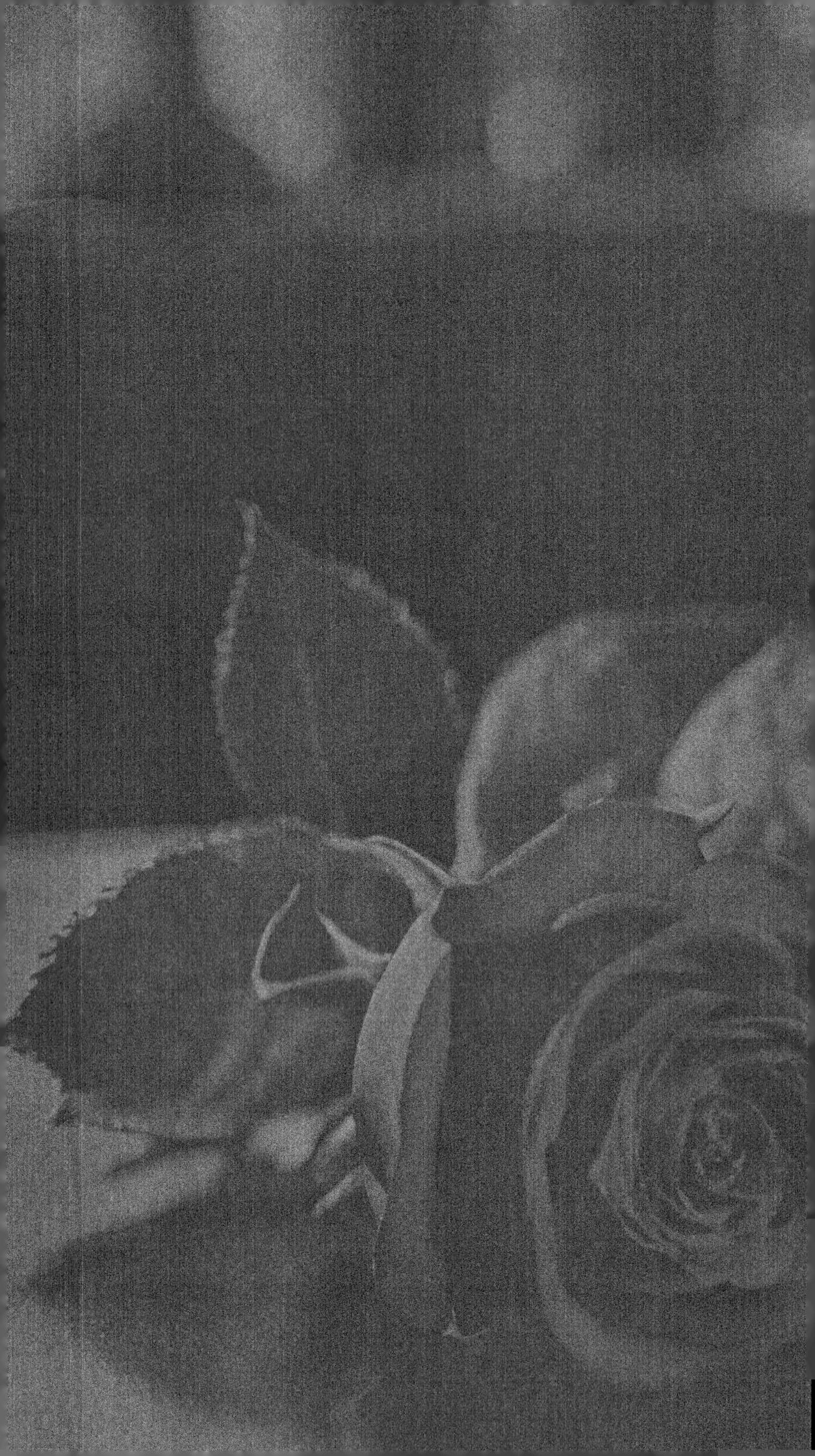

Chapter Sixteen

"What if you don't like the way I taste?"

Melanie wanted me dead. There were no ifs, ands, or buts about it. Blaze told me not to jump to conclusions stating that Melanie could simply be a pawn or not involved at all.

However, neither explanation made me feel any better.

I mean, the jaws of life? Come on! What in the hell was going on? Even if it wasn't Melanie, someone, somewhere, wanted me gone, and they were sparing no expense.

"Please go over it again," FBI Agent Swanson said to me through the screen. "Start back at the Zen's case. You must be missing something."

I was in Blazes home office, having a virtual meeting, or rather interrogation, by Agents Swanson, Divers and Steele.

I'd explained what happened at Zen's and the attack at my apartment three separate times now, and apparently I wasn't giving them the answers they needed.

"I didn't see the guy arrive," I began. "I was facing the register when—"

"We have heard this," Steele cut in. "What I want to know is, what else did the man say to you? What other discerning features did he have?"

"Did he indicate that he knew you?" Divers interjected. "Did he look familiar?"

"I... he...there was..." my thoughts were getting tangled.

I was trying to cooperate, but they were grilling me hard, and I was exhausted. Merely hours had passed since the attack in the streets, but the impact it had on me was so strong that my head was still spinning with disbelief and confusion.

"Come on," Swanson pushed. "A very dangerous person has employed some serious man power to get to you. That does not happen to people that don't know anything. Think!"

Swanson was now shouting in frustration, and I watched him rake his fingers through his thinning grey hair.

"Don't yell at her," Blaze said in an even tone. "She has had a long night, and she is trying to assist the best way she can."

He was standing near my chair, watching the three men on the screen, their faces twisted in impatience, annoyance and fear. Things were getting worse in this case and after tonight I was looked at as their only lead.

They were desperate to discover why someone wanted me dead. Well, they would have to get in line because I needed to know first.

"I can speak however the fuck I want," Swanson snapped, "Don't forget Blaze, you work for me."

"She needs to do a better job of figuring out the missing link," Divers chimed in. "She is the key to cracking this case wide open and if you think—"

Blaze hit a button to end the call, their irate faces vanishing from the screen. It rang again almost immediately, but Blaze ignored it, turning to me.

"Aren't you going to get in trouble?" I asked.

"I work *with* them," Blaze said pointedly. "Not *for* them, a fact that Swanson confuses when he gets his delicate panties in a bunch. I'll let them have some time to think it over because they need me a lot more than I need them."

"Yeah, but they need answers," I said, wanting to help.

"I'll take care of them," Blaze assured me. "Go take a shower. I have already left a towel and robe for you in the bathroom. I'll be in to check on you soon."

I sighed, appreciating this out he was giving me. Blaze looked exhausted, his clothes were still caked in dust and dried blood. He'd taken the time to wash his face and hands, but neither of us had the chance to get fully cleaned up.

My plan was to help. Even if Swanson, Divers and Steele were ganging up on me, I knew their only goal was to end this madness.

Plus, after all Blaze and his team had to endure tonight, the least I could do was to assist the agents.

The monitor chimed again with an incoming call, and I tried one last time. "Blaze I can talk to them, I'll be fine."

"An answer to a question I didn't ask," he responded, opening his office door. "No one can think without a clear head. You're done for tonight."

I slowly stood up, my legs stiff from sitting so long not just in the chair, but in the SUV and then in the van that picked us up from the scene.

Right after Blaze threw an explosive that put the rest of the assailants out of commission, a man by the name of Buck arrived. Since both SUVs were damaged during the attack, and now inoperable, Buck was our ride home.

It wasn't until Buck mentioned he was five minutes early did I connect the dots, realizing he was the pickup we were waiting for; the one the robotic voice had mentioned would arrive in twenty-seven minutes.

Buck's job was to pick up Blaze and his team, or provide additional back up when shit hit the fan and with the metal frame design of the vehicle and all the weapons hanging on the walls, Buck was prepared for war.

During my shower, I kept replaying the things the three

agents had said, analyzing their questions and word choices to build my own interpretation of the case.

Despite the lack of forthcoming information, it was evident that this investigation had been ongoing for several years, indicating the pursuit of a highly influential individual.

Based on my loose profile, they could be looking for a politician, dangerous drug lord, or anyone else with major pull and connections.

I closed my eyes.

The hot water from the shower cascaded over my shoulders, easing the tension that had built up throughout the day, allowing the warmth to penetrate every muscle, melting away the stress and worries.

Eventually, I forced myself to depart from the soothing shower. True to his word, there was a towel and robe folded neatly on the bathroom counter.

The towel was his, but the robe was mine and I didn't recall packing it, which meant Blaze must have gone by my place while I was at the hotel to get more of my things.

After pulling on my robe, I stared at myself in the mirror, a habit I'd formed over these last few weeks. The reflection that stared back at me looked distressed and worn out, more evidence of the insanity from the last couple of days.

"Today was rough for you," came Blaze's voice from the doorway. I jumped and my hand flew to my chest.

"You scared the hell out of me," I said.

"Sorry about that," Blaze replied. "Moving quietly is a habit."

He was leaning on the doorframe. His wavy hair was damp, and he was shirtless, a towel hanging around his neck and blue sweats hung low on his waist.

Obviously, he'd used his other shower, and I wished he would have insisted on joining me instead.

The twelve foot door frame made his incredibly tall height

appear normal. Like he wasn't larger than life and a malevolent force when it came to defending those that belonged to him.

My mind flashed back to watching him today. Fighting, killing, dominating. I wanted some of that fierce intensity used on me.

I lowered my hand from my chest and tied my robe around my waist.

"It was a rough day, but I am perfectly fine," I said.

Blaze's eyes shifted down to the knot, as if his gaze alone could undo it. It wouldn't surprise me if it could.

"Where do you get that from?" he asked.

"What?" I responded, touching the silk material. "My robe?"

"No," Blaze replied. "The stubborn streak. You never want to admit when things are heavy for you."

"Oh, that," I said with a laugh. "Family trait I guess."

"Well, no matter how well you are handling it. You should have never experienced it."

"Blaze, if you came in here to apologize, there is no need."

"I did not," he replied, leaning off the doorframe. "Come in here to apologize."

His words hinted at something kinky just under the surface. A slight smirk played on his lips, revealing a confidence that bordered on arrogance. He was definitely well-versed in the art of seduction.

"Why did you come in here?"

Blaze pulled the towel from around his neck, dropped it into the hamper and came to stand behind me. Our reflection in the mirror made us look like the perfect couple, two people destined to be together, a contradiction from what I knew was our reality.

"Because I need you to satisfy a craving I have," he said.

"I thought I was on punishment?" I asked.

"After the night you have had, I think you have been punished enough. I come to give you a reward."

I stared up into his dark brown eyes in the mirror and understood. He was talking about going down on me and, to my amazement; I was ready. He'd made me wait until I fantasized about it for so long I craved it.

But, and that was a huge but, being the over thinker I was, I still feared it could go disastrously wrong. A guy hadn't eaten me out in over fourteen years, because after Jamie, I was perfectly fine never putting myself in that situation again.

"I'm fighting the urge to run out of this bathroom right now," I said, giving Blaze the honesty he'd always told me I could.

"You'll never make it," he promised. "But you're ready and I know you want me to do this," he added with absolute certainty.

I was practically drooling for it, but I played it cool.

"I do want it, but how do you know that?" I asked.

He untied my robe, and it fell to the floor.

"Because I know what I'm doing. I have been a Dom for twenty years, making my subs tear down their own walls is another one of my talents."

Although it was a sexy bonus, I often forgot about our age gap. Blaze's high energy, playful personality and down right exquisite face and body made me feel like he was in his early thirties like me, instead of ten years my senior.

"I can attest to that," I said. "You are very talented."

Blaze was caressing my stomach, and now that his hands were gradually moving upward toward my breasts, my nipples were hard.

"Don't worry. We are going to take it slow. Sit on the counter," Blaze instructed.

Showtime!

Funny thing though, my legs didn't move. I swore I intended to move them, but they weren't cooperating.

"Maybe," I said with a nervous laugh. "There is just a little more of that wall left, that I didn't tear down, because as bad as I want to, I don't know if I can do this."

I was stalling, and I hated this part of myself. I needed to get over it, shake these annoying jitters and get this gorgeous man's face between my legs!

Blaze chuckled, and something told me he was about to fix my problem.

"You know, I once had a sub that had a problem similar to yours, and she didn't obey my request."

"Oh," I said, already not liking where this was going.

"Yep," he replied, that unwavering gaze of his speaking volumes.

"What did you do?"

Blaze removed his hands from my breasts and placed them on my butt, giving it a nice, long squeeze. "I spanked her until she couldn't sit on her ass for hours."

Yikes. I swallowed hard.

"That doesn't sound pleasant. So, she had to stand until the pain subsided?"

"Oh no, she sat down," he said simply.

My brows knitted in confusion. "She did? Where?"

"On my face like I originally instructed her to. Would you prefer that route?"

On his face! Wall. Demolished.

I wasn't even prepared for the less extravagant positions to let Blaze eat my pussy. The possibility of actually smothering him with it was too much.

I had never spoken so fast in my life. "Do you want me further back? Or towards the edge? Because I can do either way. Never mind," I announced, hiking myself up to sit down on the long, wide counter. "I'll just get up here and you can take it from there."

"Figured you'd see it my way," Blaze said.

He kissed me while pushing my thighs apart. I planted my feet near the edge and leaned back onto my palms.

Seductively, he dragged his fingers across my collarbone, further down my chest and toward my left breast. The soft touch made me shiver, and I was drifting into the moment, but not quite there yet.

A memory of my ex, Jamie, from college spitting all over the place, saying I had gotten too wet, flashed in my mind and nervous chatter kicked in.

"What if you don't like the way I taste?" I asked quietly.

"Close your eyes," Blaze ordered, and when I did, he kneaded one of my nipples between his fingers. "Do you trust me?"

"Yes," I said with a pleasurable sigh.

"And what is your only job?" he asked.

"To please you," I responded.

"Then do your job, because tasting you," he'd now begun using his thumb to massage my clit, "pleases me."

My moan was louder this time, and I was officially in the zone.

"I like that sound," Blaze said. "I want to hear it again when I'm devouring you."

I kept my eyes closed, which made it easier to concentrate on the pleasant sensations of Blaze's knuckles lightly brushing across my clit.

Worry no longer consumed me, but talking was keeping me from thinking and I needed not to think right now.

"Are you going to do anything sadist like?" I asked. "You know, make it hurt?"

Blaze pinched my clit and tugged on it.

It felt amazing and my back arched in response.

"Is that a problem if I do?" he replied.

I shook my head, still in a trance from his stimulating technique. "No, sir. You can do anything you want to me."

"Good girl," he complimented, "And to answer your question. No, I'm not going to do anything sadist like."

I smiled my eyes still closed. "I thought pain was your thing."

"Not tonight," he replied, grabbing my face and my eyes immediately opened. "I know that you are nervous, but I am not him. Now shut the fuck up. I want nods and moans only."

Blaze inserted a finger into me, pressing on the exact spot inside me that flipped the on switch. My hands squeezed into fists, and my lips parted, his rudeness and skilled fingers already coaxing compliance out of me.

"How does that feel?" he asked.

I licked my lips and nodded.

"And this?" Blaze added a second finger, twisted it and applied more pressure, forcing my breath to catch.

I squeaked and nodded faster, sliding closer to the edge of the counter, urging him to press deeper.

"Now this?"

It was the last thing Blaze whispered before his mouth was on my clit.

Initially, it caught me off guard, and my eyes popped open, but once I looked down and saw his head buried between my thighs, I relaxed.

I had no choice.

His tongue was magical. Licking all around my pussy, sensual and slow, before sucking my clit into his mouth and then gradually releasing it over and over again. By the time I got used to that, he switched it up. I thought it would break my flow, but it only heightened the already exquisite sensations.

This time when his tongue caressed my sensitive spot, he

sucked it firmly in between his lips, holding it there while moving his head steadily from side to side and simultaneously pumping his fingers in and out of me.

I wanted to slide off this counter and bury my pussy in his mouth. I had never felt more vulnerable yet cared for in my life.

My mind was in a haze and my body was on fire. It felt immaculate. I cried out, almost slipping up and calling him Blaze, an innocent reaction that would be disrespectful coming from his sub, but I caught myself at the last second.

I knew I was wet. I could hear it as Blaze hungrily sucked and licked me closer to my climax, and I felt it with how easily his fingers entered me.

Is this what I was afraid of? Is this what I'd denied myself that night at the wedding?

Obviously, I'd lost my mind because the sheer euphoria that enveloped me made this one of the most exceptional experiences I had ever encountered.

And then, Blaze made a sound that landed somewhere between a moan and a growl, and oh. My. Goodness. That knocked it out of the park.

It was so deep and masculinely sensual that it amplified everything, becoming its own aphrodisiac.

Now, with two fingers inside, his thumb caressing the tender spot right beneath my clit and his tongue handling all the rest, I could no longer contain myself.

"I'm...so... so... sorry," I said in between ragged breaths.

"Mmm, for what?" Blaze asked, taking a quick pause in between licks that were much too titillating.

"Ever saying..." I whimpered as his tongue danced over my center. "No to you."

Oh fuck this is amazing!

I felt the smile on Blaze's lips, but he didn't miss a beat. He continued to push me to new heights after he withdrew his fingers and held me in place with a grip that demanded obedience.

As my orgasm neared, the pressure was becoming intense, as usual, making me too sensitive, but I held my position and didn't pull back.

I knew what he liked and what was expected of me. Blaze hated when I pulled away. One of his rules is that I give into the sensations and let it take me.

Gripping the edge of the counter, I let my Dom have his way. My cries of ecstasy growing louder as my body vibrated. This was going to be yet another massive release.

"Don't stop. Please, don't stop."

If I got punished later for speaking again, I didn't give a damn. My words weren't a request, they were a plea. I had never felt this before. Never knew it existed. Never knew I wanted it so bad.

Sure, what Hannah did was wonderful, but this was on another level. It felt like his mouth was making love to my pussy.

Blaze removed his hands from around my waist and placed them over mine, encouraging me to release the counter. Once I did, he laced his fingers through mine, in a gesture that was so simple, yet so tender, it tugged at my heart.

He knew what he was doing; he was tearing down every defense I had, demanding that I give him every ounce of me even though he wasn't willing to do the same. However, in the end, he won, and without a second thought, I gave Blaze what he wanted.

With my legs wrapped around his neck and my hands clutching his, I released my fear and completely let go, once and for all.

He owned me.

The next morning, I awoke, and Blaze wasn't there. I laid my head back on the pillow and sighed. That was until I heard what sounded like a video game being played outside.

"Get em! Get em!" I heard Jolli yell.

I laughed and slid out of bed, going to the bathroom to freshen up. When I came out of the room, Jolli was sitting on the couch, game controller in hand, turning and twisting it in the direction he wanted his player to go.

"Morning, Jolli," I said, giving him a wave.

Blaze told me yesterday that when he wasn't home, he would have a team member staying with me because, although he felt I was safe here, he wasn't willing to take any chances.

Jolli paused the game. "Oh, I'm sorry. Playing this game had me happy as a hog in slop. Did I wake you?"

I grinned and shook my head. "No, you didn't. It looks like fun. What are you playing?" I asked.

"Some old zombie game," he offered, picking up a second controller. "You want in?"

"Most definitely," I said, appreciative of the invite. "Let me just get some coffee."

"Sweet," Jolli said.

Stepping into the kitchen, I stopped dead in my tracks when I noticed a cream-colored box with a familiar logo.

I knew this box.

It carried the shoes from René Caovilla. Shoes that I was only supposed to receive if I won the bet, but I didn't win. Blaze did.

I walked over to the counter and picked up the small card beside the box.

Flipping it over, I read the handwritten message:

You never lose when you are with me. Thanks for the taste, I'll be wanting more soon.

P.S. You did good, princess.
Blaze.

I swear, I almost came again.

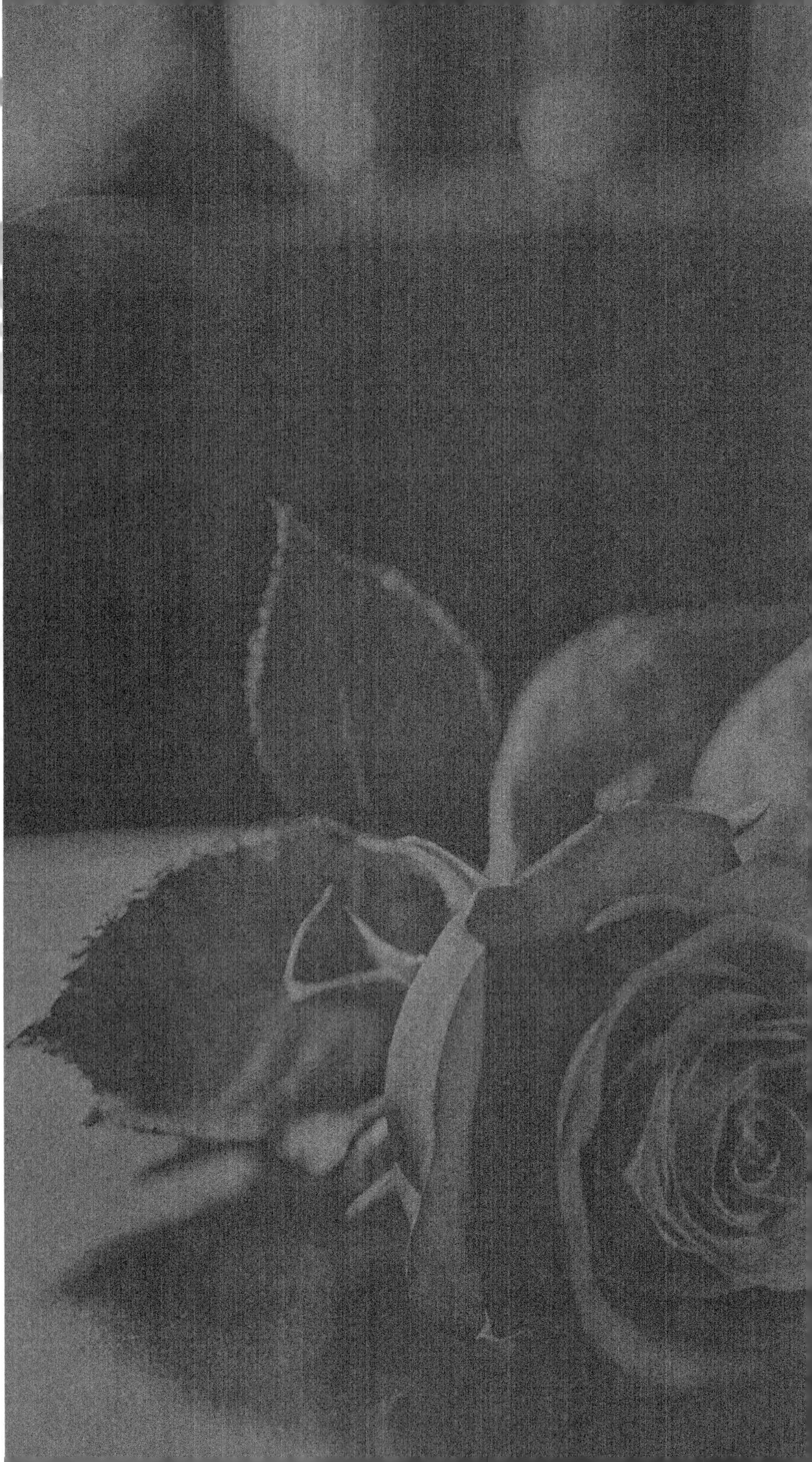

Chapter Seventeen

"STARING INTO THE EYES OF MY ATTACKER."

"Have you gone stir-crazy yet?" Jocelyn asked.

"Ugh, I'm about a quarter of the way there," I said, balancing the small phone Blaze had allowed me to use on my shoulder while trying to grab plates from the cabinet.

This phone couldn't be tracked, which didn't surprise me at all. It was so small that when I put it down, even I had trouble finding it.

I'd been at Blazes house for two days, and I was restless already. He had a five-mile trail in the back of the house, which would be perfect for my daily runs, but I wasn't too keen on the idea.

I kept thinking I would run into a snake or a deer and be so panicked I could not find my way back to Blaze's house.

As another option, I could ask Axel, my current sitter of the day, to go with me, but I didn't want to bother him. Besides, we were about to have a Jamaican inspired lunch.

My eyes shifted to Axel across the kitchen. His long locs were pulled back into a ponytail and he leaned over the island cleaning his knife with extreme precision, preparing to cut the pineapple. We were having a Jamaican fruit salad with lime and honey.

"I think all of Blaze's team members like killing a little too much," I said in a whisper.

Jocelyn laughed. "Merrick has gone to a few of their training exercises. He said they are no joke."

"Take it from me. Merrick is right."

A giant smile formed on Axel's face right before he sliced the pineapple into two halves in one quick motion.

Next, I watched him carefully dig out the insides of the pineapple. Axel loved food and all the preparations that went into it. The man was truly talented.

"Regardless," I said to Jocelyn. "They are the most amazing and kind killers I have ever met."

"Sounds like you're in excellent hands, then."

"I am," I replied. "Anyway, time for lunch. I will call you in a few days."

"I'll be looking forward to it," Jocelyn said. "Here's to hoping you get fucked senseless in the meantime."

"Hear! Hear!" I agreed and pressed the ultra tiny red button to end the call.

By the time I got to the counter, Axel had added all the toppings to one of the pineapple halves. He turned it this way and that, making sure each side was filled evenly and that it looked picture perfect. Once satisfied, he stepped back and pointed at it emphatically.

"You see dat ting? It looks cris, eh?" Axel announced, smiling brightly.

Since I had begun working at Vex, I'd learned that cris was a Jamaican term for referencing someone or something that looked good. Usually, Axel only applied it to a woman, but from how he was looking at it, I think he was rating his pineapple creation on the same scale.

I gave him a thumbs up and put the plates down on the counter. The fruit salad contained blackberries, raspberries, strawberries, walnuts, raw honey and lime juice poured into an empty pineapple shell.

"This looks yummy and artistic, Axel! I almost don't want to eat it."

Axel laughed and placed the finished fruit salad on a plate and slid it over to me.

Adding the fruit mixture with extra walnuts to his own pineapple, he said, "It tastes even better than it looks."

Traces of his accent were faint now.

That was something I noticed about Blaze's entire team. Their accents only became easily prevalent when they were excited, happy, or pissed.

With my spoon in hand, I scooped up a generous portion of the dish. To give it an extra tangy and sweet kick, I drizzled on some additional lime and honey before tasting it.

It. was. perfection.

"Mmm," I said through a mouthful.

"Good, right?" Axel said. "And this is only a fun snack. Wait until you taste my Ackee and salt fish."

I was really excited now. I loved seafood.

"Was that the meal that caused Jolli to lose the bet?" I asked, remembering that a cooking competition landed Jolli in the position of doing the late night stakeouts.

"No, him lose dat bet over da brown stew chicken."

My mouth was watering already.

"No worries," Axel promised, noticing my tongue practically hanging from my mouth. "I'll make that for you one day, too."

I took another bite of my salad and then said, "You are too kind. You don't have to make me all this food."

Axel turned towards me on his stool, sincerity on his face.

"If Blaze takes care of you. We all do," he stated.

I patted his hand. "Thanks, Axel. Now tell me more about your life growing up in Jamaica."

Serenity, joy, and wonderment sparkled in his eyes.

"Dem days, Ms. Ash..." Axel began, jumping into full

islander mode as he took me on a journey of his time growing up in the beautiful small town of Treasure Beach.

By the time Blaze arrived, a few hours later, we were still at the kitchen counter and I'd become so immersed in Axel's stories that even I had begun talking like a Jamaican.

"Wah Gwaan, Blaze," I said in lieu of hello as he entered the kitchen.

"Awww hell," Blaze said, turning his attention to Axel. "Did you give her some of your Jamaican rum?"

Axel raised his hands, collected his things, and backed up toward the door. "Me want no trouble."

We all shared a laugh and Axel told Blaze and me goodbye.

Blaze sat a large black box near the edge of the island, and I collected our dishes and the left over pineapple before heading to the kitchen sink. Since Axel made the lunch, I'd insisted on doing the cleanup.

"I see you enjoyed your day with Axel," Blaze said, removing the lid from the box.

I rinsed the suds from the first plate and dried it off.

"I enjoy time with everyone on your team. They are a pretty cool bunch." I picked up the second dish. "Hey," I said, something dawning on me. "I know where all of your team is from, and you know where I am from, but where are you from?"

Blaze retrieved a few files from inside the box and placed them on the island counter.

"I'm a military brat. Therefore, I'm from everywhere."

"Ahh! That explains how you fit in so well with everyone."

After putting the carved out pineapple chunks in the fridge. I headed towards the living room, but Blaze stopped me.

"I need your help with the case," he said.

"No problem," I replied, returning to the island. "Do you want me to go through what happened again?"

"Not this time. I have created a folder of criminals associated with the case and I need you to determine if the man that attacked you is there. And then..." Blaze trailed off, obviously hesitant, "I want to give you some insight about it."

My brows lifted. *Blaze wanted to divulge information? Now that is a surprise.*

"Sure," I responded quickly, taking a seat because I feared he would change his mind.

Blaze took a seat as well, his hand resting on top of the closed folders.

"Since the last attack, I've been thinking that you deserve to know at least the basic details about what we are working on."

I agreed, but didn't say anything, and Blaze continued.

"Whoever is behind this wants you dead because of what you know, or what they *think* you know, which means you are our biggest advantage. Being kept in the dark as much as you have been may not only be a danger to you, it could prevent us from solving this. Therefore, even though the agents wouldn't agree with me, I am making my own call." Blaze opened one folder and slid it over to me. "Do you know who this man is?"

It took me a second but then it came to me, having seen his face all over the TV, billboards and local signs begging for votes.

"Yes, it's Governor Paul Wesley." Confusion, then shock, rolled in. "Wait! Is he trying to kill me?" I asked in disbelief.

"I can't say for sure," Blaze replied, gearing up to tell me more. "For five years, the FBI has been chasing a very dangerous criminal that has escaped their grasp at every turn. This person has been running one of the biggest and most lethal organized crime rings in history. I'm talking drugs, murder, money laundering, human trafficking, illicit goods and weapons, you name it, they seem to have a hand in it."

I stared down at the picture of Governor Wesley. His

wholesome smile and speeches about being united to make changes for the better, not exactly fitting for the man Blaze was describing.

"Five years and no leads?" I asked.

"The identity of the person behind it remains a mystery, and whenever law enforcement apprehends some of the low-life criminals caught in the raids, they refuse to cooperate and if they do, they suspiciously end up dead."

A shiver ran down my spine as Blaze resumed revealing more confidential details.

"That changed a few months ago when the FBI uncovered some links between the crimes and the governor. They brought Vex in for some additional manpower and although, we too have been able to locate numerous affiliates, as I said, it doesn't end well."

"And this case is what brought you to Zen's that night when you ended up killing Louis? You were following a lead?"

Blaze nodded. "We had been tracking Louis for a few weeks, hoping he would lead us to someone bigger, but when I saw him holding that gun. I knew I would have to take him out."

There was no doubt in my mind that Blaze was correct in his assessment. Louis would not have bowed out gracefully, and I was certain he would have taken a few of us with him.

"You found Louis. I'm sure there will be others," I said.

"I agree. Problem is, whoever is behind this always remains several steps ahead, and every advantage we get turns into a dead end."

I let that digest. It was a lot to unpack. The fact that the FBI had discovered connections between the heinous crimes and the governor was shocking.

"You said whoever is behind this," I said, my mind replaying his words. "Do you not believe it is Wesley?"

"I believe the FBI is being too narrow minded. Following

some of my own hunches led me to Zen's that night I rescued you. Wesley could be involved, but I'm not convinced he is the mastermind behind this operation. And with the way this person is pulling out all the stops to get to you, combined with the recent revelation that there is a mole in my company, solidifies my belief that I am right."

"Have you told the agents this?" I asked.

"I have, but telling them I think they should broaden their scope won't persuade a stubborn group of men that have spent five years on this to listen to me."

"Even though your leads seem to pan out?"

"They may pan out, but there are still too many unanswered questions and we can't lock down in any one direction. This whole thing has us baffled. Normally, crimes like these are committed by a group of people from the same racial background, which makes it easier for us to narrow things down. Unfortunately for us, the people involved in this have been from every race and nationality."

Blaze pushed another folder in front of me.

"These are the images I need you to look over. Take your time and let me know if any of them fit for the person at your place."

Then, leaving me with the daunting task, Blaze went to the bar area and poured himself a drink.

Opening the folder, I looked down at the first one. It was a man's mugshot. The guy appeared sleepy and annoyed to have to pose for a picture and even though his eyes were strange; they didn't fit my attackers.

I flipped to the next one, taking my time and trying hard to determine if anything about him stood out. I wasn't sure and the last thing I wanted to do was choose the wrong person.

After studying close to twenty-two images in the ever-thinning pile, I was getting discouraged. The man who attacked me was wearing a mask. There is no way I could tell who was under...

I stopped.

Those eyes. The eyes of the man who attacked me. These were those eyes.

"What's wrong?" Blaze asked, standing behind me.

I didn't hear him approach, but I was glad he was there.

"This man. This is him. It has to be him," I said, my body so still I wasn't even blinking.

The faceless man from my horrible dreams now had a face. He wasn't the start of my nightmares, but he'd certainly added to it. As long as he was out there searching for me, I foresaw that this new torture would never end, because I would never truly be safe.

"Are you sure that's him?" Blaze asked.

"Yes, I mean well, no. His face was covered but his eyes, the shape of his head, even this little scar on his neck," I said, touching the picture. "Makes me feel like it is. But..."

"But what?" Blaze prompted.

"I must be wrong. I didn't see his face, and I didn't even remember the scar until I saw this picture. Eyes aren't enough to insist someone attacked you."

"True," Blaze replied. "But, being caught on a security camera two blocks from your house, clutching an injured arm, might be, though."

"What?"

I heard what he said, but it was too good to be true. They had found my intruder. Blaze sat down next to me, placing his glass of bourbon on the sleek surface of the island.

"Meet Boris Gorbunov. A hitman willing to provide his services to the highest bidder. The team and I have already started looking for him just to question him, but you identifying him makes a major difference."

I closed the folder and turned toward Blaze. I didn't want to keep seeing the bitter hatred in Boris' eyes.

"So you knew he was the guy? Why didn't you say so?"

"That would be considered influencing the witness. It had to come from you."

"That's understandable," I muttered. "What happens if you find him? Will I have to do a lineup or something?"

"*When* I find him," Blaze said. "Not if, then I will safely arrange a way for you to identify him."

I was stunned. The idea of facing Boris again didn't sit well with me, yet I would do it in a heartbeat to get us one step closer to ending this. Blaze collected the folders, putting them back into the black box and a flood of relief washed over me.

"Seeing the face of a man that haunts your dreams is indescribable," I said quietly, staring at the box as if I could still see the photo of Boris inside. "I know it sounds pathetic, but I was kind of hoping to never have to see him. Then eventually I could pretend like it never happened."

"It doesn't sound pathetic. However, it is important to recognize that the challenges we avoid can be just as detrimental to our well-being as the challenges we confront head-on. Which is why I will help you face this," Blaze promised, gently stroking my face. He pushed the box aside and said, "That's enough sharing for today. Do you want a drink?"

I shook my head. I didn't need a drink. I needed a new life. Preferably, one where I wasn't on a hitman's list simply because I was in the wrong place at the wrong time.

"Did the shoes fit?" Blaze asked, knowing exactly what to say to pull me out of my miserable thoughts.

There was no need to waste time thinking about fatalities when I could think about fashion. I was in no danger right now. Happy thoughts only.

"Yes, they did," I said, perking up. "The champagne gold

color is actually one of my favorites from the Caovilla line. Thank you again for that."

"No need to thank me. I believe in punishments and rewards. That was a reward you earned."

I tilted my head slightly, trying to determine what to make of him.

"Are you always so charming and romantic with your subs?"

"I wouldn't call it romantic," Blaze said. "I give my subs what they need mentally and emotionally to open up. It's as simple as that."

As simple as that? He couldn't be serious.

"Well, with that approach, that means you would even tell a sub you love them too, right? If that is what they needed at the moment."

I expected him to say no, that saying I love you for kinks was too farfetched, but as usual, Blaze surprised me.

"Without hesitation and occasionally I have," Blaze confirmed. "It was part of their fantasy."

That was so bizarre to me. I could never tell someone I love them and not mean it. However, I was a hopeless romantic, so what did I know?

"So you say this to these women," I asked, intrigued. "And meanwhile you feel nothing, it's just all part of the scene for you?"

Blaze sipped his drink.

"I see it like this. I could order my subs to do what I want, and sometimes I will, but I find that once a woman has been finessed, she is much easier to fuck."

The mans arrogance knew no bounds, but it was true. Being seduced by someone you wanted made the probability of sex higher. My eyes shifted to his lips, then back up to stare into his eyes.

"Brutal," I said, in a whisper, wanting to kiss him.

"Effective," he countered, looking at me like he wanted to do the same.

I broke eye contact and faced away. "I guess what you're saying is true, though, because if you hadn't finessed me, there was no way I'd be your sub."

Not even a little of that was true. Blaze didn't need to finesse me. All the man had to do was show up, and I was ready to get bent over a table.

Nevertheless, I'd decided to take my heart out of it. We were friends, and it was time I started treating him like that, instead of like the man that held my heart. He wasn't the only one that knew how to make a person crave them.

However, when I glanced at him again, the way Blaze was looking at me was anything but friendly. It was fierce and sexy as hell, but I planned to pay it no mind. I got up and left him sitting there, going to the fridge to get a drink of water.

Knowing that he was watching me, I took my time, and when I was done, I removed my shirt, sauntering around in my bra only, claiming it was too hot to keep it on.

"Do you want to help me out some more on the case?" Blaze suddenly asked. He was finishing up his last bit of bourbon and pouring himself another.

"Of course. What do you have in mind?"

I knew what he had in mind. Sex.

"Sometimes when I am having trouble concentrating, I like to get lost in physical activity to clear my head," he said with a grin.

"Physical activity, huh? I'd be game for that," I replied and grinned right back at him.

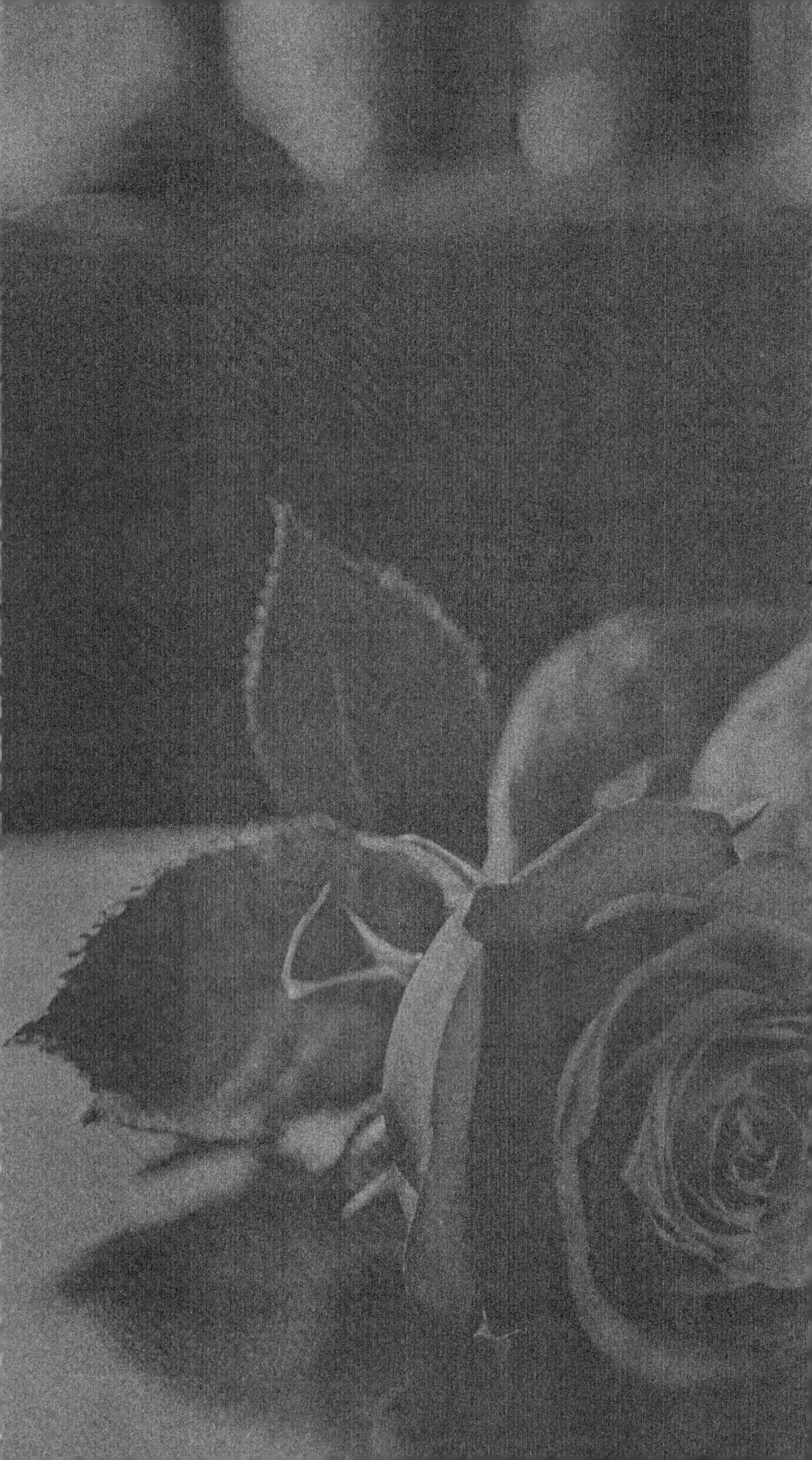

Chapter Eighteen

"THWAP! THWAP! THWAP!"

I should have known that sadistic bastard had something else in mind. I thought when he said to help him with some physical activity that he meant sex, not a flogging!

Now, here I was, strung up like an erotic symbol, naked, save for the Caovilla heels he'd bought for me.

I braced myself for the first blow. Eyes squeezed shut, muscles tense and holding my breath.

Blaze had told me to relax numerous times, but since I couldn't seem to, he left me to my own demise.

The blow came in fast and... *gentle?* I opened my eyes a little. Wasn't getting flogged supposed to hurt?

"Are you still alive?" Blaze asked sarcastically from behind me.

I rolled my eyes, thankful that he couldn't see my face, and gave him a respectful, curt response.

"I'm fine, sir."

Blaze chuckled and hit me again.

We were in the darkroom. The secret kinky room, found through a door in Blaze's bedroom. It was well equipped and pristine.

Two round tables sat opposite of a throne-like chair, inviting me to indulge in the thrills that awaited me.

Chains, whips and floggers meticulously hung from gold hooks on the wall.

Below that, on a shelf, sat an assortment of sexual toys and intriguing gadgets with odd shapes and pointy edges that sparked my curiosity. Their purpose and function shrouded in mystery.

And then, more discreetly tucked away in a far-off corner, were the torture devices. I spotted nails and barbed wire before immediately looking away.

I didn't know what they were for, but no matter how small and thin, neither of those should be present for anything sexual. Its mere existence was a chilling reminder of the darker desires that Blaze craved.

Overall, the room evoked a sense of both fascination and apprehension, like stepping into a forbidden world. It also reminded me of what a BDSM museum would look like if that sort of thing existed, because here fantasies could be explored without judgment or restraint.

However, there was no time to browse, and be in awe of Blaze's extensive collection because I was currently tied up in the Eiffel Tower position.

My arms were raised above my head, and bondage cuffs that were attached to a low hanging metal pole secured my wrists.

Although my heels were planted firmly on the floor, I had to stand very still, with my legs far apart to keep my balance.

Blaze hit me on the ass with the flogger and I widened my stance even more, the heels making my butt naturally arch up, ready for another tap.

As annoyed as I was that Blaze tricked me, I had to admit, this felt amazing.

The flogger, crafted with a sturdy rubber material, had the remarkable ability to deliver solid slaps against my skin.

Furthermore, it was designed with a fur coating that not only awakened my senses but also produced a teasing, tickling effect, ensuring a completely painless encounter.

Blaze said that this type was used for sensation play and to heighten sexual arousal. He also pointed out that the extended pieces of the flogger that brushed my skin were called falls, and they had me falling in love.

I couldn't speak for the more intense looking items he had hanging on the wall, but this one had become my new best friend.

Blaze slowly circled me, hitting my thighs, legs, and even ankles before coming to stand in front of me and striking both of my breast several times in quick succession.

"Oh, that feels nice," I said, my eyes closing.

Starting at my right breast, Blaze dragged the flogger across my nipples, down my stomach, to my pussy.

"Spread your feet further apart," he instructed, hitting the inside of my thighs with the soft tool.

I did, and he spanked my pussy using an upward motion so many times I lost count. I moaned repeatedly until Blaze hushed me, demanding I hold in my cries of ecstasy.

"Someone is turned on," Blaze finally said, inspecting the flogger.

It didn't take me long to see what he was speaking of. The white fur had a slick wetness over it, where my juices had stained it.

"It's time to move on to the next level," he announced.

Blaze tossed my new best friend into an empty black basket and I frowned. I wanted more from that pleasure inducing contraption.

He stood in front of the various whips, floggers, and paddles hanging on the wall and stroked his chin.

Blaze was shirtless and in sweats. His and my preferred style of dress for him. I loved seeing his abs, all of those tattoos, making beautiful art all over those muscles, and gorgeous brown skin.

Currently, Blaze was facing away from me and I watched, nipples hard, chest heaving and pussy dripping. The muscles in his back shifted and flexed as he picked up and put down different whips and paddles, taking his time arriving at a decision.

If this would have been a few months ago, maybe even a few weeks ago, the idea of what was coming next would have me shaking to my core.

I wasn't sure if it was growth, desire, or that I'd simply seen too much death, but I wanted to live boldly in the adventure that was now my life, and I was excited about what was to come.

I could handle some pain.

One had spikes sticking out from it. *Not that much pain.*

Another was wooden and thick, and I wondered just how much it would hurt. The next was long and leather, so shiny I felt like it was beaming at me.

Blaze picked up a red paddle from a gold hook that had a handle on each end. He folded it in half and squeezed it shut, doubling its thickness.

"This is made of natural full-grain leather," Blaze said, admiring it. "Which gives it a nice impact."

To demonstrate, he slapped it against his palm, and a loud sound echoed throughout the room. I wasn't afraid, but my knees shook a little as I wondered how hard he planned to hit me with that.

"During this," Blaze continued. "You won't need to use your safe word. Instead, we will use the light system. Green means go, yellow means slow down, or it's becoming too much, and red means stop."

Blaze picked up the glass of bourbon he'd brought in with him and took a sip. I watched him swallow and lick his lips when he was done, and I had the sudden urge to kiss and bite every inch of that masculine taut body.

"Are you ready?" Blaze asked, his gaze sliding over to me, his voice deep and alluring.

"Yes, sir," I said truthfully.

This was about to get interesting.

The first hit landed on my ass, and it was no big deal. In fact, I liked it as much as the flogger. I assumed he was going to hit me elsewhere with it too, but several smacks later, I realized that this would be a full on spanking.

THWAP!

My body jerked involuntarily, and I cried out. Blaze had increased the pressure with that one and I felt a brief sting, that subsided as soon as Blaze rubbed it.

He tilted my head back and stared down at me. "I love that sound," he said. "It makes my dick hard. Where are you now?"

"I'm at green," I replied. "I think the additional pressure simply caught me off guard."

He didn't speak again, instead he hit me twice. One in the way I'd already grown accustomed, and a second that definitely upped the pain level.

This time, I could feel my rear end getting warmer, and Blaze's gentle caresses, which had previously provided immediate relief, now seemed to take longer to ease the discomfort.

"Where are you?" He asked again. I could hear the insistence in his voice. He wanted me to give up, ask for mercy, prove to him I couldn't handle this. Well, no, sir. Bring it on.

"Green," I said.

THWAP! THWAP! THWAP!

I remember one time I stubbed my toe by accidentally kicking the edge of the bed. I knew the pain was coming, but had to wait a few seconds before it arrived. When it did, it was bad.

This was like that, but worse.

I groaned miserably, refusing to open my mouth and let the cry free. My ass was pulsating and standing in these heels made it no better. Now my ankles were hurting.

I held firm, though. He would not break me. Not this quick.

Blaze continued a few more rounds at this new burn inducing level while I remained quiet.

THWAP! THWAP! THWAP! THWAP! THWAP! THWAP!

Obviously, my lungs had stopped accepting air delivery because I could not breathe. I screamed, my shoulder slumped and my gaze fell downward while little floaty things danced their asses off at the corners of my vision.

"Where are you?" Blaze said.

It took me a second to answer, but eventually I did. I needed him to decrease the pace, but I was not ready to quit.

"Yellow, sir," I said through gritted teeth.

Blaze came around to stand in front of me.

"Sorry if that was a bit heavy. I just didn't want you to think I was trying to finesse you."

You asshole.

I knew he was bothered by my little comment from earlier. I'm glad I got under his skin... or then again, with this ever-growing ache, maybe I wasn't.

I briefly shut my eyes to avoid staring daggers at him.

"It is no problem at all, sir."

My voice did not sound convincing, and Blaze narrowed his eyes.

"You are at yellow. Would you like to remain there or see how the next level feels?"

I shook my hair from my face, and pulled against the bar my cuffs were attached to, using it to help me stand straighter. "Give me what you got." *Bastard*, I mentally added.

Blaze smirked, reading my mind.

"Are you sure that's all you want to say? I think something else is on your mind."

I was exhausted as hell. That is what was on my mind. My

butt burned, my back ached, and my legs were wobbly. Nevertheless, I did not break.

"I was just thinking I should have taken that drink you offered earlier," I said.

"That," Blaze replied, pointing at me with the paddle, "Is something I can help with."

He went over and took a large sip of his bourbon and returned to me. Gripping my chin and lifting my face, he kissed me, and with the height difference, it was like he was pouring the sweet and spicy drink from his mouth into mine.

I swallowed fast and the entire act was so fucking sexy I almost forgot I had a throbbing ass.

Once I'd consumed it all, a few droplets escaped my lips and Blaze used his tongue to clean it up. Licking a short trail from my chin back up to my mouth were he kissed me again.

I was floating.

Blaze ended the kiss and said. "I want you nice and sore when I fuck you. Let's continue, shall we?"

I nodded and once again; he disappeared behind me.

THWAP!

It was one hit. Only one hit, and that was all it took. With the way it landed, I imagined a pitcher winding up to throw the fastball and sticking it to me. Blaze no longer had to ask me where I was, because an almost unintelligible response spewed from my mouth.

"SHIT, FUCK, STOP, RED!"

Blaze tossed the paddle onto a nearby table and unfastened me. I slumped in his arms, weak, aching, and so tired.

"Red would have sufficed," he said, carrying me out of the darkroom to the couch in his bedroom.

My body felt like one giant nerve. All the spanking had me highly sensitive to his touch, and I moaned and trembled every time any part of his body touched any of my erogenous zones.

Blaze used one hand to pull his sweats down, and kicked them off, without even putting me down.

After sitting on the couch, he guided me onto his dick, entering me with ease.

I whimpered and held my breath. Stimulation of this magnitude was new to me and when he tightly gripped my butt, directing me to ride him, an actual tear fell down my cheek.

It hurt, but despite the pain, the pleasure was so extreme that it became overwhelming.

Sighing with satisfaction and exhaustion, I weakly wrapped my arms around Blaze's neck, struggling to hold on, working to keep up, but I could barely move. Despite my best efforts, my limbs betrayed me, refusing to respond to my commands.

Vaguely, I felt Blaze place a hand on my back, whispering filthy, vulgar, increasingly explicit things to me, but over time his voice became quieter until suddenly I couldn't hear him at all.

I could only feel.

His fingers digging into my skin, his teeth and tongue on my neck, his erection hard and massive, digging inside, holding me captive to his desires and freeing me at the same time.

I felt high, like the effects of a drug had taken over. My body was light as air and pleasing sensations engulfed me in a euphoric rush.

I couldn't think. I couldn't hear. I couldn't speak. Yet I was at perfect peace.

Time was no longer of importance, and I don't know if Blaze fucked me for twenty minutes or two hours, but it didn't matter because I was at his mercy, exactly where I belonged.

Sometime later, I awoke in Blaze's bed, wrapped snugly in the soft comforter. Despite the lingering pain in my rear end, I felt a sense of relaxation and renewal. I also smelled the calming scent of the aftercare oil he'd used on me before.

Wow! I didn't remember Blaze massaging me or carrying me to bed.

I tried to recall the details of our recent encounter, but beyond the spanking, I drew a blank.

Hmm.

Delicious sexual haze? Check. Feeling of being disconnected from my body? Check. Happiness beyond measure? Check.

A grin spread across my face.

I'd just had my first experience in subspace — A trancelike state experienced by submissives when they were flooded with high levels of adrenaline, endorphins, and other hormones at the same time. Apparently, Blaze's extreme pleasure and pain cocktail did the trick.

I could not wait to tell Jocelyn. She was addicted to riding the blissful waves brought on by subspace, and now I understood why.

It was otherworldly, and I needed that again. However, I wouldn't rush it. I needed to see how I did overtime. Subdrop, which was subspace's evil twin, was like a hangover.

It had the potential to bring on feelings of depression and crying fits as all your hormone levels shifted back to normal.

"Hey," Blaze said.

I turned my head to the right and there he was, pulling on his vest.

"Hi," I said sweetly. "Work calls?"

"Yeah, but I have good news. I think I know where to find Boris."

I bolted up, and the comforter fell down, gathering around my waist. "Really? Where? You're not going alone, are you?"

Blaze fastened the last strap on his vest and came to sit on the bed beside me, paying no attention to my questions.

The caring look in his gaze indicated he wanted to touch base with me before getting down to business. Blaze slid a hand beneath the covers and tenderly caressed my skin.

"How do you feel?" he asked.

"I'm good, Blaze. I can handle a little spanking," I said, waving him off. "Tell me about your lead! Did someone call you about it?"

"No, I told you that engaging in physical activity clears my head. It came to me midway through our spanking scene."

I glared at him. "And you continued anyway?"

Blaze shrugged.

"I was having a good time. Anyway," he said before I could comment. "Are you up for a ride?"

"Is it better than the one I just had?" I teased.

"Not even close, but it'll be fun."

Fun for Blaze could be dangerous, but he wouldn't put me in harm's way. As long as I was with him, I was safe, so no worries. I got out of bed and got dressed.

"By the way," Blaze said. "You're going to need a vest."

So much for safe.

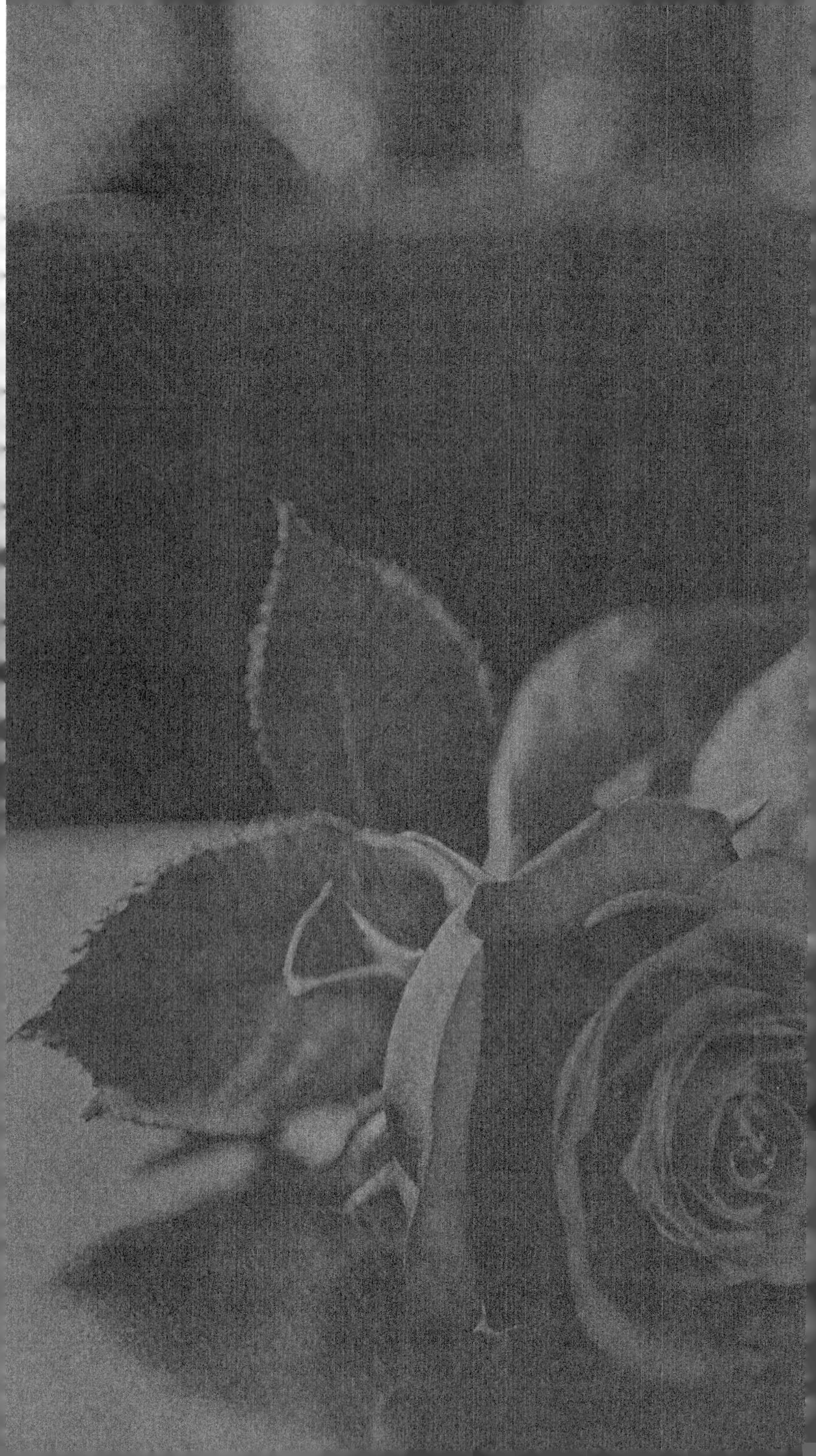

Chapter Nineteen

"I WILL CUT YOUR SCALP OFF AND FEED IT TO YOU."

I tightly gripped the card, and recognition hit immediately. The image I was staring at was an exact match to what was on the man's shirt that broke into my apartment.

Now that I was seeing it up close, what I thought was the top of the T was a hammer turned horizontally, and below it was a thin road, positioned vertically.

"How did you find it?" I said, glancing up at Blaze, the headlights from passing vehicles illuminating his face in the darkness as we drove down a long, winding road.

"Once I learned we were looking for Boris, the team and I checked all the places he's been spotted at in the last few years with no luck. But because you helped me clear my head," Blaze said with a mischievous grin. "I remembered you mentioned there was an image on his shirt that looked like the letter T, and I thought of this place."

"Glad to be of service," I said, my butt throbbing slightly at the mere thought. "So, what is Tilted T? Why the hammer and the road?"

"Tilted T was originally owned by a man named Maksim Trutnev. I think his grandfather did some type of construction back in Russia and the bar was attributed to him. Either way, it was a popular hangout spot for Russians. Vadim used to say it was the only place he could get a proper drink."

I studied the picture again before dropping it into the empty cupholder. "Does Vadim still go there?"

"That's the thing. Tilted T got shut down and sat abandoned for years, which is why it escaped our radar. It reopened last year, but no one hardly goes there anymore, which makes it the perfect place for Boris. Poorly lit and no traffic."

The possibility that we might find Boris filled me with a mix of eagerness and fear. Would he give us answers to who was behind this? If he didn't, would Blaze kill him? Would he kill Blaze?

That last thought was much too dark and hurt to even consider. I wasn't ready for more violence, but I was learning fast that it came with the territory.

Once the team arrived as backup for Blaze, the plan was that I stay in the vehicle with Jolli, where I would be safe. Assuming Boris was there, I could witness him being carried off, dead or alive, and that should bring me some peace.

"I'm curious," I said. "Do Swanson, Divers and Steele know what you're up to tonight?"

Blaze didn't even take his eyes off the road. "No, they do not. If I turn Boris into them without doing my own interrogation first, I will not get the information I need."

He made a good point, and I trusted Blaze a whole lot more than I trusted the agents.

After Blaze made a left turn at a large sign that indicated Tilted T was one mile away, the gravity of this little adventure sank in.

"Do you think tonight will be crazy?" I asked.

"Crazy is always a possibility in my field," Blaze replied. "Vadim has already laid the groundwork by talking to the only staff member on duty. The rest is up to us."

"How do you know the employee won't give your team up to Boris if he is in there?" I asked.

"I don't, but I trust Vadim. He has quite the reputation

amongst the Russians in the area. He knows how to do his job."

I exhaled audibly. There were so many questions swimming around in my head.

"Did you find out if Melanie had something to do with this?"

Blaze gave me an empathetic look. To minimize any unexpected shocks, he was striving to be more forthcoming with me, yet I could sense that his patience was wearing thin.

"I know she is your friend, so if it eases some of your worrying, I don't believe Melanie is involved. We found a listening device hidden under her desk, which I am assuming she didn't put there. But," he emphasized. "I will not rule her out until I have more information."

"That's something," I said appreciatively. "Thank you."

We turned into the mostly empty parking lot, and Blaze pulled the truck over. Less than a minute later, the rest of the team arrived, parking in a spot closer to the back of the building.

I saw the team exit the vehicle, walking off in different directions, and Jolli headed toward us. Blaze put his hand on the door, preparing to get out.

"I don't want to wait in the truck," I blurted.

"You abso-fucking-lutely will!" Blaze exploded. "It may have been a mistake to bring you along at all. You will stay here and Jolli will sit with you, just like we planned."

Assuming the conversation was over, he faced away again, and I grabbed his arm.

"Blaze, please," I pleaded, my voice desperate.

I didn't know what had come over me. Maybe I had a death wish, but suddenly the plan where I sat in the van, hiding like a coward, hoping to glimpse the man that tried to kill me, wasn't good enough. I needed to be a part of this.

Blaze sighed. "You know he wants you dead, right? He is not looking to paint nails or get runway advice."

I released his arm and crossed both of mine.

His intention was to piss me off or, at the very least, scare me so that I was reminded of the vast differences between our worlds, but it wouldn't work. His mighty roar wouldn't dissuade me.

Mainly because he was right. My life had been a lot fluffier and less complicated before all of this, but that wasn't my life anymore.

Things would never be the same. *I* was not the same. I had to take some part of the woman I was back, and that was why this was necessary.

"I know my request might seem really stupid, and maybe it is, but I don't care. I need to do this." Then, unfolding my arms to appeal to his incessant need to be in charge, I added. "You have my word that I will listen to everything you say."

Blaze studied me until Jolli arrived at the vehicle's door. Then he gave me a half smile and shook his head. "You're just as stubborn as me, I see."

"Guilty," I said with the shrug of my shoulders.

"Fine," he replied after another long pause. "I did promise I would help you face this."

"Are you ready?" Jolli asked when Blaze opened the door. "Axel, Hannah and Vadim are already in position."

"There's been a slight change of plan," he replied to Jolli. To me he said, "Good thing you wore a vest."

His words prompted me to touch the thick Kevlar. Bulletproof vests saved lives, but that didn't stop the stories I'd heard of broken ribs and excruciating discomfort from filling my thoughts. I silently prayed I wouldn't have to experience such agony, or worse.

Jolli had snuck us in through the backdoor, and we were peering out of a small area in the backroom that overlooked the bar.

The place wasn't that large, so I could see everything. In addition, because Blaze was wearing a small microphone on his vest that transmitted to the listening device we all had ear buds for, I could also hear everything.

An unfamiliar song played quietly through the speakers placed strategically throughout the bar and all the wooden tables, except one, sat devoid of customers, adding to the eerie, dimly lit atmosphere.

Axel and Hannah were on the outside of the building, blocking the exits and Vadim was waiting somewhere inside the bar, in case things escalated.

Blaze entered the building alone, just like they'd planned, and walked straight to the bar. Remaining calm, I pushed aside the thought that we were here for a killer, a hitman, and before the night was over, someone could be dead.

The bartender, who I could only see the back of from this angle wore a crisp white shirt and black apron. From his hand movements and the flashes of white I saw I gathered he was cleaning a glass.

The man looked up as Blaze approached.

"What can I do for you?" the man said.

"Вадим уже говорил с тобой. Я здесь насчет Бориса," Blaze said in Russian to the bartender.

I was so surprised that my eyes darted to Blaze's face. I didn't know what he said, but the answer was yes.

Yes, he could have me. Yes, he could keep me. Yes, I would do whatever he wanted.

Hearing his voice switch so casually to another language made something naughty and dangerous come alive in me, like this was some dark, treacherous movie scene and I was part of it.

The man didn't respond, but I imagine he made some discreet gesture because Blaze suddenly turned away and walked toward the three men sitting at the table.

All I could make out as Blaze neared was laughter and Russian being spoken in hushed tones. My eyes strained to make out their features, but the poor lighting made it difficult to discern any details.

Blaze positioned himself behind the chair of one of the men, and a sudden silence fell upon the group. The two men seated on the left and right shifted to look at Blaze, but the third man didn't bother to turn around.

"Boris," Blaze said, and I swear my heart almost stopped.

He'd found him. Blaze had found my attacker!

Since they were still in shadow, I couldn't make out who spoke, but I assumed it was Boris.

"I don't know what you want," he said, his voice emitting disgust and annoyance. "But I am not interested."

"Doesn't matter," Blaze responded. "I still plan to take you in for questioning."

"Fuck off," Boris replied and then he turned and spit on the floor.

I imagine it landed on Blaze's boot because he said, "You're going to clean that off."

My eyes widened. This wasn't going well at all.

"Fuck you," Boris said, and the three men erupted into laughter.

"Per protocol," Blaze began much too calmly, which meant trouble was brewing. "I am obligated to tell you that this concerns a case with the FBI."

"I don't care about your protocol," Boris said in a gruff tone.

And once again, like two mindless puppets, the men began laughing, as if Boris had made a hilarious joke. You could easily tell who ran that group.

In a low voice, Boris said something in Russian and things went south real quick.

The puppets, who must have been his guards, stood, but they didn't have a chance. Blaze fired off two shots, killing them both instantly, and their lifeless bodies collapsed back into their chairs.

With an angry shout, Boris rose, kicked the chair aside, and swung at Blaze, narrowly missing him. He tried again, but Blaze blocked it and delivered a powerful one-two punch to Boris' abdomen, sending him reeling backward.

I gripped Jolli's arm, instinctively, watching the fight unfold. The angry Russian now had a knife. He dodged Blaze's next punch by shifting to the left and sliced the weapon upward.

The knife must have been razor sharp and Boris used a great deal of force, because I heard a low whistle as the blade cut through the air. Boris was now facing the backroom where Jolli and I were and I got a look at his face.

It was disturbing and evil, no doubt appearing more sinister to me because of my encounter with him. Boris had long blond hair around the sides of his head, pulled back into a ponytail, and the top of his head was bald.

A beer belly protruded from the black and red shirt he wore, but even with the extra weight, he moved a lot faster than I expected.

I shouldn't be surprised.

Boris was a hitman and undoubtedly dangerous, but thankfully he was not trained to fight as effectively as Blaze. This time, when Boris executed his next strike, Blaze caught his arm, twisted the knife free, and got behind him, locking his arm around the man's neck.

Boris cursed and fought to get free and Blaze, who was at least a foot taller, forced Boris' head back and made a long, deep cut across the man's hairline.

The magnitude of Boris' scream was so strong that it compelled me to briefly remove the earbud. However, Jolli didn't move, as if the piercing sound of the man's torment had no effect on him.

"I will cut your fucking scalp off and feed it to you," I heard Blaze say when I put the bud back in. "Who hired you to kill the woman in the apartment?"

I guess there was no need for small talk. Apparently, Blaze knew Boris understood exactly why he was here, and what woman he was talking about.

Boris was breathing hard, but he was no longer fighting. He was also no longer talking because he was seething as blood dripped down his face.

Blaze dug his fingers into the cut and pulled at the man's scalp.

This time, the painful howl from Boris was enough to cause a reaction from Jolli. He adjusted the volume on his earbud and glanced back to check on me.

I told him I was fine. It was a reflexive response because truth be told; I was highly unsettled. Blaze was literally ripping a guy's scalp off right in front of me! How in the hell does someone explain their feelings about that?

Nevertheless, I couldn't take my eyes off the unfolding drama. I wondered if Vadim, wherever he was hiding, planned to jump in and help.

Although Blaze didn't seem to need any help, and I supposed Vadim thought the same thing.

"давай и убей меня," Boris said.

"No problem," Blaze snarled, lifting the knife to Boris' scalp again. "I'll make this nice and slow."

Digging the knife further into his head broke the hitman's stubbornness. I was astonished he lasted that long.

Shakily, Boris wiped at the blood oozing down his face, and bile rose in my throat.

Speaking quickly, he said, "I do not know who wants her dead. My orders came from another man that works for him."

"Name?" Blaze pressed.

I think Boris cursed in Russian before answering. "Triston, Traiton, Trenton! That's it, Trenton. He works for a security company called Vex. Ask him about it."

"Fuck," Jolli said under his breath.

It was my sentiments exactly.

Trenton! Our Trenton! The one that I greeted every morning was in on this?

Blaze forced Boris down to the ground, keeping hold of the man's head. "Thank you for your assistance. Now, clean this shit off of my boot!"

After all the moving around they'd done, I didn't think there was any spittle left on his boot, but Blaze was insistent. I guess it was just the principle of the thing to him.

Stubborn ass.

However, when the hitman refused, Blaze yanked him to his feet, forced him into a chair, and stabbed the knife through one of Boris' hands so hard, the man became one with the table.

I yanked the earbud out midway through another torturous scream. I'd gotten the closure I needed, and I was definitely going to be sick.

As far as I was concerned, justice was served. The feds were likely on the way to pick up the hitman with an altered scalp, and now that Blaze had slammed his foot down on Boris' leg, the man was using the hand not attached to the table to wipe the traces of spit off of Blaze's shoe.

One last look at the loose piece of Boris' scalp was enough for me to excuse myself. I told Jolli I needed to find a corner to throw up in. There was now only one thought on my mind.

I hope you're a praying man, Trenton, because Blaze is coming for you.

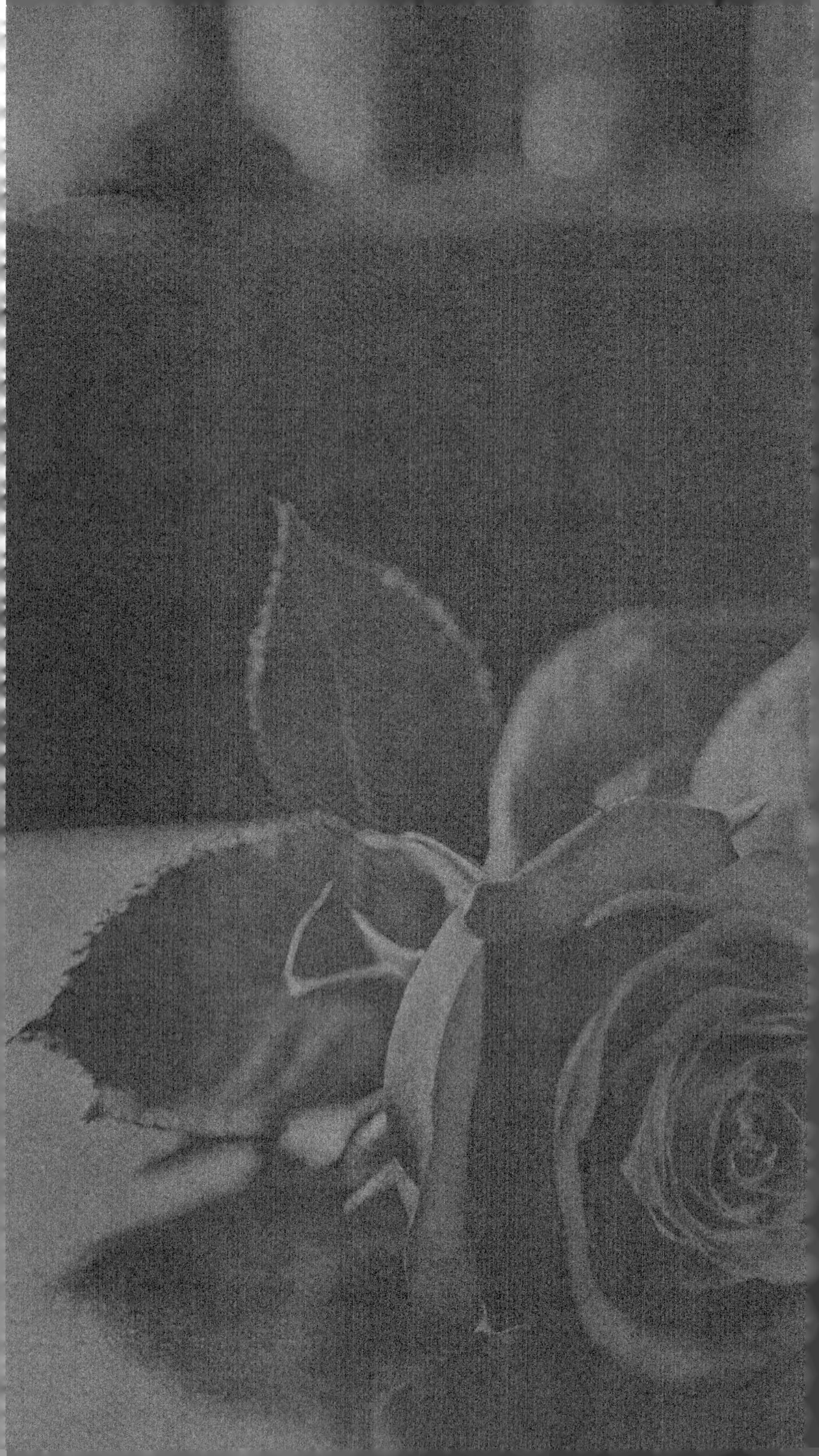

Chapter Twenty

"Crawl to me."

"Isn't it beautiful?" Vadim said.

Based on the love and admiration in his tone, one would think he was talking about a baby or possibly a sweet, defenseless kitten, but no, Vadim was talking about his gun; a Browning Black Label Medallion.

"Look," he said, his L sounding more like a V. "Don't you love this checkered rosewood-colored laminate? I can stare at it for hours. And this gold part here. It is where you grip the weapon for better aim."

I felt like I was at a gun show. Vadim was taking me through his collection of guns he'd brought to the house. It was his day to stay with me and, just like the rest of the team, Vadim was patient and kind.

However, he was also probably the craziest member.

If I thought Axel had an unusual obsession with knives, Vadim took the cake. It was unsettling to see him hold the guns, explain their differences, and pretend to fire them.

Not because I thought I couldn't trust him, but I'd officially realized guns made me cringe and I'd definitely developed a slight fear of them.

Dammit!

I didn't need any new problems, but suddenly it didn't matter that I knew how to shoot a gun, that I'd grown up around them or that I never saw them as a threat.

Thanks to all the gun action happening around me, I'd

now seen what they were capable of, witnessed the way they tore through flesh, seized lives in an instant and felt one pressed against my head with malicious intent.

Vadim shifted closer, holding up the gun at new angles for me to see, oblivious to the fact that I was moving slightly away every time he did so.

"Back in Russia, when I would go Kamchatka brown bear hunting with my father, we used a 300 magnum. This gun reminds me of that one. It, too, has heavy bullets."

Why, oh why, couldn't we go back to talking about the magnificent beauty of Moscow?

About how there are over 250 metro stations and each one has its own theme and designs. Marble walls, conical chandeliers, ornamental brackets on the ceilings. I wanted to talk about glamour, not guns.

I smiled politely, inching away yet again.

"Hunting, huh? I take it that means you don't mind the paperwork like Jolli and Blaze do?"

Vadim scratched his head with the gun and considered my question.

"I do not. In fact, I look forward to it. The paperwork lets me relive the kill. But, I am always in admiration of Blaze's control. I would have killed Boris simply because there is no need for him. A man that makes living killing innocent people is not good person," Vadim announced, his Broken English and matter-of-fact tone oddly putting me at ease.

That was until he picked up a new gun to shove into my face. "Here," Vadim said. "You can hold it if you like."

Vadim was sweet, so sweet, but there was no way in hell I was holding that gun.

"No, no," I replied, being sure to touch his hand and not the gun itself, as I nudged it away. "I wouldn't want to damage it."

"You sure?" he offered again.

"Positive." I stood. "Actually, I need to get back to work. Thanks for telling me about Russia."

"Anytime," he responded, sliding the gun back into the case. "You are very easy to talk to. I see why Blaze has taken a liking to you."

Every time someone mentioned how fond Blaze was of me, I thanked them and moved on. Blaze and I were friends. Sex with me was the only thing he was fond of.

"I'm making a sandwich for lunch after I get some work done. Do you want one?" I asked.

Vadim had already moved on to the next gun. "Yes," he replied, touching it like a delicate treasure.

Entering Blaze's office, I headed toward the workstation he'd set up for me at a table near the filing cabinet.

I was helping with the case by reviewing photos taken by the team to identify any irregularities.

Such as if there was a mysterious-looking person in the background, or if the subject they were watching carried an item into a building, but no longer had it when they came out.

I was grateful to provide some type of assistance to those that were looking out for me. Only being able to offer a listening ear or lunch got old real quick.

Learning that Trenton was a part of this continued to astonish me. Having worked for Blaze for over five years, there were no signs that he would betray him.

We all had so many questions.

Was Trenton part of this all along? If so, why? Was his role voluntary? Or did the mystery man pulling the strings have something on him?

One small victory was that after giving it some thought, it now made sense why there was no forced entry into my apartment. With all the times I'd left my purse at the security station to run back and get something in my car, Trenton could have easily made an imprint of my key.

However, besides that conclusion, getting the answers to anything else would be tricky because Trenton was nowhere to be found. The last time anyone saw him was the day Boris got picked up by the feds.

According to Blaze, the individual he was working for must have tipped him off about Boris being taken in, and now Trenton was lying low.

The only man on their list of suspects with access to that type of insight and power once again put the governor in the spotlight.

Pulling out the bottom drawer of the file cabinet, I collected more folders of pictures. I felt a rush of excitement when I noticed I had close to one hundred images left to look over. That meant I'd be able to remain busy for a while.

Right as I was about to close the drawer, my gaze fell upon a label tucked away near the back. The stuff I worked on was toward the front, therefore I never had a reason to look back there.

The folder's title tab had the words "Weaver charity" written across it. Immediately, it stood out because Loni's last name was Weaver and we'd organized a charity for her.

After retrieving the folder, I flipped it open and my hand flew to my mouth.

It was a receipt from Loni's charity for a fifty thousand dollar donation!

Shock, disbelief, and confusion swirled inside me as I stared at it.

Donating to Loni was a good thing. Why hadn't he told me? Why would it be a secret? When I told him about Loni and the charity, that was the opportune time to say, "Oh yeah, by the way, I donated fifty thousand dollars to it," but Blaze had said nothing.

Closing the folder, I shook my head. I felt a little

perturbed and that shouldn't be. This was a generous thing Blaze had done. So why did it feel so underhanded?

Blaze got home around six that evening and Vadim gathered his things, promising to return with more guns and exciting stories about his work.

Part of me wanted to tell him to skip the gun show, but before leaving, Vadim said to me, "Face your fear, or it will own you."

I laughed. It appeared he knew the guns were making me uncomfortable.

"Any recommendations?" I asked.

"Everyone is different," Vadim said, tossing his bag over his shoulder, his green eyes narrowing. "It is a reason babies are easier to teach and mold than adults. Fear works the same way. Start while it's small."

"Thanks Vadim," I said, giving him a tight hug.

Once he left, Blaze got showered while I set up the dart game for us in the living room. Usually, after work, Blaze liked to unwind by throwing darts at the board while we chatted about whatever came to mind.

"What do you want to play tonight?" Blaze asked entering the living room, referring to which version of darts I wanted to play.

He placed his gun down on the glass table next to the couch and an uneasiness crept over me. Although I was certain they all deserved it, I wondered how many lives that gun had taken.

Glancing up, I realized I hadn't answered Blaze and quickly decided. The last several times we'd played English cricket and 301 style, so tonight I wanted to play a much more fitting version.

"Killer," I said.

Blaze cocked a brow. "Teasing me already, I see."

Killer darts were his favorite. The initial goal of the game was for each player to hit within the double ring of their randomly chosen number, using three throws in a turn. Once a player scores, then they become the "Killer".

Afterward, that player aims for the doubles of opponents' numbers. I'd only played it twice with Blaze and he won both times, but I was a pretty close second. Darts was a popular game I played with my siblings growing up.

Blaze and I were in front of the couch, but I was a few inches closer to the board because Blaze figured it was fair due to me being shorter.

"Any luck today?" I asked Blaze, making my first throw.

The number I chose was eight, and my dart didn't land anywhere near that. Instead, it clung so close to the bottom of the board it almost didn't make it at all.

It was a lousy throw, and when my next two followed suit, I knew this would not be a good game for me. My mind was elsewhere.

Blaze's number was twelve. All three of his darts landed within the single score area of twelve, not in the double ring, which meant he was close, but not close enough.

"None yet," he said with a sigh. "Whoever is behind this has more connections, power and money than I have ever seen, but they can't hide Trenton forever."

That was a death threat if I ever heard one.

"Anything in the photos?" Blaze asked.

I threw my next three darts, and this time, all of them did hit the floor except one that hung proudly near the number sixteen. *Pitiful.*

"Nothing stands out yet."

Blaze nodded, looked at me strangely for my pathetic shot, but didn't mention it. Instead, he said, "Thank you for helping us out."

"You're thanking me?" I asked, astonished. "You and your team are the whole reason I am still alive. There is no need to thank me. It's the least I can do."

Blaze's next throw crowned him as "Killer," and then he turned to me and said, "We would protect you, no matter what. You don't have to work for it. If you want to work for something, that can easily be arranged," he said suggestively.

I grinned and took my turn. It landed in the bullseye of all places. That would have been a huge score if we were playing the standard game, but it meant nothing in this one.

We finished up the game, and I collected the darts while Blaze went to make a call.

Taking a seat near the bar area that was across the living room, I tucked my feet underneath me and relaxed into the large leather recliner. I was staring off into space, wondering yet again why he didn't tell me about the donation.

"Why are you all the way over there?" Blaze asked, reentering the living room and taking a seat on the couch across the room.

"Didn't you know?" I said, rubbing the buttery leather arms. "This is my favorite chair."

"Come here," Blaze said.

Based on his tone, I could tell immediately that it was an order from him as my Dom, not a request from him as my friend.

I stood and took my first step. I was unquestionably in the mood for play. However, walking wasn't what Blaze wanted.

"Crawl," he instructed.

Without hesitation, I got down on my hands and knees, the smooth carpet welcoming me, and crawled toward him.

My movements were flirtatious and indiscreet as my shirt fell low, exposing my chest.

Stopping in front of him, I placed my hands on his knees, trying desperately not to notice how close his gun was on the table. Unfortunately, my eyes kept darting over to it.

Thanks, Vadim, I thought sarcastically.

"How can I serve you, sir?" I asked, finally able to place all my attention on him.

"I don't need anything," Blaze said. "You know, I simply love seeing you on your knees."

After flashing him a smile, I sat back on my heels and asked him a serious question. "Why do you share your submissives?"

Blaze mirrored my movement and sat back on the couch. "Why shouldn't I? They are not mine to keep."

"Certainly you could have kept a few if you wanted to."

His response was blatant. "I didn't want to."

"Okay," I said slowly. "So you never formed a deeper connection with any of them?"

This wasn't even about me. This was about something far more vast. Since becoming a Dom, Blaze had trained at least fifty subs, not taking it further with even one of them was baffling.

"Wasn't your ex a sub?" I asked.

"No," Blaze said, and then added. "Well, not at first. Jasmine was a nurse. I met her after a mission had got out of hand and she patched me up."

"Sounds like a genuine love story," I said. And I meant it. A nurse that makes her way into an assassin's heart by first healing his wounds. It might be a dark romance, but a romance nonetheless.

Blaze and I stared at each other for a moment. No words were necessary because I already understood. I didn't need to know about the intricate details of his relationship with

Jasmine, what they did together for fun, or what went through his mind when she ended it.

All I knew, and needed to know, was that Jasmine broke his heart and Blaze never planned to let that happen again.

"So," I said, summing the story up. "You two were happy. She became your sub and after it was over, you took love off the table? Now, your only goal is to bring women's fantasies to life."

I smiled at him, wanting to ease the tension of this moment. Blaze smiled back. I think he was grateful that I didn't want to press deeper into what happened between him and Jasmine.

"Pretty much," he said. "I help my subs come out of their shells, explore their sexuality and learn what they're into. Sharing them helps that happen. Plus, you never know, opening the door for them to be with another might be how they meet the one for them."

"So kind of like pushing the birds out of the nest."

"Pretty much," he said, staring into my eyes.

"How long do you suspect I will be your submissive?"

"Until you grow tired of it," he replied.

"Ah, but what if I never do?" I countered.

This time, Blaze leaned forward and took my hands. With sincerity in his eyes and gentle movements, he shared his truth.

"You will, once you accept I am not the man to fall in love with," he assured me, his thumb brushing across my knuckles. "They all do."

I would not fight what he said, because I believed it. Blaze was not the man for me, as he'd said so many times before, and that was okay. I placed my hand over his and gave him a truth of my own.

"I understand, and until that happens, I'm going to enjoy this experience. I am yours to control."

He kissed me, and every obstacle, or excuse that separated

us vanished. That was until he broke free and said, "Is my gun making you uncomfortable?"

"Why would you say that?" I asked, flipping the tables to avoid answering.

"Because you have been stealing glances at it all evening."

"Well, you're mistaken. I'm not uncomfortable."

Blaze made a tsk-tsk sound. "You know, if you lie to me, all I am going to do is call you out on your shit." He picked up the gun, bringing it closer to me. "I ask again, does this bother you?"

I nervously bit my lower lip. It looked so menacing.

"I'd never seen a gun as a threat before," I finally admitted and then laughed to myself. "I mean, I knew what they were capable of, but seeing it, being in danger of it..." I shook my head.

"Do you want to hold it?" Blaze asked.

I wanted to say no, but then I heard a familiar voice.

"Face your fear," Vadim had said.

Taking it from Blaze's hand, the gun was cold and heavy in my hesitant grip. I could feel the weight of its power, the potential for devastation it held. But amidst the fear, there was a strange sense of empowerment.

Blaze watched me closely, his eyes filled with a mix of interest and determination.

"Take a deep breath," he encouraged, his voice steady. "Remember, it's a tool for defense. The only danger lies in the hands that wield it."

With a newfound determination, I gripped the gun tighter. As each second passed, the familiar feel and memories of practicing at the range with my grandad returned, helping me reclaim a sense of control and resilience.

"How does that make you feel?"

"Better," I said honestly. "More in control."

"That's a relief," Blaze replied cooly. "Since you're aiming it at my chest."

Oh shit!

I looked at the gun in my hands. I was simply trying to get more comfortable holding it, and as a reflex I guess I'd aimed it.

Lowering the gun, I shook my head. "Do you even have a pulse? You could have said, don't point that thing at me!"

Blaze shrugged. "Guns are aimed at me all the time. It's oddly comforting."

"You are a strange one. How can having a gun aimed at you be comforting?"

"Because it's a familiar danger. One that I automatically know my next move to."

"So what would your next move—"

I was cut off when Blaze moved at lightning speed, retrieving the Glock from my hands, flattening me against the floor.

He stared down at me as I tried to wrap my mind around what had just happened.

"You were saying?" he mocked.

Staring up into his beautiful dark brown eyes, I regarded him with admiration.

"That you are the most maddening and sweet man I have ever met."

Blaze's brows knitted in confusion. "Go on," he replied.

"You donated money to Loni's Charity," I said quietly.

Blaze got off of me, placed the gun on the table and sat with his back against the couch. "Oh, I didn't want you to see that."

"Why?" I asked, arching up to rest on my elbows.

"Because I didn't do it for your gratitude or the way you are looking at me right now. I read the article you posted for Loni on the charity website and wanted to help. You really loved her and honoring her wishes, even in death, meant the world to you. I wanted to give you some semblance of peace inside of a horrific event."

There was no reason to ask how he heard about it. I was sure either Jocelyn told him, or he heard the story on the local news.

Regardless, his sincerity and kindness almost moved me to tears.

"You did give me that," I said. "I don't know how I can ever repay you."

Blaze fixed me with a stare and instantly, I understood that my reaction was exactly what he wanted to avoid. In his mind, knowing what he'd done would force me to look at him differently, feel indebted, or like I needed to prove my gratitude.

He wanted every exchange between us to be authentic and, although it had been, if I knew about what he'd done early on, Blaze would always question why I was doing it.

"I get it," I said, sitting up to lean against the couch next to him. "And even though you don't want gratitude. Your generosity at least deserves some insight about what happened."

"You don't owe me anything," Blaze insisted.

"Yeah, but maybe this is about me. I'll bet my therapist would say it is healthy to talk about the amazing friend I lost, with the amazing one I've gained," I said, nudging his shoulder with my own.

"In that case, I'm all ears," Blaze agreed.

I took a deep breath and went back to a time I'd tried so hard to forget.

"Loni was one of my closest friends. We'd begun modeling together when we were teens and clicked immediately. On the night of the accident, we were celebrating. It was a tradition of ours anytime one of us scored a new contract."

I paused, the weight of guilt relentless. I didn't know if I would ever forgive myself for that night.

"Anyway, we would go out to dinner at a restaurant that shared the same initial letter as the company we had just closed a deal with. For instance, when Loni got the contract with Tailored Clothing, we went to Tommy's steak house. On my two-year contract with Bare it Bikini, we went to Bella Cuisine, and so on."

I stopped again; the story approaching a more heartbreaking turn of events.

Taking hold of my hand, Blaze pulled me closer to him, enveloping me in his embrace, allowing me to find comfort as I laid my head against his chest.

A wave of emotion washed over me, threatening to bring tears to my eyes, but I fought against letting them escape.

"That night we were celebrating my contract from X Travels. They marketed clothes and accessories for flight attendants and pilots. I even think they had a line for tennis players and gymnast."

The details of my contract didn't matter, but I needed to buy time. At this point in my memory, Loni was alive. Her laugh was still infectious, her smile still bright and her heart still beating. She hadn't died yet... or rather; I hadn't killed her yet.

Blaze patiently waited. His breathing even, his hold on me tightening, helping me hold on for the scary ride to come.

"I chose Xylophone. It was a restaurant with a live jazz band, but it was an hour away and by the time I found out about the contract, it was already getting dark. Loni didn't want to go. She said we should wait until the next day because it was a long drive and it had already started to rain. I told her I would drive and even pay for dinner, but Loni still didn't want to do it." My voice cracked at the next sentence. "But I begged, and eventually she caved."

Squeezing my eyes shut, I gripped Blaze's hand.

"We had almost made it to Xylophone, and I was going around a steep curve, when a deer jumped out. I swerved to avoid hitting it, but I was going too fast, and the roads were too slick, and I couldn't stop," I spoke faster, trying to get to the end of this nightmare. "I wasn't wearing a seatbelt, and the impact threw me from the car, but Loni..."

I opened my eyes. The visual of seeing the medics trying to remove Loni from the car burned in my mind.

"Part of a tree pierced through her, pinning her to the seat. I'd passed out when I hit the ground, but I woke up for the briefest moment as the paramedics were getting me in the ambulance, and I saw her. I saw Loni, pale, broken, dead. There was so much blood... so much blood."

I'd returned to that dreadful night.

My body shook with uncontrollable sobs. The scars on my back suddenly seem to ache and burn like they had for so many nights after the accident. The weight of grief and guilt pressed heavily on my chest, as I once again processed that I had survived while Loni had not.

"Shhh, shhh. No more," Blaze said, trying his best to soothe me. "You don't need to tell me anymore."

I cried and cried, like I had countless times. Each tear that streamed down my face carried with it a piece of the pain and anguish that had consumed me for so long.

I miss you so much, my dear friend.

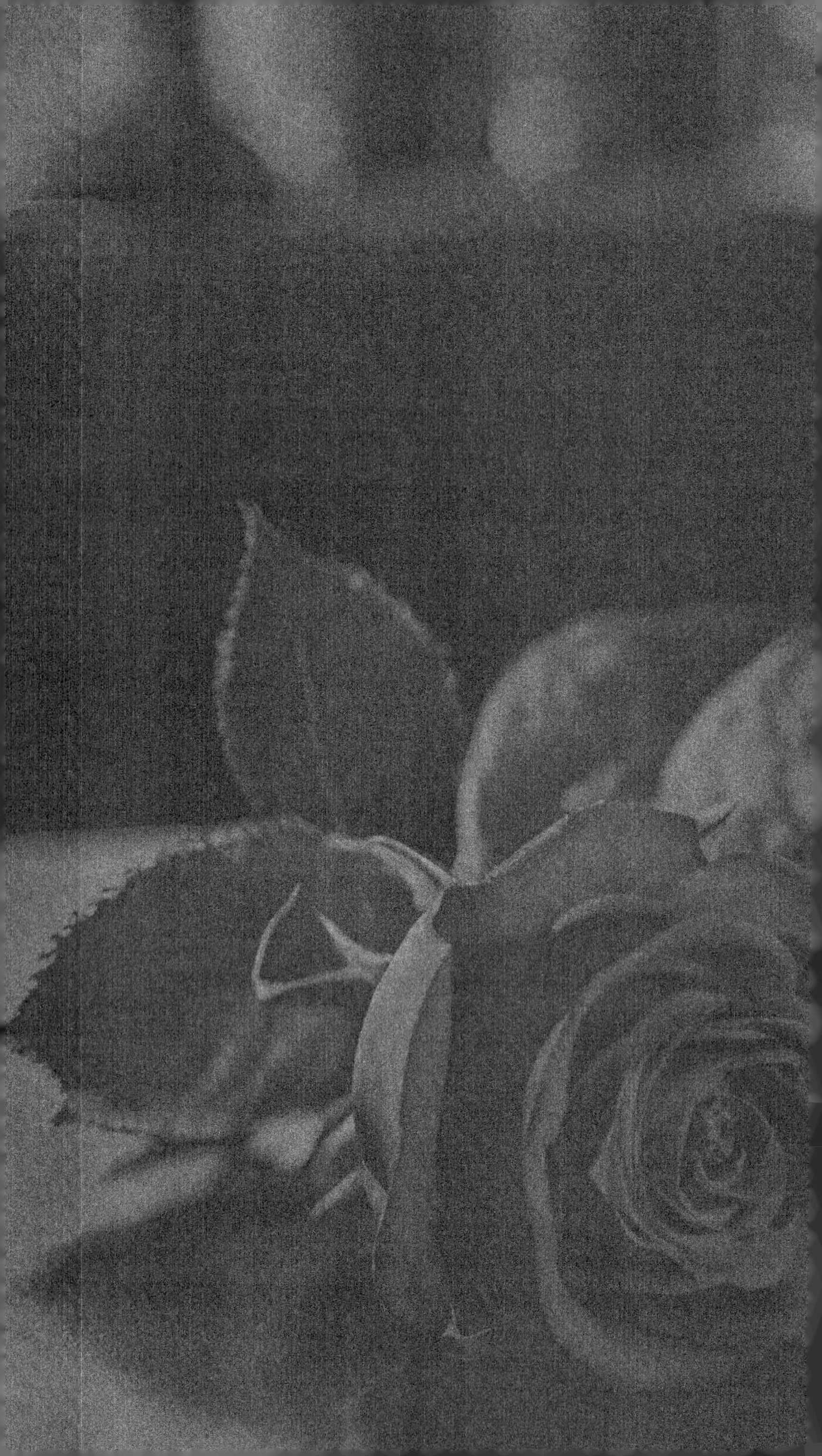

Chapter Twenty One

"I SUGGEST YOU RUN."

I had fallen down a rabbit hole.

About seven hours ago, I started reviewing case briefings. It was a new assignment that Blaze had given me, in addition to the photo work I was doing to assist with the case.

However, in the last hour, I'd gotten sidetracked and begun researching anything and everything under the sun and it was all this case's fault.

Apparently, after reading notes all day, simple words no longer made sense and instead of focusing on the diabolical and illegal details of the summary, I was questioning pointless things.

Such as, why radar was spelled the same backward and forward? And what were words like that called?

Then I came across the word knowledge several times. "To his knowledge", "to my knowledge", "to their knowledge." Why was the k silent?!

Surely, if it was necessary to make it silent, it should also be invisible!

So here I was an hour later, and I now knew that words spelled the same backwards and forward were called palindromes, and the reason there are silent letters is because of old English.

The pronunciation of certain words required these letters, but after aphaeresis, which is the dropping of the initial sound of a word, they left the useless letter, but changed the way we said it. Pointless.

From there, I moved on to the perplexing and interesting world of phobias. In conclusion, I wasn't being productive at all.

Guess it's time to close the laptop and get back to the case.

I was about to push the computer aside when I saw a suggestion to learn what the longest word in the English language was.

I shut the laptop... but then opened it again.

The word was pneumonoultramicroscopicsilicovolcanoconiosis.

And before I fell down an even deeper rabbit hole, concerning the fact that it referred to lung disease contracted from inhalation of particles from volcanos, I pushed the laptop away.

Blinking several times, I got up from my worktable and went to grab more photos to review. I simply could no longer stare at words, even though the summaries were astonishing and highly entertaining, reminding me of the security reports at Vex.

In one bust, the FBI tracked down a gang member named Val Pablo and arrested him in his home. The insane part was when they got there, they were surprised to find the dead body of one of Val's associates that he'd stabbed fifty times over a video game.

Sheesh. And these people were looking for me?

A few days thereafter, the team apprehended a big time coordinator of the drug trafficking organization, who was moving approximately 3.5 tons of cocaine, worth 300 million dollars hidden inside furniture.

I had to read the amount several times.

300 million dollars!

No wonder drugs were an overpopulated market. Many

people wouldn't say no to money like that, even if it were being split in many ways.

Opening the folder of photos, I looked down at a picture of Governor Wesley standing beside a suspicious-looking man. The man was wearing a dark blue baseball cap and sunglasses, holding a black bag.

I moved to the next picture, and this time, the guy was facing the governor with the bag extended. The mystery man was absent in the third image, leaving Governor Wesley on his phone and holding a black bag.

I flipped through the three photos again... and then again.

Blaze entered his office, talking on the phone to someone in Swahili, one of the five languages he spoke fluently. As usual, he sounded ridiculously sexy, but I had no time to be turned on. Something was weird about these pictures.

"Asante sana, kwaheri," Blaze said before dropping his phone on his desk.

"Blaze, can you come here for a second?" I asked, my eyes still glued to the images.

"What's up?" he said, his deep voice filled with concern.

Turning the three photos in his direction, I pushed them towards the edge of the table so that he could get a better look.

"Take a look at these," I said, my voice tinged with a mix of curiosity and unease. "If I'm not mistaken, they're photoshopped."

Blaze leaned down, scanning the images. He picked up one and eyed it closer.

"Something looks off," he agreed. "But are you sure it's photoshopped?"

"Pretty positive. During my modeling career, I worked closely with the graphic designers. Images taken during photoshoots are often digitally altered and I would sometimes assist with what looks worked best for the final result. I got pretty good at spotting the differences between the fake and the real."

Blaze lowered the photo and considered what I was saying.

"We have looked over these photos and no one else has said anything."

"Maybe they don't have an eye for it," I said. "Besides, I'm not saying I can spot any Photoshop job ever done. A lot of work is incredibly polished. I'm saying when they are really basic or of poor quality like this one, then I can usually tell."

Placing the photo back on the table, Blaze took a seat next to me.

"How can you tell?" he asked.

I pointed at the area in front of the guy in the hat and shades.

"Alright, see these shadows? They are inconsistent and the physics of it doesn't make any sense, especially since the mystery guy is facing the sun. Also, the sidewalk between the governor and the guy appears excessively smooth. Typically, that is done when images are being blended. It stands out because other items in the photo are not this perfect."

Blaze picked up the photo again. "Now that you say it, I see what you mean."

He studied me, as if he didn't exactly know what to make of me.

"I didn't know you worked with graphic designers."

"Because you didn't ask," I said with a smirk. "I also went to school for a brief time to be a cybersecurity expert."

"Well, excuse the hell out of me," Blaze replied, impressed. "Did you really?"

"Yup. My sister is a cybersecurity expert, and I find it so fascinating. Which is why, when Jocelyn mentioned working for Vex, my interest was piqued."

"This is news to me," Blaze said.

I looked at him, perplexed. "I thought you did an extensive background check?"

"The HR team did, but they only provided me with your major highlights to review."

"No wonder you didn't see it. It wasn't exactly major. I only went for a semester, if that."

"Why didn't you continue?" Blaze asked.

"Modeling kept me way too busy, and to be honest, it was very lucrative. I would have done both, but between the contracts, traveling and the long hours, I couldn't keep up."

"You are a phenomenal woman full of surprises," Blaze complimented.

I blushed. I couldn't help it. Any compliments from Blaze went straight to my head and between my legs.

"Thank you, but the biggest surprise is that these images are fakes."

Blaze checked his watch. "Yeah, I'm going to get my tech guy to check them out."

I nodded and then something odd occurred to me.

"Wait, didn't one of your team members take these pictures?"

"No. Some images are from stakeouts done by the FBI before we came onboard."

"So from Divers, Swanson or Steele?"

Blaze shook his head. "No, they would consider these types of duties beneath them. They would assign it to either a rookie agent or a cop from a local district."

The significance of this sank in as I considered the implications. It meant the information I was analyzing might not be as accurate as initially assumed, and Blaze would need to verify the data with additional sources.

"Maybe you were right. Governor Wesley may not be the top guy after all."

"Seems we're going to find out," Blaze said, rising from his chair. "I'll get this processing, and then you and I are going to take a break."

I closed the folder. "Yes, a break sounds good. What did you have in mind?"

"When is the last time you went running?" Blaze said.

I was staring at the thick, long imprint of Blaze's dick through his sweats.

Blaze snapped his fingers. "Hey, my eyes are up here," he said with a grin.

Feeling a bit embarrassed, I laughed and briefly averted my gaze. Yes, the shyness in me was practically nonexistent after all we'd done, but the old me still peeked out sometimes.

I'd already stretched and warmed up for our jog and I couldn't help it if watching him in all of his masculine glory was keeping me occupied.

The sun was setting, but the area where we stood remained well-lit because of the lights on the back of Blaze's house.

What I didn't understand is why he had us out this late for a run. The woods would be almost pitch-black.

"How fast can you run?" Blaze asked.

"Not sure, but certainly faster than you," I teased.

Blaze glanced down at his watch and pressed a button to dismiss an alert that had appeared on the screen.

"Is that so?" he replied, moving closer to stare down at me.

"It is," I challenged, further tightening the gap between us. I really had to strain my neck being this close, but I had to let him know I wasn't intimidated.

"Most people don't run as fast as they think. Why should you be any different?" he asked.

I tapped my chin. "Let's see. I can run two miles in nine minutes. I did it in the park with no problems every day."

"That's cute, but it's not fast enough," Blaze said confidently.

My hands shot to my hips. "How so? That's a damn good time."

"For a leisure run, maybe so." I watched him, confused, until he said, "Let me rephrase, princess. Have you ever been hunted?"

Ah, now I got it. I was about to have some spicy, adrenaline inducing fun.

"Outside of those hunting me on this case," I joked. "Never."

"Well, tonight is your lucky night," Blaze announced. "And in order to make it fair, I will give you a one minute head start."

"I don't need that long."

"I suggest you take it," Blaze warned. "Because when I catch you, I'm going to fuck you and I will not be gentle."

A fierce wave of erotic sensations rushed over me. I welcomed Blaze's amorous advances.

"If," I said, accentuating the word. "you catch me. It will be because I wanted you to."

Blaze narrowed his eyes at me. "One."

I didn't move, merely stared at him. Tonight, I was going to be a brat. The countdown had begun, and I would take my precious time.

"Two," he said.

I glanced at my nails, unbothered.

"Thirty-five," Blaze said.

I got my ass out of there. Running at full speed into the bushes doing my best to remain on the dirt trail that twisted, turned and lead me deeper in to the woods.

The glow of the lights from the house was still offering me

some illumination, but as I ran faster, the darkness rained down on me.

Ducking low to avoid a branch that was sticking out, my feet pounded the pavement hard as I tried to listen for Blaze behind me. I wasn't scared, but my adrenaline was through the roof.

The excitement and possibility of being captured at any second was thrilling and exhilarating.

I zigged left and right before stealing a glance over my shoulder.

Nothing.

That meant either Blaze hadn't started or was too far behind.

I pushed myself even harder, my legs burning from the exertion. The trail seemed to stretch on forever; the trees closing in around me like a maze. Long branches whipped at my face and arms, leaving stinging scratches in their wake.

If we did this again, I would definitely wear a 2-piece workout set with pants and a long sleeve shirt, instead of the running shorts and t-shirt I was currently sporting.

Increasing my speed and focusing on what looked to be a bush up ahead.

Thankfully, there were small path lights placed throughout the trail, but their soft glow only provided enough light to see a few feet ahead of me. I still had to squint and slow down periodically to avoid running headfirst into a tree.

Running two miles in nine minutes was an impressive speed, but maybe tonight I could do it in eight.

Crack!

From somewhere around me there was a sound within the trees, but when I looked back, I didn't see anything.

Maybe it was a cute squirrel... *or an angry fox,* my mind offered.

Alright, now I was getting a little afraid. My heart was

beating faster, and between the sprinkles of lights and the overwhelming darkness, shadows that looked like monsters were being cast all around me.

Crack!

I glanced back again. There was nothing. I felt the burn as I pushed myself to run faster.

Truthfully, I wasn't sure why. I wanted Blaze to catch me, at the same time I did not want to lose. Rounding a curve, I stepped on a pile of pebbles and almost slipped, but caught myself just in time.

If I could keep up at this pace, I may outrun him after all.

My premature thoughts of victory abruptly shattered when Blaze, who moved as silently as a ninja, skillfully wrapped his arm around me from behind and forcefully pulled me backwards. My feet shot into the air as Blaze spun me around, bringing me to the ground on top of him.

Blaze rolled so that he could pin me down in a patch of grass. As I felt his weight pressing against me, a surge of excitement coursed through my veins and I refused to surrender.

Instead, I tried to break free and run away again. Knowing that I was safe with him made this scenario much more arousing. I was going to enjoy this.

Blaze wasn't saying a word; he was all about action.

He yanked my shorts and underwear off and, as promised, it was not gentle. Blaze pulled my hair, bit me and playfully, yet firmly, wrestled with me.

Sticks dug into my back and my hands slipped on the strips of dirt as I fought not to relinquish control.

Blaze pinned my wrists down above my head and said, "Relax, little slut. You're mine."

His words halted me.

Despite the playful undertone, there was a menacing aura surrounding him, which emphasized his savage nature. I knew

Blaze liked this type of power, keeping me in the dark and speculating about his next course of action.

He pulled out a knife, and I didn't even flinch. In fact, I remained in the position he'd put me in. Hands above my head, legs bent at the knees and him between them. My gaze shifted from his face to the gleaming blade, back to his face again. I was on the edge of my seat.

What would my dangerous Dom do?

"You've seen me do things I know were frightening for you," Blaze said. He slid his hand and the knife underneath my shirt, taking his time slicing it open. He moved on to my sports bra, holding the blade in the center, using just enough force to lift it away from my skin, but not enough to cut it. "So I must know, are you afraid of me?" he asked.

He pulled upward, and the blade was so sharp, it cut through the supposedly resistant to tear fabric, effortlessly, revealing my breasts.

There was no thought necessary for his question. My response was immediate.

"No," I said. "I am not afraid of you."

"You should be," Blaze replied with a wink.

I couldn't tear my eyes away from him. His dark eyes filled with a sadistic pleasure as he continued to toy with me.

It was difficult to determine whether my excitement stemmed from knowing what was about to happen or the undeniable sexual tension that Blaze was building. Every move he made seemed calculated, designed to keep me on edge.

He traced the edge of the knife down my neck, over my nipples and then further down my exposed skin, leaving a trail of goosebumps in its wake.

I lie motionless, fully aware of how sharp the blade was, but certain Blaze knew how much pressure to use. It was a game of trust and being teased this way felt electric, igniting a primal desire within me I didn't even know I had.

With a flick of his wrist, Blaze discarded the knife, his lips crashing onto mine in a feverish kiss that stole my breath. Raw passion consumed the surrounding air, and when he entered me, it was rough, animalistic, and fulfilling.

I let him ravish me, urged him to take me, and begged him to wreck me. I came twice, my fingers digging into the dirt and my mind lost in a world that only Blaze could produce.

He was everything I had ever wanted in a lover; passionate, demanding, caring, and remorseless.

The experiences I had with Blaze allowed me the opportunity to explore my true self, unbounded and unrestricted. No matter how our story concluded, I would always be eternally grateful.

As I entered the house, I found myself completely covered in leaves, twigs, and dirt, which made me realize how desperately I needed a shower. Blaze decided we should take one together so that he could care for any cuts or bruises that I'd received amidst our passion.

I was perfectly fine, but since Blaze insisted, there was no way I would argue with being spoiled and cared for by him.

Afterward we ate dinner, and since I wasn't quite ready for bed, I planned to look over more photos.

"I have some new ones for you there on the shelf," Blaze said, turning off his desk computer.

My eyes scanned the various books while I pulled the stack of photos down. One book was on meditation, another on tactical planning, and a third... *what was this?*

After pulling the book down from the shelf, I studied the

cover. It was all black and thin with a woman on the front. The title said Blaze's Little Black Book.

"What is this?" I asked, holding up the slim booklet.

Blaze laughed. "Oh that. I always keep a record of the women who want to be my subs whether I refuse or accept them. My friend Nicki thought it would be a hilarious idea to turn those notes into an actual book."

"You mean like a book she printed for you as a gift?"

"No, I mean like a book that you can actually purchase at bookstores."

I opened my mouth, shut it, then started again.

"So you're saying the women that wanted to be your sub allowed you to print information about them for the world to see?"

Blaze regarded me thoughtfully. "It's not a deep dive. Only their names, kinks, why they wanted to be my submissive, and notes about what I did to them are listed." Then he glanced at the book in my hand and added. "And of course they agreed to it. Even if I didn't choose them, they wanted to make me happy."

Putting the book down, I stared at him in disbelief and opened the laptop. Was this real? The idea was wild.

"I don't believe you," I said, typing in the title on the site of a popular book retailer.

No one would really sign up for... and there it was. Blaze's Little Black Book was actually something I could purchase online.

"I think I've officially seen it all," I said to Blaze. Glancing down at the book, I asked, "May I look through this?"

"Knock yourself out," he said. "I'm going to bed. I have an early morning."

I had an early morning too, but sleep could wait. I was about to dive into this book.

BLAZE'S

THE EXPLICIT COMPILATION OF

LITTLE

SIR BLAZE'S SUBMISSIVES

BLACK BOOK

KRISANGELA

KINKS
CNC
VOYERISM
EXHIBITIONISM
BREATH PLAY

WHY SHOULD I ALLOW YOU TO BE MY SUBMISSIVE?
I want someone to take control and show me just how much I can truly handle. I want to experience all that you have to offer.

NOTES...
I used a latex breathing hood on her. With this toy, Krisangela only had fifteen minutes' worth of air before breathing became completely impossible.

With each passing minute, it became harder and harder to breathe. Most of the time I would fuck her all the way up to the max of fourteen mins and fifty-nine seconds before pulling the mask off.

Fun times.

LORILEE

KINKS

BLOOD PLAY
ANYTHING BDSM
HUMILIATION

WHY SHOULD I ALLOW YOU TO BE MY SUBMISSIVE?

I need someone to teach me how to navigate my kinks. I'm too scared to tell anyone what I want for fear they'll think I'm crazy.

NOTES...

The sex was very aggressive and wild. Once Lorilee got past the fear of judgment, we did lots of scenes that bruised or cut the skin.

Typically, I accomplished this by using a single tail whip or paddle adorned with spikes measuring less than a millimeter, to elicit both a physical and auditory response of pleasure from her.

Definitely appealed to the sadist in me.

LYSSA

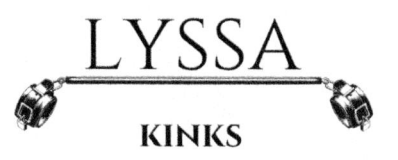

KINKS
BONDAGE
BREATH PLAY
PRAISE
ORGASM DENIAL

WHY SHOULD I ALLOW YOU TO BE MY SUBMISSIVE?
I need punishments for my crimes. Tame me and you can have all of me. Well, if I can have all of you.

NOTES...
Lyssa liked to think she could have it her way. During our first scene, I told her not to cum without my permission, but she did anyway, stating that it was hard for her to control her body and that she orgasms easily.

Well, since she was always so turned on, I cooled her way down by submerging most of her body in an ice bath, while she leaned toward the edge, and I face fucked her from outside the tub.

She couldn't get out until I came, furthering my point that the only person in this dynamic that may cum without permission is me.

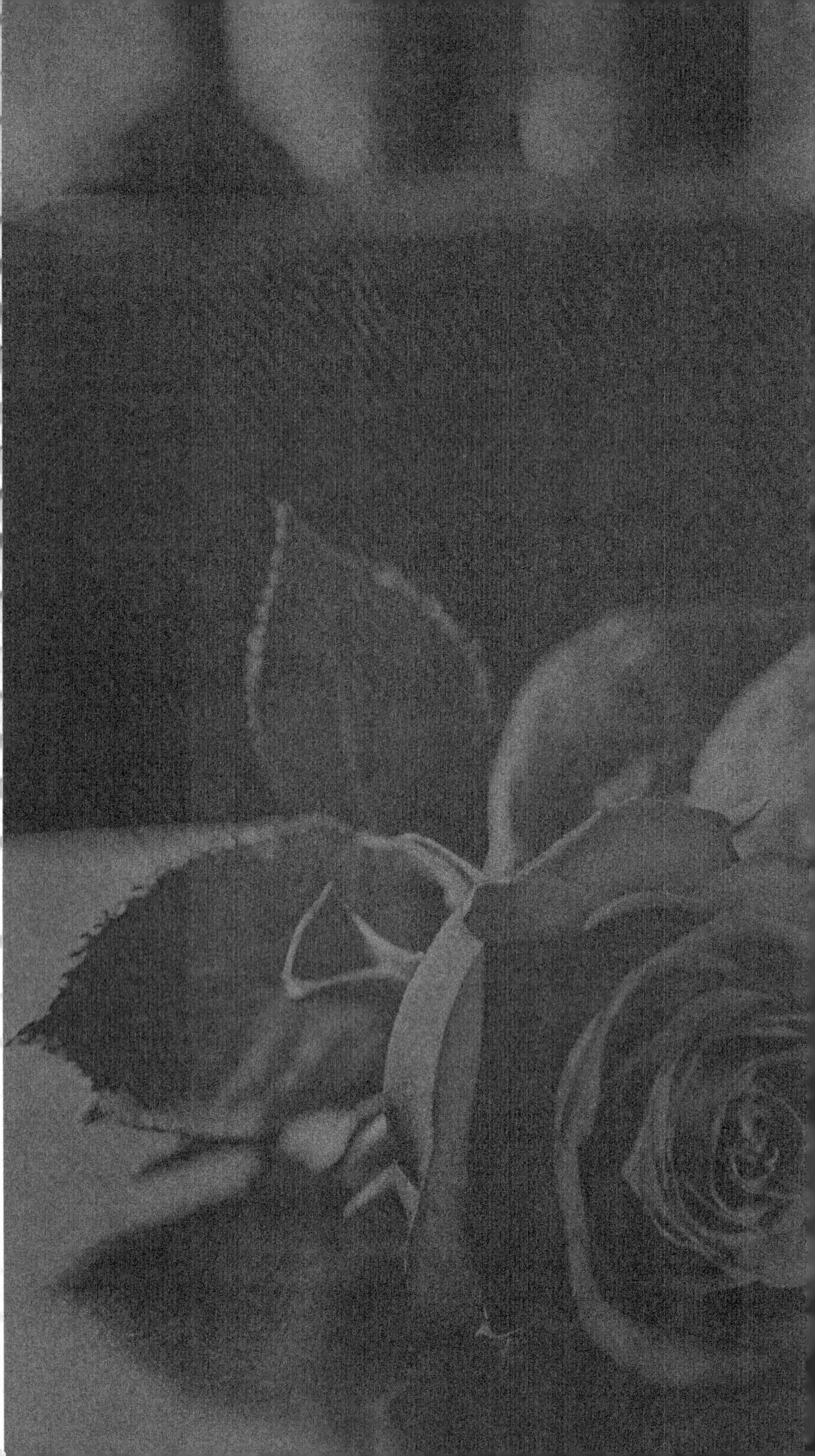

Chapter Twenty Two

"You're getting your nipples pierced today."

Latex breathing masks, blood play and ice bath punishments... wow.

Entries from Blaze's Little Black Book inhabited my dreams all night. I was nothing like most of those women, and yet I understood their compelling desire to please him. Blaze was a walking formula for disaster.

He was complex, edgy, dominant and so handsome and charming one couldn't help themselves and reading through his notes only solidified that belief.

Although I didn't get to read the entire thing, I did skim through it in search of one name in particular: his ex, Jasmine. I didn't find it, which meant, as I suspected, some people Blaze was not interested in sharing.

I picked up the book. Right as I was on the verge of indulging in a few more pages, Blaze entered the bedroom and said I needed to get ready for my appointment.

I got to my feet and dropped the book on the nightstand. "Appointment?" I said.

"Yeah, you're getting your nipples pierced today and Jag will be here in..." he checked his watch. "About ten minutes."

He said it so casually and nonchalantly, as if getting one's nipples pierced was the most ordinary thing in the world. I stared at him in disbelief, processing what he had just said.

"I'm getting my what? WHAT!?" I asked incredulously.

Blaze grabbed a pair of jeans from the drawer, then faced me.

"Based on your reaction, I think you heard me. Also, don't bother getting dressed," Blaze added. "You can keep your robe on."

"Umm, were you going to ask me if I wanted them pierced?"

"I am asking you right now," he said with a smile.

"No, you already made the appointment. Sounds like you have already decided for me."

Blaze pulled on his jeans, that fit him way too perfectly, and then went back to the dresser to grab a shirt.

With his back to me, he said, "Raquel, no matter what I come up with, you can always say no. The question is, do you want to?"

I stood there, watching those tatted muscular arms flex as he checked inside drawers, pulling out clothes to wear.

Eventually I turned away, facing the nightstand to consider this request. I couldn't think rationally while looking at that gorgeous man. If I did, my answer to everything would automatically be yes.

I laughed at myself, because I didn't need to physically see Blaze to want to surrender to him. The image of him in my mind would be just as persuasive.

Regardless, the question was, did I want my nipples pierced?

The only women I knew that had those piercings were Jada and Jocelyn. They seemed to like it, stating not only did it heighten their pleasurable sensations, but that their men loved it and the decision to do it was not one they regretted.

All great pointers for the pro list, but Jocelyn and Jada also agreed it was painful. A major con.

I didn't like pain.

Okay, that wasn't completely accurate. I had learned that I

enjoyed sexual pain, but anything outside of that I wasn't interested in.

So should I do it? I wondered again.

"What's it going to be?" Blaze asked, coming up behind me.

I was about to express my uncertainty, but then he slid his hands down through the top of my robe and massaged my breasts.

His touch was always so precise.

Delicate when it needed to be, but firm and most importantly, convincing when he wanted to make a statement and, with the way his fingers expertly kneaded my nipples, his point was being made.

"That feels good," I confessed, my head falling back onto his chest, my eyes closing.

After warming me up a bit, Blaze applied pressure to my nipples, twisting and squeezing them hard.

Sucking in a sharp breath, I moaned and my hips moved of their own volition. If it felt anything like this, I wanted in.

"I think you just decided," Blaze said, releasing me. "Let's go."

I shook off the sensual haze his touch induced and went to freshen up. Afterward, Blaze lead me from the bedroom to his office.

The first thing I noticed was that his desk was completely clear. All items that usually sat there, such as his computer, files, calendar, etc were on a nearby table. There was also a smaller empty table on the side of his desk.

The doorbell rang and Blaze went to answer it with, "Wait here," being his only instructions to me.

In less than a minute, he returned with a tall, attractive woman that made me think of a professional basketball player. She was shorter than Blaze but taller than me, so I figured she must have been around six feet.

The woman had honey brown skin and platinum colored hair that somehow looked natural and not strange, as one might presume. Her head showcased a striking contrast, with one side completely shaved and the other adorned with long, luscious waves cascading down.

There was a piercing in her nose, right brow and cheeks, where two deep dimples were located. To top it all off, she wore minimal makeup of lip gloss and eyeliner that made her long, full lashes stand out more.

Facing her, Blaze said, "Jag, this is my sub," then turning to me, he said. "This is Jag. She does all the tattoos for me and my team and will do your piercings today. She is a Dom, which means be respectful and only address her as mistress or madame."

Wow! She was not only a brilliant tattoo artist and ridiculously beautiful, she was a Dom, too. I loved this woman!

I extended my hand to Jag.

"It's nice to meet you, Madame."

Jag switched the orange case she was holding from her right hand to her left and shook my hand.

To Blaze, she said, "She is stunning. Do you share her?"

Blaze briefly studied me, and my stomach tightened.

Initially, I gave little thought to the sharing aspect of our agreement. However, now that I was no longer entertaining any delusions of a romance with Blaze, I was refocused and ready to do exactly what I'd set out to — broaden my sexual horizons and fully experience all it meant to be Blaze's sub.

Threesomes, orgies, one-on-one interactions. I wanted it all. I was sowing my wild oats, as my grandma would say. Therefore, when it happened, it happened.

But was it going to happen today?

"Eventually," he said to Jag. "She is very obedient, and a whore is meant to be used, after all."

Why were his dirty words so appealing to me?

I was learning fast what my kinks were, and it seemed, degradation, praise and floggings were my favorite. It was something about switching off my brain, tuning out the world and giving Blaze full control that relaxed me.

Usually during sex, I'd end up thinking about the laundry, shopping or my plans for the following week, but Blaze kept me engaged and so eager to be naughty.

Blaze and Jag continued their conversation, and I did exactly what was expected of me. Remained silent. It wasn't hard because they spoke as if I wasn't in the room, anyway.

I snapped back to attention when Jag asked, "Does she perform well in front of an audience?"

Blaze's gaze shifted to me, and his eyes filled with a mischievous glimmer, deciding something.

"Well, let's find out," he said.

Blaze took a seat near the office door. He then, unbuttoned and unzipped his jeans, before freeing his impressive length from its confines, and gesturing for me to come and take care of him.

I felt a surge of heat engulf me. Being watched would be a different and thrilling task, and I was up for the challenge.

Instinctually, I did the three things that Blaze had taught me before getting started.

First, without taking my eyes off him, I opened my robe. I was naked underneath, and Blaze was very visual.

Being able to glance down at my body while I was servicing him only excited him more. I would have completely removed the robe, but I still wasn't comfortable showing strangers my scars.

Next, I got down on my knees in front of him and placed my hands behind my back. My way of surrendering all of my control to him.

Last, I waited for his cue for me to begin. Blaze sometimes

liked to instruct me on how he wanted things and, apparently, today was one of those days.

"Make me cum fast," he ordered.

I smiled. "Yes, sir."

He glided my mouth down onto his dick, twisting his fingers in my hair and pushing or pulling as needed to direct how fast or slow he wanted it. I relaxed my throat, sucked hard when he pushed me lower and eased up as I neared the top, gliding my tongue over the tip hungrily.

I moaned and sucked, enjoying the feel and taste of him repeatedly sliding between my lips. Time seemed to fade away as I got lost in the pleasure I derived from getting him off. I didn't know how long I'd been at it, but suddenly the sweet taste of Blaze's release filled my mouth.

Swallowing fast, I drained every drop, savoring the taste, and a little sad that it was already over. However, there was no need to be disappointed. Blaze wasn't done with me yet.

"Fuuuuuccckkkk," he groaned in one of the sexiest voices I'd ever heard. "Keep going, I'm about to cum again."

Blaze pushed my head all the way down, forcing his entire length down my throat, and held me there. I didn't gag or resist. I was used to this.

When he removed his hand, I happily obliged his request, sucking him off fast and greedily.

"That's it whore, work that cum out of my dick."

I did my job, making him unload into my mouth a second time and not stopping until he removed his hand from my head and said, "That's enough of a treat for you. You'd suck my dick all night if I let you. Stand up."

I gave him a sultry grin, because he was absolutely right. I'd become pretty addicted when it came to giving Blaze blowjobs.

It was the sounds he made, his unique taste and the oddly

powerful way it made me feel to please a man as hypnotic and cutthroat as he was.

Licking my lips, I thanked him for allowing me to service him, got to my feet and awaited his next instructions.

"Oh, she is good," Jag said. "She would be the perfect gift for my male submissives when I want to reward them."

"I'll keep that in mind," Blaze responded, zipping up his jeans.

Setting up her tools on the empty table beside Blaze's desk, Jag signaled to him she was ready.

Blaze directed me to sit on top of the desk, facing him.

He sat in a chair directly in front of me, but rolled back to give Jag space to perform a quick examination to determine the ideal placement for the piercings.

Her eyes traveled over my breasts, down my stomach and stopped at my pussy, before she lifted an appreciative brow. Nonetheless, besides that brief gesture, she said nothing, keeping her mannerisms and choice of words professional.

"It could prolong the healing time, but do you want me to use numbing cream?" Jag asked.

I almost responded, but then remembered she was likely talking to Blaze and not to me.

Say yes, please say yes.

"No," Blaze said. I rolled my eyes. In my mind, of course.

Jag gave a curt nod and the powerful smell of antiseptic filled my nostrils as she wiped off both nipples, dotted them with a marker of sorts, and asked me to lie down. I deliberately avoided looking at her tray of piercing tools and kept my eyes on Blaze's smooth, extremely high ceilings.

She positioned herself on the opposite side of the desk and stood near my head. As I looked up, an upside-down version of Jag stared back at me.

"Keep your hands flat at your sides and don't move," she said. Glancing at Blaze, she added, "Tell me when."

I was unaware that Blaze had come back close to the desk until I felt his hands caress my thighs. It was such a pleasant feeling any time he touched me. Parting my legs, Blaze dragged his fingers over my pussy. After giving him oral earlier, I was already wet.

"You'll know when she's ready," he said to Jag.

Then, without warning, his tongue swept over my center and I sighed with pleasure.

How on earth was I supposed to remain still if he was eating me out while Jag was piercing my nipples?

You horrible... twisted... infuriating... His lips brushed across my clit. *Oh, so talented, asshole!*

I closed my eyes and struggled internally, willing my mind to focus all my strength on being still and not on how skilled he was.

But it was useless. Blaze was an expert at this. He found my most sensitive areas in no time and sucked it delicately, then aggressively, drawing circles and erotic mazes with his tongue all over it.

My hands itched to grab his head and force him deeper, but I resisted. However, once his fingers pressed into me, getting in on the action, I arched my back, practically shoving my breast in Jag's face since she was now hovering over me. She took that as her cue to begin.

I opened my eyes just in time to see her unwrap a sharp instrument, and that was when the most bizarre thing happened.

"Yes, please, Mistress," I cried out.

The involuntary urging escaped my lips so quick even I wasn't sure I'd said it.

It was official. I'd lost it. Blaze had pulled me over to the dark side. Less than an hour ago, I wasn't sure I wanted any part in this. Now I was begging for it?

What. The. Hell.

Blaze had proved to me time and time again that pleasure was intensified when pain was present, and not only did I want it. I sought it out.

Jag pushed the tiny tool through my nipple and it stung, but the jolt of pain felt from the initial entry only lasted a second or two, similar to a quick bite or pinch.

It may have been worse, but while she was adding pressure to my upper half, Blaze was simultaneously pleasuring my lower half.

He sucked harder on my clit and I sighed and moaned, not sure which of them were evoking which reaction.

I felt a light tugging and a cool sensation that wasn't really painful, and I imagined Jag was inserting the actual ring into my right nipple.

It would be simple to confirm this by opening my eyes, but I wasn't interested in watching her gloved hands bejewel my nipples. I was riding the wave of sensations and was already nearing my climax.

Jag moved on to my left nipple, gripping it firmly. Blaze stopped tasting me, but kept his fingers moving inside, rubbing up against what must have been my G-spot because it felt exquisite.

I heard his chair roll back and my eyes popped open.

Blaze was watching me.

"Do me a favor," he said to Jag, his gaze locked on mine. "Go slow with that one. I want her to feel every second."

I didn't have time to mentally curse him. I was too busy bracing myself for the pain that would run parallel to the sexual gratification.

Nevertheless, the Madame obliged, taking her time, pushing the point through. I sucked in a sharp breath and trembled, but my hands remained flat against the desk.

"Don't focus on what she's doing. Focus on what I'm doing," Blaze said.

And I tried. I swear I tried, but it hurt way worse this time around.

With his free hand, Blaze massaged my right inner thigh. It was an interesting trick that loosened the tiniest bit of the tension and eased some of the pain.

"What do good girls say?" Blaze prompted, as I gradually zoned back in on the phenomenal job his hands were doing.

"Thank you, sir," I said, my breathing heavy and short.

"And to Jag," he pushed.

"Thank... you, Madame," I said through clenched teeth.

I wasn't angry. Far from it. I was slipping into subspace again.

I could tell because talking had become difficult. My mind was reeling, and all the sensations were threatening to overpower me and cause a blackout. I didn't know whether to scream or sigh, to cry out in ecstasy or curse because of the pain.

"You're right," Jag said to Blaze. "She is very obedient."

Blaze didn't respond. His eyes were fixed on my chest, where I could still feel Jag pulling the sharp tool through. She was definitely taking her time.

"Do you like being treated this way?" Blaze suddenly asked.

I nodded.

"Use your words," he instructed.

It took a moment, but I understood he was gauging how far gone I was. Eventually I said, "Yes... yes, I do."

"Good. Are you close?"

"Yes, sir," I said in a rush.

"Hold it," Blaze ordered. "Do not cum until she says she is done. Are we understood?"

I opened my mouth. No sound. I opened it again. Nothing. Finally, a weak agreement tumbled free.

This was torture. Blaze tells me not to cum, Jag tells me not to move.

Were they trying to kill me?

With a seductive smirk on his lips, Blaze sat back down, and in an instant, he resumed passionately licking and sucking all over my pussy.

I had no idea he could swirl his tongue that fast.

Jag locked the second ring into place and finally said, "I'm done."

Which meant I was free, and I came so hard, Blaze had to tighten his grip on my thighs to keep me in place. However, my gracious Dom didn't stop. He kept feasting on me, producing multiple orgasms as I slipped further and further into bliss.

"That's it," Blaze encouraged, taking a quick pause. "Keep cumming for me."

Vaguely I noticed Jag collecting her things and exiting quietly, but the icing on the cake was when she switched off the lights and the room was bathed in darkness.

I lie on the desk panting, my legs spread wide, Blaze working his magic, but now I also noticed that my extravagant new nipple rings glowed in the dark.

Pretty, I thought, as everything went black.

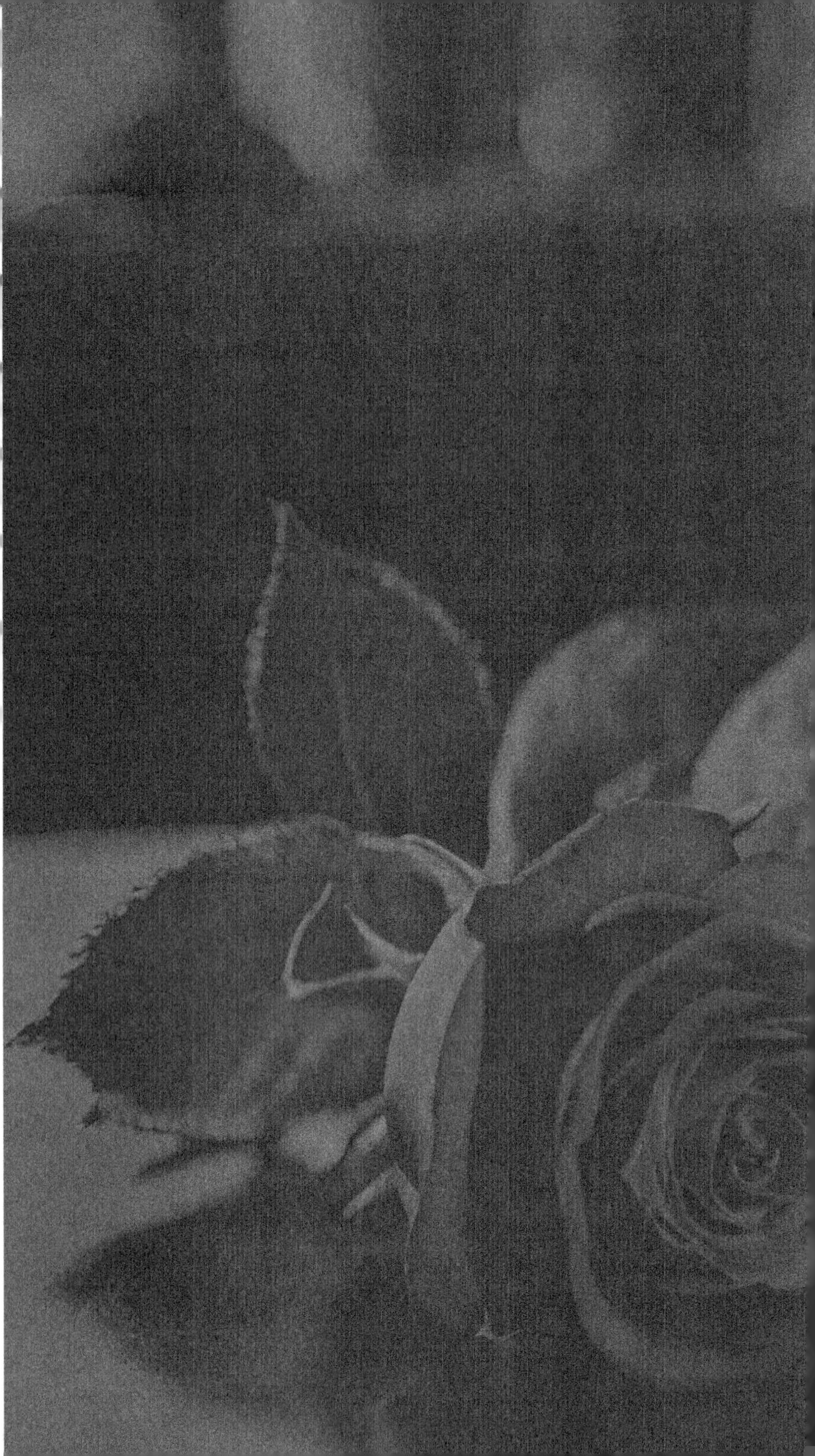

Chapter Twenty Three

"Hannah, are you flirting with me?"

I woke in a panic with a terrible headache.

There was blood all around my legs and this time it was not a dream.

I know because I pinched myself several times and not only did it hurt, the blood-covered sheets had not disappeared.

Where had the blood come from? Where was Blaze? Was he hurt? Was I?

I only remembered waking once from a nightmare about Loni and the accident before going back to sleep, but nothing after that.

Talking to Blaze about it the other day must have reignited the bad dreams, but there was no way the blood from my nightmare had seeped into my reality.

Jumping out of bed, logical thinking finally caught up to me.

It was my damn period.

Taking a second to put my heart back into my chest, I surveyed the mess and pulled off the sheets, only to experience a new wave of dread. I had ruined Blaze's bed!

Normally, all I would need to do was wash the sheets, because the mattress protector spared the actual bed, but last night we had an intense session and I once again squirted everywhere.

Blaze removed the mattress protector and sheets to clean them, but because I was so tired and couldn't wait for the protector to finish drying, he only put on fresh sheets and left the mattress protector off.

I glared at the large spot of blood. This was karma for lying to him that night at the wedding. I just knew it.

Rushing to the bathroom, I quickly showered, in the dark of course, because the light angered the throbbing in my head. Afterward, I returned to the bedroom, gathered the sheets, and tiptoed to the laundry room.

Blaze was home today, but he was in his office handling business. Hopefully, I could get back to the mattress and clean it up a little before I told him what happened.

Opening the lid to the washer, I tried to hurry, but I was moving a lot slower than intended. My head was pounding like two angry men from the stone age were having a rock fight.

I had just poured some bleach on the stain and dumped part of the sheet into the washer when the door opened.

"Hey," I said, glancing up, casually shoving the rest of it into the machine. "Done with your meeting already?"

The sudden movement slid the headache from behind my right eye to pounding behind the left.

Blaze leaned against the door frame. "I have another in an hour and then I have to go to the office for a bit. Why are you washing the sheets?"

"Just had a little accident," I said. "No biggie."

"Was the accident your period?"

I stopped.

"Does anything get by you?"

"If it did, you shouldn't feel safe here because I wouldn't be a very good protector, now would I?"

Blaze came over and pulled the sheet from the washer, the giant blood stain disgusting and embarrassing.

"I have a process for removing blood," he said.

A process for removing bloodstains? Exactly how much

blood would one need to remove before they develop a process?

I got ready to say something, but tossed up my hands instead. "You know what? I'm not even going to ask."

"You shouldn't," Blaze said with a laugh. Taking me by the shoulders, he turned me toward the laundry room door. "I'll take care of this. You go sit down."

I was almost out of the door when I froze.

"Umm, I hope your process works for mattresses, too," I said over my shoulder, revealing he had bigger problems.

"I'll take care of it," Blaze repeated. "Now go."

With a sense of ease, I walked towards the inviting couch and extended my legs, stretching them out across the entire expanse of it. As I settled in, I let my head sink back into one of the plump soft pillows, closing my eyes to fully immerse myself in relaxation.

This migraine was working me over big time.

"Hey," Blaze said a few minutes later.

I opened my eyes, and he was standing there with a cup of tea, a bottle of water and pain meds.

He put it down on the side table closest to me before sitting on the couch. I pulled my legs closer toward me to make room for him, but once he sat down, he took my legs and put them on his lap.

Then the man completely shocked me by massaging my feet.

"I feel like I'm in the twilight zone," I said.

This was weird. No guy I'd ever dated had pampered me during my period and the fact that I wasn't romantically involved with Blaze made it even stranger.

"With the way this case is going, I feel like I'm right there with you."

We were talking about two different things, but it didn't matter. I took the medicine and almost drank the entire bottle of water. The tea smelled of lavender and citrus, making me feel cozy.

"How does this feel?" Blaze said, his finger pressing into the soles of my feet.

"Heavenly," I replied. "Am I in trouble and this is some evil trap?"

"If you were in trouble, you'd know it."

I sighed blissfully. "I don't think even one of my boyfriends has ever massaged my feet before."

Blaze kept carefully kneading his fingers into my foot.

"Good thing I am your Dom and not your boyfriend."

"True," I replied. "You wouldn't make a good boyfriend, anyway."

That made him stop.

"Really?" Blaze asked, one brow lifted.

I smiled. "It's nothing bad. I mean, don't get me wrong, you're great. Perfect even. But you are a one-man army. Some people do better alone and others need companionship, that's all."

"I need companionship," Blaze said.

I looked at him suspiciously. "I'm not talking about sexual companionship."

"Oh well, count me out."

We shared a laugh, and I leaned back again. "This headache is threatening to split my head in half. You got any cool stories to keep my mind busy?"

Picking up the tea, I took a long sip while Blaze considered what to share.

"I once got into the world's smallest car," he stated, landing on something that instantly spiked my attention.

"A beetle?" I asked.

"No. It's called The Peel P50, and it is definitely smaller than a beetle."

"Wow!" I said, glancing at his long legs. "How did you manage that?"

"Painfully," Blaze responded, seeming to relive the moment.

I giggled. "Okay, I have a better question. Why would you do that?"

"The team dared me and I had to do it. I couldn't let them down."

I couldn't stop laughing, as I imagined Blaze getting into a car that looked like a toy next to him. "The Peel, huh?" I said.

"Yes, and the name was fitting because they almost had to peel it off me."

As Blaze continued sharing more torturous details of his time in the world's smallest car, we both couldn't help but laugh until, finally, the medicine took effect and I drifted off into a deep sleep.

I heard a quiet humming and sat up. Thank God my headache was gone.

Bless you, Blaze.

Glancing toward the kitchen, I spotted Hannah at the table. She was flipping through a magazine and once she saw me, she stopped humming.

"Oh, I'm sorry, did I wake you?"

"No," I said, getting off the couch and joining her at the table. "It was nice, actually. I thought Jolli was my babysitter today."

Hannah chuckled. "He was, but Blaze asked if I could switch with him. He said you might prefer feminine energy today. Whatever that means."

I shook my head. "It's that time of the month," I said.

Hannah closed her magazine with extreme animation.

"Well, I guess we better get to male bashing then. Wouldn't want to disappoint."

I laughed and felt totally at peace. Blaze's team was so down-to-earth. I see why he loved them, would die for them, and trusted them with his life.

"Oh," Hannah said, suddenly remembering something. "Jolli claims he wants a rematch because you lied to him about not being good at race car games."

"I didn't lie." I said, smiling. "Jolli never accepts when he loses."

"And he never will," Hannah added. "He is still losing to Axel over cooking challenges, but keeps requesting a rematch. It's his way of keeping us all on our toes."

"Gotta love him for it," I said.

"Yeah, Jolli is the best. He is the heart of this team and a much needed light in this dark world."

I agreed. Jolli was everyone's reminder to find happiness and positivity, even in the toughest of times. His unwavering optimism and ability to uplift others made him truly irreplaceable and loved by all.

"Hannah," I said, turning the conversation more serious, "I never got the chance to thank you that day when they bumrushed us. You saved my life."

"It was nothing. I'd do it again in a heartbeat."

"Well, I hope you won't ever have to."

Hannah looked appalled. "Where's the fun in that? I like a good fight."

"I bet you do. You're good at it."

"I'm good at most things," she said with a wink.

Not wanting to read anything into that statement, I got up from the table and went to make myself another cup of tea.

"The only people I can handle in fist fights are schoolyard bullies. Anything beyond that and my ass is grass."

"Don't worry, I can protect your ass," Hannah said.

I added the water and tea bag to my mug and faced her. She was watching me with an interesting expression on her face.

"Hannah, are you flirting with me?"

She laughed and opened the magazine again.

"Chica, I'm always flirting. It's part of my Colombian charm. Don't pay me any attention, but I could teach you some defense moves if you'd like."

"Yeah, I would appreciate that," I said absently, and even though I meant it, my mind was back on the statement about not paying her any attention.

That was the problem.

She now had my attention and my mind was vividly recalling her on her knees, pleasing me at Blaze's demand. Rejoining her at the table, I put my mug down.

"Did you want any tea?" I asked.

"No, I'm good."

Hannah's eyes continued to scan the page. It was a magazine about classic cars. The title above the one she was looking at was Muscle cars of the 60s.

I wanted to talk to her about that day in my apartment, her time as Blaze's sub and what ended it, but I wasn't sure how to bring it up.

"You were right about being good at most things," I said, going out on a limb.

"It's true I am," Hannah replied, still engrossed in the article.

"I'm talking about a more specific thing," I replied.

Hannah glanced up, her brow lifting. "What thing would that be?"

"Umm, the thing Blaze asked you to do," I said, mentally willing her to take the hint.

Hannah stared at me, silent for a few seconds, but then she suddenly smiled.

"Oh, you're adorable," she announced, sitting back in her chair and folding her arms.

With that uniform, the identical tattoo on her arm that all the team members shared, and the confidence she eluded, Hannah reminded me of the female version of Blaze. And then she spoke, confirming it.

"I ate your pussy like it was my last meal. Could even smell and taste you for hours after it was over and you can't even say it."

I fanned myself. "That was very descriptive."

"Does that make you uncomfortable, princess?" Hannah said with a grin.

I narrowed my eyes at her. "Not you, too!"

She laughed. "I couldn't help it. Don't worry, it's only a nickname we made up for you. It's all in good fun. We mean no harm."

"We?"

"Just the team, not people at Vex."

"I hate that nickname."

"Why?" Hannah asked.

"It makes me sound so delicate, sweet, and a little naive."

"Raquel," Hannah said directly. "You are delicate and sweet, but I wouldn't call you naive. I think you are looking at it the wrong way. Nowadays, everyone is so damaged and broken, it's nice to know women like you still exist. You're strong, confident, and smart, but you're also soft and humble. The world hasn't ruined you."

I considered Hannah's perspective.

"I guess I only saw it in a negative way."

"You shouldn't. It was the reason why, when Blaze asked if

I would go down on the princess, I agreed. I'd never done anything with a woman and I wanted to see you squirm and what was beneath the surface. You are always so put together and polished."

"Ha! I'm anything but put together," I said.

"Trust me. You're doing great. I've watched people who have gone through much less fall apart a lot easier."

"Well, thanks, but I hope I seem less polished and more relatable to you now."

"Of course," Hannah stated. "Us subs have to stick together. You just needed someone like Blaze to make you feel safe enough to open up, and I'm so glad you let me be a part of it."

Her accent became extremely noticeable toward the end of that sentence. Yup, Hannah was definitely flirting again.

"It was nice," I admitted. "It's hard to believe you have never done anything with a woman before. You've got skills, girl, and you're gorgeous."

"Says the model," Hannah countered.

"Yeah, but you would put a lot of the models I've worked with to shame. You're not only tall, with a nice body and attractive face, you have this tough, sexy edge. Now, that belongs on a cover."

"All facts," Hannah responded confidently, "But that's not my world."

"It's no longer mine either," I said in a low voice. Getting back to all the nosey questions I had, I said, "So Blaze asked you to go down on me and you just went with it?"

"Pretty much," Hannah replied.

That was a wild thought.

"No pushback? Hesitation? Or anything?" I prodded.

"None at all. He *was* my Dom, he *is* my boss and I respect him. If he asks me to do something, I do it."

This had me fascinated. I mean, I was pretty much the

same way when it came to Blaze, but I had to understand it from someone else's point of view. What hold did this man have?

"That's my point though," I continued. "He's not your Dom anymore, so how does that work? Is it like he has lifetime rights to order you around?"

Hannah laughed.

"No one orders me around. I do what I want, when I want. But I see you have a lot of questions and I am happy to answer them all. I was once in your shoes."

"Thank you," I said, relieved that my questions weren't bothersome.

Hannah sat forward. "This is how it works. Since Blaze is no longer my Dom, if he wants me to do something sexual, then out of respect he asks my current Dom, Vile, if he can borrow me. If Vile will allow it, then he asks me. At any time I can obviously say that I am too uncomfortable and everything stops there, but I wouldn't deny a request from either of my Doms, past or present."

"Vile?" I said, needing a second to highlight that little detail.

Hannah nodded cooly and, with a dirty grin, said, "He lives up to the name."

"I will not ask," I said, moving on. "But why wouldn't you deny a request?"

"I live this lifestyle to give up control and I'm a daredevil. Blaze shared me and Vile shares me, and I love it. Fucking a room full of men is not only hot, but a major stress reliever for me. In my opinion, running scared at every wild request would be boring."

She made a good point. A major factor that added excitement to being a sub was the act of obeying demands and relinquishing control.

"How many Doms have you had?" I asked.

"Only two, Blaze and Vile, but I am very selective with who I give that type of power to."

That hit home with me. The Dom/sub dynamic was a very thrilling, yet risky, idea to me in the beginning. Even though I gave it a try, I sometimes wondered what stops a Dom from going too far.

"When you first became a sub, were you ever afraid that being so free could lead to a guy abusing that type of control over you?"

"You mean with Blaze?!" she asked as if the question was insane.

"Not necessarily Blaze, but in general, with any Dom."

"I never knew anything about BDSM before Blaze, but I will say this, he would never, ever abuse a woman. If she isn't into it, then neither is he. He may be a sadist, but he is not evil, and trust me, I know evil. He was my stepfather."

Uncertainty filled me. I was hesitant to ask anything else, because it occurred to me that the trauma she dealt with at the hands of her stepfather may have been a contributing factor to why her agreement ended with Blaze.

"I'm sorry to hear that," I said empathetically.

"It's no problem. He's dead now."

She said it so casually that one troubling thought came to mind.

"No, I didn't kill him," she said, reading my thoughts. "Wish I had, though. It would have been slow and painful."

Hannah grinned, rubbing her hands together.

No comment was suitable for a statement like that, so instead I said, "How on earth are you a submissive?"

Hannah shrugged.

"While it's true that I feel more comfortable with a gun than in a gown. I love being dominated in the bedroom," she gave an expression of pure pleasure. "That's my jam."

I nodded in agreement, and then Hannah eyed me.

"You want to know about my time with Blaze?"

"More than I want to take my next breath," I said desperately.

I took another sip of tea and pulled my chair up closer to the table.

Story time.

"It was fun, *real* fun," Hannah admitted. "Blaze is aggressive, passionate and someone I look up to. He showed me parts of myself that I never knew existed and helped me to be stronger in every area of my life. I will forever be grateful because he wasn't just a good Dom, but an excellent friend."

"What were some of your favorite experiences?"

"Let's see," Hannah said, tapping her chin. "There was that time I was being a brat at this party and Blaze dragged me into the bathroom, pinned me against the wall and fucked me so hard I had to lean on him to get around the rest of the night. Or the time he gave me a delightful massaged with a magnificent body butter before flogging me."

Hannah seemed to remember that one fondly. She laughed, paused, shook her head, then laughed again.

"That sounds nice," I said.

"It was painful as hell," Hannah confessed. "The body butter contained peppermint oil, and he used a flog with the stiff leather strips. So before the first hit, my skin was already sensitive and tingling, with a cooling sensation."

"I misspoke. That wasn't nice at all," I said.

"It was exciting, though. I screamed, cried and came so many times that night."

"Alright, what was the scariest thing he ordered you to do as a sub?"

Hannah thought about it. "That would have to be the first time he shared me. I was left to get screwed every which way by a room full of strangers."

My mouth fell open.

A room full? Could I handle that?

I was game for one, maybe even two, but a room full?

"How many guys was that?"

"Ten," Hannah said without hesitation.

Shit!

I better do some squats and learn to fit more than one hotdog in my mouth at a time.

"Where did it happen?" I asked.

"At Gated Domination, it's the BDSM club Blaze and Vile are members of. They are big on discretion and safety, so you don't have to worry about stuff like that. My biggest issue was my nerves in the beginning. If I failed to get all the men off, I got punished."

"Did you ever fail?"

"A few times," she said. "And as punishment, I might get a serious flogging, or Blaze would hog tie me and edge me until I was crying and begging to cum. Then once I came, he would keep going until I was crying and begging him to stop."

"And he didn't?" I asked.

If my eyes got any wider, they would eject from my head.

"No, because I refused to use my safe word. I'd rather pass out first, which I often did."

"And you didn't run away screaming?"

Hannah leaned in, rested her elbows on the table and grinned provocatively.

"Never. I loved that shit. And the next time Blaze sent me back, I made sure every guy came twice."

Wow!

I wondered what would happen to me when I failed. Because I most certainly would fail. I moved on to something else. I'd fear that experience once I faced it.

"It sounds like you and Blaze worked well together as Dom and sub. What ended things?"

"My stupidity," Hannah said, her eyes shifting from mine to stare at the wall behind me. "I tried to fight him."

"You're kidding, right!"

"Nope," Hannah said. "And I'm not talking about a slap or a few love taps. I don't do those. I tried to beat his ass, even landed a punch or two because he was trying to take it easy on me."

I made a sound that fell somewhere between a gasp and a laugh. Astonished at this.

"What did he do to make you so angry?"

"That's the thing. It was nothing serious. Blaze simply tried to tell me that this guy I knew was bad news and that I should leave him alone and I don't know," she said, as if unclear. "It reminded me of my stepfather and all his rules. Rules that he used to isolate me so that he could get into my bed every night."

Hannah paused and said what sounded like "Ese maricón" under her breath before pushing on. "Point is, when Blaze said that to me, it's like I transported back to my childhood and I could now fight the monster."

"Oh, Hannah," I said, genuinely heartbroken for her. "I am so sorry."

She gave me a weak smile and waved a hand. "Forget about it. Turns out Blaze was right about the guy, anyway."

"And that was where you called it quits."

Hannah's gaze remained locked onto the wall behind me. I didn't know if opening up like this was hard for her, but I wholeheartedly appreciated it.

"No, Blaze ended it. I still wanted to be his submissive, but he wouldn't hear of it. However, he did give me one last punishment for my blatant disrespect, and I accepted it."

"What was it?"

"To see a therapist. He wanted me to heal, and it took a while, but eventually I did. He even expected weekly progress reports and talked me through the rough patches." Hannah's eyes shifted back to me then. "Like I said, I have nothing but respect for Blaze. If he asks, I'll do it and he'd never abuse that."

I let what she said sink in. It all fit who I understood Blaze to be, and I felt just as willing to do anything he asked as well.

"I'm glad he has you," Hannah said. "We all worry about Blaze finding someone that he is willing to have a deeper relationship with. I know he is terrified of getting too close out of fear that he will put someone in harm's way, but he should get past that."

"He lives a dangerous life, so his reservations make sense, but there is nothing between Blaze and me. I am just passing through, but I hope with all my heart he meets the woman for him."

Hannah tilted her head. "But it isn't you?"

I answered honestly. "No."

"I wouldn't be so sure about that," she said.

I wouldn't debate this. Besides, I needed to eat and start work. With a smile, I said to Hannah, "Are you hungry?"

"Mmm," Hannah said, licking her lips, "I could always eat."

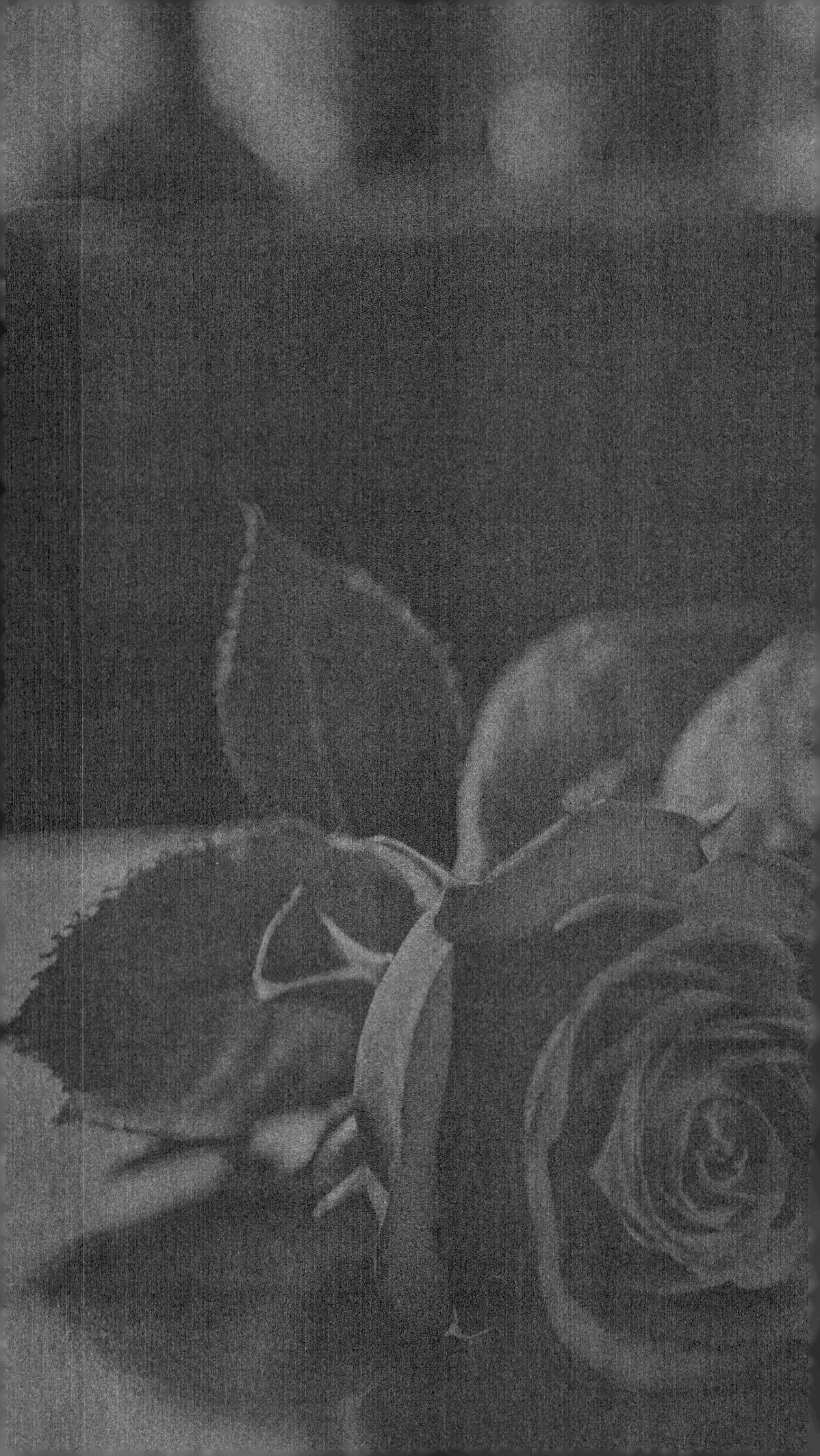

Chapter Twenty Four

"She breasted boobily away."

Excited, intrigued, tense and terrified.

Yup, that just about covered all the emotions I was experiencing at this very moment, and by the end of the evening, I think there will be a lot more added to the list.

Currently, I was in the passenger seat, sitting on one hand, with the other tightly clutching the door, while Blaze drove us in silence to a club.

No correction, not *a* club, *the* club. Gated Domination. The BDSM club where Blaze was a member, shared his subs, and Hannah had been countless times.

I didn't have the guts to ask him if he was going to share me tonight. I didn't want to know. Let it be a hot or horrific surprise, depending on the outcome.

Blaze looked over and smiled at me.

Yup, I was fucked... and I was getting fucked. Who would be the lucky guy, or guys, had yet to be determined.

Per Blaze's request, I was only wearing two things: heels and one of his white, button down business shirts. No underwear, no bra and no idea when the shirt would be taken out of the equation.

Blaze said my long legs looked perfect, peeking out from underneath his shirt, which stopped slightly above my knees. He'd also instructed me to leave the three top buttons undone.

The shirt only had seven buttons, so although you

couldn't officially see anything, If I sneezed too hard, I'd end up in my birthday suit.

When Blaze had walked into the living room an hour ago. I'd been reviewing my twentieth briefing for the day with a fine-tooth comb and drawing my usual blank. I was going stir crazy and needing something more riveting than reading and re-reading conversations.

One look at the smile on Blaze's face and I knew he'd gotten a major lead.

There had been an entire week of no new gang activity, updates from the surveillance team, or Blazes' contacts. It felt like we had been spinning our wheels, but finally there was a break.

"I'm about to meet with Zac Littleton, he's an undercover agent and has some information that may point us to where Trenton has been hiding out. Do you want to come with me?"

"Yes," I'd said, jumping to my feet.

I had unintentionally walked into a trap, and since Blaze never missed an opportunity, we would indulge in some playfulness once his business was concluded.

So here I was waiting for my next step in sub training. Open to all the possibilities while freaking out on the inside.

"You good?" Blaze asked, pulling my attention from staring out the window into the dark night.

"Yeah, I'm fine. Why wouldn't I be?"

"I want to make sure you know that your safety isn't compromised by being out."

If he was picking up on any apprehension, it was about how this night would unfold and nothing else. I released my grip on the door and faced him.

"Blaze, if there is one thing I know you do well, it's your job. I'm not worried." I turned away, but then had a thought. "Just out of curiosity, how many trucks are following us?"

Blaze laughed.

"You are learning how I operate. I like that. There is only one behind us and Axel is in it. Jolli is ahead of us, and do you see them out there?" He nodded out the window.

It was dark so I couldn't see anything. Therefore, unless he was referencing the trees as people, I was at a loss.

"I don't see anything," I said.

"Exactly," he replied. "I have snipers hidden strategically throughout the woods from my house up to the club. In case we encounter any trouble on the road."

Wow.

"That's taking every precaution," I said, a bit stunned. "There are really snipers out there?" I squinted, straining my eyes in the darkness, even though I knew I wouldn't see a damn thing.

"Yup," Blaze confirmed. "Also, the club is only fifteen minutes away and I take all deserted roads, so we're good."

Blaze was a crafty one, always one step ahead when it came to safety measures.

"Do the agents know you are using their resources?" I asked, replaying the last conversation I heard between Swanson and Blaze a couple of days ago.

The agents expressed their desire for him to seek their authorization before carrying out any actions related to the case, but Blaze firmly rejected the request, asserting that he did not get involved with how they did their jobs and expected to be treated with the same level of respect.

"It's not their resources. Those snipers are on my payroll," Blaze said.

"Damn, do you have an entire army, too?" I asked, astonished.

"Just about," he replied.

Blaze preferred to remain in charge, which made sense because he was so good at it.

Listening to him talk about snipers, demands, and safety

routes really up my sex drive. I was beginning to wonder if I had a danger kink.

Was that even a thing?

I didn't want to be in danger, I just got massively turned on by knowing Blaze fearlessly faced it every day.

We arrived at a huge medieval castle-looking building, out in the middle of nowhere.

Blaze said that Jolli was already there, and that Axel was pulling in, but I didn't see them, which I assumed was the point.

We walked to the front door, and I kept glancing down at my shirt, wondering if Blaze would notice if I closed at least one of these buttons.

No one could see any of my most private areas, but still I was barely leaving anything to the imagination.

Blaze pressed a button that looked like a doorbell and a voice came over the speaker and said, "Your name, please."

"Sir Blaze," my alluring Dom responded.

I got chills.

The door made a buzzing noise, and we were in.

Blaze guided me down a long red hallway that had elegant art drawings of people in all sorts of submissive positions — on their knees, in the air, against a wall. It was very intriguing.

Each drawing was skillfully crafted, capturing the raw emotions and intricate details of the human form. The hallway invited curiosity and contemplation, drawing me further into its enigmatic allure. Blaze placed a hand on my lower back, guiding me further down the hall of exploration.

At the end of the hallway, we made a left and Blaze led me through double doors filled with people.

The focal point of the room was a bar area where a few men and women sat having drinks, while their subs lie on the floor licking their feet.

Well, I'd just found one kink I wasn't into.

Leading us around the bar area, we arrived at a long couch where a guy sat, watching two naked women touching and kissing each other.

When he spotted us, he said, "Alright, you two go find someone else to play with. I have work to do."

Both women kissed him on the cheek and he slapped one of them on the ass before she left. Her breasts bounced around so dramatically I had to hold back a laugh, because I recalled some crass satire about men describing women's breast movements.

They would say "She breasted boobily away."

In this case, they would be right. If ever there was an image to go with that description, it was the girl who'd just left. Those breasts had gone rogue, as one went left and the other went right, making up their own rules.

Zac, I presumed, stood and shook hands with Blaze.

"Thank you for meeting me on such short notice," Zac said. "I think you are really going to want to hear this."

He sounded like he was from Australia, a place I'd been to several times and really enjoyed. Zac was around five feet, nine inches, slim with short cropped sandy brown hair.

"No problem," Blaze said.

Zac turned his attention to me, his eyes doing exactly what I expected, scanning me from head to toe, pausing in all the appropriate places. The shirt wasn't see through, but I imagined Zac could see thorough it just fine.

"Who is this?" Zac finally asked.

"This is my sub," Blaze said, turning to me. "She is going to wait for me at the bar while we talk."

I lifted a brow and smiled. "Yes, sir," I said and made myself scarce.

I'd hoped I could stay and listen to the details, but I wasn't privy to that. Blaze did share information with me, but it was what he deemed relevant and necessary.

Taking the last seat in the corner, I avoided eye contact with anyone at the bar and instead took in the activity around the room.

Subs were on their hands and knees, being led around by their Doms on leashes.

Some were taken to cages and others were used as furniture, with their backs serving as a convenient surface for dominants to rest their drinks and food upon.

This truly captivated me. I didn't want to be furniture or locked in a cage, but seeing others so freely commit to it was like watching a horror scene that you couldn't bring yourself to look away from.

I continued to be awestruck with all that I saw happening around the room, but suddenly I noticed an older guy with a bad toupee and a weird expression ogling me hard.

Without thinking, I shifted in my seat, closing up one of the shirt buttons. I didn't have a problem with being almost nude, but this was my way of saying, "Look elsewhere, buddy. There is nothing to see here."

I'd become aware of Blaze and Zac approaching from behind solely because of Blaze. Whenever he was near, my senses perked up and even if I couldn't see him, I could feel him.

Spinning around in my seat, I faced them.

"It's time to move on to the more festive part of the evening," Blaze said with his signature dirty grin.

Zac's eyes raked over me for the second time that night.

"Alright," Zac said to Blaze as if he'd just decided something important. "I have to know. Do you share her? Because I would love to have her for the evening."

I stopped breathing. Wondering what Blaze would say. If ever there was a perfect time to start this, it was now.

But was I ready?

Turns out it didn't matter because Blaze was.

"You're the second person to ask me that. And I think it's time." Blaze shifted toward Zac. "Tell you what. I'll have her ready for you in the service room in ten minutes."

The service room?

"I'll be there," Zac said and exited the room we were in.

And there was my answer. Tonight was the night.

Okay, I thought. *No problem. Zac is cute. This is going to be fun, really fun.*

Blaze maneuvered me through twists and turns that led me to a room with his name on it.

We entered, and I did what I had been doing all night, inspected my surroundings.

The room was standard size. There was a bed, a couch, a table and a huge treasure chest type box.

Its polished mahogany exterior hinted at the mysterious contents within, and I imagined it was some array of the same kinky toys Blaze had at home.

"Nice room," I said.

It was the first words I'd spoken since we left the room with Zac.

Zac... I tried to put him out of my mind, which was ridiculous because soon he would access parts of me much more tangible than my mind.

But something was wrong. Very wrong.

I thought that I'd welcome being with another guy, experiencing more than just Blaze's version of sex, but something was off. Somehow, it seemed wrong to be touched by any man but him.

Which was absurd, because Blaze was not mine and I most

certainly was not his.

"Thanks," Blaze said in response to my comment about the room, but I think we were both just being polite, filling the charged silence between us.

Didn't he feel something was off?

Blaze went to grab a box off the table and opened it. Inside were two things: a blindfold and a gold necklace. The necklace held a small, red charm with the word "owned" engraved on it.

"Turn around," he said.

I complied, lifting my hair, and Blaze placed the necklace on me.

As the light metal touched my skin, I couldn't help but feel a shiver run down my spine.

"Wearing this lets the members of the club know you are a new sub and that you belong to someone. That way, if you do something considered disrespectful, you will be warned before being punished for it."

He fastened the necklace in place and turned me around to face him.

"From now on, I want you to always wear this. When you are in public, I will allow you to tuck it underneath your shirt, but while you are mine, this does not leave your neck. Do you understand?"

I looked up into his eyes, melancholy washing over me, as I suddenly understood what was wrong. I loved him.

Not just in the friendly way I'd convinced myself of, but head over heels, wanted no one else, and could imagine spending the rest of my life with him, type of love.

Fuck! Fuck! Fuck!

This hurt so bad, because I was just another sub to him.

And whose fault is that?

Blaze told me from the start that this wouldn't be love. Training me to be his submissive was only a fun hobby until he moved on to the next.

He'd said that he never had a connection to any of the women he dominated and that he never wanted to keep them, and what I thought I'd understood, accepted and moved past was that his words also applied to me.

But I hadn't understood at all. I wanted to be special. I wanted the man I loved to see that there was no one for him but me.

"I understand," I finally said, my voice confident and steady, revealing none of the hurt, devastation or brokenness I felt inside.

Blaze gently rubbed his knuckles down my cheek.

"Good girl," he replied. "Oh, and one more thing." He pulled a switchblade from his pocket and flipped the knife free. "Did you think I wouldn't notice you buttoned up the shirt?"

"I...uh..."

"Don't speak," Blaze warned me. He held the knife at the first button and sliced it off, then moved on to the second and did the same.

"I don't want any excuses," Blaze said, cutting off the third button. "You are always expected to do what...," fourth button. "You...," fifth button. "Are...," sixth button. "Told." And there went the last one.

The shirt fell open, and I looked down at my naked body. My nipple rings giving off a soft glow because, with Blaze standing this close, he was casting a shadow over me.

I was officially going to be on display for everyone in the club to see and with my heart in shambles, I couldn't care less.

Besides, objecting to this might make Blaze tell me to lose the shirt altogether and then the scars on my back would be exposed. My broken heart was in enough pain. I didn't need to add to it and I would not give Blaze the satisfaction.

"You will once you realize I am not the man to fall in love with. They all do."

The response Blaze had given me when I asked him what happens if I never grew tired of being his submissive sounded off in my mind.

Tonight, would mark the beginning of the end of us.

And while I could say no to being shared, it wouldn't matter. I needed to move on at some point. Who knows, maybe sleeping with Zac was exactly what I needed to get the ball rolling.

"I'm ready whenever you are, sir," I said, with my shoulder's back and chin held high.

Blaze stared at me intently before flipping the blade closed and pushing it back into his pocket. "Let's go," he ordered. Then, referencing our conversation about how easily he detached from his subs, he added, "It's time for you to leave the nest."

The service room was enormous and round. It held at least double the amount of people than the first room, and they were definitely engaging is some very lewd behavior.

Lavish couches filled the space, hugging the wall of the circular room on two levels, giving it an odd stadium seating effect.

But then when I noticed the bed in the middle of the room, sitting on a stage lit up by spotlights, I understood the reason for the design.

The room was setup so that people could watch the show, while possibly creating a mini version of their own in the stands.

A raw, carnal energy pulsated through the room as moans

and whispers filled the air, intermingling with the seductive music that played in the background.

Anal sex, oral sex and aggressive sex were unfolding all around me between the salacious guests. Those that didn't have anyone were watching those around them and, I guessed, possibly waiting for the show.

That's when I noticed that quite a few people were staring over at me. Several sets of eyes were locked on my body and my face, and amongst those eyeballing me was Zac.

He was sitting alone on a couch on the first level. Watching me. Waiting for me.

"This is where I leave you," Blaze said. "Remain standing here until Zac comes to get you."

I nodded.

Blaze left my side, and I thought he'd left the room, but then everything went dark as he covered my eyes. I suddenly remembered the blindfold he'd tucked into his pocket.

"This should make it easier for your first time," Blaze said. "Remember, don't think just obey. I expect a good report. So, make me proud."

Moments later, I heard the door close behind me as Blaze, the man I loved, threw me to the wolves.

Filled with every emotion under the sun, I put my hands together, unsure of what to do, how to stand, or what to think.

I reminded myself of the original giddiness I had when I started this arrangement with Blaze. I wanted to experience what it felt like to be sexually free, and I would need to hold on to that feeling right now.

It didn't take long before I felt someone gently pull my hand. I jumped.

"It's alright. It's alright," the man said in a soothing voice.

It was Zac. I recognized his Australian accent and, with my eyes covered, it was even more pronounced.

He stroked my face and even though my eyes were covered; I closed them, already comparing the stark difference between his and Blaze's touch.

"You are so fucking hot," Zac said.

He took both of my hands and placed them on one of his arms. "Hold on to me. I'll guide you to where we are going."

We hadn't walked far before Zac stopped us, and using my shoulders, he shifted me in the direction in which he wanted me and I imagined I was facing the couch I saw him sitting on before Blaze put on the blindfold.

"I want you on your knees," he said, keeping hold of my shoulders to press me down.

Once I was on the floor, I heard what sounded like Zac adjusting on the couch, and then he reached forward and guided me to him.

Automatically, I placed my hands behind my back, certain that if he wanted me to do something different from what Blaze had taught me, he would say so.

At this point, I was numb and merely going through the motions.

Part of me wanted to do this with Zac. It was a change of pace and actually exciting to be used by someone else.

However, the other part of me wanted to go home, not Blaze's home, but my own. Where I could crawl into bed and try to remedy my broken heart with ice cream.

When I felt Zac's dick brush against my lips, I knew he was ready to get started.

Concentrating on the task and not the man, I took him into my mouth. My rhythm was steady in the beginning as I got a feel for him, kissing his dick and running my tongue over the head.

Zac's dick pulsated, which meant he liked it, so I did it a few more times, teasing him and tasting his pre cum before getting into some heavier action.

With my eyes covered, I found it easier to get lost in the sensation of pleasing him and tune out everything else — The music, the people that were definitely watching, and even the fact that he wasn't Blaze, everything.

In addition, I couldn't help but notice that his touch was noticeably gentler than what I was used to, more affectionate in some way, like he wanted me to feel safe. That was a gesture I appreciated.

I worked hard to make it good for him, transporting myself back to all the times I'd been on my knees for Blaze, sucking him fast, deep and practically begging for his release.

Zac tasted good. I'd give him that. He had me craving his cum and using all of my skills to get him there and once he finally exploded into my mouth; I swallowed all of it.

In that moment, one thing became very clear — I truly enjoyed embracing my submissive side and, in due time, I would hopefully find one special man to submit to, but not right now.

For now, I would continue living out my sexual fantasies while giving my heart time to heal. I'd had sex without love before, certainly I could do it again.

I was still blindfolded with my hands behind my back, but I didn't forget my manners.

"Thank you," I said, licking the slight traces of his cum from my lips.

Zac didn't respond, but suddenly, I felt his hand on the back of my head, his careful movements aimed at loosening the knot that kept the blindfold securely in place.

No, no, no, no, no.

It took every fiber of my being not to protest aloud, but I suppressed it, fighting against my instincts.

I wasn't ready to see his face or look into his eyes. I wanted to stay in the dark, where I could pretend he was someone else.

When he lifted the blindfold, I blinked a few times,

waiting for my eyes to adjust to the light and once they did, it wasn't Zac I saw, but Blaze.

Fully nude, dick still hard and the most satisfied look on his face. My heart literally skipped a beat while my mind tried to catch up. I knew it was Zac's voice that I heard.

"But... How... Zac was...," I blurted, unable to find the right words.

I glanced around. I didn't see Zac, and I didn't know where Blaze had come from, but I was relieved he was here.

"It seems I can't let you go, little bird," Blaze confessed with sincerity and longing in his eyes.

Happy tears blurred my vision, then rolled down my cheeks. Blaze reached out, tenderly wiping them away.

With a gentle tug, he drew me closer to him and claimed my lips with the sweetest, most romantic kiss I had ever experienced.

"However, I do still have to share you," Blaze announced with an impish grin.

Confusion and slight panic flooded me. "What do you mean?"

Blaze nodded toward the bed and that's when I realized that most of the people in the room were eagerly watching us.

"The people want more," Blaze said.

Arousal laced with apprehension filled me, and I scanned the room again. There was at least thirty people in here.

Giving Blaze head while blindfolded was a lot easier than being on a bed in the center of the room, getting my brains fucked out.

"You can always close your eyes," Blaze offered, reading my thoughts.

I leaned forward and kissed him again, shoved my nerves aside, and remembered something Hannah had said about why she didn't run from a challenge.

"Now, where's the fun in that?" I responded with a wink.

To anyone else, I would have been convincing, but Blaze knew me and even if I planned not to show it, he could sense my anxiety in this moment.

Blaze stood in all his naked glory, pulling me to my feet.

"Don't worry, love," he said with a smile. "I'll make you cum fast."

He led the way to the bed, awaiting us on stage.

The idea of what I was about to do was highly indecorous in the world I'd come from. Intimate acts should be kept private, not broadcasted for everyone to see.

So why did the idea of strangers watching me provide such a high level of enticement?

It goes to show I'd come a long way from my old self since I agreed to be Blaze's submissive, and his advice of "don't think, just obey" had served me well.

The buttonless shirt I wore only covered my back because my naked body, the main attraction based on the way people's eyes were glued to it, was easily visible.

Once we made it to the bed, Blaze picked me up and laid me down on the plush mattress. My eyes flickered to the crowd, then back to him.

Unlike me, Blaze looked completely in his element; the nudity and his dominant control over me feeding into his scandalous desires.

His dick was rock hard and his body was a work of art, as the spotlight cast a glow over every muscle and curve he possessed in the most perfect way.

To sum it up, Blaze was... Blaze.

Confident, intentional and focused, and the crowd loved him.

They shouted his name, obviously already familiar with his reputation, and knew what to expect.

I turned my head to the right and saw a woman fingering herself while staring directly at me. Next to her was a guy stroking his dick, fully mesmerized in anticipation of the show.

Placing a finger under my chin, Blaze shifted my face, so that I was once again looking at him.

"Don't worry about them. Worry about me. I am the one you answer to."

"Yes, sir," I said.

He leaned down and kissed me, occupying my mouth and my pussy at the same time as he entered me.

I let out a whimper, unable to deny how incredible he felt, and my arms instantly closed around his hard body and the crowd cheered, this time amping me up as well.

Blaze's ear was close to my mouth and my tongue darted out, licking it and sucking the lobe.

"Destroy me," I whispered in his ear, egging him on.

I needed him to know that I was surrendering wholeheartedly. I didn't want him to take it easy, consider my shyness, or offer me any comfort.

I wanted to be ravaged, objectified and marked.

"Would you expect anything less from me?" he replied in a gruff tone.

Blaze went from mild to manic in seconds. He pulled out of me, flipped me over so that I was on my knees and reentered me again so hard it made my teeth chatter.

The lower half of my shirt pooled around my mid back, exposing my ass and every few seconds he would slap it, sending a delicious burn throughout my lower half.

His thrusts were aggressive and precise, stretching my pussy to accommodate him and his fingers dug into my waist, holding me immobile while he reached forward to massage and tug on my nipple rings.

My temperature was skyrocketing, and the spotlights weren't making it any better.

Sweat trickled down my forehead and back and I clawed at

the sheets, trying to keep balance and some level of composure under the rising pressure.

Thunderous screams and applause erupted from the crowd as if the fascinated onlookers were watching a fighting match, and with the way Blaze was bending me into submission, I wasn't certain they weren't.

Their faces had blended together, turning the spectators into one giant blur that encouraged Blaze to "make her scream", "make her hurt", "make her beg" and "make her cum" and my Dom was fulfilling every request.

I was dripping wet, panting and disoriented from a sexual high.

Blaze roughly grabbed my hair, yanked me back, and put his arm around my neck in a tight, unforgiving chokehold.

I couldn't breathe and instinctively my hands flew to his arm, but I didn't try to loosen his grip. I trusted him and what happened next should be his decision.

Besides, I was on the edge of the cliff, preparing to drown in my orgasm.

However, it was the next words to leave Blaze's lips that sent me over the edge. "I'm not letting you take your next breath until you cum for me."

And fuck did I cum.

Combine my astronomical climax with my suppressed oxygen supply and I also passed out, bringing this match to a close.

The last thing I remember was Blaze releasing me and falling face down onto the bed, the cheering and excitement from the crowd becoming nothing more than a distant whisper.

Blaze 1, Little Bird 0.

Total knock out.

Chapter Twenty Five

"Trenton is escaping!"

I leaned forward and watched as Axel and Hannah entered the building from the rear. Once they fully disappeared from view, my only way of knowing if they were okay would be through audio.

A fact that was not very reassuring when I knew they could be walking into a trap.

Blaze was still waiting for me to confirm no one was approaching the front of the building. While Vadim guarded the side entrance.

Jolli wasn't on this mission. His son, Sam, had to be rushed to the hospital because of issues concerning his tonsils, and there was no way Jolli could make it.

Therefore, we were putting forth our utmost effort, determined to execute this plan smoothly.

And by we, I meant the team, because being in the safety of the house, nervously biting all of my nails off, while they were the ones risking their lives, wasn't exactly even.

Blaze said what I was doing was a big help, but it didn't feel that way to me.

It all started this morning when Blaze was developing a new strategy to enter the building, since Jolli wasn't available. I'd taken a break from work and brought him breakfast to his office.

Expectantly, Blaze had a lot on his mind. I could see the

intensity in his eyes as he meticulously studied the layout of the apartment building.

His desk was covered with various blueprints, maps, and surveillance photos, and he had a pen in one hand, carefully tracing the different entry points and potential escape routes.

Normally, being down a team member was no big deal, it's not like all of them weren't capable of holding their own, but there had been so many issues, leaks and burdens with this case that Blaze wanted to cover all his bases.

"Anything I can do to help?" I offered, sitting the breakfast tray down near his desk.

I knew there wasn't, but it only felt right to ask.

Blaze laughed humorlessly and said, "You could be the lookout since we are down one set of eyes."

"If it was a virtual job, then I'm your girl," I replied, and that sparked an idea for Blaze.

"You said you knew a bit about cybersecurity, right? Any chance you had to do some surveillance exercises, too?"

And the rest is history.

I stared at my computer screen. It was split to display four separate angles of the building that were being transmitted from four strategically placed cameras.

Each quadrant featured a comprehensive view of the building's surroundings. In the top left corner, I could see the front entrance of the building, capturing anyone approaching, entering, or leaving.

The top right corner exposed the back of the building, revealing any activities happening in the rear vicinity, and the bottom left and right showcased their respective sides.

At the moment, on the front view, was a man pushing a grocery cart. I could make out the plastic bottles, shoes, and garbage bags inside the cart.

Once he arrived at a trashcan, he spent a few minutes rummaging through it, collecting some cans and a pizza box.

My heart ached for him, but I couldn't break my focus. Yes, this could truly be a homeless man, but it could also be a gang member planted there to notify someone of the arrival of Blaze's team.

Finally, when the man gripped the cart and began pushing it in the opposite direction of the building, I could breathe easier.

"You're clear to go, Blaze," I said.

Blaze entered the building, and I held my breath. Not just for him, for all of them.

If something awful took place, I likely wouldn't see it, but I would definitely hear it and the last thing I want was to be an audible witness to one of them getting injured, or worse, taking their last breath.

I got up on my knees, shifting even closer to the laptop.

When this started, twenty-five minutes ago, I was in the kitchen with a nice little setup at the table, but as the time for them to enter the building drew closer, I'd relocated to the living room; sitting on the floor and placing the laptop on the coffee table.

Somehow, already being on the floor gave me a sense of stability.

"First floor, left side clear," I heard Hannah say. "Retreating to the rear to watch for the target."

A few moments later, I heard Axel. "First floor right side clear, advancing to stairwell."

Now that they'd cleared the first floor, Blaze could move to his area.

"Proceeding to second level," Blaze chimed in.

I hope this plan worked.

The big grey structure had two floors and three ways in: One at the side, one in back and another in front. According to Zac, Trenton was on the second floor in apartment 2E.

The building's layout placed that apartment at the third

window from the right. From here I could see a light on in the apartment, but no movement. It seemed quiet and still, raising my suspicions about what could be going on inside.

"In position," Blaze whispered.

Which meant he was in front of 2E. I watched the outside of the building, no one was approaching.

"Entering 2E," Blaze said in a low voice.

I didn't hear anything unlock. Blaze had gadgets that allowed him to quickly and quietly open locks if they were the standard deadbolt. Therefore, I didn't know exactly how long he was inside, but there was a silence that lasted fifteen seconds... thirty... one minute... two minutes.

I wished someone had gone in with him. However, the building was small, with only twenty-five units, so it was decided that Blaze would capture Trenton and the rest of the team would watch the exits in case he escaped or trouble showed up.

"Front room and first bedroom clear," Blaze suddenly said.

I was on the edge of my seat, prepping myself for the commotion that would be heard once he was face to face with Trenton. I think the plan to get him out of the building quietly involved some type of tranquilizer.

This was going to get crazy.

While observing the lower right square, I noticed an individual making their way towards the building. In less than a minute, they would arrive at the side entrance Vadim was guarding.

"Vadim. You have someone approaching," I said. "Dark jacket, hands in their pockets and I can't see their face."

"On it Princess," Vadim replied.

The official nickname I'd been given made me smile. It was a much-needed feel-good reaction in a tense moment like this.

"Hey man, do you have a smoke?" I heard the guy ask once he arrived at Vadim.

"I do not," Vadim said, irritation already evident. "Keep moving."

"Come on," the guy begged, rubbing his hands together. "Don't treat me like that."

Vadim took a step toward him. "I said, to keep moving," he repeated, his voice sterner this time.

The guy didn't seem interested in leaving. As a matter of fact, Vadim's disinterest seemed to egg him on.

The team couldn't hear each other unless they pressed a button to do so, which meant they likely weren't listening to this unfold with Vadim.

I didn't know if this was a ploy or an unfortunate coincidence, but Blaze, Hannah and Axel needed to be alerted to the trouble brewing.

I pressed the button that allowed me to connect to them all at once.

"Vadim is having an issue with a man on the side of the building. Stay alert, will keep you abreast of the situation."

"Yeah, I'm not getting good vibes," Hannah replied. I could see her standing near the back door, constantly checking her surroundings.

"Trenton is not here," Blaze said. "We should pull out."

Vadim and the man had begun to argue and maybe it was innocent, but Vadim took it as a threat when the guy shifted closer and suddenly a fight broke out.

Vadim hit the guy several times, his blows sending the man staggering backward, wiping at his face. With most people, punches like that would have them out cold, but to my surprise, the stranger seemed unfazed. He regained his balance and relentlessly pressed forward, displaying an unwavering resolve to continue the fight.

"Shit," I said, holding the button down to inform the team. "Vadim is —"

A deafening continuous beeping blared from my computer. Its piercing sound filled the room, causing my ears to ache.

Was that the fire alarm?

I backed away from the screen, trying to put distance between myself and the overwhelming noise so that I could think. It was so loud I doubted anyone would be able to hear me, and since Axel and Blaze were saying something that I couldn't make out, apparently, I couldn't hear them either.

They were still in the building, and I was watching the screen, praying that they would materialize soon.

The man who Vadim was fighting must have had enough because he was now limping away, and Hannah, still in the rear, and always ready for any situation, immediately sprang into action.

With urgency, she reached for her weapon, her eyes scanning the area for any signs of danger. Something was amiss. I could feel it. I searched every side of the building and didn't see any smoke.

Residents began pouring out of the building in waves, rushing, knocking each other over, covering their ears and yelling to communicate with one another.

I actively searched the crowd for Blaze and Axel, but I didn't see them. Instead, I saw Trenton.

He was lowering himself out of the second-floor apartment window, next to the apartment he was supposed to be in.

My eyes darted across the screen, diligently looking for Hannah. She was to the far left of the building and Trenton was coming down on the far right. Once he jumped to the ground, he would mix in with the other people and disappear.

I had to reach her.

"Hannah, Hannah!" I shouted into the speaker.

The level of noise was so high that it was clear she wouldn't be able to hear me. I could barely hear myself, and I wasn't even there.

"Hannah!" I tried again. "Trenton is escaping!"

I hit a few keys and tried to reach the others.

No response.

In the camera I watched Hannah and Vadim back away from the building, staying amongst the crowd but still alert. Then, to my relief, Blaze and Axel emerged, looking inconspicuous and casual. Moving away from the building with the crowd.

My heartbeat could at least slow down. None of the team was in danger. Too bad Trenton was gone and who knew when, or if, we'd get this close to him again.

Axel, Hannah, Vadim and I were sitting around Blazes' kitchen table drinking beers and playing dominos. Hannah was in the lead, but I was close behind.

Blaze was on the phone with Agent Steele, his fingers pressing into his temples. No one was in a good mood. Different expressions were formed across each of their faces, but the goal was the same: figure out who tipped Trenton off.

I picked up a tile and stared at the layout for a long moment, trying to find the best place for my domino, but my mind wasn't on the game. A major lead had been lost, and I feared we wouldn't find Trenton again.

As I suspected, there was no fire.

The fire alarm was pulled while Blaze was in Trenton's supposed apartment, which meant Trenton snuck out of a different apartment and activated it. But how? Did Zac feed Blaze the information only to mislead him?

Blaze said he was certain that Zac wasn't involved in this, but if he wasn't, then why was this mystery person always one step ahead?

My head hurt.

Sliding my tile in position so that it touched one end of the domino chain, I prepared to add up my score when...

"Fuck!" Axel suddenly shouted. No one at the table jumped or batted an eye. "We had him. He was right there."

"Calm down, my friend," Vadim said, patting him on the shoulder. "Trenton may live tonight, but only because he is meant to die a different day. And he will die," Vadim promised.

"I've got to get some air," Hannah said.

She pushed away from the table and walked out the front door. I stood and walked over to a large window. It granted me an unobstructed view of the vast expanse of the night sky, adorned with shimmering stars.

This view gave me hope and a smidge of peace. Something I desperately needed.

Would I have to live the rest of my life looking over my shoulder?

Whatever important information this mystery person thought I had, I needed to uncover it quickly because we were running out of time. I couldn't hide forever. Eventually, this killer would find me.

Blaze approached, wrapping his arms around me from behind.

"I promise you, I will figure out who is trying to hurt you, even if it kills me."

Instead of responding, I faced him, laid my head on his chest, and listened to his heartbeat because I feared he may be right. This mission just might kill him.

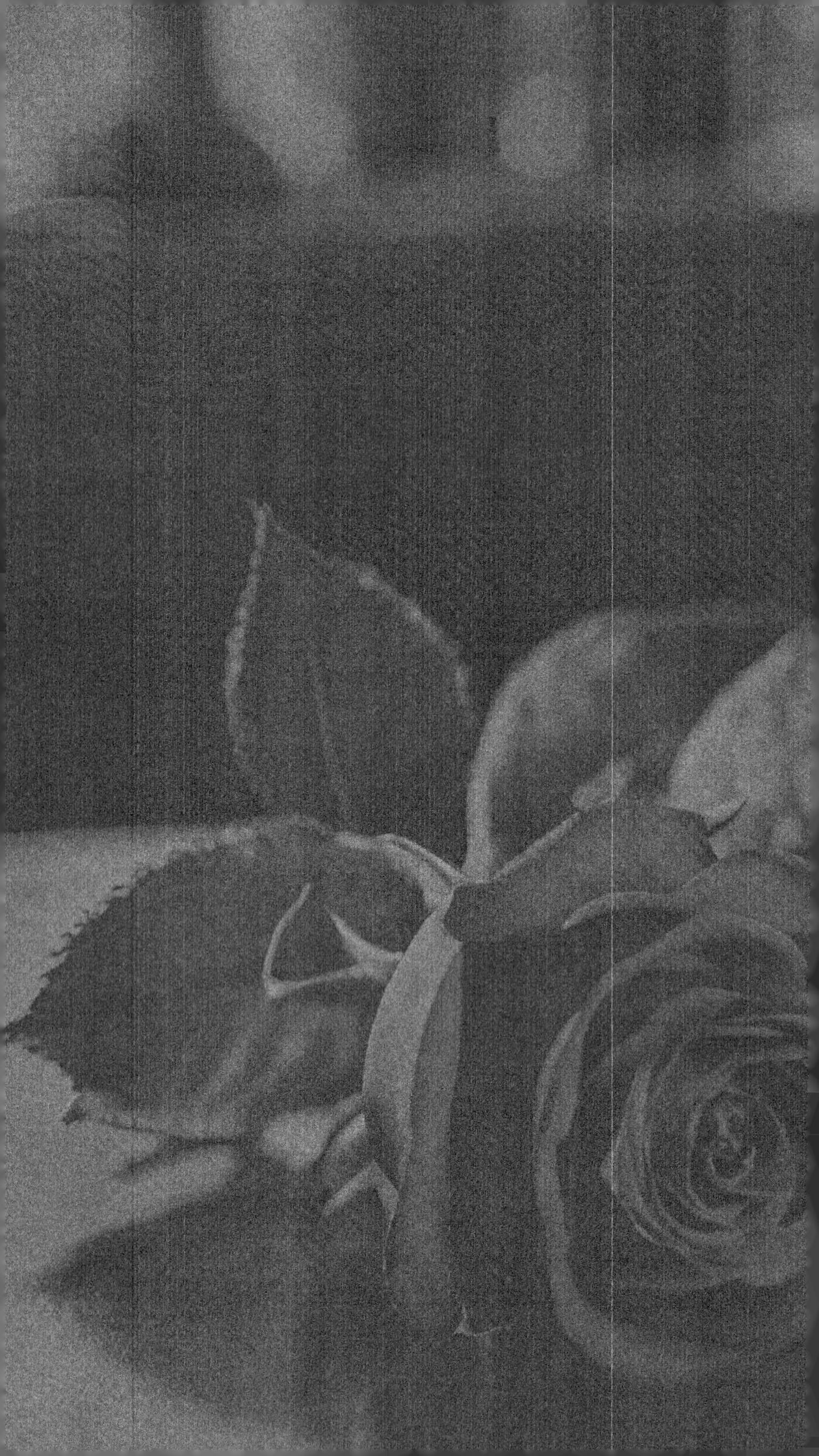

Chapter Twenty Six

"Trouble was coming."

Blaze had me in the darkroom, completely immobilized.

I was blindfolded, tightly bound in the crab position, and placed on a large, sleek table. This position brought about a heightened sense of vulnerability because it created an entirely new level of exposure.

Blaze had bent my right leg and tied my thigh and ankle together with an easy release two column tie. Then he repeated the process again on the left leg. For good measure, he had also tied my wrists to my ankles.

Long story short, I was at his mercy.

Small weights hung from my nipple rings, while Blaze alternated hot and cold items over my body, applying them to my most sensitive areas and erogenous zones.

The delicious torture had gone on for over an hour. Blaze had started at my nipples, teasing them with an ice cube until I shivered uncontrollably.

Next, he dripped warm wax on them, and once that dried, he slowly and carefully peeled the wax off with a knife, only to start with the ice cubes again.

The method was called temperature play, and he was using it to make my body sensitive so that I would be more susceptible to orgasm from his touch.

Incorporating the knife into the mix was merely Blaze's way of making this already unique experience highly sensuous.

The fact that he hadn't cut me even once was wild to me.

Then again, I think when we started he said something about using a duller blade to perform this task but, all I heard was blade, which was enough for my mind to assume the worst.

Nevertheless, I didn't object. If Blaze thought I'd enjoy it, he was probably right.

As usual, his idea of making me wear a blindfold was a good call. It may have been difficult for me to soften to the idea of using a knife to scrape wax off my skin if I could see it.

From my nipples, Blaze had moved on to my lower abdomen, neck, shoulders, the bottom of my feet, lower back and, currently, my pussy.

He was massaging my clit with ice-cold fingers and a slowness so excruciating I wanted to scream.

Eventually, he stopped using his fingers and picked up another instrument to use on me.

At first, confusion overwhelmed me as I tried to figure out what it was.

However, as soon as the tiny prickles rolling up and down my inner thigh registered, I realized it was a sensation pinwheel designed to tantalize and awaken my nerve endings.

I shuddered so hard that Blaze had to place a hand on my shoulder to keep me from falling over.

He continued, rolling the wheel over the top of my feet, my arms and sides, making me so wet, I had formed a puddle underneath me.

Blaze lifted the blindfold from my eyes, dropping it on the table next to me. The room was dimly lit, so it barely took any time for my eyes to adjust.

Despite that, I preferred my eyes closed; it intensified the sensations. Besides, I'd already cum four times in this last hour. I was working on a fifth.

"I want you to do something for me," Blaze said.

"Anything, sir," I replied with a breathy moan.

Blaze rolled the pinwheel up and down the delicate skin of my inner thighs. I trembled and jerked every time he maneuvered it all the way down and it touched my labia.

"Say my name," he ordered.

My eyes opened slowly, comprehension temporarily lagging.

His name? As in, call him Blaze and not, sir? Was this one of his tricks?

"I... uh."

Blaze put the tool down and switched to using his hand. With skilled fingers, he twisted and tugged my clit. Then, with his free hand, he tapped the weight hanging from one of my nipple rings. I shook in ecstasy.

If this was a trick, looks like I was falling for the bait.

"Blaze," I said in a whisper.

He gave me a long, soft kiss on the lips.

"Not that name," he said in a deep, suggestive voice. "I think you know what I mean."

I stared up at him. We hadn't talked about what had happened at the club. I didn't know if his admitting that he couldn't let me go meant for that moment or for forever, and the oddest thing was, I didn't care.

If being his sub had taught me anything, it was to live in the moment. And in this instance, I was experiencing a sincerely poetic and heartfelt one because the last person to use Blaze's real name was the woman he was in love with.

My lips parted, my heart thudded, and my knees shook, or tried to, I was tied up pretty tight.

"Adrian," I said, my voice dropping much lower than I intended, because Blazes touch had me in the clutches of my next release.

"Mmm," he moaned with satisfaction. "That sounds so sweet on your lips."

He kissed me again, the speed of his hand increasing, but his touch so light, it was as if he wasn't touching me at all. Like he was manipulating the air and sparking an electrical current that was doing wonders to my body.

I felt high on passion and desire.

This time, something else was fighting its way out of me at the same time as my orgasm. It was a confession and in all the bliss and ecstasy, I couldn't hold it back any longer.

The words that had been locked away in the depths of my soul spilled out from my lips as my climax exploded from my body. "I love you, Adrian," I said.

However, nothing was more satisfying and pure than his reply. It gave me reassurance, it gave me tranquility, it gave me fulfillment when Blaze said, "I love you too, princess."

"That was the best pizza I ever had," I said, lying back on the thick grey blanket.

"I told you," Blaze replied, lying down beside me.

He thought we needed a change of scenery and a break from staring at case details, and his four walls. So, Vadim dropped off a pizza for us from Blaze's favorite spot and then, Blaze brought us to a secluded park to eat it.

Aside from the random impulse to glance around, because I still feared for my life, this was probably the most romantic date I'd ever been on.

"Do you have guards out here too?" I asked, glancing around at the thick, tall trees.

"I sure do," Blaze confirmed.

I slid my hand in his and stared up at the sky, my eyes immediately finding a cloud that looked like a heart. After our romantic confessions, it was no surprise that I had love on the brain.

"This is a place that I come to sometimes when I need to think. It never really has many people, and it reminds me of something you see in a portrait."

I could tell what he meant. The park we were in was a hidden gem, tucked away from the hustle and bustle of the city. Its serene atmosphere provided the perfect backdrop for our intimate conversation.

We had spoken little since we arrived, and that was fine with me because I had been starving. After a scene with Blaze, I was always starving.

The man drained my body of every ounce of energy, and once he was done, my appetite overshadowed everything else.

"I see why, it's perfect," I said.

"No," Blaze corrected. "That would be you."

I giggled. "Stop it! You are making me behave like some love sick school girl."

Blaze shrugged, lifted my hand to his lips, and kissed it. "It's not my fault you don't know how to handle compliments from me."

I rolled onto my side to face him and wiggled a little. The bullet-proof vest he had me wear was still taking some getting used to, but it was the only way he would let me come out and I eagerly agreed.

"Should I call you Adrian from now on?" I asked.

"That's up to you," he said.

I thought about it, but decided that referring to him as Blaze was much too reflexive for me. I'd probably stick to calling him that, but use Adrian if I'm feeling extra kinky.

"How about I use Adrian when we are having sexy time?" I said playfully, running my fingers up and down his leg.

Blaze reached out and touched the necklace he'd given me at the club. I was expected to wear it at all times, and I did.

Lifting the charm on the end, he twisted it around so that I could see the word "owned" etched in the red box before he responded.

"If you want to get punished, then go right ahead," Blaze said, his playful tone matching mine. "Otherwise I suggest you stick to sir."

I heard a branch snap, and my eyes darted over. It was only a squirrel, a cute innocent squirrel, but in my mind, it was a masked killer, sneaking up on me to end things once and for all.

"Raquel," Blaze said, instantly drawing my attention. "It's okay, my love."

My heart melted, and my shoulders slumped. He had never called me that before, but to that truth, I had never been *his* before, and now I was. I searched his eyes and found determination, love and... *helplessness*?

For the first time, I recognized the ache and torture it was causing him to watch me live in fear, constantly on edge, and it was taking its toll on him.

Blaze was a warrior. Known for his bravery and unwavering determination.

He solved crimes, protected the innocent, and was my shield against the darkness. But more and more lately, we faced the unsettling possibility that even he might not be able to keep me safe.

It tore at my heart to consider what that must be doing to him.

Kissing him on the cheek, I tried my best to appear less rattled. "Tell me more about life as a military brat," I said.

The conversation lasted for at least an hour, as Blaze recalled the places he lived for short periods throughout his life. I'd actually visited many of them before, but hearing about them from his perspective was like experiencing it all over again.

He was just about to tell me about a funny incident that happened one year at school when his cell rang.

"What's up Jolli," Blaze answered.

"I found Trenton," Jolli said.

He was loud, out of breath, and pissed. Blaze didn't even have him on speakerphone, and I could make out every word he was saying.

Both Blaze and I sat up.

"Where?" Blaze asked, already gathering our things. I followed suit, taking the blanket from him, folding it quickly and collecting the pizza box and our drinks as Jolli continued.

"A place I remembered him mentioning years ago. I guess after the raid he hid out here, but listen," Jolli said, speaking a mile a minute. "That doesn't matter. Trenton told me who is behind all this and boss, it's bad. Really bad."

Blaze froze and so did I.

"Who?" Blaze said, the edge and distaste in his tone unmistakable.

"Not on the phone," Jolli replied. "Now that I have found Trenton, I don't know who could be listening in. This has to be in person. You will understand when you get here."

"I'm heading to the truck. Send me the address."

"Already Done," Jolli confirmed. "But watch yourself. Now that I have Trenton, anything could happen."

Jolli ended the call and Blaze pressed the button on his earpiece, informing the well-hidden bodyguards he was leaving and that they needed to follow.

The entire drive, I felt on edge. We were finally about to learn who was behind this and why Trenton was involved. All fantastic news, but in the back of my mind, I couldn't shake the sense of uneasiness.

This could be a trap. Blaze had considered it too, but what choice did we have?

There was no way we would skip finding out, and asking

Jolli to bring Trenton to Blaze also carried its own risk. He could be attacked during transport, which was dangerous because at the moment, Jolli had no backup.

Then again, all of this could simply be false paranoia. Given that everything about this case had been treacherous, it was only natural that a lead of this magnitude would be met with uncertainty.

It took us twenty-two minutes to do a drive that normally would be substantially longer.

A few minutes before Blaze turned on the street leading to the warehouse, he instructed me to get into the backseat and stay low.

Although the windows were tinted, Blaze was not taking any chances. If this were a setup, it would be just our luck that the bad guy would see him exit the vehicle and glimpse me in the passenger seat.

Stopping near the abandoned warehouse, I waited until Blaze closed the door and the vehicle locked before I peeked out of the backseat window. Instantly, I heard a second click and rolled my eyes.

The vehicle locked automatically, but it had a second feature that locked the vehicle from the inside. Meaning I couldn't get out.

There was no need for the glorified child lock, as I'd named it. Nothing would make me get out of this SUV. However, Blaze knew how impulsive I could sometimes be if I wanted to help, therefore he didn't trust me.

In order to get to Jolli, Blaze had to walk across a concrete type bridge that connected the building to the parking lot. I spotted Jolli coming towards Blaze, heading away from the building, but he was a little distance away.

Despite that, I could still make out the expression on Jolli's face. It was pure anger. I'd never seen Jolli so furious.

The man had a smile that could light up a room. Whatever

information he had for Blaze must have been highly unsettling if it had him this upset.

My eyes shifted to a few feet behind Jolli, and I instantly recognized Trenton.

I gasped, but remained low, my hands clutching the top of the door right beneath the window.

Jolli really found him.

Trenton's hands were cuffed around a tall metal post, effectively restricting his movement. Ironically, he was wearing his Vex uniform. There was a hole torn in the right pants leg, and the surrounding fabric appeared to be stained with blood.

A fight with Jolli, perhaps?

One thing that was unmistakable was his expression. Trenton didn't look too happy to see Blaze and although Blaze's back was to me as he was still heading towards Jolli, I imagined Blaze didn't look too happy either. Murderous would likely be more fitting.

That's when I noticed it, a high tension in the air, like something bad was about to happen. I spun around and glanced out at all sides of the vehicle.

Nothing was there, yet trouble was coming. I knew it.

Time appeared to slow down as my surroundings took on a surreal, sluggish quality, and that's when I realized my intuition had been right all along.

It wasn't just the way the birds suddenly dashed from the building's rooftop, the alarming way Jolli lifted his hand, or the immediate halt in Blazes movement that forewarned me. It was the terror in Trenton's eyes seconds before thunderous sounds cracked through the sky and a spray of bullets tore through his flesh.

I screamed Blazes' name, forgetting that he couldn't see or likely hear me. I pulled at the door handle, in full disregard for my life as I tried to warn, get to and save the man I loved, but the door didn't open and more gunfire rained down.

The people firing must have been up on a hill, with a much better vantage point. Every fiber of my being screamed for me to help, but I was trapped on the other side of the impenetrable door.

Blaze and Jolli dropped to the ground, and I stopped breathing, only able to start again when Blaze rolled over and began firing back.

Speed reversed, now moving much too fast for me to fully comprehend what was going on as suddenly several men came to Jolli and Blaze's defense, returning fire to the attackers.

It took me a minute to realize it must have been Blaze's bodyguards that had followed us from the park. I was so relieved I cheered.

The group of men banded together and created a protective barrier around Blaze, working as a cohesive unit, and retreated towards the SUV.

Confusion set in as I watched them move closer and closer. I could only see the back of Blaze's head, which meant he was facing away from the vehicle, but walking backward like he was pulling something... or someone.

The wall of men made it to the door, and it clicked, automatically unlocking.

I immediately moved out of the way, consumed with horror as they placed Jolli's lifeless body on the backseat.

I had it wrong. Jolli wasn't dead, but he was dying, or he would die if we couldn't get him to the hospital quick enough.

Too much blood. Too much blood. My mind kept screaming on an endless loop.

Jolli's face was pale, his breathing shallow, and every

passing moment felt like an eternity. Panic and fear gripped my heart, but I refused to let it show. I held his hand and spoke words of reassurance, promising him we would be at the hospital soon.

Blood soaked his shirt and the seat as Jolli coughed and choked. Globs of it landed on his face and stained his sandy brown curls, making the scene before me even more horrifying.

No one lived after losing that much blood.

"Hold on man, hold on," Blaze shouted, driving so fast I was surprised all four wheels were still connected to the ground.

Jolli's desperate eyes locked onto mine.

"It's going to be okay, Jolli. Stay with me alright. Just stay with me."

His mouth opened, trying to speak, but he coughed hard and his face contorted with pain and fear.

"Die... die," Jolli finally choked out.

Tears stung my eyes.

"No, you are not going to die, Jolli. You won't die. Sam needs you. We need you. You will not die," I stated again, willing it to be true.

"No way, man," Blaze said from up front. "I can't do this without you. You are going to be around for a long time, so that you can lose a lot more bets."

Jolli tried to smile, but it faltered and then fell flat. His gaze shifted upward, and he tried to speak again, but this time not only did his mouth close, his eyes did too.

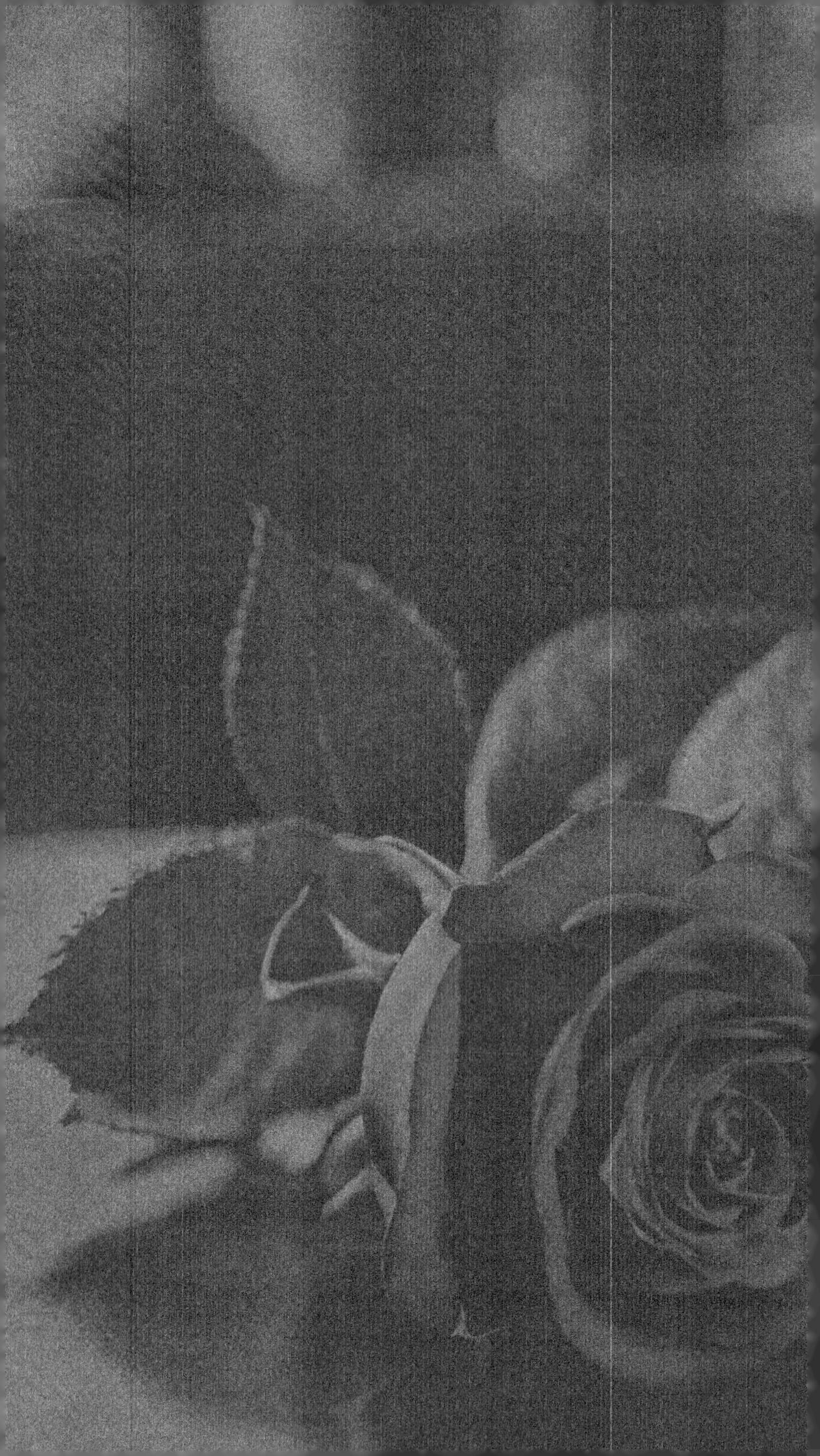

Chapter Twenty Seven

"I HAVE A CONFESSION."

I paced the bedroom, biting my lower lip while my fingers absently traced the square charm on the necklace Blaze had given me.

Should I go to be by his side on the deck? Or let him have some alone time?

If I were him, the last thing I'd want to do was talk to anyone.

Yet, no choice felt right. Nothing seemed like enough. Jolli could die. *Jolli could already be dead,* I thought with a disturbing realization that stopped me in my tracks.

I kicked the thought out of my mind and slammed the metaphorical door behind it. Jolli was going to make it... he had to.

Officially, we'd come to the conclusion that Jolli finding Trenton was part of a setup, or at the very least, someone had a tracker on Trenton and sent in their men once they knew Blaze and his team had located him.

And now, not only would Jolli die, the answers he had would die with him.

I squeezed my eyes shut, trying to shake the distressing thought of losing Jolli, but that only brought back the vision of watching him bleed out on the backseat. A few tears fell from my eyes and I wiped them away, praying and pleading for Jolli's full recovery.

Although Jolli was wearing a bullet-proof vest, he'd gotten

shot in the arm and the bullet had penetrated through to his lung.

Me, Blaze and the rest of the team had spent the last few nights on standby in the hospital's waiting area for progress, updates, or at least a guarantee that Jolli would be fine, but so far, his condition remained critical.

Currently, Vadim and Hannah were on their shift at the hospital, while the rest of us were supposed to be resting.

Of course, we were not.

Axel was with Sam, getting pizza and trying to keep the poor little guy's mind off the possibility that he might lose his dad. He'd already lost his mom, and Jolli was the only family Sam had left. If Jolli didn't make it... *nope! I wasn't going there.*

Blaze was out on the deck.

Ever since we returned home this morning, that is where he'd been, either engrossed in case files or lost in thought, his gaze fixed on the distant horizon.

And then there was me. In the room, pacing, trying to determine the best way to be useful.

Blaze was due to return to the hospital tomorrow morning and I would go with him. My relationship with Jolli wasn't nearly as deep as the rest of the team, but I cared about him and I cared about them.

If all I could do to make things easier was bring food and keep their coffee cups filled, then sign me up.

Ultimately, I decided to check on Blaze. Tiptoeing to the back in case he'd fallen asleep. He wasn't.

"Hi," I said, stepping outside.

Blaze nodded his head in greeting and picked up the bottle of bourbon that rested on a wicker and glass table in front of him.

"Do you need anything?" I asked.

"No, I'm good," he replied, lifting the drink.

This was awkward. I loved him, but I didn't know this side of him. Was there anyway I could ease the hurt? Likely not.

Accepting there was nothing I could do, but give him time, I gently said, "If you need anything. I'll be inside, okay?"

Blaze put the bourbon down. "You should stay," he said, glancing over at me.

Grateful for the invite, I took a seat beside him on the comfy outdoor couch. The wooden deck creaked slightly under our weight. Together, we sat in silence for a moment, allowing the sounds of nature to fill the space between us.

"Jolli has been on my team for longer than anyone," Blaze finally said. "We met ten years ago when he came to work for me at Vex and he stood out as only Jolli can. He was extremely dedicated to the job and kept everyone laughing and in good spirits, which is how he got the nickname."

"And the fact that he looks like an assassin, but has the heart of an angel, makes the name even more comical," I added.

"Exactly," Blaze said. He cracked the first semblance of a smile, but it faded fast. "It was Jolli who convinced me to accept jobs from the FBI. He even volunteered to work with me, in case I needed someone to have my back."

I remained quiet, allowing Blaze his time to reminisce.

"When his wife Jenny died, Sam was two. I assumed Jolli would stop working with me because the job was too dangerous and now Sam only had him. But he told me that if he quit doing something he'd given his word on because of fear, then he wouldn't be the type of father that Sam could look up to, or be proud of."

That made us both smile and silence filled the air again. Jolli was a really good guy. He didn't deserve this.

"Fuck!" Blaze suddenly shouted. "They will not get away with this."

"They won't," I assured him. "As horrible as what

happened to Jolli is, it also means we were getting too close. The best thing we can do is figure what clue we are missing."

Blaze nodded and took my hand, intertwining his fingers in mine. His breathing slowed and the irritation from mere seconds before dissipated.

"You bring me peace. Did you know that?" he asked.

"I did not, but I'm not surprised," I replied arrogantly.

"Oh," Blaze said, clearly entertained by my cocky response. "And why not?"

I turned to him, my lips twisting into a playful yet sincere grin. "Because you bring me peace as well."

That earned me a genuine smile and a warm embrace from Blaze.

"I have a confession," Blaze said.

"Alright," I replied, filled with curiosity and concern.

"That night at the club, I fully intended to share you with Zac."

My eyes widened slightly, and I sat back on the couch a bit. I didn't know how to feel about that.

True, the outcome had been in my favor, but somehow hearing that choosing me was an unexpected occurrence on his end wasn't exactly comforting.

"Oh," I said. "What changed your mind?"

"You did," Blaze declared, his eyes softening. "Up until that very moment that I almost left you in the service room, I was lying to myself. I'd noticed my feelings growing for you over the past few months, but I pushed them aside. I didn't want to admit to myself that you were different."

"Because you didn't want to fall in love?"

"Partially," Blaze admitted. "But more so because I didn't want to love you and know that the life I live might cause me to lose you."

I could understand the battle he had fought within

himself, trying to resist the pull of his feelings for me because of the woman who had hurt him.

Getting my heart broken wasn't a fear I had, but I was grateful that he'd been honest with me.

I'd learned a lot from him since we'd been together and because of that, I had the perfect response to his confession.

It was the exact one he'd given me when I was afraid to get oral. It was blunt, to the point, and solidified that past hangups had no place between us.

Cupping his face with my hands, I leaned in close and said. "I am not her, so shut the fuck up and kiss me."

Blaze laughed. "You are so fucking perfect," he said before kissing me so passionately it left me breathless.

Once we ended the kiss I said, "Finish telling me how you got Zac to be part of your evil plan."

Blaze sat back, adopting a casual tone as he recounted the events.

"I went over to him, said I'd changed my mind and if he ever asked me about sharing you again, I'd break his nose and that was that."

"You threatened him?" I asked.

"Zac knows how I am," Blaze replied with a shrug. "He wasn't offended. Anyway, I asked him to go get you and bring you over to me."

"And that's when you thought it was a good idea to trick me into thinking I'd sucked Zac's dick instead of yours?" I asked, crossing my arms.

"You call it tricked. I call it training."

"That was not training," I countered, getting in his face, ready to kiss those soft, sexy lips of his again.

"Training," Blaze emphasized, "Is whatever I want it to be."

I observed him closely, my eyes narrowed. He only smirked. So I got back at him another way.

"I guess you're right," I replied, indifferently. "It's a shame, though. Zac looked like a lot of fun."

Blaze grabbed my chin and turned my face to him. "You are going to pay for that," he promised.

"I certainly hope so," I responded, further engaging in our playful banter.

And just like that, we went back to kissing, but nothing more. I think we both yearned for the comfort of the simple, yet highly intimate exchange to provide a buffer between the macabre feeling that hung over our heads.

Nonetheless, a few minutes later, we found ourselves back staring off into the distance. Sadness, anger and pain of Jolli's condition resurfacing.

"What do you think we are missing?" I asked, not needing to preface the question with anything else. Blaze knew it was about the case. Everything nowadays was about the case.

"I'm not sure, but I have a new theory," he said, sitting forward and picking up a folder from off the table.

He opened it, and there was Louis. The man that attacked me at Zen's.

For some reason, seeing his face no longer gave me that knotted feeling in my stomach or quickened my heartbeat. After watching Blaze nearly rip Boris' scalp off, my fear of masked villains had diminished significantly. I felt stronger and braver somehow.

"What's your theory?" I asked.

Blaze lifted the photo of Louis to display several sheets underneath it. A brief scan revealed it to be his background details.

"This all started with him," Blaze began. "For the longest time, we all assumed that you saw or heard something that you simply couldn't remember, but what if you were the wrong person to concentrate on?"

I felt perplexed. "I'm not sure I'm following. Are you saying Louis should have been the focus?"

"Exactly," Blaze said.

"But I thought you already searched his background."

"We did, and nothing about him stands out. He had the typical upbringing you would expect. Raised by an alcoholic mother and abusive father. Around eight to eleven years old, he spent some time in foster care. From there, he was constantly kicked out of school for fighting. Then, he was in and out of juvenile detention for petty theft and assault, until it eventually escalated to jail sentences for robbery and attempted murder."

I leaned in closer, eager to examine the pages. "But you think something about him may point us to the answers we seek?"

"I do, and I'd like you to look through it. There may be something in his background that connects the two of you."

I liked where this was going. Finally, we had a fresh way to view the case.

"Is he part of a gang?" I asked. The snake tattoo I saw on Louis' hand that night clearly photographed in the picture.

"He was," Blaze confirmed, "And so was the guy that came to attack you at the hotel and several other men we have seized. We think that whoever he is working for is using the gang to facilitate more criminal activity."

I stared at the image of Louis. I didn't recognize him from anywhere.

Not consciously, anyway. He didn't appear to be a student at any school I attended or work at any of the jobs I'd been on, however that didn't mean we hadn't crossed paths.

Blaze gave me the folder, and I settled in, tucking my feet beneath me and flipping to the first page.

As Blaze had said, these sheets summarized Louis' life from birth until death.

He was born at a local hospital at 6:17 am, weighing six pounds and four ounces. There were no additional medical records beyond some of the basic vaccinations, until the reports of random hospitalizations at ages five, six and eight.

My heart ached as I read the reports of a kid that suffered broken bones, burns, and more disturbing injuries, no doubt, inflicted by the hands of his neglectful parents.

At age eight Louis lived at Heavenly Hands Children's Home for six months before being moved to Divine Door, another children's home, until the age of eleven.

I read the name of the two facilities again. Specifically, Divine Door. *Where had I heard that name?*

I glanced up at Blaze. "Have you ever heard of Divine Door Children's Home?"

He slowly shook his head. "Not until reading his file."

"Are you sure? It sounds familiar and I feel like I heard it recently. Is there any chance Vex donated some money to a charity that worked with them?"

"I can look into it," Blaze said, "but I don't think so."

Not being able to place where I'd heard the name bothered me. Even though it could have been from something as simple as a billboard or a commercial, neither of those answers seemed to fit.

And since it pertained to this case, and every detail mattered, I wanted to know for sure.

"Thanks. Looking into it might help."

I continued reading Louis' file in order to gain further insight. The schools he attended, which included elementary, middle, and high school, didn't ring a bell for me and neither did his places of employment.

The further I pushed along, the more discouraged I became. Nothing stood out. A few hours later, I had completed the file. The ending of Louis' life summed up into 2-3 sentences.

"Any luck?" Blaze asked, returning from grabbing us a drink.

I dropped the folder back onto the table. I felt defeated. Why in the hell couldn't I figure this out? Someone was after me for some reason, and I was too blind to see it.

"I'm sorry, Blaze. I got nothing."

He placed his arm around me and passed me a glass of wine.

"It's okay. Tomorrow, before we leave to visit Jolli, I will double check that Vex has had no business with the children's home."

I nodded and took a sip of wine. The rich aroma and smooth taste, paired with Blaze's comforting presence, momentarily distracted me from my thoughts, but I couldn't shake the feeling of failure.

Jolli was in the hospital room fighting for his life and if we couldn't put an end to this mysterious evil villain, he was going to put an end to all of us.

I was wearing a long, beautiful silk dress that was a vibrant shade of emerald green, standing outside on a balcony, enjoying an enchanting view of the city. I turned my head to the right, and he smiled at me, a compliment falling from his lips.

All night he had been showing up here and there, creating small talk and although I was polite, I never returned his interest. I didn't want him. I wanted Blaze.

However, Blaze was nowhere to be found. I'd seen him earlier, strutting around with some beautiful woman on his arm, but hadn't seen him since.

"I enjoy coming to these events," the man beside me said. "Charities are dear to me."

I gave him a gentle smile.

"I know what you mean," I said. There was a heavy sadness tugging at my heart and in the back of my mind, but I couldn't figure out why. "Charities hold a special place in my heart, too."

"Do you have a favorite one? Maybe I can put in a good word, and we can donate to it."

I thought about his offer. There was a charity that meant a lot to me, but every time I tried to think of the name of it or why it was special, things got hazy, like there was a part of my memory I wasn't allowed to access.

A sudden breeze offered me some solace, like an embrace from a lifelong friend. I glanced up at the night's sky and in that moment everything felt right.

"I can't remember the name," I said, "But once I do, I will be sure to let you know."

"Well, since you shared the name of your favorite charity, it would only be fair if I did the same."

I looked at him, confused and uneasy. What was he talking about? I hadn't told him the name of my favorite charity. I told him I couldn't remember it.

Suddenly everything felt out of place, upside down and alarming. I wasn't safe here. The man's face was in shadows and no matter which way I moved, he remained hidden.

"Do you know my favorite charity?" he asked, oblivious to my discomfort, as if he were talking to himself and I wasn't there at all.

It was important that I hear this. I wanted to run, but I needed to stay put. Keep him talking, make him say it.

"No, what is it?" I replied.

"Divine Door Children's Home. No one knows this but, I

spent some time there when I was a young boy after I lost my parents."

"Oh, I'm so sorry for your loss."

"It's okay," the man said. "These things happen. But now that you know, I have to kill you."

My eyes popped opened, and I bolted up in bed, fists clenched and heart racing. It was only a dream, but now I knew who we were looking for.

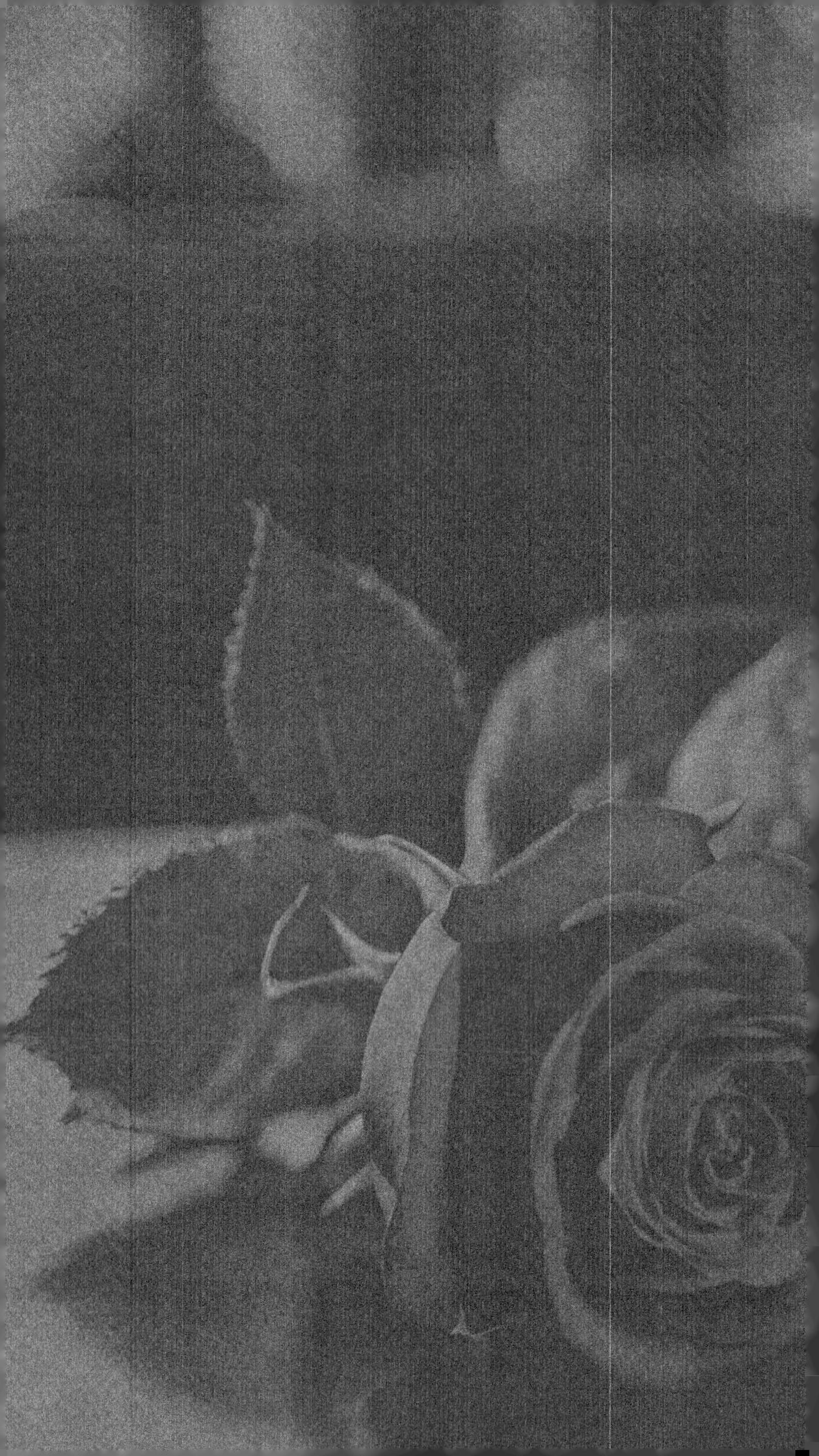

Chapter Twenty Eight

"Please forgive me, Blaze."

"Michael Divers," Blaze said in a calm, controlled voice for the second time. "And if you make me repeat myself again, I am going to come down there and bang your head against that fucking keyboard."

"Umm o...okay... I'll... get right on it," Ben said.

Blaze was pissed and so was I.

We were in the kitchen and Blaze was standing with both hands planted on the counter, staring down at his phone as if it were Ben, the now terrified FBI administrator that was assigned to helping us locate all known addresses for Agent Divers.

I was sitting at the table, writing all the clues that connected the dots of this case. We were now one hundred percent certain that Agent Divers was behind all this. He'd had us fooled by expertly playing both sides at the same time.

After the warped dream version I'd had last night, I woke up to recall the very real encounter that I'd had with Agent Divers at a charity event almost ten months ago.

It was the first one I'd been to since I started working for Vex. I got a chance to meet Divers as well as Steele and Swanson and learn that Vex was more than a security company. They really cared about making the world a better place.

During a conversation that took place on the balcony, Divers shared his deep affection for charities. I figured he was trying to use it to get to know me because he had been extra friendly all night and each time I'd found a way to excuse myself.

Regardless, this time, when he mentioned charities, it made me think about Loni, and unlike in the dream version where I didn't share the name of Loni's charity, I shared the name with him that night.

I think he felt it connected us because he then divulged that his favorite charity was Divine Door Children's Home, and that he'd spent time there.

Obviously, I didn't think much of it after the conversation ended and neither did Divers. Who would have believed that almost a year later, I would find myself in an unfortunate situation, being in the wrong place at the wrong time, held hostage by Divers' foster brother, Louis?

This entire revelation was blowing my mind.

After I told Blaze about my dream, he immediately contacted Swanson and Steele. Blaze needed no convincing, because, according to him, it all made perfect sense.

He believed that placing all the blame on Governor Wesley was too simplistic and convenient, overlooking other factors. Not to mention, the governor's background had many gaps that did not align or correlate with details of the case.

Who else but an FBI agent, turned villain, would have access to the manpower, know-how and determination to chase down a witness and pull off such an elaborate scheme while not getting caught for five years?

Swanson and Steele's skepticism came as no surprise. It was hard for them to fathom that their colleague and respected agent could be behind all this.

However, their tune changed when Blaze pointed out that if Divers was guilty, maybe they were too.

Proving their own innocence became a top priority as they

sought to find Divers to clear this matter up, but Divers wasn't in the office.

In fact, he hadn't been in since the day Trenton was caught. Suspicions were raised even further when Swanson and Steele received clearance to look into Divers background and confirmed that his time at the children's home overlapped with Louis Murphy.

Coincidence?

Blaze and I didn't think so and even if the agents did, Blaze had raised enough attention to officially bring Divers in for questioning.

The problem was, he also wasn't at his home address.

At this point Swanson and Steele's boss caught wind of it and desperation took hold.

The two agents were instructed to scour phone records, financial transactions, and even reach out to informants, searching for connections between Divers and the case, while Blaze was transferred to Ben, the administrator, assigned to locate another address for Divers.

The higher-ups did not want this to get out. If the public learned an FBI agent had gone rogue, using taxpayers' dollars and inside information to run a major crime ring, it would be a scandal of epic proportions.

They wanted to apprehend Divers and bring him to justice before the truth came to light.

But were they too late? No one knew where Divers was.

"Mr... umm... Blaze," Ben said nervously. The guy had to be new to the office and young. He sounded so intimidated he would piss his pants.

"Yes," Blaze said.

"I am working on some connection that may give me another address, but it could take a while. I don't want to leave you on hold, so can I call you back with the information?"

When Blaze said nothing.

Ben hurried to add. "Please, sir." His voice was squeaky and cracking.

"Sure, no problem," Blaze said, scrubbing a hand over his face. He was oblivious to the fact that he had Ben shaking in his boots. I could tell he'd already moved on to something else.

The call ended, and Blaze walked over to me.

"Make any more connections?" he asked.

"Not really. I am still trying to find out where Boris fits into all this."

Blaze thought about it. Another angle we had brought to the FBI's attention was finding the connection between Divers and Boris, the man that broke into my apartment.

He was currently being detained somewhere unknown and last we heard, still not cooperating.

"Maybe the connection wasn't between Divers and Boris," Blaze said. "It could have been between Louis and Boris. They both had conditions with their eyes, right? It is highly likely that Louis knew Boris and brought him in to work for Divers."

I nodded, letting it sink in. "That adds up. I wonder if we could find out if Louis and Boris had the same doctor."

"It's worth looking into," Blaze said. Then he smiled at me. "We are finally getting somewhere. Thanks to you."

I said a brief "you're welcome" and steered the conversation elsewhere. Even though it wasn't my fault, I felt bad that I couldn't connect this quicker.

"Any updates on Jolli?" I asked.

Blaze's entire demeanor physically transformed, his shoulders stiffened and his eyes hardened. He was going to kill Divers if he got his hands on him first.

With a deep sigh, Blaze said, "No updates. Axel is there now with Sam, and I plan to go a little later. Considering what we have learned, it was a better idea for me to hang back and see what I could do here."

"He's going to be okay," I reassured him, and myself, for what felt like the millionth time.

Blaze's cell rang and he went to answer it, holding the device that appeared so tiny in his large hands to his ear.

He listened intently, and a few moments passed before he said, "Tell her yourself."

Hitting the speaker button, Blaze placed the phone on the counter and motioned me over.

"Ms. Ash," came the voice from the other end. "I owe you an apology."

It was agent Swanson. I stepped closer to the phone and Blaze crossed his arms, annoyed.

"Why is that?" I asked.

"Steele and I weren't exactly on board with your belief that Divers is behind all this."

Wasn't on board was an understatement. When Blaze first told them, Steele said I should have my head examined.

"But you had your head up your ass, didn't you?" Blaze asked, offended enough for the both of us.

"We weren't being open-minded," Swanson said, wanting to make the truth sound a little less harsh. "However, we obtained a new development that we can't ignore."

As Swanson continued to speak, Blaze and I listened attentively to his explanation about their conversation with someone named Ms. Anne at the children's home.

She had worked at the facility for forty years, and it turned out she remembered both Louis' and Divers' time there, particularly because Louis had an eye condition called Coloboma. It was a defect in the iris that gave his pupil its unique shape.

The other kids teased Louis over the condition he was born with, but Divers took up for him and, over time, the two became inseparable, almost like brothers.

"So, as you can see," Swanson said in conclusion. "We shouldn't have been so eager to disregard you."

"I see," I said, while Blaze appeared so disinterested I couldn't help but laugh a little.

Swanson resumed speaking, eager to stay neutral while also pointing out that he wasn't the bad guy.

"Now, I'm not saying Divers is guilty, but things aren't looking good. You can understand our hesitation in believing the worst, right? I mean, it's Divers."

I let him cling to his delusions.

"Sure, I get it," I said, giving Swanson an easy out.

Honestly, he could feel how he wanted to feel. Divers was guilty, and Swanson's attempt to justify his doubts about his friend fell on deaf ears.

The truth was, Divers had been weaving a web of deceit for far too long, and it was finally unraveling before our eyes.

Despite Swanson's and Steele's reluctance to accept the reality, the evidence was mounting against their long-time colleague.

"We will be in touch," Swanson said before disconnecting the call.

Blaze looked at me.

"They want to cover their asses."

"I know," I agreed. "That was a mountain of information, though. No wonder Divers wants me dead. Not only did I know something that put the spotlight on him as the prime suspect after all these years, he blames me for getting a man that was like his brother killed."

"Well, I pulled the trigger," Blaze stated. "And I'd do it again. Divers should take his frustrations out on me and me only. Trying to kill you crosses the line."

I was still in shock that the guilty party was right under our noses this entire time.

Divers was the one who sent his minions to attack us on

the street, at my apartment, the hotel, and the parking lot at Vex.

"I guess now, you know who sent you that threatening letter that warned you to "Back off or else," I said. "You were making headway and Divers didn't like it."

Blaze's jaw tightened. "The man isn't only a criminal, he's a coward."

Witnessing the reemergence of his anger, I softly caressed his face, sensing the tension dissipating as our eyes connected.

"I'm alive and safe because of you. Divers can't hurt me."

"And he never will," Blaze said pointedly.

That raised a question in my mind.

"Doesn't the FBI know your address? Couldn't he have searched their database or something?"

"No. As I told you before, my information is scrambled for my safety. However, if there was a reason they needed to pull my address, clearance from the higher-ups would be necessary and Divers wouldn't risk asking for that."

The explanation made me feel even better than I did before, but out of curiosity I had to know. "What if by some chance he got clearance?"

Blaze laughed.

"Then he'd get an address for my place in New York because that was the information I gave them to scramble. I don't trust them, so they have no idea where I really live."

Knowing Blaze, I'd bet he knew someone that helped him out when it came to keeping his privacy private and the FBI really was none the wiser.

Just because Vex was in Atlanta didn't mean he couldn't live somewhere else, especially since he traveled all over the world for his missions.

I didn't know he had a spot in New York, but I could tell his real sanctuary was this place. Far away from prying eyes and unwanted visitors.

We sat down and tried to have some lunch, but it turned into us pushing the plates aside and playing a game of darts instead.

When Blaze's phone rang again, it was Ben with a new address for Divers, and Blaze immediately kicked into action. Heading to the bedroom to get dressed.

I followed, watching him pull off his pants and shirt, uncovering that gorgeous, mouthwatering body, before covering it again with his uniform.

"I'm going to drop by and see how Jolli is doing. Then Vadim, Hannah and I are going to go check out this new location Ben sent over," Blaze said, pulling on a black shirt over his white one. "Are you sure you don't want me to have Axel come over? He could bring Sam with him and the nurses would keep us updated on any changes."

I shook my head. "Blaze, sweetie, my love, I will be fine. Stop being extra. I am safe here. Something that you clearly pointed out. Let Axel stay with Sam and Jolli, and as backup if you need it."

Blaze fastened his vest and then came over to me.

Grabbing the collar of my shirt, he pulled me closer to him, leaned down and said, "I love you and you mean everything to me. I don't know what I'd do if something happened to you and I never want to find out, so I will always be extra when it comes to you. Get used to it."

Meeting him the rest of the way, I got up on tiptoes and kissed him. "I love you, too."

I was sitting on the couch flipping through the channels on the television. I was in search of something to hold my attention and transport me to a different world for a while, when my phone rang.

It took me a few seconds to find it because I only used it to check in with my mom, brother and have quick conversations with Jocelyn.

Assuming it was one of them, or maybe even Blaze, calling to give me an update, I answered.

"Have you been looking for me?" came Divers' slimy voice from the other end.

I was so startled I didn't say anything for several seconds. When I spoke again, I sounded much calmer than I felt.

"How did you get this number?"

"It took a while," Divers admitted, his voice light and jovial as if we were friends. "But I have my ways."

"You mean the same ways that have allowed you to run a crime ring for the last five years?"

Divers sighed, but he didn't really seem bothered. "So it's true. My secret is out. When my men told me to lie low because Trenton was dead, I'd hoped this was all a simple misunderstanding, but now I'm glad I heeded the warning."

"What do you want?" I snapped.

His answer was simple. "You, of course."

Now I laughed, although nothing was funny. I was scared shitless. "Oh, well, in that case, come and get me," I bluffed.

I was talking a big game here. Praying that what Blaze said about not being able to locate his place was true.

Divers grunted in disapproval. "Now, you know I have no idea where you are. Blaze wouldn't be so careless. Locating this number was even a stretch, and my readout says it is pinging from a tower in Texas. You wouldn't happen to be in Texas, would you?"

I quietly sighed with relief. "Yup, you got me. I'm in Texas."

Divers announced his distrust.

"I don't believe you." He said. "I'll bet you are somewhere close by. Nonetheless, where you are doesn't matter, because you are going to come to me."

I started to hang up, worried that being on the phone with him too long would suddenly allow him to locate me, but I was hesitant to end it. If Divers was calling, it was for a reason.

With the phone pressed close against my ear, I asked. "And give me one good reason why I would come to you?"

"I could give you five. One of which is in intensive care right now, hanging on for dear life. It would be a shame if he didn't make it through the night. What would poor little Sam do?"

Jolli, I thought desperately, and my heart sank.

Divers continued speaking, knowing I would not only listen, but comply. "It goes without saying that you should not tell anyone about this, especially Blaze. If you alert him, or tip him off in any way, I will know and it's goodbye, Jolli. So come now and come quietly."

There weren't many things Divers could have said to tear me away from the safety of this place, but threatening Jolli worked.

Please forgive me, Blaze. I have to do this.

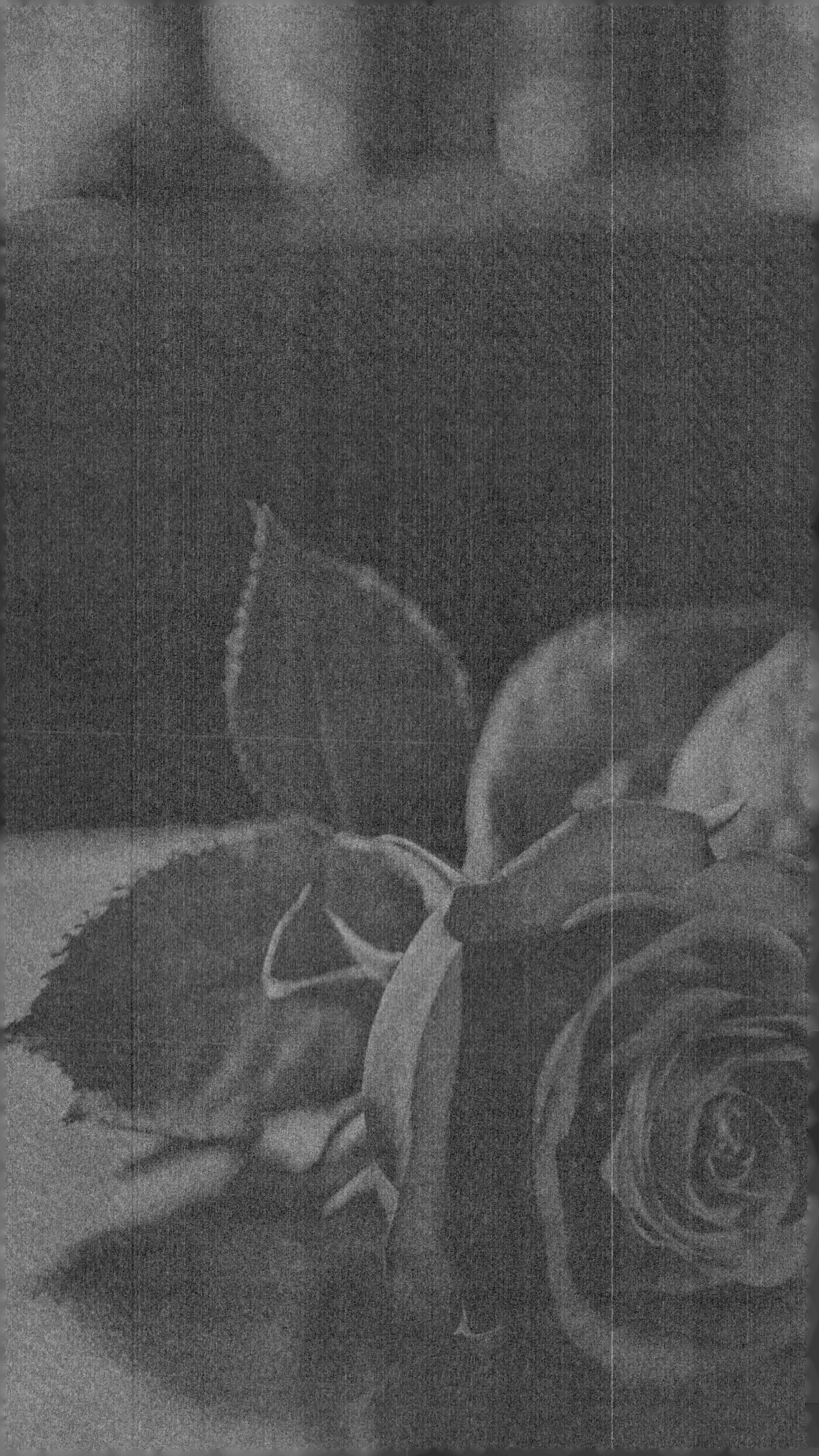

Chapter Twenty Nine

"Arms aren't supposed to bend that way."

I was nervously driving to the location Divers had instructed, and I was terrified.

Not for one second did I believe I could trust that he wouldn't hurt Jolli if I sacrificed myself, but I literally had no choice. I could not in good faith remain hidden in the safety of Blaze's home, knowing there was even a chance that I could have prevented Jolli's death.

Even so, I tried to call Divers bluff, stating that he was lying and there was no way he could get to Jolli. He put an end to that disbelief by letting me hear a recording of medical staff discussing Jolli's prognosis.

"I have ears everywhere, you see, and many people are on my payroll. So Ms. Ash, don't test me. It would be so easy to get someone to 'accidentally' give Jolli the wrong medication. Or," he added in a sinister tone. "Would you rather I set my sights on Blaze? I imagine he is coming to the hospital to visit Jolli soon."

What could I do? How could I stop him? Simply put, nothing and I couldn't.

My only choice was to do what he said. Therefore, I grabbed the keys to one of the two vehicles Blaze had parked outside and accepted my fate.

I love you Blaze.

For the entire drive, I'd been chanting that to myself. I also left Blaze a letter apologizing for leaving and telling him I loved him.

However, it didn't make it any easier because, officially, I wouldn't get to say goodbye.

My heart shattered when I realized I would never again witness the adoration in his eyes, taste the sweetness of his soft lips, or find comfort in the embrace of his muscular arms.

Without question, I knew it would break Blaze's heart as well, but I hoped he would understand why I had done this.

Reaching into my bra, I adjusted the knife I had brought with me. It kept digging into my skin because the bullet-proof vest I was wearing may have been too tight.

I knew neither the knife nor vest would save me once Divers got his hands on me, but I still felt compelled to protect myself.

Turning into a deserted parking deck, I waited close to five minutes before the phone rang.

I tried to get my breathing under control before answering. I was scared to death, but Divers didn't deserve to hear that.

"I'm here," I said, using a voice filled with fury instead of fear.

"Good, you know how to follow directions. There will be a truck pulling in right about... now," Divers said. And just like magic, a black SUV similar to the one Blaze drove for work entered the garage, stopping in front of me. "Get out of the vehicle, pass him your phone and I will see you shortly."

It took several attempts to move, but finally, I exited the vehicle. My mouth was dry and my hands shook. Weakened legs threatened to give out on me because I was essentially walking to my death.

Putting all my weight on the door, I balanced myself, forcing a level of dignity to override my dread as a big bald, burly guy the size of a linebacker approached.

He immediately snatched the phone from my trembling hands, dropped it, and stepped on it. The sound of the phone shattering under the man's heavy boot echoed through the garage, intensifying my sense of despair.

An involuntary devastated whimper escaped.

There goes any hope of Blaze tracking me through the phone.

The man's intimidating stature sent shivers down my spine, as he stepped towards me, further weakening my already trembling legs.

I mustered the strength to meet the man's gaze, refusing to let him see the full extent of my vulnerability. Deep down, anger simmered within me, fueling my determination to survive this ordeal... or at least survive it for as long as I could.

Linebacker guy scans my body and then gives me an evil smile.

"Face the car. Arms up," he said.

When I was in position, he used a metal detector over the front and back of my body. I lost another ounce of hope when it beeps at the discovery of the small knife I have folded in my bra.

Laying a heavy hand on my shoulder, he spins me around. "Hand it over," he growls.

I didn't move.

"I don't mind getting it myself," he said.

The speed at which I retrieved the knife shocked even me. The last thing I wanted was this man's filthy hands on me.

Noticing my bulletproof vest, he said, "You can leave that on. He plans to do much worse than shoot you."

A knot formed in my throat so big I almost couldn't swallow. I'd read the details of some of the horrific case reports. Many of them were killed in a slow, savage, sickening way.

The guy swiped the detector over me again, and once satisfied, shoved me inside onto the backseat, then got behind the wheel.

The entire drive I tried to map out ways that I could escape or survive this, but my plan was mentally cut short every time I realized that if I escaped, then Jolli definitely wouldn't.

Poor Sam.

We arrived at an old-looking building and I was yanked out of the vehicle and led inside.

The air grew heavy with a sense of foreboding. The interior was dimly lit, revealing cracked walls and dusty furniture, and every creaking floorboard echoed through the harsh silence.

If Divers had been hiding out here, it couldn't have been for long. The place appeared filthy and neglected.

The big guy took me into a room where the walls were peeling and the floor was grimy, littered with discarded trash and broken furniture, giving off a musty odor.

The pipes, which were exposed and rusted, snaked along the corners of the room, adding to the overall atmosphere of neglect and decay.

A single flickering lightbulb hung from the ceiling. It cast eerie shadows over the room that were so realistic I almost didn't notice the man with his back to us looking out of a tiny square window into the night's sky.

When the man faced us, all the courage I had left abandoned me. I was now face-to-face with Divers, which meant I was going to die tonight and no one could save me.

My legs gave out, and I almost collapsed, but the linebacker tightened his grip on my arm and held me upright.

"Raquel, so glad to see you," Divers said excitedly. "Shall we?"

He motioned to a chair that sat a few feet away and the big guy forced me into it, immediately tying my hands behind my back.

"Why?" I asked.

It was the only word I could form at this point. However, it needed no further explanation.

"Why? WHY?" Divers repeated, his voice rising to a shout. "Because you got my brother killed, because you opened your fucking mouth, because you..." he walked over to me, his fist raised in fury. "Have threatened to destroy all I have worked for!"

I expected all of those answers, but it was still frightening and surreal to hear him say it. Divers really was a liar, a criminal, a vicious killer. His fist was still in the air, and I tensed, waiting for the blow, but it never came.

Instead, Divers lowered his hand and straightened out his suit jacket. Closing his eyes for several seconds to collect himself.

The linebacker finished up with my wrists. They were tied so tight I could already feel the loss of circulation and Divers nodded for him to leave.

"Is there anything else you would like to know?" Divers asked. He was back to his calm, psychotic self.

"All these people. All these crimes. All these years," I said in disbelief. "How could you?"

"Power," he replied simply. "I craved power, control, and the satisfaction of seeing others suffer at my command. I built my empire through lies, manipulation, and bloodshed. And anyone who stood in my way, well... they paid the price. Much like you will."

His words sent a chill down my spine. I couldn't bring myself to ask what he was going to do to me.

"You know," he said, coming closer, "things were going smoothly before you came along. My brother Louis was helping me recruit people from the streets and I was making deals with those in higher positions. I was forming my own army and soon I would be unstoppable."

Now he was bent down, directly in front of me. I could smell the stale stench of cigarettes and whiskey on his breath.

"I liked you. I even wanted to ask you out on a date, the night of the charity, but you wouldn't give me a chance. Always finding an excuse to leave, like I wasn't good enough for you."

Spittle flew from his lips, landing on my face, and I almost threw up, but held it in and kept quiet. He was already so angry and his green eyes bore into mine, narrowed and cold, like an evil monster.

"It is going to be such a waste to ruin this pretty face," he said, sliding his fingers down my cheek. "But the satisfaction I am going to get by taking someone from Blaze the way he took someone from me makes it worth it. Initially, I planned to kill you both, but now I think killing you first will be much more devastating for our wannabe superhero. Don't you agree?"

I vaguely wondered how he knew Blaze and I were even together, but realized it couldn't have been that hard to figure out. Blaze took me into his home, argued with the agents for me, and openly protected me with his life. Anyone could see that he loved me.

Oh, Blaze, I am so sorry.

Divers was still breathing on me, staring me down, his ominous gaze causing me to avert my eyes.

I shuddered in disgust. "You're sick," I said, my voice shaking.

"What's that?" he asked, cocking one hand behind his ear.

I didn't repeat my insult. There was something else I wanted to know.

"Will you leave Jolli alone?"

Divers straightened and paced the room.

"Hmm. I don't see why not. My issue isn't with Jolli, it's with Blaze and you." He laughed. "Do you know how much it is going to destroy Blaze to find you crumpled and beaten to death?"

Beaten to death? That was my ending?

Vomit rose in my throat and I closed my eyes, all the case details of broken bodies, fractured skulls and crushed limbs flooding back to me.

Divers continued in his rant. "That arrogant bastard has solved every case he has worked for the FBI, but this time I will win and he will lose everything."

The smile that formed across Divers' face was pure evil. He hated Blaze, and this was about more than vengeance for his brother. This was jealousy.

I uselessly pulled at my restraints trying to free my hands, but gave up. All my struggling did was make the ropes dig in tighter and when Divers faced me again, I knew it was over. Even before he said the most disturbing words I'd ever heard.

"Say hi to my brother for me."

Then he hit me so hard the chair fell sideways. I didn't have time to react or protect my head from connecting with the floor, but fortunately, or unfortunately, my shoulder caught the brunt of the fall and a sharp pain ripped down my back.

Nevertheless, I didn't have time to scream or cry out. Divers sat the chair up and hit me twice more.

Once across the face and the other in the stomach.

I doubled over in pain as far as my restrained hands would allow, and the only reasons sobs didn't pour out was because I couldn't catch my breath.

Sorrow, fear, and dismay flooded me as he hit me again, and again, and again.

"Please," I choked, blood leaking from my mouth, tears spilling from my eyes. "No... mo... more."

I didn't plan to beg for my life, knew that he wouldn't care, but everything hurt so badly. I could barely see out of my right eye, but the smell and stickiness of blood trickling down my face was unmistakable.

Open cuts burned from being exposed to the air. Taking a breath hurt because one or more of my ribs must have been broken, and my shoulder, on which I had landed, hung unnaturally loose, throbbing so viciously that I could feel it in my head and throat.

Divers yanked my head back, so that I was forced to look at him. Through blurred vision, I saw his crazed face as he said, "But we are just getting started."

And then everything went black. I assumed it was because I had closed my eyes, but when a fresh wave of pain didn't come and Divers released his hold on my hair, I opened them again.

The area was dark and the only light coming in was from the window, giving the room a dark bluish glow.

"What the hell?" Divers said.

He drew his gun. The only reason I knew was because it was in my line of vision. With my head sagging, I could only see his lower leg and could just make out the glint of the weapon he held.

"Don't go anywhere now, my dear," Divers said playfully, patting me on the head with the gun. My head sagged further. "I'll be right back."

I heard low whispers between Divers and the linebacker outside the door.

"What the fuck happened with the lights?" Divers asked.

"I'm not sure, sir. I got Stanley checking on—"

An explosion of gunfire ended the conversation, and shouts and screams filled the hallway. I wanted to jump up and cheer, but that was out of the question. Blaze had found me, or maybe the feds had. Either way, this was over.

After a few minutes, the door opened. I was much too weak to sit up, so I remained in the pitiful position I was in.

Whoever it was said nothing, and I was gripped with a new fear.

What if Divers had returned to finish the job?

I stiffened, waiting for the blow behind my head, against my back, across my throat, but it didn't happen.

"Raquel," came Blaze's voice. It was so quiet and terrified he must have feared I was dead.

Lifting my head a few painful inches, I saw him kneeling in front of me. Shock, torture, and pain in his expression.

"No, no no no," he said. His voice was so desperate, so broken, and his eyes filled with such anguish I cried.

The pain in my chest intensified with the effort, triggering a coughing fit that made me vomit. Blaze extended his hand, but hesitated, appearing uncertain about where he could touch me without causing further discomfort.

"I'm... o...kay," I finally said.

I wanted to comfort him. I'd never seen him look like this. It was worse than the physical pain I'd suffered, and it had the power to rip my heart out.

"You will be alright, I promise," Blaze said gently, "but Divers won't," he vowed in a menacing tone.

He visibly checked me, making sure it was safe to move me before he cut my hands free. Immediately, I slumped forward, and Blaze caught me, lifting me from the chair and cradling me in his arms.

"I'm bringing her out, Hannah," he announced, pressing the device on his ear.

"Bear with me, princess," Blaze whispered into my ear, tenderly kissing the top of my head. "I'll get you out of here as fast as I can."

He carried me outside to the truck and Hannah said, "Vadim is in there, but so far no sign of Divers. Paramedics are on the way."

Blaze faced the door of the SUV, preparing to lay me down

inside, and if my head wasn't on his chest with my gaze fixed behind us, I would have missed it.

Divers was crouched low in a corner almost hidden from view, holding a gun.

He raised it and I don't know where the strength came from, or how I twisted myself free from Blaze's hold so fast, but I did, shielding the side of his body with my own.

White hot pain exploded all over me, and my body jerked hard before I fell to the ground and hit my head.

Vaguely, I knew that both Hannah and Blaze were over me. Hannah cradling my head and Blaze tearing at my clothes. When he found what he was looking for, he sighed with relief and then he was gone.

It was so fast. Almost like magic.

"Blaze! Blaze!" Hannah shouted. "Do not kill him. We need him alive."

But Blaze kept moving.

"You're going to be okay," Hannah said, staring down at me. "The vest caught it, but you might have a concussion and help is on the way."

Vest? Concussion?

I couldn't comprehend what she was talking about. The excruciating pain radiating over my body claimed my ability to speak, coherently think and, it seemed, to stay alert.

My head lolled to the right, giving me a sideways view of Blaze approaching Divers. The man looked terrified, and Blaze was coming in fast.

My mind wasn't making logical sense of all that was happening around me. The only thing I understood was that Blaze was angry. I mean, royally pissed the fuck off.

What made him so angry?

I tried to stay awake to find out what would happen next, but I began fading in and out of consciousness, earning me snippets of Blaze's wrath instead of the full story.

Blaze made it to Divers and grabbed his arm. *Oh, that's strange. I didn't think arms were supposed to bend that way.* Darkness.

Divers on the ground and Blaze stomping on his sides and head. *Divers looks like an ant trying to scurry away.* Darkness.

Blaze slicing Divers' ear off and shoving it into his mouth. *Yuck, I'll bet that doesn't taste good.* Darkness.

Blaze tying Divers to the back of a blue car. *Aren't people supposed to ride inside, not out?* Darkness.

The blue car driving off with Divers still attached to the bumper. *Well, now, that doesn't look fun.* Darkness.

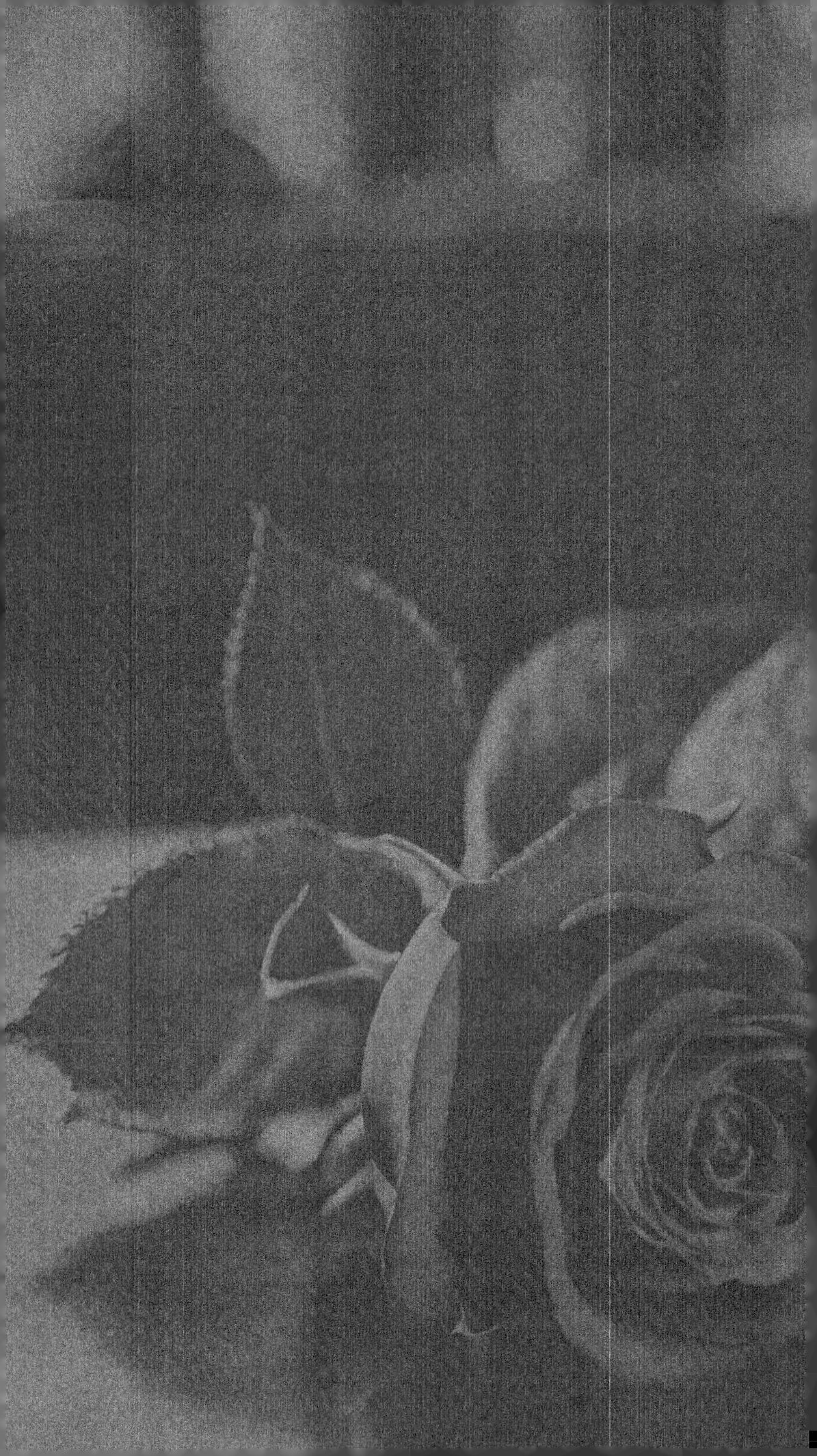

Chapter Thirty

"You will always be my whore."

Four broken ribs, two broken fingers, a broken clavicle, eye socket, sternum, left arm and jawbone. Top all that off with a missing ear, and friction burns to the right side of the body from being dragged by a car and the term bad day becomes an understatement.

Divers was in for a bad month, year, or possibly lifetime. Sheer luck was the only reason he wasn't dead.

Since I'd been awake, Vadim, Hannah and Blaze had filled in the missing pieces. When Divers shot at us, he not only hit me, he also gave away his position and Vadim, who had come outside looking for him, returned fire.

But Divers underestimated how many bullets he had left and by the time Blaze advanced towards him, all he could do was run, or try to, but he was unsuccessful.

Blaze beat him severely, and after cutting off his ear and shoving it into his mouth, he tied Divers to the back of a car, hot-wired it, and drove off.

However, Blaze didn't get far before Vadim rammed into him with one of the SUVs, preventing Blaze from gaining any serious momentum. Then, a couple of minutes later, the paramedics arrived and Divers and I were rushed to the hospital.

"I wasn't trying to kill him," Blaze said. "I simply wanted to teach him a lesson. Choosing to die after that lesson would have been his choice."

Vadim scoffed. "Any other time, I would agree with your

methods. But death is too good for him. Divers deserves to live hopefully a paraplegic life in prison where he is assaulted daily by the very criminals he put there."

Vadim's accent was so heavy by the end of that sentence I could barely understand what he said. Satisfaction crossed his face, as if he were imagining Divers in a cell, getting his due right now.

Both Blaze and Vadim were still furious and I would be too, as soon as these loopy meds wore off. They had me a lot happier than the mood called for.

"It's not my favorite option, but I guess rotting in a cell, barely alive and unable to defend yourself, is a close second," Blaze muttered.

My eyes traveled from Blaze, sitting in a chair beside my bed, to Vadim, seated near the foot of the bed, then to Hannah, comfortably lounging in a folding chair she'd brought in over in the corner.

She was knitting me a throw blanket. Actually knitting! *What couldn't this woman do?*

I laughed a little at the sight of her wearing all black, with a gun strapped to her waist, appearing to be the very definition of deadly, yet knitting me a happy, brightly colored blanket.

"Ouch!" I gasped, reaching for my fractured ribs with my good arm.

I certainly fared better than Divers, but I didn't escape unscathed. The cuts on my face burned slightly from being exposed to the open air, and in addition to that, I had a partially swollen eye, two broken ribs, a dislocated shoulder, and heavy bruising to my torso.

Blaze was on his feet in an instant. "Do you need anything?" he asked.

Ever since I arrived two days ago, Blaze had been faithfully by my side. Listening to the diagnosis from the doctors, vowing to take care of me during the healing time, and confessing his love every chance he got.

Honestly, I didn't expect him to be this way. Blaze's usual demeanor was straightforward, fearless, and unapologetic, with only occasional glimpses of his softer side, so this consistent change up from his usual behavior was truly endearing to me.

Especially since I could tell the rage and desire to permanently destroy Divers still lurked beneath his surface.

I could feel the warmth and comfort of his hand as it cradled mine, and that meant the world to me.

"I'm good. I actually feel lovely, but I have to remember the ribs don't like it when I laugh, cough or breathe," I said dramatically. "You guys finish telling me about what I missed."

Blaze didn't speak. He was watching me with a hurt yet determined expression. He was still likely thinking of ways to get to Divers and finish the job.

"So," Vadim began. "Divers had been running the crime ring for five years, as we all know. He had judges, doctors, officers, even politicians, in his pocket helping to advance his dirty work."

"That's a lot of people," I said.

"Yeah, half the damn police force by the last count we received," Hannah said, not looking up.

"How'd you find out?" I asked.

This time, Blaze answered. "Because no one wants to be left holding the bag. Now that Divers is out of commission and definitely going to prison, people are feeling bold. We received several anonymous tips, two of which gave us detailed lists of who Divers dealt with and what dirt he had on them."

"Was Trenton on there?" I asked.

"No," Vadim announced in disgust, crossing his arms. "Trenton was a lowlife criminal, a hired hand for pennies not worth any list. Divers paid him a measly ten thousand dollars to spy on you and Blaze, and to swipe the key to your place."

"Dammit and I didn't get to kill him either," Blaze said, disappointed.

"It is a pity," Vadim said, his shoulders slumping slightly.

"You can say that again," Hannah chimed in.

This time she stopped knitting to stare at the wall, clearly irritated by the realization.

I was surrounded by killers. Morally grey, dangerous, complex killers.

The bedside monitor beeped, keeping me up to speed on my body temperature, blood pressure, and blood oxygen levels.

For the most part, I barely glanced at it, but I'd caught Blaze watching it closely several times, like he was waiting for the machine to detect a sudden decline in my health before even my body had the chance to react to it.

However, at moments like this, when I was trying to think, the insistent beeping was hard to ignore.

Hmm. Something didn't add up.

"Wait," I said, confused. "If Trenton's information wasn't on Divers list, how did you learn the details of his deal?"

They all looked up then, smiling first at each other, then me.

"Jolli told us," Hannah said.

"He's awake?" I asked excitedly, sitting up straighter.

Big mistake.

I winced as a painful spasm shot through my ribs, reminding me of my injuries. Once again, I had completely forgotten that broken ribs were a buzz kill. This was going to be a long recovery.

Once the pain subsided, I realized I'd been squeezing Blaze's hand so hard there were imprints of my nails in it. He didn't even flinch, and he only smiled at me when I glanced up at him, horrified that I'd almost drew blood.

Releasing my hold, I cleared my throat and asked, "Why didn't you all tell me?"

"We wanted it to be a surprise," Blaze admitted. "Jolli woke up yesterday, but you needed your rest. The nurse is going to bring him down in a little while."

"And I spoke to him this morning," Vadim interjected. "Luckily, he hadn't forgotten what happened before the attack. He told me that once he caught up to Trenton, the man sang like a canary, wanting out of the deal with Divers and for Blaze and the rest of us to protect him in exchange for his cooperation."

Hannah smirked and said, "He thought after he had double crossed us, he could turn around and ask for our help. Well, it pissed Jolli off and he told Trenton to kiss his ass."

That explained why Jolli looked so angry when Blaze and I got to the warehouse that day.

"Also, he remembers trying to tell us we were looking for Divers. I think when we thought he was saying die, he was actually trying to say Divers," Blaze offered.

"And that was why he kept shaking his head," I recalled. "I thought it was a reaction from his injuries."

A brief sadness set in as I remembered watching Jolli fight for his life, but it went away when Vadim said. "Jolli is tough. Just like you. You see, you both made it."

"No time for bad thoughts. Look at this," Hannah said, holding up the blanket for me to see.

It was gorgeous. The knit style she was doing was called colossal ribbed, and it was light grey with touches of purple and gold throughout.

"Do you like it?" she asked.

Despite only being able to see it out of one eye, its elegance truly amazed me and it looked incredibly comfortable.

"I love it!" I said. "Thank you, Hannah."

She gave me a thumbs up and went back to knitting.

"Killers don't knit, you know that, right?" Vadim said. "It takes away from our tough exterior."

"Well, I knit and if someone pokes fun at me, I'll kill them," Hannah replied, smiling sweetly, pointing the long silver needle at him.

Vadim shrugged. "This I can accept."

They all laughed. I held back. My ribs didn't subscribe to humor.

"What are you going to do with your one thousand dollars?" Hannah asked. When she noticed I wasn't following along, she added, "You won the bet. You saved Blaze's life. I told you the first person to save him would get a thousand dollars."

"I don't need money for that.," I protested. "Give it to Jolli."

"Jolli won't take it," Vadim said. "Rules are rules."

I raised my gaze to Blaze, and he shrugged. "You did save my life."

Glancing around the room, I looked at the three of them. They weren't budging.

"If Axel agrees, then I'll take it," I finally said. "Where is he, by the way? I need his laid back island vibes."

"Axel is with Sam," Blaze said.

Vadim spoke up. "Sam prefers Axel to us because he loves Axels' cooking and the lively stories he tells. I can't blame the kid."

Blaze brushed the hair off my forehead, and I glanced up at him. "Axel said as soon as you get home, he is making you any dish you want."

I only smiled. Now that was something to look forward to.

There was a knock on the door, and then a nurse came in, pushing Jolli in a wheelchair.

Happiness filled my heart. Then a slight sadness took over as I noticed he'd lost weight.

The evidence was clear in his oval-shaped face that had now become more defined, with cheekbones that were more visible. His sandy brown curls were combed back, flattened to his head, but his greenish-brown eyes shimmered with joy, and that was all the confirmation I needed.

He was still Jolli. Vibrant, recovering and most of all alive.

"Jolli!" I exclaimed. "I am so happy to see you."

"Not as happy as I am to see you," he said. "I heard about what happened."

The nurse, an older woman with silver hair and a pleasant smile, rolled him closer to the bed. Blaze took a step back, giving us space to say hello.

"How are you?" we asked each other simultaneously.

Jolli laughed, but I didn't. I had already learned my lesson. No more pain for me.

"You first," Jolli said.

"I'm a lot better now that I have seen you," I said. "But sadly, even after all those fighting video games we played, I still didn't learn how to avoid getting hit."

Jolli took my hand and smiled, his country Texas accent coming through.

"It's cause you didn't let me teach you the proper combo move, little lady."

I was grateful that we both wanted to find humor in such a terrible situation, but Jolli's eyes told me he wasn't happy.

"I heard you sacrificed yourself for me."

"I had to," I confessed.

Jolli gave me a stern look. It was one I'd never seen before and I imagined it was the dad look he used on Sam.

"The fuck you did. Don't you ever do that again. We protect you, not the other way around."

Guilt flooded me. I felt like I'd just gotten in trouble for sneaking out of the house. Jolli's request wasn't easy because, like him, if someone I cared about was in trouble, I was coming to help.

I nodded, and Jolli's strict expression vanished. "Besides, no one cheats to win like you."

I laughed that time, accepting my painful fate, and my ribs didn't disappoint. However, it was worth it. Jolli would never admit that I played certain video games better than him and I wouldn't have it any other way.

We chatted more about our brushes with death and how blessed we were to have survived. Then the conversation naturally veered towards lighter topics like food and much needed vacations, before Jolli was rolled over to Hannah to checkout her knitting skills.

While Vadim, Jolli and Hannah were lost in their own conversation, another thing dawned on me.

"Hey," I said to Blaze. "How did you know where to find me? I was forced to ditch your SUV and the bald guy broke my phone."

Blaze reached into his pocket and pulled out my necklace. The red charm at the end twirled around and the word owned reminded my body of happier times.

The blood pressure monitor beeped quickly, indicating a sudden increase in pressure, and Blaze and I smiled.

"It has a tracker in it, enclosed in an aluminum shell that makes it undetectable to most devices."

I opened my mouth to respond, but wasn't sure what to say. There was no way I could complain and I wouldn't dare. His forward thinking had saved my life.

"I got nothing," I said. "Thanks for being overprotective, I guess."

Blaze grinned.

"I'm protective because I know I can't trust you to behave

and as long as this case was open, I wasn't taking any chances. I like my backup plans to have backup plans."

Making a come hither motion with my finger, I asked, "Have I told you how much I love you today?"

"You have, but I'm always up to hearing it again."

"I love you, Adrian," I said.

"I love you more, princess."

"What's so funny?" Blaze asked, sitting down on the couch, placing his glass of bourbon on the side table next to him.

I glanced up from my phone. "This silly dad joke Jolli sent me today."

It was seven weeks later, and Jolli had not only made a full recovery, but he'd been sending me a joke every day. It had gotten to where I was looking forward to them.

Nevertheless, Jolli wasn't the only one from the team spoiling me. Axel had taken care of all the cooking during my healing time. Hannah had knitted me another blanket and come over to do my hair when Jocelyn wasn't available, and Vadim ran all our errands.

In order to support both Blaze and me, they made sure he didn't have to leave my side and made me feel like a valued member of the team.

They included me in their recreational plans, visited often, and kept me up to date on Divers case, which wasn't pretty.

Turns out, Vadim was right. Due to extensive damage to his spinal cord, Divers was officially a paraplegic and, because of his heinous crimes, he'd been sentenced to life in prison.

A few of the FBI agents wanted to bring charges against Blaze for the cruelty and gruesome nature of Divers arrest.

However, after details of all Divers had done over these past years were brought to light, no one was coming near Blaze with any legal action. In fact, they awarded him and his team for bringing down a ruthless criminal they'd been chasing for half a decade.

"Lay it on me," Blaze said, getting comfortable. "What joke has Jolli sent today?"

I joined him on the couch, sitting between his legs and leaning back onto his chest. He immediately wrapped his arms around me and planted a kiss on my temple.

"Alright, what do a tick and the Eiffel Tower have in common?" I asked.

Blaze thought about it, then gave up.

"They're both Paris sites," I said with a giggle, giving him the answer.

Blaze shook his head. "Jolli should stick these jokes in a book."

"You mean like the Little Black Book your friend published for you?" I asked.

Blaze took a sip of his drink. "Still reading those entries, huh?"

"I can't help it. They are so addictive. Did you really do all that stuff?"

"Yes, I did."

"Do you miss it? I mean, some of it is pretty extreme and I'm not into all of it."

"Not for a second. You give me a good balance and although you will always be my princess, you are not exactly dainty anymore."

I smiled, thinking about the night he turned me down for sex, stating that I was a dainty princess.

However, my smile fell flat. He was right. I wasn't dainty anymore. I enjoyed the pain and extreme experiences that were now part of my sex life, so why hadn't he been aggressive at all with me lately?

We'd had sex twice, wanting to wait until the pain from my ribs had disappeared, but both times it was extremely romantic. Not the raunchy, rough, sex I was used to, but gentle love making filled with passion and emotions.

"Adrian," I said.

"Oh no," he sighed. "What's wrong?"

The only time I called him Adrian was when I was being serious or when we were making love and since he wasn't romancing orgasms out of me at the moment, he knew it was the former.

"Are we ever going to do intense scenes again? I know waiting for me to heal really put a damper on your more aggressive side."

"Is that a complaint?" He asked.

"Hell no!" I exclaimed. "I love the sweet and sensual, but I love the other side too."

During my healing period, Blaze had taken on a much more delicate and accommodating approach as it pertained to me. Not only did I relish in it, I fell in love with him all over again.

Even still, deep down, I still longed for the thrill and excitement of the sadistic, dominating man I knew Blaze kept tucked away. Seven weeks was a long time to be broken and weak. I needed to get down and dirty.

"Well, when you are ready, we will gradually proceed back to more extreme things."

I faced him. "It's been seven weeks! I am completely healed now. No need to be cautious."

"Let me rephrase," Blaze said. "When *I* decide you are ready, we will do more."

"But I am ready," I challenged. "Tape me to the ceiling,

spank me into submission, treat me like your little whore," I demanded, getting in his face. "I want my Dom back!"

Blaze grabbed me by the shoulders, spun me to face forward and then removed my t-shirt and bra.

I got excited. He was about to Blaze-handle me.

Guiding me back onto his chest, Blaze lifted my chin so that the back of my head rested against his right shoulder.

"I don't know why you are in such a hurry to be treated like my submissive. You already have two punishments awaiting you."

He kissed my neck and some of the irritation had left my voice when I spoke again.

"Two punishments? But... I didn't do... anything," I said, my eyes closing. The sexual haze Blaze induced was strong as ever.

His voice was low, seductive, and filled with a hint of mischief.

"You've merely forgotten princess, but you see I don't forget anything," he whispered, his warm breath sending a delightful shiver over me. "The day we were at the hotel, you tried to seduce me and I told you it was inappropriate, but your punishment was cut short by our intruder."

He kissed my ear, tugging at my earlobe lightly with his teeth. His hands playing with my nipple rings, before shifting lower and lower. Continuing, he said, "The second punishment comes from that sly remark you made about Zac looking like a lot of fun to be with."

Aright, fine. I couldn't dispute that. I was guilty, and I did enjoy pushing his buttons. Blaze slid one hand into my sweatpants and cupped my pussy.

I spread my legs and placed my hands at my sides, like I knew he expected. Giving him access and encouraging further exploration from those amazing fingers. His touch was intoxicating, making it impossible for me to resist even his unspoken commands.

"Know this," he said, driving two fingers into me. "I will always be your Dom and you will always be my whore, but first and foremost, I am your man."

Blaze's lips trailed down to the top of my shoulder. He used his free hand to tilt me forward so that he could kiss the scars on my back while his fingers continued to work their magic.

Surprisingly, I was never the type of woman to enjoy being fingered. Mostly because the men I knew had no idea what they were doing down there, but Blaze knew exactly where to touch and where to press to make it pleasurable and powerful.

"As your man, all I want to do right now is take care of you, kiss you, spoil you, and love on you, because you deserve it."

He took a long pause to brush his lips across each and every bruise that scarred my back and my breath caught. I felt special and loved.

"But most importantly," Blaze announced, digging those fingers deep into my pussy and pulling me back against him. "You are mine to control. Which means you are ready for more when I say you are ready."

Damn, I loved this man. He was beyond talented, the only man alive that could make me cum from his dick, his mouth, his fingers and his words.

"Yes, sir," I said, moving my hips against his hand. "Anything you say."

Blaze encouraged my climax by pressing harder inside me. It felt like he had practically taken hold of my G-spot with his fingers and was massaging and caressing it into an orgasm.

"Good girl. Now cum for me," he ordered.

And obediently, I did. Saying his name and telling him

how much I loved him before falling slack against him, satisfied. Serenity and completeness washing over me.

The journey that led us to this point, where we found ourselves blissfully in love, was a lengthy process that was fraught with danger, disaster, and unforgettable experiences, but it also brought us enlightenment and growth.

Blaze consistently told me that my innocence, as he called it, was something he found grounding and it served as a constant reminder of what he fought to protect every single day.

In addition, he expressed gratitude towards me for introducing him to my world of optimism, peace, and compassion.

However, I don't know if Blaze truly understood that he'd done the same for me.

By bringing me over to his side, he'd shown me a reality devoid of idealistic notions, and although it was shocking, intense and sometimes violent, it had strengthened me and definitely made me more sexually free.

Blaze's world of Doms, subs, vulnerability, and action was on a level all its own. Not too long ago, I feared that, but now I craved it. It was spontaneous, seductive, and unpredictable.

I loved it here.

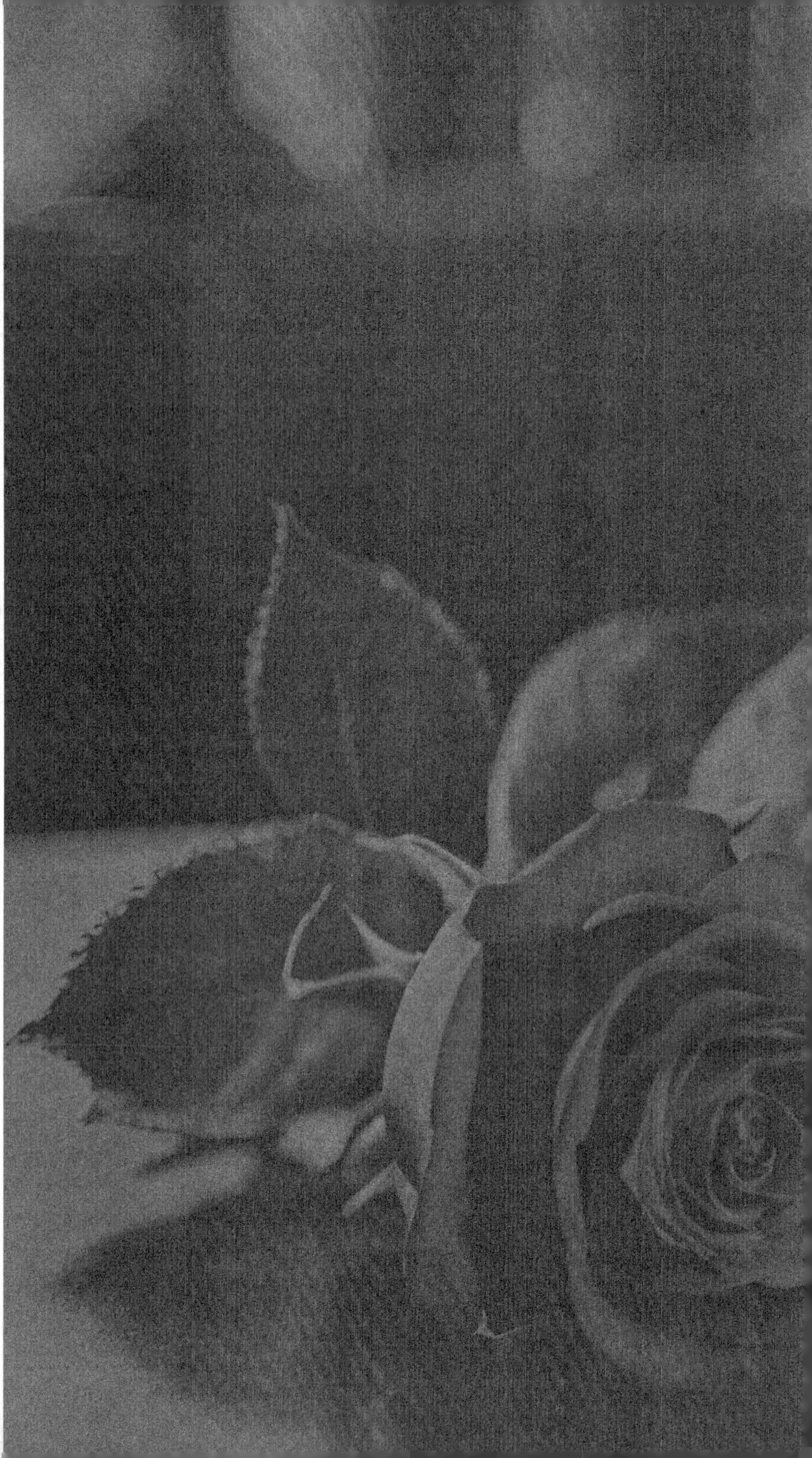

Epilogue

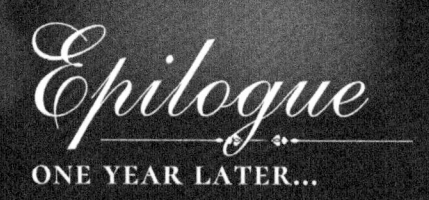

ONE YEAR LATER...

The paddle hit my ass once, twice, and then a third time before I had to come up for air.

"I didn't say you could stop sucking my dick," Blaze said. "Give her two more," he instructed to Jag.

Jag obliged, slapping my rear end two more times with the paddle. The girl was severely heavy handed. To her, light swats and hard swats meant the same thing. I couldn't see my ass, but I bet it was heavily marked.

Blaze still never shared me sexually with anyone. I was his and his only, exactly the way I liked it.

Nonetheless, sometimes he had some interesting ideas like tonight, and he would utilize Jag or Hannah to assist.

"Arch that ass up and start sucking again," Blaze instructed. "Don't stop until I'm done and if you think you need to breathe. Guess what? You don't."

"Yes, sir," I said, taking a few more deep breaths before sliding his dick back into my mouth.

I sucked, teased and ran my tongue over every inch of Blaze's hard, smooth erection.

We were at the BDSM club in Blaze's private room.

I'd wanted to be spontaneous tonight, so this is where I ended up — on my knees, butt in the air, sucking Blaze off, while Jag spanked me with a paddle and Blaze played with the remote that controlled the vibrator in the thong I wore.

I'd cum five times. Five! And Blaze hadn't cum once.

The rule was that I could stop when he finally got his release, but the stubborn man was holding out on me and Jag was back there having the time of her life.

Jag and I had become good friends since she'd done my tattoo nine months ago. It was the official "I love Chaos" tattoo that all the members on Blaze's team had, and now, so did I.

Vadim suggested that the team pay for the tattoo as an official "welcome to the assassin family" gift, but I refused, because I finally had something cool I could spend the thousand dollars on I'd won for saving Blaze.

"You're ass is red princess. It looks good," Jag said, and she swatted me again.

Blaze flipped the switch on the vibrator, turning it up to the highest notch, and I squealed, but I did not stop sucking.

"I love when you moan on it," he encouraged, turning the intensity of the vibrator from the highest level to the weakest, over and over again, just to get the reaction out of me he sought.

I gasped, whimpered, laughed and choked all without letting him slip from my mouth. I was a champ at this.

Not to mention, the pain coming from the spanking and the pleasure coming from the vibrator felt like paradise.

Finally, Blaze said, "I need to be inside you."

Pulling my hair, he yanked himself free from my mouth and picked me up.

After slamming me into a nearby wall and momentarily knocking the air out of me, Blaze ripped off the vibrating underwear and positioned himself between my legs.

"Give me all you got," I begged.

"You're going to regret that," Blaze growled in response.

He was right. I was going to regret this because I would be sore in the morning.

Blaze thrust into my pussy so deep I got dizzy, but once my

world stopped spinning, those familiar sensations of otherworldly pleasure rode in.

It felt incredible.

I shook, whimpered and moaned uncontrollably, and once I got too loud for Blaze's liking, he wrapped his hand around my neck and squeezed, silencing me for a good ten seconds, while pounding into me, before allowing me to breathe again.

I didn't know if Jag had left the room, or stayed to watch the show, but all I saw was stars.

"Does it hurt?" he asked, moving faster than I thought humanly possible.

"Yes," I squeaked.

"Good. Deal with it," he ordered. "I'll be done with you soon."

That upped the ante. I got off on the thought of Blaze using me for his own satisfaction.

At this point, I was certain there would be an imprint of my back on the wall when we were done. His glorious, hard, muscular chest was pressed firmly against mine, holding me in place.

My back hurt, my legs hurt, my pussy hurt, but I wanted more, I wanted it all and Blaze was not slowing down.

Without warning, my back arched, my toes curled, and I gripped Blaze's shoulders rough enough to leave marks.

I came again, and this time he came with me, filling me with his release and biting my neck hard enough to hurt but not enough to break the skin.

After Blaze's breathing returned to normal, he withdrew from me and I slumped to the floor in a state of euphoria with a wide grin on my face.

"You look lovely tonight," Blaze complimented.

He gracefully twirled me around multiple times, his firm grip never faltering, and then he gently pulled me back into his warm embrace.

I couldn't help but smile because I definitely felt lovely.

I was wearing a formfitting, silver backless dress, unconcerned with who saw my scars or what they would think. In addition, I was in the arms of the man I loved and celebrating a friend's engagement.

In my opinion, things couldn't be better, but of course I was with Blaze, and he always turned wonderful into spectacular.

"How are your classes going?" he asked. "Did they post the grades yet?"

I smiled so hard my cheeks hurt. I'd been working my ass off with those classes.

"I am waiting on the grade for my data communications and networking class, but in the others I got all A's."

"That's my girl!" Blaze said with pure joy. "I knew you would."

He likely did, and so did my therapist.

They were both encouraging me to live without regrets and to chase my dreams and most of the time, I did great.

However, survivors' guilt from the accident and nightmares about all of my brushes with death occasionally made full recovery an uphill battle.

Despite the challenges, I remained determined and continued to make significant progress.

I'd went back to school to get my degree in cybersecurity, and although I had a year left, I'd already begun handling virtual surveillance for Blaze on some of his top secret missions.

Doing so required that I have a station setup at home for

the cases the team worked after hours, and my own office at work.

Melanie kept making up excuses to come by when she saw my office door open because she missed having me as a cubicle buddy.

We made plans to do things at least once a month, and we went to lunch twice a week so that we could still have our fun chats about office gossip, which more often than not included me and Blaze.

I was proud of myself and the constant encouragement from my family, friends and the love of my life really went a long way.

As my head rested on Blaze's chest, I glanced over at Ashton and Jada. Ashton had his arms around her waist and they were talking and laughing with another couple.

This was their engagement party, and I was so happy for them.

"Those two are another perfect fit," I said, "Just like Merrick and Jocelyn."

"Although I agree they are a great couple," Blaze said. "Don't forget about the other perfect couple here."

I looked up at him and smiled. "Yes, Blaze, we are perfect together, but we aren't getting married."

Blaze cocked a brow. "Says who?"

I stopped dancing. "Adrian Shaw, are you saying you want to marry me?"

He pulled me back in and began moving to the music. A smooth jazz song, pouring from the speakers.

"Don't act surprised, princess. You know you are the woman of my dreams. And no, I am not saying *I want* to marry you. I am saying I am *going to* marry you."

It was impossible to control the excitement that enraptured me.

The idea of spending the rest of my life with Blaze was

both exhilarating and comforting. He was my person. He was my everything.

"And how long has this been on your mind?" I asked, my cheek splitting grin from earlier returning.

"For a while now," came his casual response. "And when I propose, you won't see it coming."

"Knowing you, I wouldn't doubt it."

We'd been through so much together over this past year. I couldn't have imagined being with anyone else.

Blaze and I supported each other through the toughest of times, and our bond grew stronger with every shared experience.

We were not just friends, boss and employee, or Dom and sub, we were soulmates, ready to conquer whatever the future held.

"You know what?" I said, shifting my gaze upward to stare into his eyes, "The last time we were at a formal gathering like this, you were shutting me down and now you are all mine."

"Hmm," Blaze said. "I seem to recall things a little differently. I didn't shut you down. You denied my request and now, I can do with you as I please."

The familiar dynamic change was upon us.

I could see it in the passion, desire, and dominance in Blaze's gaze. His lips curled up into a sexy, naughty grin.

"I'll bet your pussy is wet and throbbing right now, as you imagine what I'm about to have you do next."

I licked my lips and nodded. It was all I could do. Blaze had the ability and charm to turn me on in an instant.

Bending down close to my ear, Blaze whispered the nastiest, dirtiest, most degrading thing I'd ever heard, and my body temperature shot through the roof.

It was something I was happy to let him do, but I'd never repeat it because some things should stay between a sub and her Dom.

. . .

If you enjoyed **This Side of Wrong** please leave a 5 star review. It helps me out tremendously.

Also, don't forget to check out more books from my collection!

Check out...
Blaze's Little Black Book

Check out Jada's story...
His Mouthpiece: Ashton and Jada

Check out Jocelyn's story...
His Mouthpiece: Merrick and Jocelyn

Check out Piper's story (Raquels sister in law)...
The Love Is Series

About the Author

Nicki Grace is an Atlanta native with a bachelor's in business and a Masters in Marketing. As a wife, mother, author and designer, she is addicted to writing, spas, laughing, and sex jokes, but not exactly in that order.

Her comedic personality and unique upbringing by an illiterate but fiercely strong mother and a courageous, prideful father, made her view of the world pretty unconventional.

Luckily for you, someone gave her internet access, and now you get to experience all the EMOTIONAL, EXCITING, SHOCKING, and HOT ideas that reside in her head. She loves to have fun and lives for a good story. And we're guessing so do you! Nickigracenovels.com

facebook.com/nickigracenovels
instagram.com/nickigracenovels
tiktok.com/@nickigracenovels
bookbub.com/authors/nicki-grace

NICKI GRACE
NOVELS

USE THE QR CODE BELOW TO VISIT MY WEBSITE

Romance

The Inevitable Encounters Series

Book 1: The Hero of my Love Scene

Book 2: The Love of my Past, Present

Book 3 : The Right to my Wrong

The Love Is Series

Book 1: Love is Sweet

Book 2: Love is Sour

Book 3: Love is Salty

Erotica

His Mouthpiece

His Mouthpiece: The Prequel

This Side of Wrong - Coming soon

Thrillers

The Twisted Damsel

Break Him

Women's Fiction

Cut off Your Nose to Spite Your Face

The Splintered Doll (A Memoir)

Self-Help

The TIPSY COUNSELOR Series

The Tipsy Dating Counselor (Summary)

Book 1: The Tipsy Dating Counselor (UNRATED)

Book 2: The Tipsy Marriage Counselor

Book 3: The Pregnancy Counselor

Printed in Great Britain
by Amazon